BLOODY TWIST

Bloody Twist

A Lupe Solano Mystery

Carolina Garcia-Aguilera

OPEN ROAD

INTEGRATED MEDIA

NEW YORK

ISBN: 979-8-3372-0228-0

This edition published in 2025 by Open Road Integrated Media, Inc.
180 Maiden Lane
New York, NY 10038
www.openroadmedia.com

As always, this book is dedicated to my three daughters
Sarah, Antonia, and Gabriella,
the loves and passions of my life.
And, of course, to my beloved Cuba,
the island of my birth.

BLOODY TWIST

One

MIAMI, JULY 2010

"Let me make sure I heard you right." I sat up slowly in the bed and reached for the glass of champagne on the bedside table. I took a couple of sips, and waited for them to luck in before turning to Tommy. "Your client is the highest paid escort on South Beach—AND she's a virgin? There are so many oxymorons there in that one sentence, Tommy, that I don't quite know how to even begin to list them!"

I could see that Tommy, the poor man, was about to fall asleep in a well-deserved post-coitus coma. Hell, after our last especially vigorous romp, I couldn't blame him for nodding off but I was undeterred. When something interested me, I was relentless, a character trait that, throughout my twenty-eight years, had served me well. However, on numerous occasions, it had sunk me, too. "Lupe, please, let it go—we can discuss it later," Tommy groaned. "I shouldn't have told you about Madeline Meadows. I should have known better, I really should have." He took one of the pillows on the bed and placed it over his head. "Yet again, I've unleashed the monster."

I had no pity for Tommy. He had certainly gotten his money's worth out of me that afternoon, so I continued making my point. I took the pillow off of his face so he could see me, then raised my right hand and started to count on my fingers. "Numero uno, you have a client who is a virgin—that's gotta be a first for you; numero dos—she's a call girl who is a virgin; numero tres; she's the highest paid call girl in Miami and she doesn't have sex with her clients. I could go on, but I've just had great champagne, and even greater sex, so I think I'll quit before I start feeling sorry for her."

Tommy ignored my sarcasm. "I swear, Lupe, that's what she said. And don't ask me why but I believe her."

"So, what exactly does she do as a call girl?" I needed to know. "And how much does she charge for doing what she doesn't do?"

"Lupe, for God's sake!" Tommy was starting to lose his temper. "Let me get some sleep, or I'll give the case to another private eye."

"Sorry." I quickly backed off.

Tommy knew me well. Just the threat of assigning the case of the virginal call girl to another P.I. was enough to quiet me. Tommy didn't take simple cases—all of his clients were involved in interesting, complex situations. Although I still didn't know any facts of the case, once Tommy handed me the file, there would be lots of work for me to do. I would begin by conducting a background check of the client, and see where that led. Though I couldn't begin to guess why the virginal call girl had retained Tommy, I sensed that it would be a very interesting case.

Tommy MacDonald was one of the most, if not the most, successful criminal defense attorneys in Miami. No small feat considering that there were 128 pages of listings for lawyers in the Dade County telephone directory. I could personally attest to the fact that in the years that he'd been practicing law, he'd had more than his share of unusual cases as I'd been his private investigator for quite a few of them. But a call girl who was a virgin? Even for Tommy that was out of the ordinary. The mere existence of a virgin on South Beach—male or female—was hard enough to believe. It wouldn't surprise me if there was a law against it—but on top of that, she was a call girl? Just when I thought I'd heard it all!

I looked over at Tommy who, now that I'd stopped talking, was lying quietly next to me with his eyes closed. I examined him closely, almost as if I'd been holding a magnifying glass to his face. I wanted to see if he'd been putting me on when, earlier that afternoon, he'd told me about a young lady named Madeline Meadows, who had come to see him about a tricky situation in which she found herself.

The fact that a young woman, one who claimed to be the highest paid call girl on South Beach, had come to him seeking representation was not surprising. Tommy, after all, was a well-known criminal defense attorney and came into contact with individuals from all segments of society. That she claimed to be a virgin had been the shocker.

Tommy and I had been particularly inspired during our hours long lovemaking session that afternoon, and I hated to disturb his much-needed nap. I was hoping for an encore, so it was self-serving to let him rest, too. But I was really curious about this new client and patience had never been my strong suit. I watched him sleep quietly, and grew increasingly tempted to wake him up and start asking the many questions that I had about her—beginning with if she was for real—but Tommy did not make idle threats, and wouldn't hesitate to cut me out if I disturbed him. Just the possibility that he might not give me the case was enough to stop me and, as great as the sex had been, he was perfectly capable and willing to do just that. I knew every inch of his body, but for the life of me, I couldn't tell if he had been making up the story about the virginal, highly paid call girl. It just seemed so fucking weird.

I'd been schooled by a platoon of nuns—my own sister, Lourdes, was a nun—and they'd educated me to accept as gospel truth a number of events that defied all rational scientific explanation. So maybe I had been well-prepared to believe in such a thing as a virginal call girl.

Actually, now that I thought about it, the greatest leap of faith that the Cadiolic Church expected of us was to accept the fact that although she was married to Joseph, Mary had been a virgin when she had given birth to Jesus. Given that, and, not meaning any disrespect to either individual in question, it was possible to suspend my natural skepticism when it came to certain matters. In this case, it was another improbable claim of virginity.

It was a late Saturday afternoon in July, stiflingly hot outside, but freezing cold in Tommy's apartment, just the way we liked it. Typically, we were both busy seven days a week—the criminal element in Miami didn't take weekends off—but it just so happened that we were both free, so when Tommy had called and asked me to lunch, I had quickly accepted.

We hadn't seen each other in a while so, feeling like celebrating, we had decided to go for a long, lazy, wine-filled lunch at Emeril's, a restaurant that had opened up a couple of years before on South Beach, and had quickly become one of our favorites. Maybe it had been the gumbo, or the platters of oysters, or the redfish, or it could have been the two chocolate desserts we had consumed (the two bottles of wine we drank had certainly been a contributing factor), but, whatever the reason, we could barely keep our hands off each other before bolting back to his apartment.

It had been on the ride from the restaurant to Tommy's Brickell Avenue apartment when he had briefly mentioned the new case he'd just been retained on—the one with the virgin call girl. Tommy had warned that my reaction would probably be just as his had been upon first meeting her: the very idea of her claim being true had seemed so unlikely. Even for Tommy, with his weird assortment of clients, the situation had stood out so much so that he had been instantly interested.

I had been so engrossed in my thoughts that I didn't realize that Tommy had opened his eyes and had been watching me. He seemed much more refreshed after his nap, which pleased me greatly. Suddenly, with a burst of energy, he reached down to the floor and into the silver ice bucket for the bottle of Dom Perignon, and, in one quick, smooth motion, refilled our glasses. We toasted each other then took several healthy sips from our overfilled glasses.

"I know it's difficult to believe that I have a client who is a virgin and a call girl," Tommy chuckled as reached for me. "Knowing you, Lupe, you're probably having trouble processing it but, amazingly enough, as I said before, I mostly believe her. Of course, her story has to be checked out. That's where you can start your investigation. Only then will we begin to find out the truth about her."

I felt strange frolicking between the sheets with Tommy while discussing virgins, but not weird enough to want him to stop doing what he was doing to me. Although we had never dated, Tommy and I had been lovers for years. We always grew close whenever we worked a case together, so I suppose it might be correct to say that our relationship was opportunistic. Naturally enough, as his main private investigator, I saw quite a bit of him. All of him, as a matter of fact.

Years ago, when Tommy and I had first started working together, we had decided that given our hectic schedules it would be more convenient for us to get together and discuss our cases after regular office hours. Almost from the start, the meetings began taking place later and later in the day, and would last longer and longer, until the inevitable happened, and we became lovers. Not only were our meetings much more productive—no interruptions from cell phones, BlackBerrys, text messages, etc.—the sex was great. Few things in my life were more satisfying than reporting on an investigation to a criminal defense attorney lying in his bed, naked, and sipping champagne.

"OK, Tommy, if you say you believe that she's a virgin, and a call girl—and, one that's making lots of money at it—that's good enough for me. At least, for now." I reached for my glass, and careful not to spill one precious drop, finished the contents. "At the very least, she'll be able to pay your fees."

"That part of her story checks out in any case. She brought in a cashier's check with my retainer." Tommy looked at me and smiled. "And, Lupe, we both know I don't come cheap and, my dear, neither do you."

Truer words had never been spoken. "So, what kind of trouble is she in?"

"That's the weird part, Lupe." Suddenly Tommy became sober. The consummate professional, he took his clients' situations very seriously. "She's not in any trouble—not yet, anyway—but she feels she's going to be, so she wanted to get a jump on it. Keep me on retainer for when the time comes."

I thought about what Tommy had said. "And exactly what kind of trouble does she anticipate?"

"Being charged with two murders," Tommy told me. "The police questioned her about two men she knew—they were found shot dead within twenty-four hours of each other— shot with the same gun. From their preliminary investigation, it seems that she might be the only connection they had in common."

I nodded approvingly. "Smart client you have to prepare herself for that day." I lay back down on the bed. "Not everyone would know to do that."

It was late in the afternoon and growing dark outside, but we still hadn't turned on any lights in the bedroom. Tommy never closed the curtains to his bedroom windows. There was no need, really, as his apartment was on the penthouse floor of the tallest residential building in Miami, so he didn't have to worry about nosy neighbors or peeping Toms. The only ones who might be able to see in were the birds that glided by on the updrafts of wind that swirled at such heights, or the pilots of small airplanes, who flew by with banners trailing after them. Every room of Tommy's apartment—bathrooms and kitchens included—had spectacular views with the city of Miami to the west, and the sparkling blue waters of Biscayne Bay and the Atlantic Ocean to the east.

His apartment was enormous, large enough to take up the entire top floor of the building; it even had a Jacuzzi in the corner of the terrace. It was furnished in a minimalist style, so beautiful and understated that it had to have been exorbitantly expensive. Tommy's apartment was a welcome and calm contrast to the Cuban Rococo motif of my family's sprawling home in the Cocoplum section of Coral Gables 'More is better, and most is best' being the de facto Solano family motto.

"Yes, she seems that way, pretty savvy for a twenty-two year old girl from Dubuque, Iowa," Tommy commented idly. "That's where our virgin's from, Lupe. Iowa."

"Hmmm. I can't ever remember working a case for you with a client who was from Iowa. Or, who was a virgin, for that matter," I pointed out.

"Me, too. At least, the virgin part," Tommy agreed. "And I've been a lawyer for twelve years—and you've been a private eye for how long? Eight? God! Lupe, is that how long we've known each other?" Tommy reached down to the ice bucket and brought up the second bottle of Dom Perignon that had been chilling. With a practiced motion, he popped the cork, and poured both of us some. We tipped our glasses to each other in a silent toast before we drank the golden liquid.

"Lupe, think about it. Between us, we've been at our respective professions for twenty years and neither of us can recall ever coming across a virgin." Tommy took a deep breath, shaking his head at the wonder of it. "Now, what does that say about Miami?"

"Or, about us," I added, and pulled the covers up to my neck. I liked the temperature to be frigid, but the air conditioner in Tommy's bedroom had been turned so low that I was actually turning blue—no small feat for a Cuban with olive skin. "So, tell me again, why exactly did Miss Iowa come to you? For professional or personal reasons? I mean, being a professional virgin in Miami must be quite a burden," I teased. "She might want to get rid of her burden."

"Lupe, come on, it's not funny. Two men were murdered," Tommy scolded me. "Ms. Meadows knew the men, but she swore that she had nothing to do with their murders. At least, that's what she said."

I had worked with Tommy long enough to know from the skeptical tone of his voice that although he may have been convinced of Madeline Meadows' virginity, the same did not apply to her declaration that she wasn't a murderer. Or maybe it was the other way around—with Tommy, one never knew. In spite of his profession, Tommy wasn't a complete cynic. Yet.

"If you say so." I moved closer to Tommy. The second bottle

of champagne had made me feel particularly amorous, and I began stroking him in the way I knew he liked. As I did so, I couldn't help but giggle at the idea of our clients finding out how we discussed their cases: in bed, naked, and drinking champagne.

"I'll send the Meadows file over to your office first thing Monday morning," Tommy said, groaning softly. "That way, you'll be prepared for your meeting with Ms. Meadows at noon."

"I'll read the file as soon as I get it," I agreed.

Not surprisingly, Tommy had automatically assumed that I would accept his offer. He knew that there wasn't a snowball's chance in hell that I would turn down a tantalizing case involving a virgin who was a professional call girl. As I stroked Tommy, I made a mental note to tell Leonardo—my cousin, who also doubled as my office manager and holistic advisor—to expect the file as well as to write in the appointment with our newest client on the calendar for Monday. Suddenly, I stopped what I was doing to Tommy, sat up in bed, stretched, and then fluffed the pillows. Tommy watched as I made myself comfortable.

"Tommy, sorry, but forget about sex right now, you've hooked me on the case. I can't wait until Monday to read the file, so you might as well start telling me about it." With great difficulty—Tommy was nothing if not persistent—I gently pushed him away. "It's your fault. You started telling me about it—a virginal, high-priced call girl who may or may not have knocked off two guys."

I knew that Tommy, with his photographic memory, would be able to rattle off information about the case without consulting any files. In this one, as with all the others, he would have the facts memorized and would easily be able to recall the most minute detail.

Tommy, seeing how determined I was, sighed, and gave up trying to initiate more sex. When something piqued my interest,

I became single-minded, so there was no point in his continuing to make love to me while I was in that frame of mind.

"As I told you before, our client, Madeline Meadows, is twenty-two years old, originally from Dubuque, and has lived in Miami for two years." Tommy turned to me. "Keep in mind that our client hasn't been charged with anything. She claims not to know anything about the murders—no big surprise there, naturally—but that she did know the victims. Ms. Meadows was interviewed by the police this past Thursday, the day before yesterday, so she's taking steps to protect herself, just in case things escalate. That's why she came to me on Friday. Just in case."

"Pretty smart on her part," I repeated. For a small-town girl from Dubuque, not exactly a place known for its high crime rate, she must have been a quick learner: two years here and at the first whiff of trouble, she hired herself the top lawyer in Miami.

Any self-respecting Miamian, when faced with the possibility of being charged with a crime, knew to get in touch right away with a criminal defense attorney—a measure comparable to getting a checkup at the doctor when one starts to feel ill. In Miami, it wasn't at all unusual for someone to have contact information for criminal defense lawyers in their address book, right next to their physicians and dentists.

"All right," I said, sitting up a bit more. "You have my undivided attention. Keep talking."

"Well, according to Ms. Meadows, she's been working as an escort on South Beach for the past six months." Tommy smiled. "She was quick to reassure me that she doesn't work for one of those sleazy operations where the girls are basically hookers— in fact, it's quite the opposite. First of all, she doesn't work with any company—she's on her own. And then, of course, there's the fact that our client doesn't sleep with her clients—that's the big selling point, her hook—pardon the pun. She reports that for the pleasure of her virginal company, she can charge up to five grand an hour."

I thought for a moment. I didn't know much about the world of escorts, but what Tommy had stated had made no sense. "I don't get it. Why would someone pay five thousand dollars an hour *not* to have sex with her? What's she into?" I didn't even want to begin to speculate. In Miami, the possibilities were endless.

"I asked her the same thing," Tommy nodded. "She said it's the challenge of it, that they all dream of being her 'first.' Let me tell you, Lupe, I can see why men lust after her. She's a total knockout—tall, with long blond hair that's actually kind of silvery. She's got full lips, clear blue eyes, and the kind of body that men salivate over—and all this with the most virginal, sweetest face ever. I swear, Lupe, she looks like a schoolgirl, a veritable Lolita. Quite a combination—definitely worth the price of admission for the right guy with a fat wallet."

I considered Tommy's words. "Does she go with girls, too, or just men?" If she did, her client base would have automatically doubled. I wondered if a woman had sex with another woman, could she still be considered a virgin?

"Lupe, I swear . . ." Tommy admired how my mind worked. "No, just men—really, really, rich ones." Tommy got a faraway, dreamy look in his eyes, one which I recognized. I cleared my throat loudly to bring him back to reality—business was business—and, as far as I was concerned, I was already on the case, adding up the billable hours, regardless of how I was working— standing straight up or lying on my back.

"Apparently, she's completely upfront with her clients about the fact that it's highly unlikely they'll get anywhere with her.

After all, that's the attraction," Tommy added. "Remember, the girl does have Midwestern values. But they still make dates with her in the hopes of being 'die first.'"

"Kind of like a sexless fetish, huh?" I burst out laughing. "The male ego! Never underestimate it—even if it costs them thousands of dollars." I winked at Tommy. "So, come on. Tell me about the two murders and how our client is connected to them."

"One was her gynecologist. A Dr. Samuel Steinberg," Tommy explained. "Ms. Meadows would visit him weekly so he could confirm that she was still a virgin and give her an affidavit certifying that fact. The other victim was Woodley Robinson, a client of hers who used to see her once or twice a week."

"Woodley Robinson?" I repeated. "I recognize that name."

"Yes, you would, Lupe," Tommy replied. "He's that successful developer. You know, the guy that bought up all of the property on South Beach in the eighties before South Beach was South Beach. He made a fortune, a real killing," Tommy reminded me.

I thought about what Tommy had said. "Even with all that money, being her client must have been pricey, but then, hope springs eternal! I'm sure that a man didn't reach the successes that Mr. Robinson had without being a risk-taking optimist."

Tommy inched closer to me. "Apparently, the homicide cops told Ms. Meadows that the only thing the victims had in common was that they were both in regular contact with her. That, and they were shot with the same weapon."

"The cops gave her that information?" I had a hard time believing that the police would divulge that much about their investigation. Homicide cops in Miami were notoriously so closed-mouthed that they wouldn't make comments about the weather—even if a hurricane was approaching.

Tommy began kissing me again as he continued discussing

the case. "I told you, she's a knockout and a pro at working men. She could get any man to bare his soul, his wallet, and probably to confess to anything."

"Well, at $5,000 an hour, she'd better be good at it," I pointed out quite logically.

Tommy had started working on my right ear, a fast track to my becoming aroused, and a state which he was rapidly approaching. Was it me, I wondered, or the thought of Madeline Meadows that was inspiring all of this passion?

"Last question. Who's the lead detective on the case?" I had trouble believing any homicide detective would reveal so much information to a suspect without having an ulterior motive. If not, Madeline Meadows, the professional virgin, must have been quite the *femme fatale.*

It took Tommy a moment to compose himself before replying, "Your old friend Detective Anderson."

Tommy sure had been right when he told me I would find this case interesting.

Two

My BlackBerry rang as I stepped out of the shower. "Fuck! I hate Monday mornings. I can't even take a shower in peace."

It was my cousin Leo. "Hey, Lupe, thought you'd want to know that the courier from Tommy's office just brought a file for you marked 'Urgent.'"

I could tell from the staccato quality of Leo's speech that he'd most likely just finished his second cup of Cuban coffee. Normally, for regular people, two cups of coffee to kick-start the work week wouldn't be out of the ordinary, especially on a Monday morning. But Cuban coffee was in a different league. The amount of caffeine in a cup of Cuban coffee was enough to make the heart beat double time, and two cups was about enough to send an elephant into cardiac arrest.

I looked at the bathroom clock and groaned. It wasn't even nine o'clock—the crack of dawn for me—and already Tommy's file on Madeline Meadows was waiting. But, worse still, Cousin Leo was clearly on overdrive. All indications pointed to the fact that it was going to be a very long Monday. I wasn't a morning person so it took me a long time to wake up, and only after I consumed several gallons of café con leche.

Still holding on to the phone, I leaned against the shower

door and closed my eyes. I needed to assess what lay ahead of me: Tommy's client, I could deal with but Leonardo was a different matter. I loved my cousin dearly, but when he was on one of his weird kicks, more often than not, I wanted to hide from him or, at the very least, medicate both of us.

After a year of drinking only herbal tea—Leo had been on a Zen binge—my cousin had gone back to his Cuban roots with a vengeance. At least as far as his coffee habit was concerned. At last count he was inhaling three cups of *colados* before noon, each drink containing eight ounces of pure caffeine. *Colados* were a beverage definitely not to be consumed by a single individual, but instead poured into tiny, thimble-sized cups and shared. I'd always felt that *colados* should come with warning labels: non-Cubans beware; Cubans only consume one per sitting. The fact that Leo drank an entire *colado* by himself was yet more proof that my cousin did not know the meaning of moderation.

"Thanks for the heads-up on the file, Leo. It's a new case that I'll be working. I spoke to Tommy this weekend, so I was expecting it." I was still in the bathroom, naked and dripping wet, not exactly in the best condition to speak to my cousin. I quickly wrapped a towel around me. It might have been hard for most people to wrap a towel around themselves while holding a cell phone pressed to their ear, but I was a virtuoso at it.

"A new case?" Leo repeated. "Good. I hope it's a domestic. I want to remodel the guest bathroom. Hmm, I'm seeing a bordello theme—very Moulin Rouge."

Bordello theme! Was it coincidence that the Meadows case landed in our laps today? "Earth to Leo. Sorry, it's not a domestic." I cut my cousin off before he could start fantasizing about the Meadows case being a domestic, his favorite kind, the kind that gave him visions of dollar bills floating around in his head. "I'll be in soon. Bye."

I hung up on what I hoped would be a reassuring note. Lately Leo had started to feel insecure when I wasn't around. Not a good sign for a receptionist/manager at a P.I. firm. I hoped he wasn't going to revert to his second childhood. As much as I loved Leo, after having been shot, I had enough excitement without having to worry about a twenty-six year old sexually confused man.

Taking into account the details of my personal life, the fact that my cousin Leonardo worked for me should not have been all that surprising. After all, how many twenty-eight-year-old female private investigators lived at home with their father, divorced older sister, twin nieces, other sister, who was a nun, a pair of octogenarian housekeepers, and their assistant, a rafter called Eliza? True, our house was quite large—some might say obscenely so—but it had to be to accommodate such a tribe. It wasn't that my sisters and I still lived at home because there was something wrong with us. Rather, it had happened gradually, as a result of the twists and turns of life. Also, the fact that Papi was a contractor made building such a house easier than if he had been, say, a doctor or a lawyer. As Papi was the kind of person who loved to challenge his abilities—both personal and professional—he had enjoyed designing and building our home.

Years before, when Mami and Papi had spoken to the architect about building a house for themselves, their three teenage daughters, and Aida and Osvaldo, they had certainly never envisioned what life would have in store for them. They had thought that as we grew up, we would marry and move out of the house, only to return with our children for the occasional visit. The house had to be big enough for the three of us, our spouses, and, of course, many grandchildren. After all, one did not name one's three daughters after places where the Virgin Mary had made apparitions (Fatima, Lourdes and Guadalupe), and not expect them to get married and have lots of children. Unfortunately, life had other plans.

Less than a year after moving in, our beloved mother was diagnosed with ovarian cancer and, less than two years later, died after a long and painful battle with the disease. She never lived long enough to see all of her daughters married. Only Fatima, the eldest, had, and that did not turn out too well. Unfortunately, her good-for-nothing husband, Julio Juarez, had turned out to be even more of a loser than we had suspected. After having several affairs (one had been a sexual encounter in the ladies' room during the reception after their wedding), it turned out that he had embezzled thousands from Solano Construction, Papi's firm.

Although I'd been appalled at what a thief Julio turned out to be, in the end, it had been because of his actions that I'd become a private investigator. Papi had retained a lawyer, Stanley Zimmerman, to see what his soon-to-be-former son-in-law had been up to, and he, in turn, had hired a private investigator to check out what Julio had done. This had all taken place during summer vacation from school (yes, Fatima had been a June bride) at a time when I'd been unemployed with plenty of time on my hands. I would accompany Hadrian, the investigator, on his rounds as he gathered evidence of Julio's illegal behavior.

It turned out that, in addition to cheating on Fatima and embezzling cash, Julio had left my sister with thousands in debt, and a broken heart. As a result, Fatima swore she'd never become involved with another man, ever again, a vow she had not broken in the ten years since her marriage had fallen apart. On the plus side, he also had given Fatima two lovely, lovable twin girls—so maybe he hadn't been all bad.

Following Hadrian around had shown me that I really liked the private investigative business. So much so that, after considering my limited employment options, I decided that after graduating from the University of Miami I would become a private eye.

Until then, I'd not had a clue as to what I wanted to do after graduation, but I did know what I did not want to do: become a nun like my sister Lourdes; become a single mother like Fatima; or go into the construction business with my father. I'd majored in advertising, not necessarily because I'd had a burning desire to work in the field, but because I couldn't think of anything else to do.

I looked into what the requirements were for becoming a private eye—interning at a firm, background checks, etc.—and, after having fulfilled them two years later, applied for and was granted my 'C'-class private investigator's license. Less than a week later, under duress, I had hired Leo, my first and only, employee. Life had been good. That is, until I'd been shot. Now, I was trying to get back to where I'd been before that very unpleasant event.

My elder sister, Lourdes, was a nun, and quite a devout one, too. Although our parents had been reasonably religious, we had no idea where her vocation had come from. Lourdes had never, ever, shown any saintly tendencies growing up. In high school she'd been kicked out of two schools for drinking and smoking pot, so, clearly, her conversion from bad girl to semi-saint had happened when she'd been a student at the University of Miami.

Even though Lourdes was quite liberated (despite the fact that she was a nun), it was highly unlikely that she was ever going to marry and have children. Still, even as she devoted herself wholeheartedly to her vocation, she liked her material comforts enough to spend half of her time at home, and the other half in her tiny, single room at the convent.

I'd had a few boyfriends but none were serious enough for me to think about getting married and having children. About eight years ago, in a burst of independence, I'd moved out of the house and rented an apartment in a building on Brickell Avenue, a place where lots of young, urban professionals lived. But that had not turned out to have been a good move; after my lease had terminated, I'd returned home. True, I had missed the family a lot, but that hadn't been the only reason I'd returned. Although Papi would have never in a million years admitted it, I knew that he had missed me a lot, too.

After Mami's death, Papi had been quite lost, and even though he'd tried to be strong for all our sakes, it was as if the life had been drained from him. I knew that I was the daughter who reminded him the most of his beloved wife, so it had been rough on him when I'd left home—almost as if he'd been abandoned twice. Needless to say, I had been welcomed back home with open arms—much like the return of the prodigal son.

I had no idea how much longer I would stay living at the house in Cocoplum, but, for now, it was home. I recognized that some might question as to why I—an independent, strong woman—would choose to live at home, but I was secure in the choice I had made. I was happy living here, and from what I could tell, my family was happy to have me. The one thing I did have to put up with was hearing lots and lots of free advice, which is, as everyone knows, worth exactly what one paid for.

I took another towel and wrapped it around my head to stop the wet hair from dripping down my back. I started to dry myself and, as I always did when naked, searched out the scar on my chest, a thin line that ran from the bottom of my right shoulder, across my chest, and stopped at the upper part of my left breast. The line was smooth, save for three puncture wounds, all lined up in a row, where the bullets had hit me. The emergency room doctors in the trauma unit at Jackson Memorial Hospital had done such an outstanding job stitching me up that the scar was barely noticeable.

It had been almost two years since I was shot, but I still woke up in the night drenched in sweat, imagining Carlos Suarez's face as he raised the hand that held the pistol. I would see it all in slow motion: the arm, the gun, and then, the bullets flying. If it hadn't been for his bad aim—three other bullets had missed me altogether—I would have been dead. Lucky for me, the man was such a pathetic loser that he couldn't even shoot straight Suarez was currently on Death Row, waiting for all his appeals to run out before he got the needle. Never had I been so pleased that Florida was a 'death penalty state.'

The dream had come less often as more time passed, but when it did, it remained as vivid as ever. I supposed that someday the nightmare would stop. At least, that's what the counselors had told me. And, apart from the scar that would continue to fade, I would be able to put the incident behind me. I told myself to do as the therapists recommended and to concentrate on the fact that, against all odds, I was still alive.

Now I was going to be reminded of it once again. According to Tommy, Detective Anderson was the lead homicide cop on the Meadows case. I had known Detective Maxwell Anderson for years—the last ones in the biblical sense—a fact that I feared could complicate and potentially compromise my ability to work on this investigation.

I had spent most of Sunday thinking about all of the possible negative ramifications of Detective Anderson and me working on the same case, albeit from opposite sides. I was reasonably sure that our personal relationship wouldn't affect my work. After all, it had been over for more than a year but I still had doubts. I debated calling Tommy to tell him that not only did I know the homicide detective in a professional capacity, which Tommy was already aware of, but that I was also familiar with every inch of his body—and, of course, he with mine, bullet holes and all.

The Meadows case would be the first time since I was shot that the detective and I would be involved in the same investigation. I had taken almost two years off to recuperate, and it had been during that time that we had become involved. Detective Anderson had been the first person I'd seen in the recovery room in the hospital after waking up from surgery. Apparently, he hadn't left my bedside in the three days that I had been unconscious.

In the previous years I had known him, Detective Anderson had never shown that he harbored any personal feelings for me, so I was surprised when he had declared his love for me. So much so that I had set off my heart monitor and caused the nurses in the intensive care unit to rush into the room. I had known him for six years, but always in a professional context. To this day, I was ashamed to admit that, crack investigator that I was, I never suspected that he had loved me for all that time.

After having had such a close relationship with him during my recovery, it was strange to think that I hadn't seen Detective Anderson in more than a year, especially as he had been the only man I had been involved with during that time. Monogamy did not come easily to me. Actually, until Detective Anderson, it had been a foreign concept. The fact that I'd been with him, and only him, during that time spoke volumes of how deeply I felt about him. Not only did I come to love him, but perhaps, more importantly, I trusted him.

Having been shot, and having come within a hair's breadth of dying, resulted, not surprisingly, in my having trust issues, but I never had those with Maxwell. He had been the perfect person for me at a very difficult time.

Of course, the fact that he'd been a homicide detective for over a dozen years meant that he had seen pretty much everything, so he knew how to treat me. I couldn't have looked very attractive, bandaged and banged up the way I was, but Detective Anderson overlooked those physical impairments. He'd had lots of patience with me and always encouraged me.

I always acknowledged that one of the main reasons I'd had a full recovery was that Maxwell Anderson had been with me, never complaining, and always by my side. He had been my tower of strength. And, even though my family had been a huge source of help and support, it had been Detective Anderson, the homicide investigator, who most understood what it was like for me to be shot on the job. Empathy and understanding in circumstances such as those could never be overemphasized.

There hadn't been one single reason for our relationship to end; in spite of our best efforts, things had simply run their course. Although we were both sad about that, neither of us could deny what had happened. Thankfully, we managed to part while still fond of each other, and with only the warmest wishes. Although Miami was a large urban area—the county had a population in excess of two million—it could be a very small town in some respects, but I had never run into him after our break-up.

During the time we were together, I had made a serious effort to call him by his given name, *Maxwell*, but I had not been very successful. No matter how hard I tried, I still thought of him as Detective Anderson, the name that I'd known him by for years. Even when we were in bed together, I would sometimes slip and call him Detective Anderson. Old habits were hard to break, even when having an orgasm.

Maxwell was assigned to investigate murders, and, as those

were the kind of cases I usually worked for the defense, we would come into contact with each other during the course of the investigation. But since I hadn't worked full-time for close to two years, this had not happened. Detective Anderson played by the rules: he was honest, thorough and didn't pull any of the tricks others in his department would. Cutting corners was not part of Maxwell's vocabulary.

It was ironic that the first murder case I would be working on full-time after my hiatus involved Detective Anderson as the lead homicide investigator. The part-time cases I had been working since being shot were relatively easy and didn't demand the kind of commitment, dedication and hard work that a multiple murder case would. But, because I'd investigated plenty of these cases during my eight years as a private eye, I knew what they entailed. Before then, I didn't feel that I was up to working such a case, but now I did. And the Meadows case seemed a perfect one with which to start.

For the past year, I'd gone into the office on a fairly regular basis, mostly supervising the cases that Leo had taken on: insurance scams, domestics, wire-transfer fraud, background investigations, etc. (the bills had not stopped arriving because I'd been shot). The Meadows case would be the first murder case that I'd accepted since that awful day when Carlos Suarez had shot me. If I hadn't been confident that I could give it my best effort, I wouldn't have accepted it. But I had to acknowledge that it had been close to two years since I'd been on the front lines. I told myself that investigating a murder case was like riding a bicycle—once you learned how to do it, you never forgot.

I may have been a bit apprehensive about starting to investigate a double murder, but I was probably getting all worked up over nothing. If I hadn't been comfortable with my decision to take the case, why would I have gone to the firing range yesterday afternoon with my two Berettas—one that I kept in my black leather oversized Chanel purse for everyday use, and the other that stayed in the safe in my office—to hone my shooting skills?

Yesterday, while driving west on Route 41 to the range, the two guns were on the seat next to me. My everyday Beretta was in the Chanel bag; the office one in its case. I had been quite calm, and not overly concerned that I might need to use them. Carlos Suarez had taken his best shot at me, and, although he had hit me, and hit me hard, he had not succeeded in killing me, so maybe the Virgin had something else in mind for me. Once out on the range, I had been pleased to find that my hand remained quite steady. I hit the mark ninety percent of the time. Next time, it would be one hundred.

The situation with Detective Anderson kept bothering me. After returning from the range, I had gone swimming in our pool, something I did when I had to think. Papi had built a lap pool in our backyard, and as I swam, the answer would come to me.

I was conflicted as to what to do about telling Tommy about Detective Maxwell Anderson. If I truly believed in full disclosure, I would have told him about our affair, but I honestly didn't think it applied here. To begin with, the detective and I no longer had a personal relationship, but, more importantly, we were both professionals, so both of us could do our jobs without letting our emotions affect our work.

In the end, after much soul searching and swimming many laps, I decided not to reveal to Tommy my relationship with Detective Anderson. In all honesty, I still didn't know enough about the case to make an informed decision as to how my history with Anderson would come into play, if at all. The best approach would be the cautious one and read the file and meet the client first.

Now that I was recovered and pretty much back to work full-time, it would be highly likely that I would be coming across more cases involving Detective Anderson. After all, we worked in the same field, so I might as well find out sooner rather than later what it would be like working opposite him again. At the very least, I would be going to the same places he frequented: the courthouse, police station, crime scenes, and the like.

Still, Tommy was the attorney on the Meadows case and, ethically speaking, I had to be upfront with him about any mitigating circumstances that might affect my ability to conduct a proper investigation. Tommy might have suspected that my relationship with the detective was more than professional, but he would never come straight out and ask. We had never defined our own relationship, but it was well understood that there were certain lines that would not be crossed. I suspected that in spite of his cool and calm demeanor, Tommy didn't really want to know about me sleeping with anyone else—and the same went for me regarding him.

The predicament I currently found myself in was just one more sign that I shouldn't get intimate with men I met professionally, but I had gone through twenty-eight years of life without listening to my own logical, sensible advice, so why start now? It was highly unlikely that I would change my ways. Besides, there was no use denying that I was attracted to men who lived on the edge and led the same kind of life as I did. It was just easier that way—less bullshit.

Another problem with dating more 'normal' men was that I didn't really have much opportunity to meet men who worked 'normal' occupations. I didn't go to bars much unless I was following someone while working a case, and the only time I looked men up online was to see if they had a criminal record during the course of an investigation.

As a private investigator in Dade County who specialized in criminal cases, I didn't exactly socialize with the *crème de la crème* of society. It was no secret that what passed for respectable in Miami would be considered sleazy in most other parts of the country. In Miami, the motto of upstanding citizens would be: "Some men are discovered, others are found out". Unfortunately, most of the ones I met fit into the latter category. Some days, I would visit as many as three different jails in Dade County, so I had plenty of occasions to interact with men on a professional level, but, unfortunately, they were behind bars. They weren't the greatest prospects for taking home to meet my family, unless, of course, I wanted to pay their bail first.

Compounding the problem was that, instead of carrying on a normal conversation with a potential date, such as asking where he went to school, I'd have to bite my tongue to keep from asking him if he had any priors. I found myself memorizing my dates' license plate numbers so I could run them if they aroused suspicions.

As far as a potential date's appearance was concerned, I would look for distinguishing characteristics rather than admire his features. Maybe even worse was that if I did go to bed with him, I would inspect his tattoos to see if he was gang affiliated. I barely knew how to carry on a conversation with a man: I would interview him instead.

On more than one occasion, if a man were to ask me out on a date and say he'd pick me up at twelve, I would have to ask whether he meant noon or midnight. And then, of course, there were the men who, if they seemed evasive when speaking about them selves, I would immediately suspect that they were in the witness protection program. Given all that, it was no wonder that most of the men I had relationships with worked in the same field as I did. They understood the obstacles of regular dating. Plus, they were just as screwed up as I was.

There was no question that the Meadows case was interesting: a virgin who was a pro. No way would I walk away from it, regardless of how much the situation was complicated by the fact that Detective Anderson was the investigating homicide detective. What intrigued me, though, was how Ms. Meadows and her clients spent their time on those $5,000-an-hour dates. Crossword puzzles? Gin rummy? Scrabble?

One of my best friends, Sweet Suzanne, was a high priced call girl. Even though we didn't talk about her profession much, she had told me enough to give me a pretty clear idea of what men expected for their money. Clearly, they didn't settle for playing pinochle.

I was completely intrigued by Madeline Meadows. Tommy would have to pry the case out of my cold dead hands if he were to take it away from me.

Three

"Lupe!" Aida yelled over the intercom. As usual, her voice was at top volume and so loud that I was sure she could be heard in Homestead. "Your breakfast is ready! Hurry up! You don't want it getting cold!"

I winced as Aida's screams reached me. I knew that she would keep it up every thirty seconds or so like an annoying car alarm that went off at regular intervals until I appeared downstairs.

Our octogenarian housekeeper had never learned to fully trust the intercom, and she continued to yell into it no matter how many explanations were given to her about how it worked. Each and every person in the family had told her the intercom Papi had bought was so sensitive that it could pick up a whisper, but to no avail. It was just a matter of time before we would suffer hearing loss as a result. No wonder the neighbors hated us—the whole neighborhood probably did—and all because of Aida's loud voice. Lately Aida's shrieks through the intercom had gotten louder.

I pressed the intercom button for the kitchen extension. "Thank you, Aida. I'll be right down. I'm just drying my hair." I knew this would quiet her. Aida was obsessed with the idea that going outside with wet hair, even in the tropical weather of Miami, would result in a severe case of pneumonia.

I needed to be in the office soon, so it was just as well that Aida was hurrying me. I quickly finished drying my hair, trying not to cry out as I untangled it. Knowing what the summer humidity would do to it, really, there was no point in even trying to force it into some kind of attractive style, so I just braided it after I'd finished combing it.

Still naked, I walked over to the closet. For a normal day at the office, I would have worn jeans, with a loose T-shirt or cotton shirt. As far as I was concerned, nearly every day was office casual, one of the perks of being self-employed. I left the more flamboyant fashion choices to Leonardo, something he took full advantage of. But that day, I would be meeting Madeline Meadows, so I had to dress appropriately as I would for any client.

Looking at my clothes, I decided that it was just too damned hot for any of the Armani suits, even the cotton ones. Because of how brutally hot and humid summers were in Miami, hardly anyone dressed up for work unless they had to. As for me, I hadn't worn stockings in more than five years. I settled on a casual two-piece tan cotton suit by Nanette Lepore, my new favorite designer. Then, operating on the belief that one must be prepared in case one was run over by a truck, I put on a sexy white La Perla lace bra and matching panties. Finally, I slipped into a pair of medium-high, black leather Manolo Blahnik sling-backs.

I took one quick look at myself in the mirror to make sure I looked presentable for the day ahead and made a couple of adjustments—the braid looked kind of lumpy—then went to the bathroom to put on makeup. I really didn't wear much, but that wasn't entirely out of choice since in Miami, especially in the summer, the heat and humidity made any cosmetics slide off my face. I settled on a little moisturizer, a bit of blush, a touch of mascara and some lip gloss. I sprayed myself with Chanel No. 5, my favorite perfume. It had been my mother's scent, and in her memory, I hadn't worn any other since her death. I may not have been able to hold my beloved Mami, but after spraying her special perfume on me, I could close my eyes and smell her.

"Lupe! Child! Your breakfast!" Sure enough, just like clockwork, Aida's voice came out of the intercom loudly, startling me so much that I almost dropped the bottle of perfume. Apparently she'd decided that five minutes was enough time for me to dry my hair. "Osvaldo is on the terrace waiting for you!"

The scene was easy for me to picture. Osvaldo would be standing outside on the terrace, under the wide roof, trying to stay out of the sun. He would be dressed in his daytime uniform, the same one he'd worn for decades: a crisp white shirt over black pants, thick, black leather shoes and a straw hat. Even though he would deny it, it was too hot for him outside, so I hurried as much as I could.

Osvaldo, Aida's husband, was our butler, handyman, driver, gardener and all-around helper. I suspected that not even he knew precisely how old he was; our best guess was that he was around ninety. Aida and Osvaldo had been with our family for more than sixty years. They had worked for Mami's parents in Havana and had raised her as though she was their own daughter. The couple had never had any children, and looked upon our family as their own, so much so that they had gone into exile with Mami and Papi after Castro came to power.

Unfortunately, they were getting older, and naturally enough, were slowing down. Papi had told them that they could, of course, continue to live with us and promised that he would take care of them if they decided to retire. But they had been offended by the notion that they could no longer carry out their duties, and turned down his offer. Lately, though, it had been becoming clear that age was catching up to them.

Aida had recently left French fries cooking in the frying pan; the hot oil had caught fire and nearly burned the house down. Thank God for the smoke alarms. Last December, Osvaldo had nearly electrocuted himself while setting up the Christmas tree lights. None of us wanted to admit that they were growing old, so when these mishaps started taking place, we dismissed them and convinced ourselves that they were just getting forgetful. But as time passed and the incidents had become more serious— and dangerous—they'd become too much to ignore.

Our family had sat down for a meeting to discuss the situation, and had decided to get Osvaldo and Aida an assistant. Fortunately, my sister, Lourdes, the nun, had recently made friends with a young Cuban woman named Eliza Mendoza who had been living temporarily at the convent and was looking for a job. Like many of our countrymen, she had come to Miami with no money, so she was looking for the kind of job that included housing, which suited our needs perfectly.

Eliza was a lovely person, cheerful and hardworking, so it wasn't surprising that everyone liked her immediately. Her story wasn't all that unusual. She had disagreed with the government in Cuba, so she'd been barred from attending university there, or finding a decent job; leaving the island was the only way she could make a future for herself. She had escaped Cuba on a raft and, after five long days of drifting through the shark-infested waters of the Florida Straits, she had landed in Miami. Since Eliza had no family or friends in the United States, the good nuns of Lourdes' order had taken her in.

We didn't want to hurt Osvaldo and Aida's feelings by telling them that we were hiring them a helper, so the story was that we were offering Eliza temporary housing until she found other work and, in return, she would repay the hospitality by doing chores around in the house. Eliza was so sweet and efficient that the old couple didn't mind having her around. It had been two years since Eliza had started living with us, and, so far the arrangement had worked out very well.

In September Eliza would be starting her second year at Florida International University, working toward a degree in business administration. She was a master of tact, and being very fond of the old couple, knew exactly when to help Osvaldo and Aida, and when to pull back. However, as much as the couple liked Eliza and welcomed her help, they had made it clear that breakfast was their exclusive domain and that they weren't giving it up.

I still had one more important task left to do to complete my morning routine before leaving my room. I sat on the bed, opened my purse, the Chanel that I kept on the night table, reached inside the zippered compartment, and took out the Beretta. I checked it twice to make sure it was loaded. It was only when I'd been satisfied that the gun was in perfect working order that I placed it back in the bag. As I did, I ran my fingers over the small hole in the side of the purse, a result of having had to fire the Beretta through it years ago while working the Arango case. Yet another close call. Although the repairs had been expertly done, I could still feel the stitches where the bullet had pierced the leather. By now, the bag was more than ten years old, but it was still in such good shape—bullet hole not withstanding—that I really had no reason to replace it. Those Chanel bags sure were expensive, but they more than made up for it with their durability.

I walked over to the closet and brought out a black satin Kate Spade carry-all that I had placed on the top shelf, behind my other bags. I took out the Beretta from the case inside that bag and laid it next to the first one. I took the second gun out of its case and I checked it carefully, making sure that it, too, was in perfect working order.

The day before I had cleaned the guns, my personal one and the office one, so I knew they were ready to be used. After making sure they were fully loaded, I placed them back in their respective bags. I would return the back-up Beretta to its regular spot in the safe once I got back to the office.

Most women who carried oversized leather Chanel bags didn't keep loaded guns in them. It wasn't that I intended to shoot anyone, but after getting shot three times by that idiot, Carlos Suarez, at point-blank range, I felt naked without the Beretta. I was a firm believer in the Second Amendment, although I doubted that the Founding Fathers meant for a weapon to be carried in a French designer bag.

I pressed the button on the intercom. "Aida, please tell Osvaldo I'll be right there. And that I mean it this time."

I sensed it was going to an eventful day, but hoped it wouldn't be too eventful. It had been a while since I had a busy day and I wasn't sure if I was fully prepared for one.

Four

Driving in Miami under any circumstance could be considered a blood sport, especially given the elements of danger unique to the city: clueless tourists in their rental cars; retirees who couldn't see over their steering wheels; macho Latino guys weaving in and out of traffic; sweet young things applying mascara in the fast lane; motorcyclists who tailgated; and drivers who tried to outrace police cars in hot pursuit. And, of course, then there were the BlackBerry addicts, cell phone junkies and texting messagers.

But what I found the most frightening: drivers pumped up on enormous doses of industrial-strength caffeine. I didn't know which ones I feared the most: the drivers who had already consumed gallons of coffee which, by then, was already coursing through their veins, or the motorists with hot drinks clutched in their hands, sipping from mugs with the intensity of an alcoholic approaching their first drink of the day.

That morning, I'd already had to swerve three rimes to avoid collisions with other drivers. The most recent near-catastrophe had involved an ice blue Jaguar whose driver was a young hotshot, no doubt making a multimillion dollar deal (hedge funds? drugs?) as he talked into a Bluetooth headset. His car had come so close to mine that I had to slam on the brakes, and had nearly gotten rear-ended by the Lexus behind me, who had been, in true Miami fashion, following too close.

The asshole had not only narrowly missed slamming into my brand new car, but he had almost made me spill my steaming mug of *café con leche* all over my lap. I mean, I wasn't as annoyed as that old lady who sued McDonald's when she spilled hot coffee on her lap, but if that had happened to me that morning, I would have had to go home and change my clothes, which would have made me even later.

Papi, bless his heart, claiming it was strictly for safety reasons, had given me a new hardtop silver CL55 Mercedes that year, a car that rode so smoothly I hardly felt it move. I would have hated to have anything happen to it, especially getting hit by some idiot in the process of closing some personal or professional deal, legal or illegal, on his BlackBerry. And, who had probably let his insurance lapse.

I had just composed myself after the close call with the Jaguar when my cell phone went off for the fourth time since I had been in the car. Knowing it was Leonardo, I let it go straight to voicemail. No matter how many times I tried to disabuse him of the theory, Leonardo felt that calling me repeatedly made me get to the office quicker—sort of like Aida yelling into the intercom at home. It was a wonder that, after all these years, they still had not figured that their methods would elicit the opposite response from me.

I loved my cousin dearly, but he sure knew how to try my patience. Lately he had been undergoing a sort of transformation, an event that wasn't entirely out of character, since it was seasonal, but this time was different because he was being annoyingly mysterious. Leonardo couldn't keep a secret to save his life, so his silence was arousing my suspicions—and fears—in equal amounts.

Normally, I wouldn't worry about Leonardo and his cyclical infatuations; he'd always had a short attention span and had trouble focusing. After all, we'd survived his moon child phase (made difficult for months when the weather didn't cooperate as the moon was obscured by clouds), his organic farmer phase (for a city boy, he was quite gifted at growing marijuana), his earth mother phase (alternative lifestyle), yoga freak (short-lived due to his ADD), psychic true believer (Leo had bad eyesight and failed at both tarot and the crystal ball), and vegetarian (Cubans, who are natural carnivores, rarely eat vegetables). There had been other phases as well, but they had come and gone so fast that they were hardly worth mentioning.

From what I had managed to pick up, vinyl was somehow involved in this new kick. *Ay.* Vinyl, in the summer, in Miami. Well, Leonardo had never been very practical. He had mentioned something about painting one of the rooms 'bordello red,' which wouldn't seem to go well with vinyl, but, with Leo, I could never be sure of anything.

The drive from our house in Cocoplum to the Solano Investigations office in Coconut Grove normally took about fifteen minutes. I had timed the ride to the second, as it allowed me time to finish my *café con leche* while listening to the news on Spanish radio. I found myself listening more and more to Hispanic stations as not only did it help to keep my Spanish fluent, I especially enjoyed learning new colloquialisms and slang expressions, but it also gave me a pulse on Miami's significant Hispanic population.

I usually enjoyed the drive on Main Highway, a two-lane road covered by a canopy of beautiful old oak trees. While the scenery was spectacular, one of the main reasons why I liked the journey so much was because, typically, it was the only part of day that I had to myself.

That morning, Main Highway was so congested that, I swear, I could have walked to work faster. Not a serious consideration for me, as I never did any physical exercise (at least outdoors). I only enjoyed one physical activity that made me breathe heavily and break a sweat, and it was one that could be done in air conditioning, and did not entail a trip to the gym. Watching the long line of brake lights in front of me, it occurred to me that only in Miami, a truly Hispanic city, did the height of the morning commute peak at ten o'clock.

I had just stopped at the traffic light in front of the Cocowalk Mall when my phone rang again. I took one quick glance at the number before I picked up. This was a call I wanted to take.

"Lupe? I just called your office and Leonardo told me that you're not in yet." Tommy sounded slightly annoyed—not a good thing. "So, I guess that means you haven't read the Madeline Meadows file yet."

"That's right, Tommy. I'm not at the office yet, but I'm only a few minutes away." Tommy and I may have been lovers, but he didn't cut me any slack where business was concerned. "I'll start on it as soon as I get in. I still have almost two hours before the meeting with die client, plenty of time to read the file. I'll call you as soon as I'm finished reading it." Then, as sweetly as I could, I added. "Bye. Have a nice day."

Normally, I never would have used that phrase, but I couldn't think of anything else to say. Tommy was right, I should have been in the office hours ago, but I was never productive early in the morning. The only time I saw the early morning hours was if it was a continuation from the night before.

Less than a minute later, I pulled into the driveway of the cottage where Solano Investigations was located. I parked my Mercedes next to Leonardo's black Jeep, took the office Beretta out of the bag and placed it in the waistband of my skirt. I looked around to make sure no one was lurking before opening the car door and getting out. It wasn't that I expected trouble, but one of the consequences of getting shot was that I was a lot more aware of my surroundings and prepared for the worst. I sure didn't want to go through that ordeal again. Assuming I survived, that is. There was no guarantee that my luck would hold up a second time. I did not want any more bullet holes in my body, or need any other near-death experiences.

Solano Investigations—a grand name, considering that the firm was made up of just Leonardo and me—operated out of a three-bedroom cottage at the end of a narrow, winding road in the heart of Coconut Grove. The one-story building was painted white with green shutters (in typical Key West style), and was hidden from the street by the lush vegetation that grew all around, so thick, in fact, that after all these years, I sometimes drove right past the driveway. Leo and I had never placed a sign out front announcing our business. We figured that if someone wanted to find us badly enough, they would be able to do so.

The huge frangipani tree next to the building was quite beautiful, but the flowers that fell from its thick branches were murder on the paint jobs of the cars parked underneath, a fact that Osvaldo never failed to point out. He would constantly scold me, and tell me to park someplace else, that I was ruining the car. I would pay attention to him for a few days, but eventually, I would go back to parking in my usual space. I was nothing if not a creature of habit.

I had bought the cottage seven years before with a loan from my father, money I had since repaid, in spite of his protestations that it was a gift. In the beginning, when we had first moved in, I had planned to rentout one or two rooms to help defray the expenses, but Leonardo had made it clear to me that sharing the space was simply unacceptable. His attitude was not surprising. As the only son in a Cuban family, sharing did not come easily to him. Besides, he had big ideas for the cottage.

In order to make the most cash in the shortest time possible, decorating was expensive and Leo had the world's most expensive tastes, it was clear that we had to increase our revenue. The first thing Leonardo had done after we'd started the firm was to load me up on domestic cases: investigations involving marital misconduct. They were the cases I loathed but which paid the best. For ten months, I worked only on cases involving an adulterous spouse or significant other (heterosexual, homosexual, and even one transgendered client) which had made me a pile of money, more than enough to pay Papi back, and to remodel our offices in the grand style to which Leonardo and I would soon become accustomed.

It was great to not have any debt, but the downside of working all those domestics was that I was never, ever, going to get married. As a private investigator, few things shocked me, but the amount of infidelity taking place in Miami was truly mind-boggling. No one seemed to be satisfied with his or her partner. People were fooling around with members of the opposite sex, the same sex, threesomes, and in one particularly harrowing case, a horse. I attributed all of the friskiness to either the climate (hot) or the water (salty).

During those ten months, I had investigated all kinds of cases, but the one that stuck in my mind was a situation in which a husband was unfaithful, not just to his wife, but also to his mistress and his girlfriend. I almost had to break open a vial of smelling salts under the nose of the mistress (my client) as she viewed the tapes. Of course, she had known that her lover was married—she could deal with the wife without a problem— but the other woman was simply too much. Even in the murky world of serial infidelity, there were limits to what was accept-able behavior.

Anyway, after those long months, I had told Leonardo that we were finished with domestics. That was, unless we were truly broke and starving. Naturally, Leonardo only followed my orders for a few weeks, until the latest bill from the decorator came in. I never really understood what exactly the designer had done to deserve being compensated so handsomely, but I had dutifully paid the tab.

I hadn't been pleased when I'd found out that Leo had maxed out several of our corporate credit cards to satisfy his 'inner decorator' and I had let him know it. I worked my ass off to pay those off, but then, he had done it again. Leo had champagne tastes on a beer budget. And, once again, he accepted as many domestic cases as necessary to satisfy those expenses.

Sometimes it seemed that Leonardo thought of me as a human ATM and he had unlimited access to the funds in the account. Whenever our reserves ran low, Leo knew that all he had to do was to hand me a folder with the details of a new domestic case. I would work it a few days and the cash would magically spew out. It wasn't exactly the way to run a business, but it worked and we were always solvent. I could safely say that we had the most beautifully decorated private investigators' offices in Miami, if not the whole country.

The ironic thing about working 'domestics' was that Florida was a 'no-fault divorce' state. This meant that unlike other states where infidelity was a factor in divorce cases, the fact that one partner was screwing around on the other was not taken into account when the judge decided on monetary awards. It was for their own reasons that our clients wanted proof of infidelity.

I loved Leonardo, so I would put up with his eccentricities, although sometimes he was simply too much, even for me. Leo was my first cousin, the only son of my mother's sister, and had been thrust upon me when I started the firm. In fact, agreeing to employ him had been the only condition attached to Papi's loan.

The news that setting myself up in business was contingent on employing my unemployable cousin made me seriously consider taking out a mortgage on the building to fund my venture. However, after deciding that family came first (Papi dangling a check made out to me also helped me to see the light), I agreed to hire him as a receptionist/office manager—a job for which he was entirely unsuited. But it was all that I could offer. At the time Leonardo was twenty years old, broke, with no prospects (personal or professional), unsure of his sexual orientation, an expert at self-medication, and still living at home. He accepted my offer.

From the first day on the job, I knew exactly why Leonardo hadn't been able to find work: he was neurotic, forgetful, opinionated, self-centered and extravagant and those were his good qualities. We got along great on just about every level. After working together for seven years, he knew everything about me, as I knew everything about him, and we accepted one another, flaws and all. Our relationship was completely dysfunctional, but it worked. One thing about Leonardo: life with him was never dull.

"Hey, Leo, I'm here!" I opened the door to the office. My cousin didn't reply. Puzzled, I went past the reception area and walked into the kitchen. Still no Leo. I heard loud coughing coming from the back bathroom.

"Leo? Are you OK?" I knocked on the door. There was still no answer, but the coughing got louder. I began banging as hard as I could on the door.

"No! No!" Leonardo called out between coughs. "I'm OK. Don't come in! I'm all right!"

Suddenly, the door was flung open, and I was enveloped in a cloud of white powder so thick that it temporarily blinded me. Thinking it was cocaine, I immediately stopped inhaling. Oh God! For a second, I feared that we were going to get another visit from the DEA, which we sure as hell couldn't afford. I was still paying off Tommy's fees for defending Leo for his mishap with all those pesky pounds of weed that were found in and around our office a few years before. Thank God, Tommy had taken some of the payment out in trade. A good deal all around.

"Leo?" I gasped, detecting the scent of lilacs. Lilac-scented cocaine? God, the drug dealers were getting cuter. "What the fuck?"

"I'm sorry, Lupe," Leo said, from the depths of the bathroom. "Oh my God! It's not what you think. Honestly, I gave that stuff up, just like I promised."

Warily, I took a tiny sniff. "Is this baby powder?" I sniffed again. "Shit! It is. It's baby powder." I was so relieved Leonardo wasn't doing drugs that at that point I didn't exactly care what it was. With my cousin, I couldn't take anything for granted. "So what's going on?"

I thought I was hallucinating as, seconds later, I began to see what was inside the bathroom. Now it was as if I was the one who had been taking drugs. Leonardo was dressed head to toe in a black, shiny, vinyl bodysuit with a hood looking like a demented drag queen stuffed into a Cat Woman costume that was too small. In his right hand, he held an economy-sized bottle of Johnson's Baby Powder, lavender fragrance. I had seen Leonardo go through plenty of phases that demanded radical attire (his Pocahontas period came to mind) but this was the strangest and most impractical outfit that I could recall. He was dressed in skintight vinyl unitard—with a hoodie, no less—in the middle of summer in Miami!

Leonardo pointed to the bottle with a sheepish smile. "It's the only way I can get into the suit." I must have looked perplexed, so he continued with his explanation. "Vinyl sticks to the skin. Baby powder makes the suit slide on more easily, and lavender has soothing qualities." This from a man holding a *colado* in his other hand. Leonardo didn't wait for me to comment, he just continued to speak casually, as if we had been discussing something as innocuous as the weather. "I ordered the suit from the internet. Don't worry, Lupe, it's well made—20/25 gauge superior latex, heavy, resists tearing, totally fireproof and completely dependable."

Leonardo must have taken my stunned silence as approval. For my part, I felt as if I was watching Fashion Television while on crack. "It conies in transparent also, but for now, I think I'll stick with black—the transparent was too much." He turned around, swirling this way and that, so that I could admire him from all angles. Only when he was completely satisfied with the impromptu fashion show did he return to his desk in the reception area.

"Wow," was all I could manage to say.

There was no way I was going to ask him what he intended to do now that he was properly attired for whatever it was. Sometimes, too much information was not a good thing, especially where Leo was concerned. At that point, I could only hope that the 'soothing' qualities of the lavender baby powder would work to counteract the over-caffeinated effects of the *colado*.

"The Meadows file is on your desk," he called out over his shoulder as he flicked baby powder off of the suit.

My instincts had been correct: it was going to be a very long day.

Five

I was still blowing baby powder out of my nose as I opened
my office door. Clearly I would need some time to analyze and
digest the scene outside with Leo, but that would have to wait.
For now, I had work to do. In between sneezes, I was able to
see the file that Leonardo had placed on the middle of my desk.
From its thickness, it was obvious that Tommy had clearly done
a thorough job of interviewing Madeline Meadows.

I sat at my desk and opened the file. But before I began, I
looked up at the clock on the wall and was surprised to see that
it was close to ten-thirty. Between one thing and another (Leo
and his latex had taken up a chunk of it) half the morning was
gone. I only had an hour and a half to read the file, take notes,
and prepare for my noon meeting with Madeline Meadows. I
was fast, but, even so, it would be close.

Normally, before settling down for the workday, I would
spend a few minutes staring out of the big bay window that
lined the eastern wall of my office and overlooked the backyard.
There was very little garden there, especially since the enure
area had been taken over by an enormous avocado tree that had
grown in the middle of the space. There was no grass either,
as the tree's shadow blotted out any chance for the blades to

sprout there. Throughout the years I had grown to know the several generations of brightly colored parrots that lived on that tree and had missed them desperately during the time I was recuperating away from the office. I had thought about them regularly, envisioning what they were up to.

With any luck, I'd visit them later in the day, especially as I'd bought seeds to give them, the kind that they really liked. Sadly, for now, I didn't have time to throw them treats. Reluctantly, I gave the birds a quick wave then opened the Meadows file.

I'd been reading Tommy's reports for seven years, so I knew how thorough he was, but, even so, the notes that he had taken during Madeline Meadows' interview were more detailed than usual. I remembered how Tommy's demeanor had changed when he'd described her, and I strongly suspected that some of that could be attributed to her sex appeal.

Because of what Tommy had told me, I was somewhat familiar with Ms. Meadows' background, but the report filled in some of the blanks about her life since her arrival in Miami. I was surprised by the similarities between her life and that of my friend, Sweet Suzanne; the obvious difference was that Suzanne was definitely not a virgin, or at least had not claimed to be. And, although I did not know her exact rates, I knew that my friend sure did not charge $5,000 an hour to *not* have sex.

Both Suzanne and Madeline were tall blond women from the Midwest who had ended up in Miami after meeting Cuban men at their respective colleges. I wondered what it was about Cuban men that caused normal, level-headed women to uproot and move to Miami. None of the Cuban men I knew and, trust me, I knew plenty, could have ever convinced me to pack up and leave my family and all that was familiar and move thousands of miles away. But then again, I sure was no romantic, or swayed by Cuban men, for that matter.

Twenty-two year old Madeline Marie Meadows, originally from Dubuque, Iowa, was the youngest of five children, and had enjoyed what seemed like a normal, upper middle-class Catholic upbringing. Her father was a dentist, and her mother was a homemaker who, after the children were grown, started a catering business that she ran out of her home.

I was momentarily confused when I read that Madeline had attended St. Mary of the Hills High School: I had thought that Iowa was completely flat. Maybe it had been a case of wishful thinking on the nuns' part when they had named the school. Since the Meadows family appeared to be very religious, it wasn't surprising that our client had attended Catholic school. One of Madeline's older brothers was a seminarian studying for the priesthood and one of her aunts, her father's sister, was a nun of the Order of the Sacred Heart. I wondered if that was why Madeline was still a virgin. However, I quickly dismissed the thought as my sister, Lourdes, was a nun, and I certainly was no virgin. Could it really be true that Madeline was saving herself for marriage and that money had nothing to do with her virginity? I told myself to stop being naïve (it certainly was not becoming to me) and to continue reading.

After high school, Madeline followed in her older siblings' footsteps and had attended Iowa State University, in Ames. She had graduated magna cum laude with a degree in Liberal Arts and Sciences and a minor in Spanish; the last had occurred after reading *Don Quixote* in Spanish class in high school. According to Tommy's notes, Madeline had fallen in love with everything to do with the language: its culture, ait, music, films. It had been during her sophomore year in college, in an intermediate Spanish class, that she met the man who would be responsible for her ending up in Miami.

It seemed that Iowa State, in an attempt to diversify and

recruit students with international backgrounds, had begun offering a Latin American Studies program. As a result, one of the students who had come there for grad school was a young man from Miami named Ricardo Melendez. Ricardo had been born in the United States, but his family had arrived from Cuba during the Mariel boatlift in 1980. Ricardo had been the teacher's assistant for her Spanish class and would take over when the professor was away, which apparently, had been quite often. Madeline had told Tommy that she loved the classes and the language so much that she chose it as her minor during spring term of her sophomore year. Of course, her attraction to the handsome young T.A. hadn't hurt either. She had been so smitten by his dark, handsome good looks that she hadn't even taken any of her three allotted class cuts.

Not surprisingly, relationships between students and teachers were vigorously discouraged at the university, so Ricardo and Madeline, though clearly attracted to each other, couldn't act on their feelings and had to be satisfied with giving each other long, lingering looks. For Ricardo, refraining from dating Madeline was a practical matter: he was studying at Iowa State on a full scholarship and breaking the fraternization rule would have resulted in instant dismissal. For Madeline, to go against any established laws went against her Cadiolic upbringing. As far as she was concerned, the university's prohibition on student/faculty dating evoked the same feelings in her as obeying the commandment about honoring thy mother and father. Her parents would have disapproved of her breaking the rule, so to do so would be the same as dishonoring them, something she would never do.

Amazingly enough, they refrained from dating for two years, but in the weeks before graduation—Madeline from her undergraduate program and Ricardo from graduate school—they started to meet after class. Their relationship did not exactly explode: first, they went for coffee, then for lunch, and then Ricardo finally built up the courage to ask Madeline out for dinner, an invitation she eagerly accepted. It wasn't as though they didn't know each other: they'd been together three times a week, for two plus years in a row, during school terms.

They quickly realized how much they had in common: both had been brought up in homes with strong families, and where the Cadiolic faith was very much alive, something that ruled just about every aspect of their lives. They were attracted to each other, but they knew that sexual relations between unmarried couples went against the core teachings of the Church. Regardless, Ricardo and Madeline proclaimed their love for each other and decided that they wanted to spend the rest of their lives together.

I was so engrossed in reading Tommy's report on Madeline that I almost didn't hear Leo calling my name. Slightly annoyed at the interruption, I set down the file; by then it felt as if I was following the storyline of a novella.

"Hey, Lupe!" Leo called out again.

I looked up to find my cousin standing in the doorway to my office, still dressed in the cat suit, looking like an escapee from a bondage museum or dungeon. For about the thousandth time, I thanked God that few of our clients ever came to our office. They would have been shocked at the sight of Leonardo: one look at him, and we could kiss our walk-in business goodbye.

I wasn't too worried about our regular visitors: the mailman, UPS, the FedEx guys, the exterminator, the water deliveryman. They were all long-time witnesses to Leonardo's eccentricities. What I worried about were the reactions of first-time visitors, and to what it might do to our reputation if the rescue squad had to be called to attend to someone who keeled over from shock.

Just then, as I looked at Leonardo—a sex therapist's wet dream come to life—I had to exert some serious self-control not to burst out laughing. Whatever else Leo may have been, he sure was creative. I'd give him that. I prayed that the vinyl phase would pass soon, and not just because our entire office was coated in a thin film of lavender baby powder. Seeing him like that was just too distracting to my overactive imagination.

"That file Tommy sent over sure must be interesting. I've called your name three times now, and nada," Leo scolded. "Anyway, now that I have your attention, I'm going to run out to Gilbert's to get some *pastelitos* to go with my *colado*."

Just hearing Leonardo say the name of what was arguably the best Cuban bakery in Miami was enough to set off my salivary glands. I could already feel my hips expanding as I sat there visualizing the overflowing counters filled to the brim with yummy goodies.

Even though my curiosity was killing me, I decided that it wouldn't be prudent to ask Leo how he was going to eat anything while wearing the vinyl suit, poured into it as he was. At that point, I was so worried about what I was going to find if I checked out Leo more carefully, that I only looked at him from the waist up. I may have been worldly in the physical attributes of men, but, just then, I couldn't deal with what was going on from Leo's waist down.

"Do you need anything or not?" Leo was obviously in no mood to wait. Leo, a true Cuban, needed his hits of sugar at regular intervals or he got grumpy.

"Thanks, but I'll pass." I sighed, reluctantly remembering the three thickly buttered slices of Cuban bread with Aida's homemade mango jam that I'd devoured for breakfast. I knew I could have mustered an appetite in no time—being hungry was a chronic condition with me—but I needed to finish the report, and time was passing. Besides, I had a new philosophy: any meal I passed up would be considered a moral victory, and anything Cuban was worth double points. Sometimes I could be delusional: my near-death experience after being shoot tended to bring out those dormant tendencies.

"You sure?" Leo found it difficult to believe my refusal. I nodded, and he shrugged. On his way out he called to me, "OK, but call me on my cell phone if you change your mind."

My cousin knew me too well. I tried hard not to think about the looks he was going to get at Gilbert's when he walked in dressed in his latex unitard. I suspected that it hadn't occurred to him to put regular clothes on, or even just put something on over the cat suit as any normal person might. The management of Gilbert's was so conservative that they might not even let him in. Leo looked so weird that in the conspiracy-thick city of Miami, they might even suspect him of being an agent of Fidel Castro. Oh well, I'd find out soon enough how his trip had gone—Leo never kept any of his experiences to himself. I just hoped I wouldn't have to bond him out of jail.

I was becoming uncomfortably pressed for time, but even so, I decided to take a break from reading the Meadows file. The truth was that I was feeling a bit overwhelmed with all of the information and wanted to absorb what I had just read. Besides, going to look at the birds was just too tempting, so I stood up, stretched, and walked over to the bay window to check out what the parrots were up to. As I watched the birds go about their daily living—building nests, feeding the babies, pecking at avocados—I couldn't help but think of Tommy; it was unlike him to be so taken with a client. I only hoped it wouldn't affect his judgment.

By then, I wasn't even a third of the way through the stack of papers that made up the Meadows file and the interview with Madeline read like a cheesy teen romance story. How, in this day and age, could two people behave like Madeline and Ricardo? Not have sexual relations until after marriage? Did those types of individuals actually exist? And how did a girl who wouldn't date a T.A. because it would entail breaking one of the Commandments end up as one of the highest-paid escorts on South Beach? Assuming, of course, that she was telling the truth. There was no reason to doubt her yet. But still, quite a few critical parts of her story didn't make sense: the virginity part, for example.

All those thoughts went through my mind as I stood there watching the parrots that were definitely busier and more productive than I. Staring at the tree wasn't going to yield any answers. Tommy wasn't paying me to look at parrots, so I slowly walked back to my desk. At the glacial pace I was working, there was no way I was going to get through the entire file before Madeline Meadows' appointment. I always read all files in a slow and methodical manner the first time through, often taking notes and making comments on matters that I felt required clarification. Sometimes what wasn't in the file turned out to be more interesting than what was.

In the years I'd been working as a private eye, I'd also learned that clients often wanted to present themselves in the most favorable light possible. Even though I would explain to them right away that they should think of me in the same way that they regarded their doctor or lawyer, they still wanted me to have a good impression of them. I would explain that for me to do the best and most cost efficient work they should level with me from the beginning. I would emphasize over and over that I was not there to pass judgment on them; I was there to help. But mostly, I listened to myself speak, and all of my explanations were an exercise in futility.

Human nature usually won out. Most clients couldn't resist playing around with the truth, so they would pick and choose what information to tell me. When I would catch them in a lie or an omission, something that would inevitably happen, they would look at me sheepishly and say that they had forgotten to mention that small detail. They were oblivious to the fact that their forgetfulness might well place me in some sort of physical danger.

On a more practical level, they also didn't realize how much of their retainer money (billable hours) may have gone to waste while I was off on a wild goose chase discovering the detail they had forgotten.

The background details of Madeline's life seemed pretty far-fetched, but at the moment I didn't have any concrete reason to believe that she was lying. I would have to give her the benefit of the doubt. At least for now. After all, she was a good Cadiolic girl, and we all know they don't lie! Tommy claimed to have initially believed her and he didn't trust anyone—not even the Pope. His opinion carried a lot of weight for me, but, of course, Tommy was also a sucker for a beautiful woman. So I had to take his judgment with a grain of salt.

I had less than an hour to figure out how the virtuous school-girl had ended up as a high-paid escort, so I went back to my reading. It had been a while since I'd been this intrigued by a client, and I was enjoying the experience.

According to the file, Ricardo and Madeline decided that, as they wanted to be together, after their respective graduations, she would move back to Miami with him. Ricardo had been offered a job teaching in the Latin American Studies department at the University of Miami, a very good situation for him, and one that he had been excited about.

For her part, Madeline, although she had searched diligently, hadn't been able to find a job. A young woman with a liberal arts degree from Iowa State, even one who had graduated magna cum laude, wasn't exactly in hot demand in Miami. Still, she had cause for optimism: she had minored in Spanish, and was relatively fluent in the language, so she was confident that her skills would surely come in handy in South Florida.

Ricardo and Madeline figured that if they worked hard, saved their money and lived frugally, it would just be a matter of time before they would have enough to get married. However, if they truly wanted to follow the teachings of the Church, they knew they wouldn't be able to use birth control once married. It was, after all, the duty of every married Cadiolic to procreate, and once they tied the knot, children would quickly follow.

Even though I was Cadiolic, this all sounded unreal to me. Both the bride and groom were virgins until marriage? Would children follow nine months after the ceremony? Especially since Madeline was supposedly such a knockout and he was Cuban. And, of course, the fact that she and Ricardo had known each other for three years; it wasn't as if they were on their first date.

A few weeks after graduation, in strong opposition to her family's wishes, Madeline bid farewell to Dubuque, Iowa, and boarded the first of two flights she would have to take to get to Miami. The plan was for her to live in Ricardo's family home and share a room with Ricardo's little sister until she found an apartment. Madeline claimed that, although she wasn't particularly spoiled, she'd had her own room at home and having a bratty teenage girl with raging hormones as a roommate was a new experience for her. A couple of days of sharing a room with a fourteen-year-old girl in the overcrowded Melendez family home provided a strong incentive for her to begin to conduct an apartment search.

A week later, after a vigorous search of the real estate classified section of *The Miami Herald*, Madeline found herself a one-bedroom place in a rundown part of Little Havana. It was a small, dark, cramped walk-up on the fourth floor of a five-story building—not ideal, but reasonably safe and satisfactory for her needs. Best of all, she didn't have to look at Ricardo's spoiled sister any longer. Ricardo and Madeline were saving practically every penny so they could begin their married life—and, for the babies to come, of course—and this apartment was about all they could afford.

Madeline claimed that she hadn't minded living in such a place, but Tommy must have questioned that statement because she went on to confess that she missed her family's spacious home in Dubuque. Madeline would get especially homesick as she lay on her bed at night and listened to the loud noises and relentless salsa music that played at top volume from the street below. The noises and music were bad enough, but the sounds of her neighbor's lively sexual activity were almost more than she could take. The only way to get through it was to keep reminding herself that her situation was temporary.

Tommy had written the address of the Little Havana apartment building where Madeline had been living, so I knew exactly where and what it was. The Atlantico Aims apartment building would never, ever, have been mistaken for the Ritz. Poor Madeline! She must have experienced such culture shock: a sheltered, devout, twenty-one-year-old girl thrown into a shabby building in a rough, all-Cuban neighborhood. I had never been to Dubuque, but it wasn't hard to imagine how dissimilar it must have been to her new life in Miami. As I read, slowly but surely, her becoming a high-priced call girl began to make sense.

I looked up at the clock and saw that in less than half an hour

Madeline would be arriving at my office—that was, if she hadn't yet adopted the Latin habit of running an hour or two late for meetings. Even if I was to speed read, there was no way I would get through the rest of the file by that time.

Although I had been reading steadily, I had yet to figure out how Madeline went from being a nice Cadiolic girl in Dubuque to being a call girl on South Beach charging clients $5,000 an hour for the pleasure of her company. I reached for the telephone and punched the first number on my speed dial. Tommy answered on the first ring, as usual.

"So what do you think?" Tommy didn't wait for me to speak. "Interesting client, huh?"

"*Sí.*" I began staring at the birds in the avocado tree. The entire crew was completely preoccupied with building a structure that looked familiar, but which I couldn't quite place.

"Lupe!" Tommy said sharply.

Wait . . . I had it. I knew what I was looking at. My God, the parrots were building a replica of the Eiffel Tower!

"Lupe, pay attention. Stop looking at the parrots!" Tommy barked. The man knew me too well.

"Sorry." I flipped through the pages of the Meadows file then glanced at the clock, "listen, Madeline Meadows will be here in half an hour. Do you have any last-minute suggestions or anything in particular you want me to ask her?"

"Not for now. You know what to do," Tommy replied. "Just do your thing and call me afterwards."

Click. The phone went dead.

Well, that was really unhelpful. I had just gotten up to go to the bathroom when the phone rang. I looked on the caller I.D. screen and saw that it was Tommy.

"Ask her to tell you in detail about her Chihuahuas and the life-sized anatomically correct male doll," he said. "You'll love it."

Click.

First, a call girl who was a virgin, then Leo's 20/25 gauge superior latex, and now Chihuahuas and anatomically correct dolls.

Twelve o'clock couldn't come soon enough.

Six

I was pleasantly surprised to hear the front door of the building open promptly at noon. Ms. Meadows may have been living here for the past year, but clearly, the Miami habit of being chronically late had not rubbed off on her yet. Or, it could be that she had been on time for a more practical reason: she was paid for her services by the hour and, like Tommy and I, was aware of the cost of the ticking clock. In our respective professions, time was money.

I had just gotten up from behind my desk to go to the reception area to greet her when I heard a bloodcurdling sound, followed by the racket of small dogs yelping. Fuck! That could only mean one thing: the Chihuahuas that Tommy had told me about on the phone were here! I sprinted to the doorway of my office and raced down the hall to the reception area, wondering what they were doing to Leo to cause him to howl like that.

One look at the scene before me and I wished I'd had one of my cameras I used for surveillance. Two miniature Chihuahuas—miniscule brown dogs—were standing on top of Leonardo's desk, a scant foot away from him, poised to attack. Their tiny were mouths open, their teeth bared as they growled and barked in the direction of Leonardo's private parts. Their tails were wagging so frantically from side to side that their entire bodies shook with the intensity of a mini earthquake. Looking at them, I had no doubt that they would tear Leonardo to pieces with great glee.

Leo had not moved an inch, but it was clear from his terrified expression that he thought his days on earth were about to end. Well, at the very least, he would lose his private parts. A tall, blond young woman scurried over to the animals.

"Hi, I'm Madeline Meadows, your noon appointment. Really sorry about the dogs, they're usually better behaved than this. I'm not sure how they got out of the case. The zipper must not have been closed all the way. I'll get them off you right now," Madeline called out to Leonardo as she reached the dogs. "Napoleon! Josephine! Home!"

No sooner had the words come out of Madeline's mouth that the dogs turned and jumped back into the oversized brown canvas Louis Vuitton pet carrier she was holding open. Once inside the case, the dogs curled up on the bottom, snuggled against each other, and promptly closed their eyes. They looked so innocent that it was hard to believe that they had been ready to tear Leo apart a minute before.

"I am so very sorry about that," Madeline apologized to Leonardo. "It's the latex—especially the heavy gauge—they're trained to attack a man's private parts when they smell that kind of rubber. It's become instinctive with them."

"Leo, are you OK?" I turned to my cousin. Leo looked to be in such shock that I briefly debated calling 911, but just as quickly dismissed it. That would have just been too humiliating for Leo.

I would have loved to have asked about the dogs, but just then did not seem to be the right time. "Ms. Meadows?" I held out my hand. "Hi, welcome. I'm Lupe Solano." I pointed at Leo, who was scowling at me. "You've already met Leonardo, sort of."

In all of the excitement I had not had an opportunity to get a good look at my new client, but now that I had the chance, I saw that in describing her, Tommy had, if anything, downplayed her attractiveness. Madeline Meadows was stunningly beautiful. Well above average height, thin, muscular, but still quite curvaceous, with long, wavy blond hair. She had the kind of ethereal look that was not often seen in Miami.

Madeline turned to face me and I had my first glance of her remarkable eyes that were an amazing blue, and so clear that they seemed translucent. Madeline had naturally fair coloring, but her eyebrows and eyelashes were quite dark, making her eyes stand out even more vividly.

Madeline had come to the meeting dressed informally: khaki cargo pants, a black T-shirt, espadrilles and tiny gold hoop earrings. She dressed in the same casual style I would have, had I not been meeting her. It seemed as if the very pricey Louis Vuitton pet carrier was by far the most expensive item she had with her.

"Hi. Thank you for seeing me on such short notice. And, please, call me Madeline." Madeline held out her hand. As I shook it, I was surprised at how soft her skin was. With an apologetic look, she turned to Leonardo and addressed him. "Again, I'm so very sorry about what happened with the dogs. It's the latex, as I said. They're trained to attack."

"It's OK," Leo managed to blurt out. I could see that his anger had already begun to dissipate. Clearly, it was difficult to stay angry at someone as sweet and beautiful as Madeline.

"Madeline, would you like to come into my office? We can talk there." I indicated the open door down the hall.

Once there, I indicated for Madeline to sit in the more comfortable of the two chairs opposite my desk. She would probably be there for quite some time, so she might as well be comfortable. Instead of sitting, though, Madeline walked over to the bay window and watched the parrots. "Look at them! They're so beautiful!" She turned to me and declared, "If this were my office, I would never get any work done. I would spend all my time looking at them!"

Those parrots had always been my weakness, and anyone who admired them had my vote. In spite of her horrid dogs, I found myself liking Madeline more and more by the minute. Still, I told myself not to be too taken by her. It was still too early.

"Yes, I spend a lot of time with them." I could easily have spent hours discussing my little feathered friends—I especially wanted to point out the Eiffel Tower, which by then, they had almost finished building, but Madeline and I had other pressing matters to discuss. Reluctantly, I pointed to the chair. "Please."

Madeline walked across the room and carefully set the pet carrier down on the floor by her chair. She moved with the easy grace of an athlete. This was a woman who was comfortable in her own body. I was also able to check her out more clearly by the natural light that came in through the bay window and saw that she was even more striking than she had seemed in the reception area.

"I'm not sure what Mr. MacDonald told you about me." Madeline's face turned a delicate shade of pink as she spoke. I was not used to having clients blush in my office, especially a call girl. It was quite touching, really. "But, Ms. Solano, I've never killed anyone. I'm innocent. I have no idea why the police suspect that I had anything to do with the murders of Dr. Steinberg and Mr. Robinson."

I didn't make any comment about what she had just said, and instead said with a smile, "First, please, call me Lupe." I lifted my right hand and placed it on the file which Tommy had sent me earlier that day. "Mr. MacDonald did speak to me about your situation. He sent over a copy of your file to me today before our meeting but I think it would be best if I were to hear the story from you directly."

"Of course." Her big blue eyes looked straight at me. Sitting there across from me, Madeline seemed so young, innocent and virginal that, had I not known her true profession, I certainly would have never, ever, believed it. And, coming from someone who has seen the worst of life and suspected everyone and everything, that was saying a lot. "Where do I start?"

I wanted to see if she told me the same story she had told Tommy a few days before. "Well, maybe it would be best if you sum up what you told Mr. MacDonald about your childhood, family, education, etc." Madeline nodded. "After that, because of the unfortunate situation you're in now, I think we'll need to focus on your life since you came to Miami."

Madeline quickly repeated what Tommy had written in her file. Tommy's notes were always factual and on point so much so that sometimes his nitpicking could be infuriating. Madeline's story matched Tommy's notes exactly, something that should have reassured me, but did not.

"So, after you came to Miami, you lived with Ricardo's family for a short time, is that right?" I recalled what I had read in the file. The situation had sounded pretty stressful, sharing a small room with a resentful teenage girl, anyone in her right mind would have gotten out as quickly as possible.

Madeline rolled her eyes upward. "Yes, but I didn't last at their house very long. It was kind of difficult living there."

"So you moved to an apartment in Little Havana?" I prompted her.

"Yes. For a few months," Madeline answered. "After that, I moved to South Beach."

Little Havana and South Beach were more than just a few miles away from each other; they were miles apart in style of living, not to mention cost of living. "Can you tell me a little about that time in your life, please?"

"Well, it's kind of a weird story." Madeline sighed. "You see, Lupe, while I was living in that apartment in Little Havana, I would go out every day to try to find a job, a job in my field. I majored in liberal arts and sciences, graduated magna cum laude, you know, but nothing turned up. Soon, I was willing to take any kind of job but the only ones that I could get were as a cocktail waitress or as a hostess in a bar or in a restaurant. I would have taken any of those jobs. They paid well, but . . ." Madeline shrugged.

It was not difficult to see where the story was going. Ricardo, as a proud Cuban man, would not want his fiancée, a beautiful woman and a college graduate at that, working at a service job in which she would meet men. "So, Ricardo wouldn't let you take those?" I suggested.

"No, even though we needed the money desperately. We used to have fights about it." Madeline turned her head to one side and began looking once again out at the parrots, blinking fast as she tried to hide the tears that were forming in her eyes. "Pretty soon, all we did, really, was fight. I had no money, only had my savings, but I wasn't about to touch that, so I was dependent on Ricardo. It was a terrible time. I was so stressed out about the situation that to get rid of my frustrations, I began working out at the gym a couple of blocks away from the apartment It had just opened up and was offering three months of free membership to people from the neighborhood, you know, to build up their clientele."

"So, then what happened?" I was becoming so engrossed in Madeline's story that I had to remind myself that she was a client under suspicion for two murders.

"It was at the gym that I met the twins—Stanley and Ernest Loredo. They lived in the neighborhood, too, and were also taking advantage of the free memberships. First, we only used to nod to each other, but after we saw each other all the time, then we started talking. It wasn't long before we started meeting there every day at noon." Madeline smiled. "It was because of them that my life changed."

"How so?" Although I had already read Tommy's notes on that, I was curious to hear Madeline describe her unlikely relationship with them.

"We became gym friends—you know how people who work out together become gym friends?" Madeline looked at me expectantly, clearly expecting me to understand those kinds of friendships. I didn't have the heart to tell her that I never stepped inside a gym unless I was working a murder and there was a dead body inside.

"Sure, gym friends." I nodded. "Then what happened?"

"I found out that they worked for an escort service. No, that's not exactly true: they had worked for an escort service, but the business had closed because the owner had been selling drugs—coke mostly, to his clients. Stanley had been the driver, and Ernest was the bodyguard for the girls. Apparently their clients were the kind to get rough, and the girls needed protection to avoid getting hurt. The twins told me all about their work. I'd never come into contact with anything like that, so it was really, really interesting."

"And Ricardo, did you tell them about him?" I could easily picture the scenario: lonely, pretty girl from out of town, no job, time on her hands, a rocky relationship with her boyfriend. No wonder Stanley and Ernest hooked up with her; it was an opportunity they weren't about to pass up.

"Yes, I did. They were so nice to me, very understanding, really supportive." Madeline clearly cared for the twins. "They were the only people I knew in Miami—except for Ricardo, of course. I sure couldn't tell my family that was going on—they'd been so against my coming to Miami in the first place. I know if they thought for a minute that I was unhappy, they'd send me a plane ticket to come home, or worse, they would come and get me. I used to tell the twins everything—they were the only ones I could trust."

"I can see why you did," I said encouragingly.

"One night, I had such a bad fight with Ricardo that he actually hit me. He thought I had been seeing another man and he accused me of doing terrible things." Madeline's voice had dropped so low that she was almost whispering. "I mean, I loved him with all my heart, but I couldn't have him hit me, could I? Especially since I hadn't done anything wrong. I hadn't been with any man—just him. He was crazy! Crazy! No one had ever hit me in my whole entire life! No one!"

"Did you think about going home then? Back to Iowa?" I wondered out loud.

"I couldn't! As much as I might have wanted to, that was the last thing I could do! Not after what my family had said to me when I left: they told me going to Miami would be a huge mistake, one that I would regret. I know they loved me with all their hearts, but they didn't approve of Ricardo, or Miami, or anything else I was going to do. No, going back home like a failure was the last thing I would do!" Madeline was so upset she was almost shaking. "No, I had to stick it out here, for a while, at least."

"I can understand you not wanting to go back to Iowa," I hurried to reassure her. "So, what happened after the fight with Ricardo?"

Madeline took a quick look back at the parrots. I could tell that, like me, she was fascinated by them. "I knew the night that

Ricardo hit me that I couldn't stay there any longer—that he would continue to beat me up. I knew he had a gun, too, a .357 Magnum—and that he knew how to use it. I was petrified. When he left to go back home to his family's house, I packed some of my clothes and called Stanley and Ernest, and told them what had happened, and that I was scared. They didn't ask any questions, especially after I'd told then about the gun. They just came right over and got me. We went back to their apartment. I was so frightened that Ricardo might have been spying on me and had followed us, but thank God, nothing happened."

"And seeing the difficult situation you were in, that wasn't when they suggested you earn money by becoming a call girl, was it?" I hoped the twins would not have immediately preyed on a desperate girl in trouble.

"Well, no, not right away. First, they calmed me down and told me that they would look after me, take care of me and make sure I was safe. They talked to me for hours and made me feel comfortable. It took a couple of days for me to relax, and it was then that they spoke of how if I became an escort, with my looks, I could make so much money, and save enough to go back to Iowa with cash to set up a small business. I would be independent, not have to rely on anyone. They told me all that" Madeline shook her head at the memory. "I may have been from Iowa, Lupe, but I knew that escort was another word for call girl."

"So, what did you say to them?" Although I tried to keep my equanimity, my curiosity was getting the better of me. It was difficult for me to imagine how the twins had broached the subject to Madeline.

"I told them that as much as I wanted to make lots of money and be independent, I could not be a call girl," Madeline replied. "I told them it was impossible for me to do what they suggested.

I mean, I may have been broke, alone and scared, but I wasn't so desperate that I would do that."

"And, what was their reaction to your refusal? They must have been angry and frustrated that you didn't go along with their plan." I could picture the twins' disappointment when Madeline turned down their offer. After all, they had obviously cultivated their friendship in the gym with an ulterior motive: they had a plan for Madeline. Stanley and Ernest did not sound like Mother Teresa to me. Their goal had clearly, ultimately, been to recruit Madeline into their line of business. They recognized a meal ticket when they saw one. However, the fact that she had turned them down couldn't have totally come out of the blue.

"Actually, no. After I explained why I couldn't be a call girl, they were thrilled." Madeline shrugged her shoulders.

"Thrilled?" I repeated. "What exactly did you tell them?" I couldn't imagine what Madeline had said.

"I told them I couldn't be an escort—a call girl—not so much because it was a dangerous, sleazy business, but because I was a virgin," Madeline replied. "They thought for a minute about what I had said and then began laughing." Madeline smiled. "Then they told me they could work with that. My virginity was no problem—if anything, it would work to my advantage."

I couldn't help but smile back. Leave it to a Cuban to make lemonade out of lemons.

Seven

If it hadn't been that two men who were connected to Madeline had been murdered, I would have burst out laughing as I pictured that scene: the virginal Iowan, the two pimps, etc. The idea that the gorgeous woman sitting in the client chair across from me was a virgin—and a call girl—seemed totally preposterous. Even for Miami, where the abnormal was normal (what was normal, anyway?). The longer I lived here, the less I knew what would be considered strange in most places. People from Miami had no frame of reference for much of anything really. This city did that to people.

"So, what happened next? After you announced to the twins that you were a virgin?" I could hardly wait to hear what Madeline had to say.

"I thought they would be angry with me. After all, they'd invested a lot of time on me. I may have been a virgin and a blond one at that, Lupe, but that doesn't mean I'm stupid." Madeline reached down to the floor, picked up the pet carrier, and placed it on her lap. I sensed she needed some comforting, and her dogs, tiny as they were, provided that. She looked straight at me and continued speaking. "From the beginning, when I first met them at the gym, I'd had my suspicions that they had more in mind for me than friendship." She unzipped the top of the carrier, put her right hand inside it, and began stroking the dogs.

As I listened to Ms. Meadows speak, I began to think I'd underestimated my client. First, she had known the twins had more than friendship in mind for her; then she'd retained Tommy as her lawyer. Clearly, there was a sharp brain behind her good looks. Or, was she hiding something, and that was why she was protecting herself? I didn't know which to believe.

I watched with apprehension as she petted the Chihuahuas and hoped that they wouldn't jump out and go looking for Leonardo to finish off the job of biting his private parts. I wasn't sure if the injuries caused by being bitten by two attack Chihuahuas with an aversion to latex would be covered by my worker's comp insurance.

"Well, it seems your instincts were correct." I smiled at her. "So, after you told them that you were a virgin, they said they could 'work with that'. What happened then?"

Instead of answering my question, Madeline just looked out the window at the parrots in the tree. I was in no hurry; billing by the hour tended to make me very patient with my clients so I let her take her time. While Madeline was checking out the parrots, I took the opportunity to inspect her yet again.

Madeline Meadows was such a spectacularly beautiful woman that it was difficult not to look at her and I was straight; I could only imagine what reaction she got from red-blooded heterosexual men. Tommy, tough criminal defense lawyer that he was, had almost been babbling when he talked about her. Madeline's beauty seemed to be without artifice. This was probably what she looked like when she got out of the shower.

I'd been to enough hairdressers to know that she was a natural blonde, and was familiar enough with colored contact lenses to be sure that her light blue eyes were her own. I would have bet a month's worth of billable hours that Madeline Meadows still had her original body parts and that the rest of her had not been messed with, either. A person could not live in Miami and not be aware that the city was a center for plastic surgery: just about anyone who, could afford it had been Botoxed, Restylaned, lipo-suctioned, collagened, lifted, tightened, and veneered within an inch of their lives. As I looked at her, I realized that it had been a long time since I'd seen anyone who was a natural beauty. Not just that, but who also didn't need to wear makeup. Still, there was something not quite right about her looks—something I couldn't quite put my finger on.

According to her file, Madeline was twenty-two years old, but watching her as she stroked her dogs, it was hard to believe that she was that old. Even without makeup, her skin glowed with an incandescence that would have caused a painter or photographer to swoon. I'd always disliked harsh overhead lights, so, in contrast to the rest of the rooms in the building, which were always lit so brightly I kept the lights in my office as low as possible, giving off a glow that flattered just about everyone. Especially me. However, as far as Madeline Meadows was concerned, the intensity of the light would have made no difference: she had been just as beautiful under the bright lights of the reception area as she was sitting in my softly lit office.

"I'm sorry, Lupe, I was fascinated by the parrots. Please excuse me, my mind drifted off," Madeline apologized. "You had asked what happened after the twins told me that my being a virgin wasn't a problem."

"Yes, that was my question," I said. "Take your time, please. There's no rush."

"Thanks." Madeline, avoiding my gaze, fidgeted in the chair. It was clear that the question was making her uncomfortable, so much so that I wasn't sure if she was going to answer. A full minute passed before she finally spoke. "Believe it or not, Lupe, after discussing the situation, the twins decided that the fact that I was a virgin would work even better with their plan."

I thought about what Madeline had just said. "You know, I've been in this business for almost eight years, and, as you can imagine, during that time I've come across some pretty strange things . . . But a call girl who is a bona-fide virgin, well, that's a new one for me."

"I know, it seemed weird to me, too," Madeline agreed. "But Lupe, you have to understand, I was alone, desperate, broke: I had less than five dollars in my wallet—Ricardo had just hit me—there was a good chance he was going to kill me—and I had no place to go. The only money I had was the thirty-five hundred dollars that I had used to purchase a CD at Citibank when I first moved to Miami with Ricardo and it was paying me five percent interest. A great rate, no?" Madeline looked at me with a sad expression. "I had just rolled it over for another six months. If I broke the CD and cashed it in, I would have had to pay a huge penalty. Even though I was desperate, that was something I was not prepared to do. That was money that I swore I was never going to touch; it was my enure life's savings, from summer jobs, birthday money, stuff like that."

Madeline began to sniffle, making the weird kind of little muffled noises that a small animal might make when burrowing in the earth. I didn't want to embarrass her by staring at her while she cried, so I turned my attend on to the parrots in the avocado tree who, apparently tiring of the Eiffel Tower in the upper branches, had frenetically begun building what now looked like the Hoover Dam in the lower branches of the tree. They were reinforcing the structure to such a degree that not even a heavy wind would be able to blow it down, that was a good thing as we were entering the heart of the dreaded hurricane season.

In spite of Madeline's efforts to control herself, the sniffles quickly turned to sobs and the waterworks began in earnest. I got up and handed Madeline the box of Kleenex that I kept in the bottom drawer of my desk for just these occasions. As I watched her blow her nose, I had to suppress a smile as, even though she worked as a call girl in Miami, in the end, Madeline was still a girl with thrifty values from the Midwest who would rather sell her body before paying the penalty for breaking a certificate of deposit from the bank. Human nature never ceased to amaze me!

"I can see how you might have been reluctant to do that." I took the box of Kleenex from her and walked back to my desk. "So, how did you make the transition from living in Little Havana to South Beach?"

Madeline finished wiping her eyes with the Kleenex, and then blew her nose one last time. I always ended up looking like road kill when I cried, so I could barely contain my admiration for Madeline's appearance after her crying jag. Less than a minute after her breakdown, she looked cool and composed as if it had never happened. Had I not personally witnessed her breakdown, I might have thought that I'd imagined the whole thing. I filed away in my brain the fact that either Madeline Meadows was gifted with an amazingly quick recovery time, or she was an exceedingly cool customer. Or, she wanted to get my sympathy. In any case, whatever the reason, it was useful information for me to have.

"Ernest and Stanley told me that they had some money saved from their last job and offered to lend me what I needed until I got back on my feet," Madeline explained. "I didn't tell them about the money in the CD, of course, they thought I only had the live dollars in my purse." I thought it was interesting that in spite of the fact that the twins had saved Madeline's life, she still didn't trust them enough to tell them about the money she had hidden.

Also, I wasn't surprised to hear that the twins had money saved: the escort business was primarily conducted in cash, so there were plenty of opportunities to skim some from the boss especially since they were deeding on the side. "And then?" I prompted her.

"We discussed whether or not I should go back to the apartment to get my stuff. I mean. Nothing all that valuable, just my clothes and personal effects, things like that. But it was my apartment, and I paid the rent. I hated to just let Ricardo keep everything: the bastard!" Madeline's eyes Hashed with anger. "So, in the end, we decided that the twins would get my things and that I should stay away. I mean, Ricardo did have a gun, after all, so we couldn't be too careful. My apartment was on the fourth floor of a walk-up, so it was easy to see people enter and exit the premises. The plan was that the twins would watch the building and as soon as Ricardo stepped out, Stanley would use my key, go in, pack up my stuff quickly, and bring it out. Ernest would stay outside and act as the lookout in case Ricardo returned. We had to do it fast before Ricardo changed the locks. Even though it was my apartment, he always felt it was his. Very annoying."

"Speed was important, so you had to move fast before he knew you had moved out." She nodded. "And everything worked out OK?"

"Thank God, yes." Madeline smiled broadly. "I got most of my stuff, no problem." She then began to laugh. "Gosh, Lupe, I only wish I could have seen Ricardo's face when he returned to discover that I was gone, and all my belongings were gone as well!"

"Yes, that would have been great," I agreed. I let her savor the moment before continuing with my questions. "So, Madeline, how long before you moved to South Beach?"

"The twins said it was very important I leave the neighborhood as quickly as possible, so I moved out the very next day. I tell you, I couldn't wait to get out of Little Havana. I was so frightened of Ricardo, and what he would do if he saw me. The twins had a friend, Eddie Nunez, who was the manager of one of the older buildings on South Beach, it was on Euclid Avenue and Seventh Street. Actually, he was one of the regulars of their escort service, so they knew him pretty well. They called him asking about studio apartments for me. He said he'd just had to evict a tenant, a young girl, a model, who had come to South Beach to become rich and famous, but instead, had gotten into trouble with Tina—you know, crystal meth—and couldn't make her rent. All he had to do was clean up the apartment and it was mine."

"So, the twins helped you out with the rent?" I was fairly sure of the answer, still I had to ask.

From what Madeline had said about them, Stanley and Ernest were not planning to run a charity. I mean, their e-mail addresses didn't exactly have a 'dot-org' after it. I'd been in this business so long that I didn't trust anyone, sometimes not even myself. Of course, getting shot hadn't done much to restore my faith in humanity. At that point in my career, I had already become so cynical that if Mother Teresa had walked into my office with a referral from the Virgin Mary herself, I still would have run a background check on the nun. Even as Madeline sat in my office, Leonardo was running a check on her.

"Yes, but because Eddie knew them, he didn't require me to put down the first month's rent or a security deposit, thank God," Madeline said. "The studio apartment was actually quite nice, spacious and bright, with an eat-in kitchen. Those older buildings have much more space than the new ones. I liked it right away, but, even better, I felt safe."

"So, you moved in . . ." I looked at the file to refresh my memory. "Let's see, February before last, a year and a half ago."

Madeline nodded. "That's right. I lived there for six months, then, when I'd made some money and could afford to do so, I moved to the Portofino Towers, where I've lived for the past year. I'm renting, but I hope to buy in the future. It's really nice. I love living there. The best part is that they allow dogs. They even have a dog park."

Right on cue, Napoleon and Josephine began to make noises from inside the carrier. The more I listened to their high-pitched yaps, the more I realized that I liked my dogs to be big: the bigger, the bulkier, the sloppier, the better. Scarily similar to how I liked my men. There was no way I would ever own a dog that could fit into one of my Chanel bags. Even without my Beretta in there.

I wasn't surprised to hear that Madeline liked Portofino Towers—there would definitely have been something wrong with her if she hadn't. Located on the southernmost end of South Beach, it was one of the first and tallest high-rise buildings built there, over forty floors high. The building represented the height of luxury, with a state-of-the-art gym, saunas, in-house massage services and the like. But, what really made the building unique were the floor-to-ceiling windows that gave residents the most amazing views of the Atlantic Ocean, Biscayne Bay and Miami.

I knew the building reasonably well because my friend, Andres San Pedro, lived in one of the penthouses. Andres had once been my client, but I'd spent so much time with him during the course of our professional association that he'd become my friend. In addition to being a very charming and attractive man, Andres was an enormously successful real estate developer. Unfortunately for him, in stark contrast to how smart and canny a businessman he was, his personal life was a disaster. He couldn't choose an appropriate woman to save his life. But despite his five divorces, he was still an incurable romantic: he totally and completely believed in love and marriage. So far, he'd married, in chronological order: a lesbian, a gold digger, an illegal alien who was deported by Homeland Security, a nymphomaniac and a practicing nun. Ever the optimist, he was on the prowl for number six.

I'd met Andres when Leo, giving into one of his periodic urges to redecorate the office, had taken on several domestic cases, and investigating Andres' first wife had been one of them. Andres had been convinced his wife had been having an affair—it turned out that he had been correct: she was seeing someone on the side—but it had been a woman, not a man. Andres—red-blooded Argentinian man that he was—had been devastated, so much so that I'd spent most of the hefty retainer he'd given me holding his hand rather than working the case. I learned early on that Andres was slightly unhinged: there was something secretive about him, but as the majority of people I knew had secrets, that didn't necessarily bother me.

Although he'd been upset at the result of the investigation, he'd been so pleased with the quality of the work I'd done that he'd hired me again to investigate his second wife, then third, and so forth. Leo used to joke that Andres was my annuity. I could count on getting a yearly check from him for doing very little work. I was quite grateful for Andres' dismal marital history, as his wives were responsible for most of our office decor.

"Yes, Portofino Towers is very nice. I can see why you like living there," I agreed. Hiding my apprehension, I watched

Madeline take the dogs out of the carrier and put them on her lap. Well, I wasn't wearing any latex, so I should be safe, I reassured myself. "So, if you don't mind telling me, how did the transformation begin, you becoming a call girl? That must have been an enormous challenge for you."

Madeline looked down at the dogs, and began to blush again. Oh, God! A call girl who kept blushing! What next?

"Believe it or not, it really wasn't all that difficult. I mean, I knew that I wasn't going to sleep with the clients or anything like that. I would just be keeping company with them that was made very clear from the start. The twins, actually, I mostly dealt with Ernest, told me that I just had to be myself on dates: to pretend I was on a blind date, or that I had met the man at Match.com, or one of those other dating services. The clients just wanted my company. Really, it wasn't as bad as you might think." Madeline smiled at me as she spoke.

Not for the first time that day, I had the feeling that my client was not being completely truthful with me. She wasn't brazenly lying, that I would have known right away. It seemed to be more a case of selective omission. I wasn't buying the fact that her dates were so pure, so sexless. Knowing what I did about men, there was no way that was how it had been—men did not lay out that kind of cash to be with women who did not put out and put out in a memorable way.

During the time that I'd worked as a private eye, I'd developed a kind of antenna, an internal polygraph, which would buzz whenever someone lied to me. Right now, it was steadily humming along at a low pitch. There were ways I could double-check her story, of course, so the fact that she was not being truthful would not affect the investigation—what was interesting was the fact that she was doing it. Clearly, there was a reason. I would just have to find it—and I knew I would. I always did.

I had no doubt that the background check Leo was conducting on Madeline at that very moment would give me a starting point. Leo was so thorough at digging into people's pasts that by the time he was done, I would know what color panties Madeline wore; that was, if she wore any. But for now, time was passing. Knowing how efficient Detective Anderson was, I was well aware that we were living on borrowed time, and that he could come for Madeline at any moment. The fact that he had already interviewed her, and had given out information to her meant she was in his sights. Detective Maxwell Anderson worked very, very quickly, so I had to be two steps ahead of him at every point.

I made a point of looking at the clock on my desk, then announced to Madeline, "It's getting late, so maybe we should get right to the reason why you're here. We can discuss your responsibilities later." Madeline nodded. "Mr. MacDonald told me that a Detective Anderson had interviewed you regarding the murders of Dr. Samuel Steinberg, your ob-gyn, and Mr. Woodley Robinson, a client. Is that correct?"

"Yes, that's correct." Madeline's eyes were beginning to water again. Her eyes were such a startling shade of blue that I felt as if I was looking at the waters at the bottom of a lagoon in the Pacific Ocean. "He said they'd both been shot, and asked me if I knew anything about it."

"What did you say to him?" I already knew that. Tommy had taken quite detailed notes but I was interested in watching Madeline's reactions to my questions, and to see if she answered me in the same way.

"I said that yes, I knew both men, and that I really liked them, but that I had no idea why someone would want to kill them. But, it wasn't me, I swear!" Madeline began to cry. "Dr. Steinberg was the nicest, sweetest man; Woodley, too. Why would anyone want to hurt them? Why?"

I reached down to the bottom drawer of my desk and brought out the Kleenex box again, then walked over to where Madeline was sitting. "That's what you've retained Mr. MacDonald and me to find out, Madeline," I said as I handed her the box again.

Eight

Leonardo cracked open the door of my office and looked around the room as if to make sure Madeline had really left. It was only after he was completely convinced that our client and her killer Chihuahuas were gone that he spoke. "Background reports came back: our new client is clean, Lupe. Nada. Not even a moving violation."

"You ran her both here and in Iowa?" I asked, needlessly. For all of his eccentricities, Leo was very thorough in his work.

Leonardo rolled his eyes, as if he could not believe how stupid my question had been. He walked into my office, handed me the printouts with the background reports in it, and then made himself comfortable on the bench in front of the window, his favorite place.

"Lupe, porfavor, give me a break. Of course I ran her in both states; I also ran her nationwide using three different databases and I can tell you that Madeline Marie Meadows is as pure as the driven snow. The girl is like the Virgin Mary in more ways than one." He turned and smiled at me. "You know, Lupe, I should have run her fucking dogs, killers that they are. I bet they have priors."

I ignored Leo's comments about Napoleon and Josephine, and said, "Coño! I was hoping that something would turn up on her background." I looked Leo over. "Hey, cousin, I see you changed—what happened to the latex?"

Leonardo had taken off the unitard and was wearing what he referred to as his clueless Florida tourist outfit: a pair of shorts and a T-shirt embroidered with what looked like palm trees blowing over in hurricane-force winds. On his feet, he wore green rubber flip-flops decorated with pink flamingos, whose beaks lit up when he walked. For perhaps the millionth time, I regretted that the only dress code that I had imposed on him was that whatever outfit he wore to the office had to weigh more than eight ounces. Leo looked like a demented Jimmy Buffet as he waved to the parrots while making kissing sounds.

I watched him and I prayed that he had not succumbed to the other habits of Margaritaville, that he wasn't drunk or high. With him, it was hard to tell if he was straight or not. And not only as far as his gender preferences were concerned. For Leo, every hour he spent at Solano Investigations was 'happy hour,' something that, years ago, at the drop of a hat, had became 'happier hour.' And, on one memorable Tuesday morning, we even had 'happiest hour.' It had taken all of Tommy's skill to get the end results from that fiesta expunged from Leo's records.

"Lupe, those fucking dogs. They're killers. They were going for the family jewels. They were headed there. Even the client said they were: I saw it in their eyes." To make sure I got the point, Leo put his hands over this private parts. "It was going to get ugly! If they'd bitten the family jewels, that would have been the end of the Garcia family line."

"I don't like shitty little dogs, either, Leo. They yap, they shriek, they're all-around obnoxious," I agreed. "You know, Leo, those dogs are not just for appearances: they're attack dogs. Madeline told me they're trained to go for a man's balls if they sense she's in danger. The twins gave them to her for protection.

They attack on her command. You want to hear how that came about?" I laughed.

"Can't wait to hear this," Leo said, making himself comfortable.

Remembering what Tommy had said about the dogs, before ending the interview, I hadn't been able to resist asking Madeline about Napoleon and Josephine, and how they had been trained to be so aggressive. Madeline had explained how, after buying them from a breeder in Ocala, a farm town in Central Florida, Stanley and Ernest had trained them to attack on command. Although they, the twins, would always be near when she went out on dates, unpleasant situations might arise, and they wanted her to be protected. Madeline refused to carry a gun, so the dogs were her first line of defense.

Madeline confessed that she had been skeptical as to how much protection a pair of four-pound Chihuahuas could provide, but her doubts had vanished after Stanley put on a demonstration. The twins explained that they had some experience in training dogs, a skill they might have acquired as a result of their involvement with illegal dog fights in Dade County. And, even though the dogs being trained were Chihuahuas, not pit bulls, the methods used were almost the same. In Napoleon and Josephine's case, though, instead of the dogs going for the attacker's jugular, they would go for his balls, a strategy that the twins assured her would be much more effective.

I had struggled to keep a straight face as I listened to Madeline describe how the twins had trained the Chihuahuas to be attack dogs. First, they had gone to an adult toy store and purchased an anatomically correct, life-sized male doll made out of latex, which they then used as the 'bad guy.' They trained the Chihuahuas to attack the doll's private parts—the most vulnerable part of the male anatomy—repeating the exercise over and over until they perfected it. Madeline reported that the man-doll had been so formidably well-endowed that it had taken the two little dogs quite a few bites before he deflated.

In just six weeks, Stanley and Ernest had turned Napoleon and Josephine from lovable little dogs into formidable killing machines. As the inflatable doll had been made out of latex, when they had smelled the same scent on Leo, it had triggered an automatic response and had immediately sent them into attack mode.

"So, now do you see why they went for you, Leo? It was instinctive for them, and nothing against you: it was the latex." I wasn't about to remind him what she had said about the memorable size of the doll's private parts. Leo was fragile enough about his sexuality as it was.

"That may be, but I'm not going to forget this. And, just to be prepared for the next time, if there is a next time, I'm going to go online and look up a recipe on how to cook Chihuahuas." Leo got up from the window seat. "Maybe Rachael Ray has an easy one. Anthony Bourdain will have one for sure but that one will be more complicated: cooked the French way."

I shuddered at the thought. I would not put anything past Leo as he always did what he said he would. "Leo, right now I'm going to reread this file. Our client may be lily white on paper, but I'm not totally buying it. I suspect there's more to Ms. Meadows than she wants us to know. Listen, can you do backgrounds on these two as well?" I handed him a sheet of paper with Dr. Steinberg's and Mr. Robinson's names and information on it. "Thanks again for the backgrounds. I want to see if they have some kind of link—apart from knowing Madeline, that is. Let me know when you get something back. Oh, and keep me posted if you make any progress on the recipes!" I was going to have to monitor him.

Leo had been about to walk out when he turned and said,

"Don't forget that it's Papi's birthday on Friday. Your sisters are planning a party, and you need to get him a present. They've been calling me, asking me to remind you." Leo wagged his finger at me. "You know how you are—you leave everything until the last minute. You have four more days Lupe. Today is Monday: the party is four days away. Please get the present so I can get your sisters off my case."

"Oh my God, Leo," I cried out. "Papi is having a big birthday. He's going to be seventy years old!" Then, so he'd stop worrying, I smiled at him reassuringly. "I promise I'll get him a present, a good one, something he'll really like."

I waited until Leo left before opening the Meadows file. There had to be a reason why Madeline had said that taking up a career as a call girl had not been all that difficult. She claimed that she had not had sex with her boyfriend because she'd been a devout Catholic. Becoming a call girl, who was a virgin, had not been a difficult decision at all? I didn't buy it. Something was off. Even though she said she hadn't slept with her clients, the transition from one end of the spectrum to the other had been just too smooth. There were more holes in her story than there were in the blocks of Swiss cheese at the Publix deli counters.

I looked over the file again, hoping to find clues as to who my client was, and why she was lying to me. I alternated between rereading Tommy's notes and the background reports that Leo had given me. Madeline Marie Meadows was born in Dubuque, Iowa, one of six children, the daughter of an accountant and his homemaker wife. Six children? I looked at Tommy's notes and saw that he had written five. It wasn't like Tommy to make such a mistake. Oh well, in any case, there were lots of children, not surprising in a Catholic family. I continued reading. The family was very stable; the parents still lived in the same house they had purchased after getting married.

In addition, Mr. Meadows had worked for the same accounting firm for the past twenty-five years, and his wife, who had once been an art teacher in the local parochial school, had become a stay-at-home mom after her first child was born, nine months to the day after their wedding. Madeline's older siblings also seemed to be law-abiding, stable, contributing members of society: her eldest sister, Maria was a nurse; Magdalena, the second oldest was a high school teacher; the third eldest, Rose, was a social worker; her brother, Peter, was a lawyer specializing in real estate transactions. All were married, and all, except for Rose and her husband, had children. I would have bet my last dollar they were Republicans.

I spent the next three hours taking notes on what I had read, then, while the information was still fresh in my mind, I wrote up a report of my interview with Madeline. I also jotted down a few ideas as how to proceed with the investigation. Although Madeline had not yet been charged with any crime, I knew it would be just a matter of time before she was. The fact that Detective Anderson had already interviewed Madeline; once— and that he had disclosed crucial, sensitive information to her about the murders—well, to me, that could only mean one thing: he was getting ready to close in on her.

Of course, Madeline had not yet been formally charged with a crime, which made my investigation a bit easier. In my experience, people spoke more freely if the client hadn't been accused of anything. In such situations, I would usually say that I was just gathering routine background information. Certain individuals were reluctant to speak to anyone who held any kind of authority, and for some reason, private investigators were lumped into that category.

Generally speaking, it was advantageous for me to be able to state truthfully when there was no case pending, and that the reason for the interview was simply to find out information; that our discussion would be an informal chat. I wouldn't bring out a tape recorder, nor would I take notes. It would be a simple, non-threatening conversation.

On the other hand, if Madeline, or any other client, for that matter, were to be formally charged with murder, and the case was going to trial, then the situation was different. Under the rules of discovery, the criminal defense lawyer that was representing the client would be entitled to see what evidence the state had against him or her, and I could investigate the case based on that. In such situations, the prosecutor was duty-bound to turn over all the evidence that he or she had against the client, which always made my investigation a bit easier, as the criminal defense attorney would then have a kind of blueprint that could point to where the case was headed.

But experience had taught me that I could not always depend on the information handed over during discovery to be complete, accurate and/or thorough. Sometimes, certain facts were omitted, on purpose or otherwise; would turn up late; reports weren't filed in a timely manner; or individuals were not included on the witness list. Anything could, and did, happen. Somehow, it seemed to be the important bits of information that never made it into discovery; the kind that never favored the defense and would end up biting me on the ass.

After being in the business for eight plus years, I had become familiar with quite a few individuals on the opposing side: police officers, homicide detectives, expert witnesses, Assistant State and United States attorneys. I knew who could be trusted, who performed shoddy work, who was not above playing fast and loose with evidence, and who thought they were above the law and did as they pleased. Florida was a death penalty state, so the stakes were very high for anyone who'd been accused of murder and, naturally, the prosecutor who was assigned to the case became critical.

Given my profession, it shouldn't have come as a surprise that I enjoyed reading books and articles, as well as watching films and television programs, in which private investigators were featured. In most cases, the writers of such entertainment would get it right, but I was often puzzled at how private investigators were often portrayed as they went about their jobs. I realized that the writers have to be given a certain amount of leeway because of such realities as time constraints; however, it seemed that it would be possible to stick closer to reality and still have been able to tell an interesting story.

To begin with, none of the private investigators I knew would willingly break the law for the sake of uncovering information during the course of an investigation. It was simply not worth going to jail for a client; there were other ways to find out what he or she needed to know. Private investigators did not routinely break into homes or offices in the middle of the night to read files.

I wasn't exactly naïve: I knew that sometimes lawyers would try to persuade a private eye to do something that would break the law, for example, interview individuals to the point where it could be considered witness tampering, something that a seasoned investigator would refuse to do, A reputable private eye (an oxymoron to some, I know) knew that no case, no matter how many billable hours would be racked up or how much repeat business would result, was worth going to jail over.

Another pet peeve of mine was when private investigators were portrayed as having adversarial relationships with law enforcement officials. Sure, there were some that we got along better with than others, but no private investigator could afford to alienate anyone in law enforcement: we were too dependent on them when working a case. Most private investigators that

I came across would exchange information, not only with law enforcement officials, but also with other investigators. We would and could work a case in a way that law enforcement individuals could not. As public officials they were bound by too many rules and regulations.

On more than one occasion, I'd helped out a homicide investigator with background information that he or she would have had to go through formal channels to acquire. Cooperating with each other, whether formally or informally, saved time, effort and money: the sort of 'you scratch my back, and I'll scratch yours' mentality. It was important for those of us who worked within the criminal justice system to develop trust and respect among ourselves, and an adversarial relationship would not benefit anyone.

Unfortunately, the only person with whom I could not get along with was Assistant State Attorney Aurora Santangelo. Most, though, were helpful. Needless to say, for a variety of reasons, I considered Detective Anderson to be the most cooperative.

Even though Detective Anderson had given Madeline quite a bit of information during her interview, he hadn't mentioned the name of the prosecutor assigned to Dr. Steinberg and Mr. Robinson's case. If Madeline were to be charged with the two murders and, from what we could see, Tommy and I were under no illusions that she wouldn't be, we could only hope it was someone who was a straight shooter who didn't play games.

The best choice, of course, would be if the prosecutor was a fair and seasoned individual like Charlie Miliken, an ex of mine, a man I still cared for deeply, and who, I suspected, still had feelings for me. In any case, that had been how he had acted in the weeks after I'd been shot, but I'd been so out of it during the first few days in the hospital that I didn't recall much of what had happened. According to Lourdes, my sister the nun, Charlie sent a massive bouquet of so many white flowers that it resembled a funeral arrangement so impressive that she almost suspected that he'd thought I'd passed away. Charlie had also come to see me at the hospital several times.

The worst choice of prosecutor would be someone like Aurora Santangelo, an old nemesis who always went out of her way to try to screw me over. Unfortunately for her, five years ago, her actions had finally caught up with her, resulting in her being busted down to prosecuting traffic violations in Hialeah. It had taken her years to claw, screw, backstab and sleep her way back to prosecuting major crimes. Aurora was just smart enough at ass kissing to hold on to her job, but it was no secret that she was completely incompetent. She should have been fired years ago. True, there were lots of incompetent people who held important positions, but the most frightening aspect about Aurora's personality was that she thought she was smarter and more deserving than everyone else, a belief that made her a dangerous adversary.

The fact that Detective Anderson, the best and most senior homicide investigator on the Miami Police Department, had been assigned to the case showed how serious the authorities were taking the unsolved murders. Having Detective Maxwell Anderson on the opposite side of the case presented a double-edged sword for me: on the one hand, he was about as honest, thorough and decent an investigator that existed; on the other hand, he was smart, driven and relentless—a deadly combination. I knew that he would not let our previous personal relationship affect his judgment. Maxwell would work the case the same way as if I was a three hundred pound former NYPD detective, and not the woman he had once loved.

Tommy had told me that the main focus of Detective Anderson's interview with Madeline had been on the nature of her relationship with the two men. She claimed to have answered his questions truthfully: Dr. Steinberg was her gynecologist, and Woodley Robinson was a personal friend, perfectly reasonable explanations as to why her name had appeared in both of their address books and cell phones.

Madeline reported that the detective had asked her profession, and she had replied that, although she was currently unemployed, she was in the process of looking for a job. Madeline, needless to say, had not volunteered the fact that she was a call girl, albeit a virginal one. Instead, she had implied that she was living off her savings, and whatever money her family sent her.

I was confident that Detective Anderson's bullshit antenna had been doing the same thing mine had done upon first meeting her: buzzing like crazy. Detective Anderson, for all his bumbling Lieutenant Columbo fumbling act, had a razor sharp mind and unerring instincts. There was no way he would buy Madeline's story without checking it out every which way. To begin with, unemployed twenty-two-year-old girls who looked like Madeline did not live at the Portofino Towers unless they had won the lottery, had a sugar daddy or had last names like Trump, Hilton or Rockefeller.

Detective Anderson was normally very closed-mouthed during his investigations, so the fact that he had divulged confidential information about the murders—both men had been shot with the same gun one day apart—indicated that he found Madeline's behavior suspicious.

I knew that the first thing he would have done after leaving Madeline was to conduct a background check on her to see if she had told him the truth about her past. Then, after having come up with the same results that Leo had, *nada*, Anderson would have begun asking around about her, just as I was about to do. A girl with Madeline's looks and personality would go far in Miami's thriving underworld.

Detective Anderson had some pretty good contacts, but I felt comfortable that I had better ones. After writing up my notes, I called Tommy.

"Lupe. I was expecting your call," Tommy greeted me. "So, what do you think of your newest client?"

"You mean the fact that she looks like the Virgin Mary?" I teased him. "Or, are you referring to the fact that she's bullshitting us?"

Tommy chuckled. "Both."

"Well, I hope you asked for a significant retainer for investigative fees. Not only am I going to have to work on the case, but I'm going to have to begin at the beginning with our Miss Meadows, right back to when her mother brought her home from the maternity hospital in Dubuque," I announced. "I don't believe much of what came out of her mouth."

"You don't believe one of your clients? I'm shocked! Shocked!" Tommy asked in mock horror. "Don't worry about the money, Lupe. I've got you covered. Tell Leo he's going to be able to have more than enough to landscape the front and back of the building like he's been dreaming of doing. Maybe even add a hot tub." Tommy knew my cousin and his preoccupation with money. "So, Lupe, how're you going to start the investigation? I assume Leo's already doing the background checks?"

"They're already done. He crosschecked all three databases: our Miss Meadows is clean as a whistle. But, Tommy, I don't buy it. Leo's running Dr. Steinberg and Mr. Robinson, as we speak," I reported. "I'll keep you posted, but right now I'm off to meet my secret weapon."

Tommy began to laugh again. "Let me guess. Anyone I know?"

"Yes, but not, I hope, in the biblical sense!" I warned him. "Bye. I don't want to keep her waiting."

After hanging up, I realized I had not told Tommy about Leo's close call with Napoleon and Josephine, nor had I asked him a question about the number of siblings in her family. Was it five, or was it six? If she had been lying about such a trivial matter, what else was she lying about? Regardless, that all could wait. I reached again for the phone, and pushed the third number on speed dial.

"Suzanne? Hi, it's Lupe. You hungry? You want to have lunch?" I was fairly certain what her answer would be, so didn't wait before continuing. "Versailles?"

"Hi, Lupe. Of course I'm hungry. You know I always am, especially for Versailles, my favorite. My mouth is already watering," Suzanne chuckled. "Versailles—half an hour? See you there."

Nothing ever changed—I knew I could always count on Sweet Suzanne to be chronically hungry, always ready to go to Versailles. As I was.

Nine

Versailles Restaurant—the unofficial center of all things relating to Cuba and Cuban exiles—was on Calle Ocho, in the heart of Little Havana. It was a huge, sprawling place: the main building, cafe, bakery, walk-up/take-out window and parking spaces, almost took up an entire city block. It was packed twenty-four hours a day.

The patrons ran the gamut of Miami residents, from society ladies to the lowliest truck drivers. For years it had been a 'must-stop' in tourist guidebooks, no trip to Miami was complete without a visit there. It didn't take a card-carrying private investigator like me to figure out why: the food was tasty, plentiful and cheap, same as the gossip. Miami politicians, hell, all politicians, knew that if they wanted to get elected, then they'd better put several visits to Versailles on their schedule.

No matter how crowded it was during regular hours, nothing compared to how jammed it became when new developments regarding news from, or about, Cuba; events that may or may not have been happening, surfaced. During those times it wasn't unusual to see television trucks three deep surrounding the place, with reporters looking for patrons' reactions to whatever information was making news.

Like clockwork, minutes after any kind of breaking news came out of Cuba—Fidel Castro's death, or from Washington, lifting of the embargo—the trucks would be out in force looking for comments, statements and reactions from the men and women crowded around the take-out window.

It was no secret that getting hard news out of Cuba was difficult, if not impossible, to come by, so the reporters did the next best thing to verify a report: they would interview the patrons at Versailles to find out what was happening on the island. Time and time again, those people had better sources than the American intelligence service, and, on certain occasions, the Cuban ones, too.

I went to Versailles as often as possible (especially when I felt I could afford the calories), and considered myself a regular. I usually sat at one of the tables in the main room, the ones located in a row by the mirrors. Although those tables were set for four people, the maitre d', an old friend of my father's, would let me sit there regardless of how many were in my party, even if I was by myself.

I had gotten Sweet Suzanne hooked on Versailles, and she went so often that she had become a regular, so much so that she, too, was allowed to sit at those same tables. We joked that if we kept it up, we would soon have to join a 12-step program to control our addiction to the restaurant.

Although I was five minutes early, Suzanne was already seated at one of 'our' tables. I walked towards her and noticed, as I usually did when we ate at Versailles, how much she stood out among the other patrons. Suzanne was very tall, she cleared six feet, broad shouldered with long, platinum blond hair and light blue eyes. She resembled a Viking goddess. Never shy about calling attention to herself, Suzanne claimed that was how she had attracted and kept some of her best, most generous clients.

She also dressed in such a provocative way that men would fantasize and salivate at the thought of being with her.

It was a good thing that I did not suffer from any kind of inferiority complex, otherwise being seen with Suzanne would have made me want to jump into Biscayne Bay and drown myself. When we would go out in public together: she, tall, blond, Nordic; me, short, olive-skinned, Latina, we looked like poster children for the joys of multiculturalism. Kind of like a Benneton ad.

That day, Suzanne had chosen to wear a light blue cotton sundress made out of such filmy material that it was possible to make out the outlines of her body. Suzanne's voluptuous body was the stuff men's dreams were made of, and women's nightmares. Although Suzanne had never stepped inside a gym, her perfect body brought to mind hours long sessions with personal trainers, aerobic instructors, Pilates teachers and yoga coaches.

Suzanne's diet consisted of lots of fats and carbohydrates; fried foods; fettuccine Alfredo topped with pounds of parmesan cheese, anything served at a drive-through fast food establishment; 16 oz. soft drinks; alcoholic beverages and lots and lots of chocolate. The words 'BMP and 'cellulite' had never crossed her lips; and neither had fresh fruit or vegetables. Her entire calcium intake came from Haagen-Dazs ice cream. Her diet was so totally horrific that I sometimes suspected that in her previous life, Suzanne must have been Cuban. Suzanne had an iron constitution and was healthy as a horse—she would no doubt live to be a hundred. She must have been doing something right, though, for in the years I'd known her, I'd never known her to be sick.

It was usually freezing cold in Versailles and that day was no exception. The management kept the air-conditioning turned down to an Arctic chill so regular patrons knew from experience that unless they wanted to get hypothermia, they'd better bring some kind of sweater to keep warm. My teeth were beginning to chatter as I pulled on the black cashmere sweater I kept in the car for exactly this kind of occasion. Suzanne, however, seemed quite comfortable wearing the ivory colored shrug that she had casually thrown over her shoulders, one so thin and transparent that it could only be used for decorative reasons. I had decided years ago that all of the winters that she had spent in Minneapolis had clearly prepared her for Miami air conditioners.

As I slid into the chair across from her, I couldn't help but notice how similar Madeline Meadows and Sweet Suzanne were in appearance. What was it about the Midwest that produced such Nordic looking women? It had to have been the Scandinavian blood, or the water in all those lakes. Either way, the end product was very attractive: both women were stunningly beautiful.

"Hi, Suzanne." I poured myself a glassful of sangria from the pitcher that sat in the center of the table. "Thanks for meeting me on such short notice." I drained the glass and poured myself another.

"Sure, Lupe. I'd had a hankering to get my weekly fix of Versailles, so I'm happy." Suzanne reached for a slice of bread that dripped with gobs of melted butter from the basket in front of her. I watched as she inhaled the entire slice, not stopping until she'd finished it. God! I was so envious of Suzanne's ability to eat as much as she wanted, whenever she wanted. None of that 'no carbs or no eating after midnight' crap for her. I would have easily given anything—money, my precious Chanel bags, my first-born child—even one of my Berettas—for Suzanne's metabolism. I could pack on the pounds just watching her eat. Life was so unfair!

"Good." Fuck the calories. I reached for a fistful of mariquitas, the thinly sliced plantains coated with layers and layers of
the hot oil they had been fried in, and then generously salted.

Just then, I was so happy that I was positively orgiastic:
strong sangria, Cuban bread dripping with butter, greasy, salty
mariquitas. Life was good. And, to think that if Carlos Suarez's
bullets were to have hit their mark, and I would have died, I
would never have been able to go to Versailles and pig out again.
I shuddered at that horrible thought; it was simply too awful to
contemplate.

"So, Lupe, not that I'm not happy to see you, but what's the
emergency?" Suzanne asked between bites. "Don't take this the
wrong way, I'm fine with it, but I'm assuming it has to do with a
case you're working." Suzanne took a sip of her sangria. "That's
the way it is when you call asking to meet me right away for
lunch at Versailles."

"You're right, Suzanne. You know me too well," I replied with
a smile. "It has to do with a case I'm working."

I was about to ask her about Madeline Meadows, but just
then, the waitress came over to take our order. Neither Suzanne
nor I looked at the menu. We knew everything that was on it.
Even if there had been specials, we wouldn't have been tempted
to order them as, on the few occasions that we had deviated
from our regular orders, we had regretted doing so. Suzanne
chose the *palomilla*, a very Cuban dish of flank steak that was
thinly pounded so that it covered the entire plate, and served
with tiny chopped onions and paisley on top; I ordered one
of the many specialties of the house, *Polio Versailles*, chicken
breasts cooked in oily onion sauce. Both our choices brought
plenty of sides: the black beans and rice and 'maduros', sweet,
ripe plantains that accompanied just about every dish. We
didn't have to worry that we might not have enough food. As far

as I knew, no one in the forty some year history of Versailles had ever gone home hungry.

We waited until the octogenarian waitress shuffled away towards the kitchen to place our order before resuming our conversation. As I watched her, it occurred to me, yet again, that the median age of the waitresses at Versailles seemed to be well over seventy. I had long suspected that none of them ever retired: they just dropped dead with their hair shellacked into place and thick pancake make-up slathered on their faces, wearing green polyester pantsuits while carrying trays of fragrant Cuban food.

"So, what is it that you need help with?" Suzanne turned serious. "You know you can count on me for whatever you need."

"Thank you." I smiled at her. "A couple of days ago Tommy was retained on a case and he asked me to be the investigator," I explained. "Two men were murdered, and cops paid his client a visit to ask questions."

"Two men were murdered? You're working a double murder?" Suzanne repeated. Suddenly, a look of concern came over her face. "Lupe, so does this mean you're back to working full-time?"

"Yes, I'm back! Watch out, Miami!" I laughed. I reached over and patted my friend's hand. "It's OK, Suzanne, honestly. I'm ready. I feel well, and I need to get back to work. Two years is a long time to be off."

I could see that in spite of my assurances, Suzanne remained skeptical. "Well, I guess I have to take your word for it, but, at least, promise me that you won't take on too much at one time. And that you'll pace yourself."

"I promise." I nodded solemnly, though we both knew I was lying. I drank some sangria, refilled our glasses then continued. "The client hasn't been charged with anything yet, but Tommy thinks it's just a matter of time before that happens and, based on some very preliminary investigations, I agree with him. He just wants to be prepared when the time conies."

Suzanne nodded. "That sounds like Tommy. Always prepared. He must have been a Boy Scout." She took another piece of bread from the basket and began chewing it slowly. "So, what can I help you with, Lupe?"

"Our client, well, it seems as if she's a colleague of yours," I said as delicately as possible. "She's a working girl."

Of course I knew what Suzanne did professionally, after all, that had been how we'd met, but it was a subject we seldom discussed. It wasn't that I passed judgment on her, or that she was ashamed of what she did. There was just really no need. I'd always thought that Suzanne would make a terrific investigator, she'd even helped me out on a couple of cases, but for whatever reason, she didn't want to explore becoming one further. She'd enjoyed working with me, but that had been as far as it had gone. Still, I had not given up hope, and would bring up the subject from time to time.

"Oh, a working girl?" Suzanne asked, not skipping a beat. "What's her street name?"

"Her street name?" I thought back to the file on Madeline but couldn't recall seeing any reference to any name other than the one she had given Tommy. "I don't know. I only know her as Madeline Meadows."

"A tall blonde with baby blue eyes? Real innocent looking?" Suzanne chuckled knowingly. "Farm girl type?"

"That's right." I nodded. "You know her?"

"Oh, God, Lupe, sure I do, not personally, though. I couldn't stay in business if I didn't know what girls were working." Suzanne poured herself the last of the sangria from the pitcher. "Everyone is aware of the professional virgin from Iowa. She landed quite a good gig."

It was reassuring to know that even though I had been away from the business for a while, I had not lost my instincts; I had figured right when I had come to Suzanne to ask about Madeline. I looked at Suzanne, trying to discern how she felt about her fellow Mid westerner. If my friend knew about Madeline being 'die professional virgin from Iowa', it wouldn't be a reach to assume that she also knew how much she charged for the pleasure of her company. I was aware of how hard Suzanne and her girls worked for their money, so it couldn't be easy for her knowing that there was a woman out there charging thousands of dollars per hour to not have sex with her clients.

"What can you tell me about her?" I was most eager to hear what Suzanne would say.

Suzanne shrugged. "Well, as I said before, I don't know her personally so all I can tell you is gossip."

"Anything you can think of will be helpful; I'm kind of flying blind here." I smiled.

"Sure, but remember, Lupe, this is what I've heard and not what I know firsthand," Suzanne warned me. She took a deep breath. "Your Madeline Meadows arrived on the scene December before last, about a year and a half ago, I think. Two brothers, the Loredo brothers, they're twins, manage her." Suzanne laughed. "They're both so ugly, years of taking steroids will do that to someone especially if they were ugly to begin with!" Suzanne shook her head at the horror of it.

"It's hard to tell which one is uglier. Anyway, they set her up in a studio apartment in one of those old buildings on Euclid and Sixth or Seventh Street, can't remember which one, but it has undergone a condo conversion since. She lived there for a few months. The twins paraded her up and down South Beach—not pimping her out—just letting her be seen. Those guys may looked like roided-up thugs, but they're marketing geniuses, I tell you!"

I thought about what Suzanne had said. "So, as far as you know, she wasn't working then?"

Suzanne shook her head again. "No, they were just showing her off. They used to work for Carlos Montoya. Remember him? He owned the L'Escort Deluxe Services until he went away for trafficking, dealing, manufacturing: the whole nine yards, courtesy of the American taxpayer. He's doing federal time out in Colorado, he'll have to serve his entire sentence. That's the problem with federal time, conditions inside are better, but there's none of this time off for good behavior shit," Suzanne pointed out. "Lupe, all this talk is making me thirsty. If you want to order another half pitcher of sangria, I won't object."

The words were barely out of Suzanne mouth before I raised my hand in the time honored gesture to request that the waitress to come over to our table. "Thought you'd never ask," I told Suzanne. "While we're ordering, you want to have a *flan de coco* for desert?" I tempted her. "This is a working lunch, so I'm going to charge the client."

"*Flan de coco*, sure, why not, especially if it's free." Suzanne smiled. "We might as well eat a little something to go with the sangria."

The waitress came over, and we gave her our order for yet another half-pitcher of sangria, plus two desserts. She beamed with approval; there was nothing the servers at Versailles liked more than watching their clients eat and drink themselves under the table. From the smile on her face that stretched from ear to ear, I could tell that Suzanne and I were making her deliriously happy. In contrast to her happiness, all I could think of was the indigestion I was going to get.

"So, after the twins showed her around and let everyone

know there was a new girl in town, then what happened?" I prompted my friend.

"What didn't happen, you mean!" Suzanne began laughing. "An 'Open for Business' sign was hung around her neck but it was all about the 'look-but-don't-touch' business. My understanding is that she would go out on calls with Johns, but there was no actual sex involved—just fooling around—whatever that means. It was made very clear she was a virgin, and if the clients wanted to have the pleasure of her company, to be with her—that's all they were paying for—no sex. I guess the deal was that they could each hope she would break down, and eventually have sex with them—and, they all wanted to be the first! Men are so stupid, really, so competitive. Any one of my clients who would pay that kind of money to be with one of my girls would be very, very happy at the end." Suzanne shook her head in wonderment. "And, Lupe, may I point out how expensive being with her was? Five thousand an hour!"

"Jesus, Suzanne, this is all so weird. That's exactly what she claimed," I said. "Madeline had said that she was a call girl, but one that didn't have sex with her clients." The waitress brought us the half pitcher of sangria, and I poured us both a glass. I took a sip, and then spoke again. "Suzanne, have you ever heard of anything like that before? A virgin call girl who charges thousands of dollars to her clients just to be with her?"

"Nope, and Lupe, honey, as we both know, I've been in the business a long time," Suzanne replied. "It's fucking marketing genius! I wish I'd thought of it first. I kick myself every night that I didn't think of that hook first! Who would have thunk! Fuck! Those twins aren't as dumb as they look; some of the steroids they took must have gone to their brains, made them smarter." Suzanne finished her sangria. "And those shitty little dogs of hers. Brilliant! Just brilliant!" There were no secrets in Miami. "But, you know, Lupe, her ride won't last forever. Pretty soon, she's going to have to put out," Suzanne stated in a matter-of-fact tone.

"Yeah, they're the escort business' equivalent to Donald Trump selling promises," I agreed, beginning to dig into the *flan de coco* that the waitress had just placed in front of me. "So, who are her clients? Obviously they're wealthy men, but how many can afford to pay her price for her virginity?"

Suzanne also began to dig into the flan. "Well, I don't think she had too many clients; no surprise there, really, those prices were passion killers, especially in today's economy, but the few she had were regulars. At least, that's the word on the street."

"Can you give me some names?" I saw Suzanne's look of alarm, so I hurried to reassure her. "Don't worry, I won't contact them. Whatever you tell me is privileged."

Suzanne smiled. "Yeah, I remember—Florida Statute 493— attorney/client privilege and all that."

"That's right," I said. "What happens in Versailles stays in Versailles, and all that."

"OK. Well, I heard that Thomas Champion, the developer, was a regular, so was Mark Gutierrez, the record producer. I saw her out once with Frankie 'Underpants' Carrillo, the underwear king," Suzanne revealed. "Sorry, Lupe, those are the only ones I can think of right now. But I'm not sure they're still clients. I mean, they're my clients, too, and, my girls, well, they're not virgins!" Suzanne chortled.

I wrote down the names in the small notebook I had taken out of my purse earlier. "Do you know a Woodley Robinson?"

"Woodley Robinson?" Suzanne repeated. "No, sorry, the name doesn't ring a bell. Is he one of her clients?"

"Not is, was. He was one of the two men who were murdered," I corrected. "According to Madeline Meadows, he was her best client."

"Oh, God! That's terrible," Suzanne exclaimed. "Does she have anything to do with it?"

"The cops think so," I told her. "As I said before, they came to see her, ask her questions about his murder."

Suzanne appeared to think about what I had just said. "You said earlier that two men were murdered. Who was the other one?"

"Dr. Steinberg, her gynecologist," I answered. "He was the one who would verify that she was a virgin."

I looked up from my notes and saw that Suzanne had gone pale. "Dr. Steinberg? Dr. Samuel Steinberg?" I nodded. "That can't be true! He's my doctor also. And my girls' doctor, too! We've been going to him for years—he's the best—the nicest man!"

What a small world! "I'm so sorry to be the one to tell you this, Suzanne, I had no idea you knew him." I reached over for her hand and patted it. "It's been in the papers."

"I don't read the papers, Lupe, I should, but I don't." Suzanne's eyes filled up with tears. "I can't believe this, Lupe, Dr. Steinberg was the nicest man, a family man, too, with a wife and four children." Suzanne sobbed quietly into her napkin.

I let her cry for a few minutes before speaking again. "I'm sorry, Suzanne."

"Yes, he was the doctor for a lot of working girls. You know, few of us have health insurance, but he would give us a break; he said it was more important that we be healthy than he get paid." Suzanne looked up at me, her eyes red from crying. "Lupe, I was going to help you out on the case because you're my friend, but now that Dr. Steinberg was your victim, it's personal for me. I'll do anything I can to help you find his killer. Anything!" Suzanne blew her nose loudly.

"Thank you. I need help. This is a world I don't know too much about, Suzanne, so I really would appreciate any information you can give me," I told her.

I closed my notebook and looked around for the waitress to order coffee and ask for the bill. I felt bad about giving Suzanne the bad news about her doctor, but it was time to go. Detective Anderson surely was not taking a couple of hours off for lunch. Besides, I was eager to get back to the office and see what Leo had uncovered about the other players in the case. I had to move fast.

The check at Versailles always came quickly, same as the food, so we were out in the parking lot less than five minutes after we had finished. It was scorching hot in the blazing sun, so we quickly began walking toward our cars, heading in the same direction as I had parked my Mercedes next to her black Escalade.

I opened my car door, then remembered that I wanted to ask Suzanne one last question. "Hey, Suzanne, seeing as how you know so much about Madeline Meadows, do you remember her street name now?"

Suzanne tossed her head back and began laughing. "Mary. Her street name is Mary."

Go figure.

Ten

I drove back to the office after lunch, garlic oozing from every pore in my body, and thought about how fortunate it was that I didn't have plans to meet with any clients or men, for that matter, in the near future. Anyone standing less than two feet away would have passed out from the fumes emanating from me. Although I could have happily eaten at least one meal a day at Versailles, I had to reluctantly acknowledge that patronizing that restaurant on a regular basis was definitely not recommended for anyone who wanted to expand, or for that matter, keep, their social and professional circles.

Traffic on Douglas Road—it was a straight shot from my office to Versailles on it—was almost at a standstill, so I was forced to creep along at ten miles an hour. I lowered the driver's side window to see if I could pinpoint what the problem was ahead, but all that I was able to observe was a mile long line of brake lights. There was no point in getting exasperated. Given Miami's kamikaze traffic, the slow up was because there was an accident somewhere along the road. So as not to act on my road rage, I decided that I might as well take advantage of the time and the fact that the car was almost stopped, to do something constructive. After popping a couple of breath mints, I reached for my cell phone.

"Leo? Hi, just to let you know, I'm on my way back to the office, but I'm stuck in fucking traffic. Douglas is a parking lot so I don't know when I'll get there. Hopefully before dark," I complained.

"Lupe, you're calling first to bitch at the Miami traffic, then, after you've vented to your heart's content to get my sympathy. You're going to ask me if the backgrounds came back, right?" Leo knew me too well.

"That's right; the bitching is now officially over." I laughed. "Now, what about the backgrounds? Anything interesting come back?"

"Well, the doctor, Dr. Samuel Steven Steinberg, d.o.b. 7/14/50, had a completely clean record: pillar of the community, family man, wife, Cecilia Maria Sanchez, four children, two in high school, two in college. He volunteered with various organizations helping supply ob-gyn services to low-income women in inner-city clinics: hookers, junkies, drunks, homeless. On paper, the guy was a saint."

What Leo was reporting went along with what Suzanne had said earlier, that the good doctor was in the habit of caring for women who would probably not have access to other kinds of medical care.

"And, the other victim, Woodley Robinson?"

I could hear the rustling of papers in the background before Leo spoke again. "The other victim, Woodley William Robinson, d.o.b. 12/18/52, well, he's not as clean or as saintly as the good doctor, but still, I couldn't come up with much for him as far as the criminal background. I mean, he was a businessman, a very successful developer so he'd been sued dozens of times mostly, though . . . I'm going to get the court records." The rustling of papers became louder as Leo flipped through the printouts. "By people that he's done business with:

contractors, customers, etc. Oh, and a couple of ex-wives. His divorces were none too friendly. Lots of money involved. It's estimated that he was worth a couple of hundred million. The divorces were really sordid: charges of adultery, physical, emotional and mental abuse, that kind of stuff, boilerplate accusations. The kind of normal charges that are found in bitter and contested splits."

Leo's voice drifted as he rattled off more details of the Robinson divorces; however, he mostly focused on the finances. With Leo, as with me, it was always a case of 'follow the money.' As I listened to him, I stifled a chuckle. I could picture my cousin salivating as he contemplated what he would have done with all the money we would have earned if we'd been retained to do the investigations for a domestic case of such magnitude. After five minutes, I decided that rather than letting Leo torture himself with those very materialistic thoughts, I should bring him back to reality.

"You said he had a couple of ex-wives? What was his marital status when he was killed?" I wondered.

"He was married to a Daniela Maria Sarmiento, a former Miss Venezuela, a finalist in the Miss Universe Pageant 2003. No kids with her, but four by his first two wives," Leo reported.

I thought about Woodley Robinson's marital situation. It didn't make much sense that a man who was married to a beauty queen—and all those Venezuelan beauty queens were gorgeous (Caracas was the plastic surgery capital of the world for aspiring pageant queens)—would pay to be with a call girl; even a knockout such as Madeline Meadows. A man as rich and as powerful as Woodley Robinson could have had virtually any woman he wanted. He had a beauty queen wife at home, but he had still felt the need to seek the company of Madeline Meadows. The fact that Woodley Robinson had strayed reinforced my long held belief that I would never go wrong overestimating the power of the male ego.

"Thanks for the update." Just then, the car in front of me began to move, and I was actually able to take my foot off the brake. "Hey Leo, guess what? I'm clipping right along; I must be going all of fifteen miles an hour now! I might get a speeding ticket!" I announced. "See you in a few minutes. Bye."

Leo had only given me a very brief report on Dr. Steinberg and Woodley Robinson. I knew there would be many pages to sift through on my desk awaiting my return to the office, but still, it had been a start. More importantly, it had given me something to contemplate while trapped in my car instead of giving me time to look at my fellow motorists, all of whom were busy talking on their cell phones, texting, applying makeup, or eating and drinking. It was a miracle that these people had drivers' licenses, but, then again, this was Miami.

I may have been a seasoned investigator that had worked all kinds of cases, but there was something about this one that captured my curiosity, and it wasn't only because I was having and/or had had affairs with Tommy MacDonald, and Detective Maxwell Anderson. The more I thought about the case, the more convinced I became that there was something not right about my client and I was determined to find out what that was.

No question about it: Madeline Meadows was in deep trouble, the kind that Napoleon and Josephine couldn't bite their way out of. The fact that the two dead men knew Madeline could have been attributed to coincidence, somewhat far-fetched, but still, it could have happened. But that they had both been killed with the same gun could not be explained away as coincidence. Anderson had not told Madeline who the gun had been registered to, knowing that would have answered a lot of questions. Or, for that matter, whose prints were on it.

The more I thought about it, the more convinced I became that the virginal Ms. Meadows had come to us because she fully expected to be charged with the murders. She had denied any involvement to both Tommy and me, but she had not retained a criminal defense attorney on the chance that she would be arrested. It had not been a preemptive action on her part; she had known for certain that she was going to be charged with the murders, and that it was only a matter of time. What I wanted to know was how she knew that was going to happen, and why.

The fact that a client was withholding information from me was not particularly unusual; at one point or another during the course of an investigation pretty much all my clients either lied or failed to divulge information that would have been helpful to me, but that usually happened after they had been charged with a crime. In contrast, Madeline Meadows was not being open and straight with us from the very beginning, prior to having been charged with any crime. I had enough confidence in my investigative abilities to know that sooner or later I would uncover whatever it was that she was hiding. Her acting secretive, though, was an annoyance that would ultimately backfire. The extra time I would have to spend investigating whatever it was she was concealing would not just add up the billable hours I would be charging her, but, more seriously, slow down any progress I might make. Detective Anderson was going at full speed, and I was being hampered by a client who was not cooperating.

Finally, what seemed like an eternity, I swear it would have been quicker to walk to and from Versailles than drive there, I pulled into the driveway of our office, remembering to go all the way to the back, so I would not park under the frangipani tree and have to hear Osvaldo's complaints about how the sap from the tree ruined the paint on the Mercedes.

In the eight years that I had parked under the tree, I had never even seen one little tiny drop of sap fall on the hood of the car, but Osvaldo would swear that he knew the killer liquid was there, just waiting to poke holes into the black paint. I loved Osvaldo with all my heart, but sometimes he fussed just a bit too much. Still, asking me to park away from the tree wasn't really too much to ask, and just in case it turned out he was correct, I did as he requested. I owed the old man at least that much consideration.

Before getting out of the car, I looked around to make sure no one was lurking around. I knew I was being overcautious, but being shot did that to people, I guessed. It was only after making sure no one was around that I got out, and walked toward the building.

As soon as I opened the front door I was greeted by the sight of Leo, who was leaning back in his chair, still dressed in his Jimmy Buffett outfit, feet up on the desk, eyes closed, snoring lightly. In his right hand he clutched a tall, green-colored ceramic tumbler that was decorated with clay figures of manatees frolicking in blindingly blue waters. As I looked at him, I briefly debated whether I should wake him up and ask what was in the glass, but decided against it. Sometimes ignorance was bliss, and I'd found out that with Leo, that was the prudent road to take. Instead, I just thanked God for the thousandth time that few of our clients ever came into the office.

I tiptoed past the reception area, went into my office, and gently closed the door behind me. The reports of the background checks were on my desk, waiting for me. There was no point in waking Leo until I'd had a chance to read them over, so I decided to let him catch up on his beauty sleep. He'd had a rough morning, starting by having been attacked by Napoleon and Josephine.

Before tackling the reports, though, I couldn't resist glancing out the bay window to see how much my little feathered friends had progressed on their construction project. The parrots, however, were nowhere to be seen, not really surprising, as it was the hottest part of the day. They usually retired deep into the branches of the avocado tree to take a siesta until the temperature cooled off enough for them to resume work. I was tempted to do that as well, but couldn't, so instead, I sighed and began my reading.

The first file I tackled was the easiest: the saintly Doctor Steinberg. Leo had summed up the contents of the report quite well. There was nothing in the file to indicate that the doctor was mixed up in anything questionable. The only thing that caught my attention was that the Steinberg family owned a lot of pricey real estate. In addition to their three million dollar house that abutted the Coral Gables Country Club, they owned a house in Blowing Rock, North Carolina appraised at just over a million dollars. A lot of Miami families had second homes in North Carolina, a place where they spent summers to escape the oppressive heat (and hurricane season, of course), so I wasn't surprised that they would have owned property there. What was surprising to me, though, was to read of how much money the Steinbergs had tied up in real estate.

Not just that, but they had four children, the two eldest in private colleges: boy at Duke; girl at Columbia; the youngest two in private school in Miami: boy at Ransom Everglades; girl at Gulliver. It did not appeal' that any of the four had scholarships or financial aid. I quickly worked the numbers, and my preliminary figures showed that the Steinbergs were paying full freight for their children's education, north of one hundred thousand dollars in tuition alone.

Nowadays, with HMO's and managed care, I was aware that doctors didn't make that much money, but maybe the Steinbergs had other sources of income: family money or investments that had paid off, or some other kind of windfall, for example, an inheritance or winning the lottery. Still, the numbers had stood out, so I made a note to myself to ask Leo to look into the Steinberg finances a bit more thoroughly.

In contrast to the good doctor, Woodley William Robinson's personal and professional life seemed to be an accident waiting to happen. True, he was a very successful businessman, but his three wives—two ex's and a current—were a huge drain on his finances. Mr. Robinson also had four children: two in college; one in high school; and one, the youngest daughter who seemed to have spent the majority of her life in rehab. So his tab for his children was also very high. None of the wives or children seemed to have ever worked, so at the time of his death, Mr. Robinson had been the sole support of seven people, not counting himself.

Apart from the lawsuits, some speeding tickets and a DUI, Woodley Robinson's record was clean. In Miami's loosey-goosey, rough-and-tumble society, he had been considered a model citizen who probably would have been given the keys to the city at some point in his life, and had a 'Woodley Robinson Appreciation Day' designated in his honor, if he hadn't been killed. Well, Miami being Miami that could still happen, postmortem honor and all that for a developer: Miami's equivalent to a god.

However, the real estate market in Miami had cooled quite a bit so maybe Mr. Robinson was not doing as well as he had been in years past. Maybe one of his creditors had gotten tired of waiting for the lawsuit to grind its way through the court system, and decided to speed things up by bumping him off. It's easier to sue an estate than a litigious person such as Woodley Robinson seemed to be.

Nothing in the file even hinted at why a man like Woodley

Robinson would seek out the company of someone like Madeline Meadows. Background checks only gave a glimpse, a cold and objective one, into someone's life. However, unlike other cases where I'd been able to glean a tidbit of information which would lead me to uncover something more than what was on the report, in the Robinson situation, I couldn't find anything that would point to why he'd been killed. I would have to get to know Woodley Robinson, the man, from other sources. As my late, sainted mother used to say, "Lupe, dear, there is more than one way to skin a cat."

I wrote a note to Leo to see if he could find out what was in Mr. Robinson's will. Leo had a friend at the clerk's office, so he might be able to get a peek at it before it was filed with the court. Seeing the cast of characters in Woodley Robinson's complicated life, it would be interesting to find out who would benefit from his death.

Before leaving to have lunch with Suzanne, I had sent Leo an e-mail asking him to also conduct a background check on the twins—Stanley and Ernest Loredo. Their files were also on my desk. I set aside the Steinberg and Robinson files and opened the Loredo ones in such a way that they lay side by side on my desk. One quick glance told me right away that the files were almost identical, not really surprising, as the twins followed the same life trajectory.

Born in Miami, at South Miami Hospital, the men were the youngest of Carlos and Lucia Loredo's six children; the others had been born in Santiago de Cuba. The twins were twenty-five years old, and Ernest was older by ten minutes. The family had come to the U.S. from Cuba as a result of having won visas in the lottery, a system allowing them to legally immigrate to the United States thirty years before. Educated in Miami public schools, the twins had graduated from Miami Senior High in

1996, at the age of nineteen. They had taken courses at Miami-Dade College, but there was no record of them having received any kind of degree.

As far as their criminal history, there were several entries for them as juveniles, but as was normally the case with juvies, those were sealed. Still, the fact that there were records of some sort indicated that they had gotten into trouble at an early age. Criminal behaviors were usually established at a young age, so the fact that they'd started off on their careers while children told me a great deal.

As adults, apart from having horrible traffic records: speeding, reckless driving, several DUI's each, they also had numerous arrests for fighting, fraud, bad checks, drunkenness, several for possession. I had to laugh when I read they'd been arrested during a raid on an illegal dog fight on a farm in Homestead, charged with running a criminal enterprise and suspicion of animal cruelty. No wonder they had known how to train Napoleon and Josephine! I hoped the Chihuahuas had been quick learners. The twins may have been Madeline's 'saviors' in her trouble with Ricardo, but they sure were no choirboys.

So far, nothing of what I had read in their files surprised me; I could have predicted what the background checks would reveal from the little that Madeline had told me. As I continued reading, I saw that their only employment listed had been at L'Escort Deluxe Services, LTD., a company with a South Beach address. Even though that had been the only job that had shown up, I had no doubt that the escort service had not been their only place of employment, and would have bet serious money they had been involved in many other activities: organizing dog fights and dealing drugs, etc. But the escort service had probably been the most legal, so that had been the one they had chosen to list.

The twins, from what I could tell, may have been relatively uneducated, but as Sweet Suzanne had pointed out, they certainly were not stupid. No amount of book learning would have taught them that they had a gold mine in Madeline.

I spent the next couple of hours rereading the five backgrounds—beginning with Madeline's, then going on to Dr. Steinberg's, after that, Woodley Robinson's, and finishing up with the twins. I jotted down a few more notes in the margins of the files, facts that I wanted Leo to follow up on; things I wanted to check out; any statements or inconsistencies that jumped out at me. Procedures I usually followed when I began working on a new case. It was only after I was satisfied that I'd done all I could at that point that I picked up the telephone and placed a call to Tommy.

"Hey, Lupe, what's up?" I could tell from the clipped, almost abrupt tone in Tommy's voice that he was busy.

"I just wanted to check in with you on the Meadows case," I replied.

"Anything I need to know right away?" Tommy sounded distracted. "I'm going to trial tomorrow on that aimed home-invasion case I told you about and I'm up to my ass in alligators."

"No, nothing critical, I just wanted to give you a quick update," I explained. "And tell you what I was planning on doing next."

"Lupe, sorry, but you're on your own for now on that case; do whatever you think you should. I have faith in your judgment." It was clear that Tommy was in a hurry to get back to his trial preparation. "Sorry, but I have to jump now. I'll try to call you later, but I can't promise. I still have a shit load of work left to do."

"Good luck with your trial", was all I managed to say before hanging up.

Less than a minute later, I picked up the phone again, and punched in the eighth number on speed dial. Nestor Gomez, my contract investigator, answered on the first ring as he usually did when I called.

"Nestor? Hola, it's Lupe. How are you?"

"Lupe! Great to hear from you! How are you? How're you doing? How're you feeling?" The delight at hearing from me was evident in his voice.

"I'm fine, Nestor, thank you," I replied. "And you? How are you? How's the family?"

"I'm fine, thanks. Working hard. I'm on surveillance right now. Fucking domestic. Old story. Husband banging the secretary. What a cliche. Shit, I hate domestics, but they pay well, you know that, immigration attorneys aren't cheap. You know the s.o.b. just gave me another bill. Two grand this time."

Originally from the Dominican Republic, Nestor was the eldest of twelve brothers and sisters, and he was in the process of bringing them all into the United States legally. Last I had heard, he only had three to go—his youngest sisters. As far as I knew, Nestor only worked so he could pay the immigration attorney's bills, and now, with all this Homeland Security stuff and new rules and regulations, his family had to jump through even more hoops to get here. I swear, throughout the years, he had forked over so much money to the man, he had become like an annuity for the lawyer. Kind of like Andres San Pedro, my serially married client, had become for me.

"I know that lawyers don't come cheap, especially the ones that practice immigration; they charge pretty much what they want." I agreed. Thank God Nestor didn't know what Tommy charged—he would have gone into cardiac arrest.

"The family is fine, thank you for asking. Everyone working real hard and staying out of double. Hey, Lupe, I only have two sisters left to bring over, thank God. Then I can retire!" Nestor laughed.

I heard the soft click of a camera as Nestor took pictures in the background—the man was a master at multitasking. "Well, it's good you only have two sisters left, but don't retire just yet, please. I have a job for you."

"A job for me? You working full-time now, Lupe? No more part-time?" Nestor sounded concerned. "Are you sure you're up to it? The doctors said you were OK to work?"

"Yes, I'm fine, Nestor, don't worry," I hurried to reassure him. Although I was touched by his concern for me, sometimes Nestor could be a bit of an old lady. "When can you come by the office so I can give you the file, and tell you what needs to be done?"

"Well, I can probably wrap up this domestic this afternoon, or at the latest tonight, when I give the report and video and pictures of her husband *inflagrante delicto* with the secretary to the wife. I hope she takes it well, and I don't have to spend hours holding her hand. I tell you, Lupe, infidelity pays well, but I hate it," Nestor said with a huge sigh. "I could come by tomorrow morning. Unless it's an emergency, then I can meet with you later on tonight, after I finish with the wife, if it's not too late."

I thought for a moment, sometimes those domestics took the longest, and I was getting quite tired. "Tomorrow morning is fine. About ten o'clock, here?"

"See you at ten. And, Lupe, it's good to have you back. Good to work with you again," Nestor said.

"Thanks, Nestor. See you tomorrow and good luck with the wife. Bye." I gently hung up the phone.

Nestor Gomez was one of the best, if not the best, investigator in the business. His specialty was in conducting any kind of surveillance—video, camera, whatever—and was as skilled in a moving surveillance as in a stationary one; the man was amazing. I had total confidence in him, and knew that he could deliver the goods on anyone. Unlike other investigators who slacked off, or who fell asleep on the job, if Nestor said he'd followed someone all night and nothing had happened, I knew that was exactly the way it had been. However, he didn't come cheap. He had to pay the immigration attorney's invoices, so, unless I had a huge budget, I used him sparingly. From what Tommy had said, Madeline Meadows had coughed up a large chunk of change as a retainer, so we could afford Nestor. I didn't pinch pennies when the client was looking at a double murder charge.

Tommy had told me to use my judgment and that was what I was doing. Madeline Meadows was lying through her teeth, and if anyone could help me to find out what she was up to, it would be Nestor. I could hardly wait for him to get started.

Eleven

The first full day back at work must have taken more of a toll on me than I had thought, as I was totally exhausted when I left the office; in the shape I was in, there was no way I could make it through an entire dinner with my family. If I were to have joined the family for dinner in the dining room—whenever possible we would all eat together—they would have noticed my exhaustion, and I would have been inundated with free advice, with them going into overdrive telling me that I had gone back to work too early, should have taken more time off, and so on. Just then, free advice was worth exactly what I paid for it.

As I turned into the driveway, I saw that my sister Lourdes' car was parked in its usual spot over by the far entrance, a sight that made me smile. Although I knew that it wasn't right to favor one family member over another, I had to admit that Lourdes was my favorite. I missed her a great deal, as for the past month she'd mostly remained in her office at the convent, keeping busy running a new program that helped recent immigrant arrivals to Miami. I hadn't seen her in over a week, and would have normally jumped at the chance to spend time with her, but getting out of my car and going inside the house would require just about all the effort that I could exert. A visit with Lourdes would just have to wait.

Once inside the house, after making sure the coast was clear, I headed for the kitchen to speak with Aida, to request that she please fix my dinner on a tray so I could eat in my room. I was pleased to see that Aida was alone, puttering around the room, moving pots and pans, placing them on the different burners on the stove, then looking at them for a few seconds before picking them up again, and returning them to their cupboards.

Even though it was almost seven o'clock, and dinner at our house was served promptly at eight, Aida had not yet begun to prepare the meal. More alarmingly, by the vague and aimless way she moved, it was obvious that she didn't have any real plan in mind.

As I watched her shuffle around, the fact that Aida had grown truly old hit me, and my eyes filled with tears. Less than ten years ago she would have heard me coming, and would have called out a greeting. No one could ever sneak up on Aida, she claimed to have been born with 'dog ears', and could hear someone approaching from yards away. It was a talent my sisters and I hated when we were growing up, because she could hear us sneak in and out of the house when we would break curfew.

In the past, when dinner was an hour away, instead of moving slow and without purpose, Aida would have had at least six pots and pans on the stove, each bubbling away with some wonderful creation. She may have been grateful for Eliza's help in many things, cleaning, washing and ironing, but she drew the line at having the young woman assist her in the kitchen. That had always been her domain and she wasn't about to cede one inch.

A couple of minutes passed and still Aida had not noticed me standing in the doorway to the kitchen, so I took a few steps inside. "Aida," I called out as I walked toward her, but in spite of my having spoken, she still had not heard me, so I tapped her on the shoulder. "Hola, Aida. Como estás?" I bent over and kissed her.

Although I wasn't exactly a giant—I was a smidgen over five feet tall if the wind was blowing right, and my hair was teased—still, I had to lean down to kiss Aida. When the hell had she shrunk so much? We used to be eye level with each other.

"Lupe! My child!" Aida's eyes sparkled with delight. "When did you get here?"

"Oh, I just walked in," I lied as I held her hand, then leaned over and whispered in a conspiratorial way. "Listen, Aida, I'm going to ask you a favor. Do you think I could have dinner on a tray up in my room?"

"Of course, why, what's wrong, Lupe?" Aida's eyes narrowed as she examined me. "You're tired, aren't you? You went back to work too soon! I knew it! We told you to stay home, but no, not you." Aida wagged her finger at me, much as she used to do when I was growing up.

I shook my head. "No, Aida, no, it's not that. I just think I'm catching a cold, and I don't want to give it to anyone in the family." I started to back away. "I shouldn't even be here talking to you. I don't want to get you sick. I know I should have used the intercom, but I wanted to see you." I blew a kiss at her. "Gracias. I'm going upstairs to take a hot bath now, and slather Vicks VapoRub on my chest to stop the cold before it gets worse."

Aida believed that the combination of a hot bath, a healthy amount of Vicks VapoRub spread all over the chest, followed by dinner on a tray was a cure for all lung-related ills, from the sniffles to double pneumonia.

"OK, Lupe, child. I'll send Osvaldo with your dinner in about an hour. I'll fix your tray when the family is having their dinner, after he's served them, OK?" Aida winked at me. "And, Lupe, don't forget your father's birthday on Friday. We're having a special dinner for him."

"I love you, Aida," I called out to her as I walked out of the kitchen. "And don't worry, I won't forget Papi's birthday."

I hated having to lie to Aida, mentioning the Vicks VapoRub had been a particularly low thing to do, but if I'd told her the truth, that I was so exhausted that I'd barely made it home, she would tell Papi and my sisters, and they would have lectured me. If they'd had their way, I would still be in intensive care at the hospital being cared for by nurses around the clock.

I loved my family dearly, but being suffocated by familial love was the price I paid for being Cuban. I knew they meant well, but sometimes I needed a little breathing room. But, when one is female in a Cuban family, breathing room, or, the concept of privacy, for that matter is an oxymoron.

Once in my room, I stripped off my clothes and headed for the bathroom, where I ran a tub with water so hot that it turned my skin a delicate shade of pink. As much as I loved Aida, I couldn't face putting Vicks VapoRub on my body, so I just opened the jar and placed it by my bedside table, so the smell would permeate the room, a trick my sisters and I came up with years ago. I knew that Aida would grill Osvaldo about what I was doing, so to make my story stick, I had to play the part to the hilt. Soon, my room reeked of menthol.

Although I was still full from lunch with Sweet Suzanne, I somehow managed to put away the meal that Aida had prepared for me: a healthy serving of steak, an entire baked potato dripping with butter and sour cream—the way I liked it—and Caesar salad. I polished off the meal with my second flan de coco of the day. I don't know how Aida managed to produce such a wonderful meal in minutes, but however she did it, I was most grateful for it was perfect. Aida had also sent up a half bottle of red wine, a California Cabernet from Papi's cave, a very thoughtful gesture on her part.

As I drifted off to sleep it occurred to me that I was behaving much like a little child would: after having had a hot bath, and with a full stomach, my eyes had promptly closed. The wine helped to guide me to slumber land, too, of course. My last thought was that Aida was not as far gone as I'd feared just a couple of hours before.

Twelve

That night, I slept like a baby—no dreams, no nightmares—a wonderful, much-needed sleep. The first of the two alarms I had set before going to sleep woke me at eight o'clock. As I turned it off, I realized I had slept for ten full hours without moving, a record for me. I had clearly needed it, for I felt great, rested and refreshed, and ready to tackle the Meadows case again. I'd been so eager to get going that I had showered and dressed in record time.

Choosing an outfit to wear that day didn't require much thought, as the only meeting I had scheduled was the ten o'clock with Nestor, and, that would be a casual affair, so, thankfully, I could dress in my usual attire of blue jeans and a T-shirt. I didn't have to be a meteorologist to know that it was going to be another hot, humid day. During July, the temperature in Miami seldom dipped below ninety degrees with equally high humidity. I didn't even bother to put on any makeup; I only braided my hair to keep it off my face.

My preparation took such little time that I arrived at the table on the terrace even before Osvaldo had had my breakfast ready. Once I had stepped outside, the wall of hot, moist air that hit me let me know that it was going to be an especially miserable, scorching day. It wasn't nine o'clock yet, but by the time I made it to the table under the wide overhang, I was already damp. Not even the ceiling fan set at top speed could cool off the area, it just moved the hot air around.

"*Buenos dins*, Lupe." Osvaldo, who had just spotted me, hurried to greet me. "Did you sleep well? Are you feeling better?" He spoke in his usual formal way. "Aida said you were feeling a cold coming on, that's why you stayed up in your room last night instead of coming down to dinner with the family." Then, Osvaldo winked at me, letting me know that even though he had brought up my dinner on a tray, he had been on to me from the start.

I loved the old man, he and I had always had a special bond. It had begun when I was a little girl, when he would take me fishing off the Key Biscayne Bridge. There was nothing like waking up at dawn and spending hours discussing fish and fishing to create a bond between an old man and a little girl. Osvaldo would have made a terrific father, but unfortunately, he had not had the opportunity. I guess working with a family with three girls, and now, with my eldest sister Fatima's twin daughters, was the next best thing for him.

"I feel much better, Osvaldo, thank you. Please thank Aida for the dinner again. It was delicious." I took a sip of the orange juice he had poured into a glass for me. "Any of the family around?"

"No, sorry, Lupe, you're the last one up: the Señor, your father, left very early for the office, he said he had a meeting; Señora Fatima left for the gym, then she was going to her office; Señrita Lourdes left at dawn. She didn't even have breakfast!" Osvaldo put his hands up to his face in horror. "And, the twins, as you know, the camp bus picks them up at eight-thirty."

"That's too bad, I wanted to see them," I replied, then smiled with anticipation at what would be coming next. Osvaldo and

I had a morning routine, one which seldom varied, which we both enjoyed enormously.

I watched as Osvaldo poured half a cup of frothy steaming hot milk into an oversized cup in front of me, which he topped it off with ink black coffee from the pot Aida had prepared. I added two heaping spoonfuls of sugar to the mixture and stirred it until the sugar had melted. I inhaled the aroma of café con leche; at that very moment, if I were to have keeled over, I would have died a happy woman. I took a sip and closed my eyes, trying to prolong the moment. I definitely was in heaven.

After finishing the first cup of café con leche, I poured myself another, which I drank much more slowly. "Perfect, Osvaldo, like always." The old man beamed. "Thank you so much."

"You're welcome, Lupe." Osvaldo smiled back at me, then, just as he was about to walk away, turned and said, "Don't forget your father's birthday on Friday. Your sisters are planning a special celebration."

"I won't Osvaldo. Don't worry." I blew him a kiss. Next, I picked up a slice of toast from the basket in front of me, spread a thick layer of mango jam on it, and began eating. Aida made the jam herself using the mangoes that grew in our backyard. I saw a copy of *The Miami Herald* sitting on the table, but didn't stop to read it, as I was eager to get to the office. Nestor was due at ten, in less than an hour, and I wanted to be prepared for the meeting.

I finished my breakfast quickly, and after thanking Osvaldo and Aida, made a quick stop at the downstairs bathroom, to brush my teeth before leaving.

For some unknown reason, but one for which I wasn't about to question, the traffic that morning on Main Highway was very light and I was able to clip along at thirty miles an hour. Not exactly a high rate of speed, but quite quick for the commute.

I was just passing St. Hugh's Catholic Church when my cell

phone rang. I looked at the caller I.D. and saw that it was Leo. Normally, I would have let it go to voice mail as I knew that he most likely didn't have much to say, probably just wanted to be sure I was on my way but I decided to answer it. I didn't want Leo to be any more insecure than he had to be.

"*Buenos días*, Leo," I said. "*Cómo estás?*"

"Hey, Lupe, I hope you're on your way. You have a visitor," Leo announced.

"Yes, I know." Surprised, I looked at the clock on the dashboard. It was only nine-thirty. Nestor was half an hour early, something that was not like him at all; I could usually count on him being at least fifteen minutes late. "Tell him I'm on my way, and, Leo, please . . ." I was about to ask Leo to give Nestor the file I had prepared for him on the Meadows case so he could start looking at it, but I was almost at the office, so there was no point in calling back. Instead, I just drove on, thinking about the Meadows case, and what else I was going to do that morning.

As I turned into the driveway, I noticed an unfamiliar dark blue Lincoln Continental parked under the frangipani tree, and it occurred to me that Nestor must have bought himself a new car. I reminded myself that I hadn't seen him in a while, so I shouldn't have been surprised that he had changed vehicles.

However, it seemed unlike him to have gotten such a large car, especially one that was so very conspicuous and a huge gas guzzler to boot. Investigators who specialized in moving surveillances usually drove small, nondescript, forgettable cars—not ones that a mark would be likely to remember. Oh well, I thought, as I got out of my car and walked toward the office, maybe he got that car so he could fit his ever increasing number of family members in it. Or, maybe it was his personal vehicle, and not his work one. He could still have the shitty, dented silver Toyota that he drove and parked someplace else.

I opened the door to the office, expecting to see Leo and Nestor waiting for me, but the reception area was empty. Instead, I was immediately hit by a wall of delicious smelling coffee coming from the back of the building. Nestor had always loved Leo's coffee—he thought that my cousin made the best *café con leche* in Miami, so it wasn't surprising that Leo was making some for him.

"Hey, Nestor. Boy, do I have a job for you! You're going to owe me big time for this. For the next few days, you get to follow the most beautiful call girl in Miami around. She's gorgeous, Nestor, you'll love this job!" I called out as I walked towards the kitchen.

"Sorry to disappoint Nestor, Lupe, but he's not going to be following any 'beautiful call girl' today." Detective Maxwell Anderson announced as he casually strolled out of the kitchen, sipping from a mug.

"Detective Anderson!" I almost passed out from the shock. Leo took one look at me and scurried away, much like a rat deserting a sinking ship, leaving me to continue the conversation with Detective Anderson in the hallway. "What are you doing here?" was all I could manage to ask.

"Well, Lupe, I thought I would have the courtesy of giving you the news about your client personally, seeing as how you're probably still not totally recovered from your injuries," Detective Anderson replied in a soft, kind tone of voice.

What did he mean when he said I had not recovered from my injuries? I was fine, just fine. Was he patronizing me? Now wasn't the time to psychoanalyze Anderson. I had bigger problems right now, and having blurted out in front of the lead homicide detective on the case the fact that I was having my own client followed was at the top of the list.

"What news?" My heart was beating so fast and so loud that I could barely get the words out.

"Your client, Madeline Marie Meadows, was arrested at her residence at the Portofino Towers at seven o'clock this morning," Detective Anderson solemnly announced.

"Arrested? Madeline was arrested?" I repeated rather stupidly. "On what charges?"

"Three counts of first-degree murder," Detective Anderson replied.

"Three," I said, then thinking of Dr. Steinberg and Woodley Robinson I went on to ask. "Not two?"

"Three," Detective Anderson repeated. "The murder of her old boyfriend, Ricardo Melendez, brought the count up to three."

My heart dropped like a stone, but I didn't let on. Instead, I asked, "Would you like to continue this conversation in my office?" I invited him as sweetly as I could. In spite of having just learned that my client was in the Dade County jail, charged with a triple homicide, I couldn't help but notice that Detective Maxwell Anderson looked quite attractive. His blue eyes still had an effect on me.

"Sure," he said as he followed me in.

Thirteen

Detective Anderson glanced toward the bay window as he crossed the office toward the visitors' chairs. "So, what are the parrots working on now, Lupe? Last time I was here, if I recall, they were putting the finishing touches on the Empire State Building."

I couldn't help but chuckle at the memory of that huge enterprise; the building had been so architecturally accurate that I had taken photos of it. Although the parrots had constructed some pretty amazing buildings, the Taj Mahal, the Tower of London, the Golden Gate Bridge, and more, they had paled in comparison to the Empire State Building. My little feathered friends worked on that one for months—adding this, subtracting that—and then, one day, without warning or fanfare, they demolished it. I shouldn't have been surprised as, being true Miamians, after growing tired of the 'old' building, they had decided to tear it down and the hell with any architectural significance it might have had.

"I think this one is the Hoover Dam, but I'm not really sure. They still have a ways to go, I think." I told him. "It's so sad. They just finished with their last one, the Eiffel Tower, when they decided to tear it down and start another one, the one before this one. I loved the Eiffel Tower. It was my favorite." I shook my head at the shame of it all.

We watched as the parrots went about their business, flying to the avocado tree, carrying sticks and twigs in their mouths, items that they would then hand over to their colleagues who were responsible for building the structure. Then, having delivered the necessary supplies to the building site, the parrots would fly out again to forage for more building materials. I never tired of observing them; the truth was that I was addicted to my little feathered friends, so much so that I had missed them most during my convalescence.

"Well, good luck to them with the dam," Detective Anderson said. "I have no doubt they'll succeed."

"I'll tell them." I smiled and sat in the chair behind my desk.

Detective Anderson looked terrific. I hadn't seen him for the better part of a year, not since that awful heartbreaking conversation about how it was time to go our separate ways. Although we had been fond of each other, and we had truly tried to make our relationship work, it hadn't.

Sometimes I felt that our breakup had happened because, among other reasons, we had come together at the wrong time of our lives. I had been shot, hovering between life and death for days, and Detective Anderson, being the honorable man that he was, had felt the need to be at my side. The first thing he told me after I had come out of my coma was that he loved me, that he had always loved me, and that he would take care of me. How could I not have responded to such pure sentiments, especially as they had come from such a tough guy?

We still had not fully discussed the reasons why, in spite of our best efforts, we had not been able to be successful, but then, really, there hadn't been a need to do that. At the end of the clay, I suspected that the main reason was that we were both loners, and unable to commit to a long-term relationship. However, while we'd been together, it had been a truly wonderful time, and I had no regrets whatsoever. I still held Maxwell Anderson in the highest regard and would trust him with my life.

Although I hadn't seen him in over a year, Maxwell did not seem to be any different, well, at least as far as his choice of clothing was concerned. He was wearing a khaki cotton suit, a blue shirt and a slightly faded reddish tie. Judging from his bleary eyes, tousled hair and live o'clock shadow, he probably hadn't been home yet to change his clothes. I was a bit surprised to find that, even though I hadn't seen him in so long, he still appealed to me.

I'd always thought that Detective Anderson looked like a modern version of Columbo, the rumpled and slightly muddled detective on television. And, just like the fictional Columbo, Detective Anderson hid a razor-sharp brain in that befuddled exterior.

I reminded myself to be on guard. Although we'd had a pretty serious relationship, he would not let our history affect his judgment. Still, in spite of my wanting to keep the meeting on a purely professional level, I couldn't help but wish that I had known I would be seeing him that morning; I would have liked to have been more prepared for the occasion. For one thing, I would have dressed better, worn makeup, tweezed my eyebrows and had a manicure/pedicure. Girl stuff. I may have been a gun-carrying private eye—one who had just barely survived being shot—but, in the end, I was still a woman. Flirting was in my genes; the tight ones.

"Lupe, although I always enjoy visiting with you and discussing the parrots, this is an official unofficial visit." Detective Anderson was now all business. "Your client, Madeline Marie Meadows, is in big trouble."

"I realize that, Maxwell. Being charged with a triple homicide is not exactly like not paying parking tickets," I replied.

Detective Anderson was not just there to give me information, but to extract some from me as well. He wanted something and my job was to make sure he didn't get it, whatever that might be. My first, huge mistake had been earlier when, thinking he was Nestor, I'd called out that he would be following Madeline. No question, that lapse in judgment had placed me at a definite disadvantage. Now Detective Anderson knew that I had retained Nestor to check up on my own client. I couldn't afford any more screw-ups, and not just because it would be Madeline Meadows who would pay the price.

"That's right, Lupe, it's not like unpaid parking tickets," Detective Anderson agreed. "Being charged with three murders in a death penalty state, that's serious. She's looking at a needle in the arm."

I shuddered at the image of Madeline lying on a gurney, strapped down, awaiting execution. "But, please, tell me why, exactly, are you charging her with the three murders? What evidence do you have against her?"

"She knew the three men; she had access to the murder weapon and the opportunity. All three were shot with the same weapon: a .357 Magnum," Detective Anderson told me. "Oh, and Lupe, by the way, her prints were on the gun."

Oh, God—not good, not good at all. I thought about the implications of what Detective Anderson had just said. Obviously, as I had not seen the 'A' form, the arrest form, I was at a disadvantage, but there were still questions that I could ask. "Who was the gun registered to?"

"A Mr. Ricardo Mario Melendez, Ms. Meadows' former fiancée," Detective Anderson informed me.

"He was shot with his own gun?" I blurted out. I recalled that Madeline had mentioned that Ricardo owned a .357 Magnum, but, of course, I wasn't about to volunteer that information to Detective Anderson.

"That's right. An officer found it hidden in one of the hedges by the side of the house where he lived, in South Miami." Detective Anderson informed me. "This was the same gun that was used in the other two murders, Dr. Steinberg's, and Mr. Robinson's."

Madeline shooting Ricardo didn't make sense; she told me she hadn't seen Ricardo since she had moved out of the apartment in Little Havana two years before. He was out of her life; he lived in South Miami, thirty minutes away from her. Why would she shoot him? Surely it wasn't revenge for having hit her two years before. Self-defense? Then what about Dr. Steinberg and Woodley Robinson?

I didn't feel I should comment about the three murders just then. There really was nothing for me to say. Instead, I pointed out, "Maxwell, you know a .357 Magnum is not normally a woman's choice of weapon."

"That's right, but then again, Madeline Meadows is not a normal kind of pro now is she, Lupe?" He pointed out quite reasonably, "I mean, a working girl who is a professional virgin? At five grand a pop for not putting out? Fifteen years on the job and I thought I'd heard it all!" Detective Anderson laughed.

I decided to ignore any comments about my client, so I did not join in on the laughter. Instead, I asked, "So, from what you've told me, all you really have is that Ms. Meadows knew all three men, and her prints are on a weapon?" I made it seem as if it wasn't much, though I was perfectly aware that Tommy was going to have his work cut out for him. Rather than acting even remotely spooked, I said smoothly, "You know, Maxwell, there is such a thing as motive in murder cases."

Detective Anderson's blue eyes sparkled with delight, which sent a chill down my back. I recognized that look; it meant I was royally fucked. "Ah, Lupe, that's where your crack investigative skills come in." He chuckled. "And, of course, with Mr. MacDonald's formidable legal talents, I'm telling you, both of you are going to be earning every cent of your sizeable retainers in this case." He leaned over, and looked at me closely. "I wonder, though, Lupe, why did Ms. Meadows feel she had to retain Tommy MacDonald when all I had done was pay her a friendly visit? Why did she feel the need to hire him right after that? All I did was ask her a couple of questions, that's all. Just an informal interview. In my experience, most people who have nothing to hide don't sprint over to the most expensive high-profile criminal defense attorney in town just because a homicide detective paid them a visit. Why didn't she assume she was a witness?" Then Detective Anderson asked, "And, by the way, Lupe, why are you having one of your investigators follow your own client around?"

Oh God. "Well, you know I can't answer your questions, but I can assure you, Maxwell, you don't have to worry about Madeline. Our client is in capable hands." I smiled brightly, and then I added. "This is all a misunderstanding, one that will be cleared up very soon."

"I hope so, for all your sakes." Detective Anderson nodded. "But, that's enough of the official visit; I know you're not going to tell me anything about Ms. Meadows, so I'm not even going to try. I'll just change the subject, and begin the unofficial part of the visit." He looked at me with concern. "How are you doing? Are you sure you're up to working?"

"Thank you for worrying about me." I felt like getting up and kissing him, but given the situation, that he had just arrested my client I didn't think it would be appropriate. "I'm fine, thank you. It's good to be getting back to work."

"It's just like in the old days, Lupe. You working for the defense; me for the prosecution," Detective Anderson said.

"Speaking of prosecution—who caught the Meadows case?" I asked.

Detective Anderson looked so stricken that I knew there was only one assistant state attorney whose name could result in such a visceral reaction. "Oh, Lupe, I'm sorry. I'm so very sorry."

"Aurora Santangelo," I said flatly.

"Yes, it's Santangelo," he confirmed. "The minute she read the file and learned that Tommy MacDonald was the defense attorney representing Madeline Meadows, she knew you would be the investigator." Detective Anderson shook his head slowly. "She's gunning for you, Lupe; she's out for blood. She still holds you responsible for all those years she had to do penance in traffic court in Hialeah and all the asses she had top kiss to get out of there. Please watch out for her. Please."

"Thanks for the heads-up, Maxwell. I appreciate you looking out for me. I really do." I smiled at him, then stood up and walked around my desk until I was just inches away from him. Fuck professionalism. I bent down and slowly kissed him full on the lips. Maxwell instantly responded, kissing me back, long and slow, just the way I remembered.

"If you hadn't done that, I would have." Detective Anderson stood up and pulled me toward him.

"Wait." I sprinted toward the door to my office and locked it. Without saying a word, Detective Anderson and I began stripping off our clothes as we headed for the couch in the corner of the office.

I had just finished helping Detective Anderson out of the last of his clothing when I heard the front door open, and Nestor's voice in the reception area, calling out my name. Oh God! How could I have forgotten our meeting?

"Lupe! *Buenos días.* It's Nestor, I'm here."

A few seconds later, I heard Leo's voice. "Nestor, hi, sorry, but Lupe's in a meeting—she'll be with you in a few minutes. I just made some café. Come to the kitchen with me while you wait."

As I gave in to Detective Anderson's expert hands, I made a mental note to give Leo a raise. Sometimes, my cousin did the right thing.

Fourteen

"What the hell did I just do?" I asked myself as I looked at my reflection in the mirror in the bathroom of my office. "Lupe, girl, those three shots that you took to the chest must have done more than just pierce the skin. They must have affected your judgment, too." I splashed water on my face, and continued to scold myself. "How could you have sex with Detective Anderson on the couch in the office? How could you? God! Two days back on the job, and you're fucking up, in every sense of the word."

Shaking my head in disbelief, I slowly walked back to my desk. I was still shaken, so it took a moment to compose myself enough to pick up my cell phone and check the voicemail. I wanted to make sure I hadn't missed any messages while I'd been in the bathroom repairing any visible effects as a result of my cavorting with Detective Anderson. Although I really did need to speak with Tommy and let him know Madeline had been arrested, I thanked God that I hadn't missed his callback to me. I sent Tommy another text message; this one a bit more urgent than the first.

This time, rather than texting me back, he phoned. "Lupe, what's up? You have to talk fast—I'm only on a ten-minute break—and it took forever to get outside. I still have to give myself time to get back inside."

I could barely hear Tommy with all the noise in the background. As cell phones were not allowed anywhere in the courthouse, he had to call me from outside, which meant that he had to use valuable minutes of the break the judge had granted. The elevator in the Richard E. Gerstein Justice Center, the courthouse where Tommy's trial was taking place, was the slowest in the county. Not only did it stop at every floor, but when it moved, it did so at a glacially slow pace, which also took up valuable time.

For those who did not have the patience to wait for the elevator, there were six escalators in the building, but they functioned so erratically that among the workers there was an informal 'escalator pool' where people could bet on the date in which all six were working on the same day.

In addition to the elevator/escalator situation, everyone who entered the courthouse had to undergo a rigorous security check, a procedure that, given the amount of traffic in and out and the not-so-bright individuals who carried their weapons on them, took forever. Miamians were a notoriously gun toting bunch, so the machine would light up periodically, bringing the screening process to a standstill.

Tommy's trial, the armed home-invasion case he had told me about, had begun that morning, so I was on notice that getting in touch with him would be difficult. Still, he needed to know that Madeline Meadows had been arrested at dawn. She had retained him for exactly that eventuality, so her arrest wouldn't come as a surprise. But the fact that it had happened so soon would. The booking process in the Dade County jail took forever, so it would be hours before Madeline would have had the opportunity to make her one phone call.

Detective Anderson had indeed done me a huge favor when he'd told me about Madeline's arrest, allowing me to get the information to Tommy right away as now he could begin the process of getting his client out of jail sooner than he would have if the normal procedures had been followed.

"Tommy, Detective Anderson stopped by the office a little while ago to tell me that Madeline Meadows was arrested this morning, charged with three murders: first degree." Time was of the essence, so I spoke quickly. "She's being processed right now. Detective Anderson said that the only statement she made to the police was to tell them you're her lawyer."

Tommy didn't make any comment about Detective Anderson having paid me a personal visit Instead, he just said, "Good girl; she followed my orders. Three? Who's the third?"

"The ex-boyfriend, Ricardo Melendez, the guy she moved to Miami with. He was shot last night; same M.O. as the other two," I replied. "According to Anderson, all three were shot with the same .357 Magnum, which was registered to Melendez. And, get this, Madeline's prints were on the gun."

"Fuck!" Tommy exclaimed. "Triple homicide—boyfriend's gun—her prints on the alleged weapon. With that, I doubt I can get her bonded out but I'm going to try, Lupe."

"Anderson seems pretty confident she's the shooter," I told him.

Tommy chortled. "Come on Lupe, I hope you didn't buy that. You know that it's his job to make us quake in our boots."

"And that's not all." I took a deep breath. "My old friend Aurora Santangelo is the ASA on the case."

"Santangelo! Fuck! She has a stick up her ass for you, Lupe. Our poor client drew the short straw, didn't she?" Tommy asked. "It's going to be tough going."

"Yeah," was all I could say.

Being charged with first-degree murder on three homicides was bad enough, but having Aurora Santangelo as the prosecutor in the case made Madeline's situation significantly worse. Even under normal circumstances, when she didn't have a personal vendetta against anyone involved, Santangelo was neither reasonable nor professional. However, it was a given that she would be even more irrational now that she knew I was working with Tommy on the Meadows case.

If I thought it would help Madeline's situation, I wouldn't have hesitated to offer to resign, but the sad truth was that with Aurora, that probably would not have made any difference. If anything, now that she tasted blood, she would be tough on Madeline regardless of whether I stayed on the case or not. Besides, on a professional level, if it ever became known that Aurora had frightened me away from a case, lawyers would think twice before hiring me. Fuck, I'd already been shot once; I couldn't have doom and gloom hanging over me forever.

The criminal defense community in Miami was very small, and word of my pulling out because of Aurora was certain to spread like wildfire. The prosecutor would gloat about her power over me, something I absolutely, positively, could not let happen.

No, I had to remain on the case regardless of how much of a living hell Aurora would make my life. I would just have to watch my back, front and sides, too. Aurora had her long knives out for me, and she would not hesitate to plunge them into me and twist the handle, smiling as she did so.

"Listen, Lupe, I'm down to my last minute so I can't talk anymore. I'll see what I can do during the lunch break about getting Madeline bonded out. It'll be a long shot. Continue with your investigations and I'll try to keep in touch. Bye." Tommy hung up before I had a chance to wish him luck on his trial.

I sat back in my chair, and looked out the window at the parrots that were flying to and from the avocado tree, with twigs and branches in their beaks, busy building their structure. I envied how they went about their business, working together beautifully, intent on what they were doing, seemingly without a worry in the world.

As I observed them, I couldn't help but picture Madeline being booked into the Dade County Jail; I could only imagine how frightened she must have been, and how alone. I knew Tommy would do his best to get her out, but given the circumstances, I wasn't exactly hopeful he would succeed. The best way I could help Madeline was to continue with my investigation. And if that meant that I would uncover evidence that she had, indeed, been responsible for the three murders, well then, that's what I would report to Tommy.

Even though I'd tried to pry additional information about the case—before, during and after our session on the couch—from Detective Anderson, he had not said much more than he had when he'd first come into the office. I think he'd been just as surprised as I had that his visit had ended the way it had. After all, we had not seen each other in over a year. Truthfully, though, it had felt perfectly natural to have sex with him. Actually, it had been great. And, although I was pretty certain I did not want to embark on a relationship with him, now that I'd had the opportunity to calm down, I didn't regret what I had done. However, I was quite aware of the fact that our having sex could complicate matters. I would just have to force myself to put personal feelings aside.

I studiously avoided thinking that less than three days before, I'd been in bed with Tommy MacDonald, sipping champagne, discussing Madeline Meadows' situation. I knew myself well enough to be sure that, for me, there was no percentage in being introspective. Navel gazing was not something I did often, or did well, for that matter.

I looked up at the clock and was surprised to see that it wasn't even noon. I'd had quite an eventful morning. Leonardo, bless his heart, had told Nestor that I would be tied up in my meeting for quite some time, so it would be best to come back later and that I would call him to reschedule. I knew Nestor really didn't care; I'd given him so much business in the past that he knew I would make it up to him. Now that Madeline had been charged with triple homicide, he would be kept super busy with all the work I would be assigning him.

I flipped open the Meadows file and read through the notes I had taken during the business part of my meeting with Detective Anderson. Certain facts jumped out at me and they were all related to the .357 Magnum, the gun that Detective Anderson had said was the murder weapon, and Madeline's apparent access to it.

First of all, Maxwell had said that the primary reason why Madeline had been arrested in the murders was because her prints had been on the murder weapon. The only way he could have known that those were her prints was because they had been in the system. One of the first things crime-scene techs did upon finding a weapon was to run any prints they found on it through the different databases—to see if they got a match, and because they had, that could only mean she was already in the system.

Leo had run a background check on her in all fifty states and had come up empty. Leo, for all his quirks and eccentricities, was very thorough in his work, so I knew that he hadn't screwed up or had missed anything. I didn't believe for a second that her prints were in the system due to an error or coincidence. Certain professions required individuals to submit a copy of their fingerprints as part of their background checks, for example: police officers, federal agents, teachers and social workers. But Madeline hadn't mentioned having worked at any of those jobs.

As much as I disliked the fact that we had become so dependent on computers for everything, for, in spite of my profession, I was kind of an old-fashioned girl, I did rely on the information they supplied, and for the most part, believed them to be accurate.

The fact that Madeline Marie Meadows was in the system sent up a red flag. The first, hell, the only time I had met with her, I had sensed that she wasn't being completely truthful, something which, unfortunately for her, had turned out to be correct.

It was reassuring to know, despite my extended leave of absence from work, my bullshit antenna was in fine working condition.

Second, Madeline had said that she hadn't had any contact with Ricardo since the day she'd bolted out of the apartment in Calle Ocho. How could she have had access to the gun? Had she stolen it from Ricardo before leaving? And, why was she at his house in South Miami? She hated him—and feared him—or, so she had said.

I highly doubted that Ricardo, at some point, had made her a gift of the gun. I didn't know the man, but from what Madeline had said, he didn't seem the type who would give her a gun. First of all, it was too macho of a gun, and next, he might be scared she would use it on him. It was safe to assume that he hadn't given her the gun, especially after how she'd walked out.

Detective Anderson had said the gun was registered to Ricardo. Had he shot Dr. Steinberg and Woodley Robinson, and then, somehow, he, himself, in turn, been killed by Madeline? Anderson also said that all three men had been killed with Ricardo's .357 Magnum. I simply could not picture a scenario under which our client could have committed those murders. However, it was still early in the investigation; the truth was that I'd only really, actively, started working the case the day before.

The three reasons why people are charged with a crime are because they have the means, motive and opportunity to commit it. My job as a private investigator was to look into all three, and if it turned out that it had been Madeline who had pulled the trigger on the three men, well, so be it. At least she'd had the sense to retain Tommy. Whatever else Madeline Marie Meadows may have been, she was definitely smart and savvy.

I was about to get up and head out to the reception area to discuss our next steps on the Meadows case with Leo when my cell phone rang. I looked at the number on the caller I.D. and pressed the talk button. It was Sweet Suzanne.

"Hi, Suzanne, what's up?" I greeted my friend.

"Hey, Lupe, I heard that our Virgin Mary was picked up this morning. Three murders: that's excessive, even by Miami standards," Suzanne pointed out.

"Word gets out fast, Suzanne," I replied.

"Yeah, well, you know, our world is small." Suzanne took a deep breath then spoke again. "Three men in one week. The girls and I were wondering; does that make the Virgin Mary a serial killer?"

Oh, Jesus, Mary and Joseph.

Fifteen

Napoleon and Josephine, Madeline's Chihuahuas, were very much on my mind later that afternoon as I drove across the MacArthur Causeway heading toward Miami Beach to meet with the Loredo twins. Instead of thinking about the tiny terrors, I should have been mentally preparing for my upcoming interview, but I couldn't help but wonder what had become of them after Madeline had been arrested. Detective Anderson had said that she had been picked up at her Portofino Towers apartment very early this morning, so it was likely that the dogs had not been outside yet to do their morning business. Not only would they probably have been scared, I had a feeling they were not left alone too often, but their tiny bladders would have been exploding.

It was already past one o'clock, which meant that the little guys would have been alone for approximately seven hours. I wasn't particularly worried that they would mess up Madeline's apartment after all, how much pee and poop could two tiny four-pound dogs excrete, but I was concerned that they might not have enough food and water to last until someone came by to care for them. Detective Anderson had not indicated whether Madeline had been alone at the time of her arrest, but if she had,

I figured that she hadn't been able to make any kind of provision for them.

From the way they had interacted with each other in my office yesterday, it was very obvious that Madeline and her dogs had a close relationship. Clearly, they must have been very upset when they had been separated from her, especially in such an abrupt and frightening manner.

During the course of my career as a private investigator, I had had the unfortunate experience of personally witnessing the arrests of several individuals at their homes, and, although no one was harmed during the process, I was positive that Miss Manners would not have approved of the way in which the arrests were carried out. Getting picked up by the cops could never, ever, be categorized as a kind and genteel operation.

In situations where arrested individuals had been unable to make arrangements for their pets, the police would call Animal Services to take charge of the animals, which would then be transported to the pound until other, more permanent, arrangements could be made. I'd been to the Dade County Animal Services facility, a huge, sprawling place just west of the airport, so I was familiar with the conditions under which the animals were housed. The shelter workers did the best they could with the limited resources they had to operate the facility, but, still, it was not the kind of place a pet owner would want his or her animal to end up. I feared that Napoleon and Josephine would not do well there. Animals that were considered troublemakers were not kept for very long, as, although tiny, the Chihuahuas had been trained to attack. And, of course, God only knew what would happen if anyone wore latex near them.

In any case, I would find out what happened to them soon enough as that was going to be one of the first things I planned to ask the Loredo twins. However, given their participation in the ugly sport of dog fighting, it was probably safe to assume that the brothers weren't exactly animal lovers, so they might not have been overly concerned for the tiny terrors' well-being. Even so, I hoped for Madeline's sake, and for the sake of all they'd invested in the animals, that they had made sure that Napoleon and Josephine had been taken care of. While I doubted the twins donated to the Humane Society or supported PETA (I did recall that Hitler was both an animal lover and a vegetarian), I really could not be sure of their attitude towards animals. However, as they had been responsible for training the Chihuahuas to be Madeline's first line of defense, the twins had a vested (financial) interest in their well-being.

After speaking with Suzanne, the first thing I had done was to look into the Meadows file for a contact number for either Ernest or Stanley Loredo. I was familiar with the ways of twins, and how the hierarchy worked; my sister, Fatima, had twin daughters so I had telephoned Ernest, the oldest, first to request a meeting with them. Judging from the matter-of-fact way in which he spoke to me, I had the sense that he had been waiting for my call, so probably Madeline had confided that she had retained an attorney to represent her.

Ernest told me that he and his brother had already heard that Madeline had been picked up by the police and was being booked into the Dade County Jail. He said she was waiting for the paperwork to be completed before being escorted to a holding cell to await arraignment.

Ernest had been quite chatty, volunteering a lot of information about Madeline's status. When I commented about that, he told me that the reason he was so well informed about what went on at the Women's Detention Center was because he had a good contact there, one who passed information on to him. He explained that one of the corrections officers who worked at Intake, the department where arrested individuals were processed, had, in a previous life, been employed by L'Escort Deluxe Services, LTD, as a call girl at the same time the twins had been associated with it.

According to Ernest, the corrections officer had conveniently forgotten to include that particular work experience when she had filled out the employment application for her current position. The twins, needless to say, took full advantage of that, holding the knowledge over her head, threatening to 'out' her if she didn't help them out.

Although I certainly didn't approve of blackmail, for that was surely what the twins were doing, I was quite thankful for the information the corrections officer had provided. I had dealt with plenty of unsavory individuals, and although I'd only spoken to Ernest on the phone, he'd already succeeded in creeping me out. Just his smarmy voice alone sent shivers up and down my spine. It wasn't very professional of me to feel that way, but I had to admit that meeting him and his brother, Stanley, in person, was not something I was looking forward to.

Nothing about them was even remotely appealing: not their petty criminal backgrounds, not their sleazy profession, not the way they had used Madeline, nothing. Madeline Meadows was a grown woman who was quite capable of making her own decisions, but I still felt that they, in a way, had coerced her into becoming a 'working girl.'

Yet, however despicable that had been, I supposed I could get past it. What had really gotten to me was their connection with dog fighting. But, like it or not, the twins were pivotal to the investigation, so I resigned myself to having to spend time with them.

Ernest had suggested that we meet at his and his brother's apartment in Little Havana, the same one where Madeline had spent her first night after running away from Ricardo, an offer I politely turned down. For a variety of reasons, I did not want to go there: my safety, for one. A neutral place would be better, so, instead, I countered with a suggestion that we meet on South Beach at Puerto Sagua, a Cuban restaurant located on the corner of Collins Avenue and Seventh Street.

In addition to being a public place, I had proposed that particular restaurant because it had the advantage of being just a few blocks from Portofino Towers, the building where Madeline lived. I was hoping that the twins, provided they had a set of keys, would agree to take me to her apartment so I could check it out for myself. At the very least, we could do something for Napoleon and Josephine.

As I drove past the restaurant on Collins Avenue searching for a parking space, I saw two very large men who, by their tough and swarthy appearance could only have been the Loredo twins, standing outside. One look at the twins: shaven heads, tattoos, dressed in tight, shiny black clothes, and enveloped by clouds of smoke from the cigarettes they each held and I felt a shudder go through my body. Even though I had the Beretta in my purse, I questioned the wisdom of even meeting them in a public place. If I'd gone to their apartment as Ernest had suggested, there was no way on God's earth I would have taken a step inside the place.

I wasn't able to find a spot to park anywhere near the restaurant—not exactly surprising, as parking was a bitch on South Beach so I was forced to drive to a garage two blocks away. As a result, I was ten minutes late to the meeting.

As I walked towards them, I thanked God that they had not seen the Mercedes, for if they had, they surely would have jacked it. The twins looked so disreputable that if I were to shake their hands, I would want to count my fingers to make sure that all ten were still there. Ernesto and Stanley were identical twins, complete mirror images of each other, so they doubly frightened me.

Part of my training to become a private investigator required that I take courses in areas necessary to do the job: surveillance, document searches, Internet research, witness interviewing techniques, etc. I quickly learned that one of the most important requirements to be successful was to have the ability of identifying an individual by his or her appearance. To do so, I had been taught to seek out distinguishing characteristics in a person's appearance that would help recognize them at a later date. The drills to acquire that skill had been quite tiresome: I would be shown photographs of the faces of dozens of individuals. Then, some time after that, anywhere from thirty minutes or even days later, I would be shown the same photos again, but this time, with a feature or features changed: a mole added or removed from the face; longer/shorter/darker/lighter hair, etc., subtle changes to see if I could identify what was different. As far as clothing was concerned, though, I quickly learned that, although most individuals who changed whatever it was they were wearing to alter their appearance, invariably, they would keep the same pair of shoes on their feet.

I thought I had done quite well in that part of my training, that was, until I came face to face with the Loredo twins. For the life of me, I could not tell them apart. Madeline had said they were twins, but she sure had not said that they were carbon copies of each other.

"Ernesto?" I extended my hand to the man who reached me first. "Hi, I'm Lupe Solano." I resisted the urge to look down at my hand after his grasp.

"No, I'm Stanley." The man laughed; not a pleasant sound. "He's Ernesto." He pointed a finger at his brother.

"Sorry—hi, Stanley." I smiled apologetically, and then turned to the other brother. "Hi, Ernesto." I held out my hand to him as well. "Well, shall we go in?" Not waiting for an answer, I opened the door to the restaurant. I followed them inside, and as I did, I thanked God that it was highly improbable that anyone I knew would be in Puerto Sagua at that time.

Puerto Sagua was a 'down home' Cuban restaurant, no 'tall' food served there, so unpretentious of both style and substance that, by comparison, Versailles seemed like a Michelin Guide rated, five-star establishment. The place was decorated (if you could call it that) in someone's vision of Havana in the '50s, or, maybe, even earlier. Dozens of dark brown tables made from thick Formica, mostly set for four persons, were placed around the room in a haphazard fashion, with wooden chairs around them that had been carved in a maritime style. The coffee-colored wood-paneled walls were covered with peeling posters and photographs of individuals, scenes, and monuments, the only items that, as far as I could tell, had Cuban motifs.

The owners had not bothered to upgrade anything in the place for decades and it was easy to see why. The restaurant was almost always full, so there really was no need to invest money into updating it. 'If it ain't broke, don't fix it' was clearly a mantra they firmly believed in.

Like Versailles, the food was plentiful and delicious, with the most expensive entrée costing less than ten dollars. Plenty of tourists came to Puerto Sagua, not only for the cheap food, but also for the 'authentic' Cuban atmosphere, something that every tourist visiting Miami seemed to be seeking.

I led Ernesto and Stanley to a table in the back of the main dining room, not only because it was quiet there, and we could talk undisturbed but also for privacy. I didn't particularly want to be seen sitting with the Loredo twins in the unlikely event that anyone I knew were to come into the restaurant. I usually made it a point not to be judgmental about someone's appearance, but in the twins' case, they were so freaky and thuggish looking that I made an exception.

I waited until we had made ourselves comfortable at our table before speaking. "So, have you heard anything else about Madeline?"

Yes," Stanley replied. At least I thought it was Stanley. "Anita, our contact at the jail, said her lawyer was trying to get her bonded out, but the bitch prosecutor was requesting the judge not to set bail. She wants Madeline to stay locked up. The lawyers are fighting it out. It's ugly."

So, Aurora Santangelo was being a hard ass. No surprise there. Tommy could out lawyer her with his eyes closed and both hands tied behind his back; if anyone could get Madeline bonded out, it would be him. Still, Aurora, as a prosecutor, had enormous power, something she wielded with great glee.

"Well, hopefully, Mr. MacDonald can prevail, and Madeline will be granted bail," I commented. "You know, even if Mr. MacDonald can get Madeline a bond, that doesn't mean she's out of trouble. Being charged with three counts of murder one. That's very serious," I pointed out probably unnecessarily.

Ernesto and Stanley nodded their heads in unison, the up-and-down motion they made was making me feel slightly dizzy. Thankfully, the Cuban sandwiches we had ordered arrived, sparing me from having to look at the twins any longer.

At the same private investigator courses I'd taken prior to being awarded my license, I had also been taught that, when interviewing an individual, to look at him or her directly in the face, focusing on the eyes as, in many cases, it was possible to learn more from a person's facial expressions and body language than by what he or she was saying. That afternoon, if I'd been getting graded on my interviewing skills, I would have definitely flunked. For the first time in my eight years of working as a private investigator, I'd been so put off by the individuals I was interviewing that I could barely look at them, something I would have to get over, and pronto.

The twins attacked their sandwiches with ferocity, as if they had not eaten in weeks. My stomach repulsed as I listened to the noises they made as they ate.

No sooner had the twins cleaned their plates, the dishes were spotless, than they began hungrily eyeing my own sandwich, making it clear what was expected of me. I quickly pushed my plate across the table to them. Less than a second later, Ernesto and Stanley each grabbed a half of the sandwich and began stuffing their mouths.

Watching the twins inhale the sandwich reminded me of a field trip I had taken with my fourth-grade class to the Miami Seaquarium, where we had stopped at the shark tank and watched them get fed. The sharks had ripped into the fish provided to them in the same way that Ernesto and Stanley Loredo were eating their Cuban sandwiches at Puerto Sagua. Neither occasion had been a pretty sight.

"Hey, that was really good." Stanley beamed at me.

Ernesto agreed. "Yup, that was good."

The twins looked at me with expectant expressions. I figured that now that they weren't distracted by food I could to get on with the interview.

"So, before lunch came, we were talking about Madeline and how we hoped she'd get out of jail soon." I forced myself to look at the brothers. "As I explained to you on the phone, Ernesto, I've been hired by Mr. MacDonald, Madeline's attorney, to investigate the case on her behalf." I smiled brightly at them, first Ernesto, then Stanley or, was it the other way around? Well, no matter. I continued, "In order to be able to do that, I'm going to have to ask you some questions, OK?"

"OK," they answered simultaneously.

Good." I took out a pen and a notebook from my purse, and opened it to an empty page. I labeled the top 'Interview at Puerto Sagua with Ernesto and Stanley Loredo.' Then, after looking at my watch, just underneath that heading, I jotted down the date and time. The twins watched what I did as if they were medical students watching a world-renowned surgeon performing an operation. "Let's start at the beginning."

And they did. At the very beginning.

Sixteen

"For God's sake, be quiet! You keep up that yapping, you're going to make me crash. Then, you'll go to the pound for sure!" I warned the Chihuahuas in the back seat of the car.

Napoleon and Josephine paid absolutely no attention to me; if anything, they began to yap louder, at a higher pitch. My head began to throb, and I debated rummaging around in my purse for the bottle of Advil Gels that I carried for emergencies. I decided against that; the Beretta was also in the bag, and I might be tempted to shoot the mutts. Instead, I conjured up an image of a silver pitcher filled to the brim with Osvaldo's mojitos. If my day continued the way it had started, I would certainly need every drop.

I headed back to the office in Coconut Grove, driving as if I were in a fog. Regardless of the racket the tiny terrors were making, I still could not believe that they were in their carrying case in the back seat of the Mercedes. What the hell had I done? How had I managed to get myself into this situation? Had I actually volunteered to take the Chihuahuas with me until more permanent arrangements could be made? God! I was such a sucker!

I tried to ignore the noise coming from the back seat, but, in spite of my best efforts, failing miserably. Threatening Napoleon and Josephine with a visit to the pound was clearly not working, so I decided to change tactics. I fiddled with the icons on the screen until I found the one for the Satellite radio, and located the station that only played '60s music, my most recent preference, and turned it up full volume to drown out their shrieks. Almost immediately, to my shock and delight, of course, the horrible sounds stopped.

I was so taken aback by this pleasant turn of events that I actually held my breath, just in case they started up again. I wondered why they had settled down. Maybe turning on the radio was how Madeline quieted them down while in the car. Whatever the reason, I wasn't about to turn down the volume to test my theory. I was perfectly happy to take full advantage of the lull. I had a lot of thinking to do and needed to have a clear head.

First, I replayed my meeting with the twins at Puerto Sagua. I had taken copious notes to keep a record of our conversation. Ernesto and Stanley had repeatedly stated that there was no way that Madeline could have killed the three men, but, unfortunately, they could not provide a proper alibi for her during any of the times that the murders had taken place. Still, they were positive that she had been in her apartment at the Portofino Towers.

I pointed out that Dr. Steinberg and Mr. Robinson had been murdered on the same day, just a few hours apart, on the night that Madeline had seen Mr. Robinson for a date. The twins acknowledged that Madeline had been on a date with Woodley Robinson earlier that night. After all, they had escorted her to and from his condo, but swore up and down that once they had taken her home, she had not left her building. They said that Madeline didn't like to go out alone at night, that she was frightened of the crime on South Beach, and, as the Chihuahuas were paper-trained, she didn't have to walk them outside, ever, unless she wanted to.

In spite of the twins' protestations that Madeline had absolutely nothing to do with any of the murders, I smelled a rat, so I kept pressing them for answers. It wouldn't be long before Detective Anderson discovered Madeline's relationship with the twins, so I figured that they might as well be prepared for what lay ahead. It was time for a reality check; the twins had to know how much trouble Madeline, a.k.a. 'Mary,' was in.

"You know, Ernesto and Stanley, one of the first things the prosecution will do is subpoena the management of the Portofino Towers for the surveillance tapes from that night if they haven't done so already. They'll find out soon enough if Madeline entered or left the building at any point during that night, when she was supposed to be in her apartment." Difficult as it had been, I had looked both of them straight in the eyes to make sure they understood what I was saying. Just in case, I repeated what I had just told them. Then, for good measure, I added, "If those tapes show that Madeline entered or left the building at times that were different than what she had told Detective Anderson in her initial statement, she's screwed."

The twins avoided my eyes, and instead, focused on the items on the table. For some reason, they both seemed to find the salt and pepper shakers especially fascinating. They began to shift their bodies around on the chairs, their considerable bulk straining against them so much that the wood began to squeak. I needed answers, and fast, so I wasn't about to make it easier on them. I just stayed quiet and stared at them: first one then the other.

Five full minutes, the longest five minutes ever, must have passed before Ernesto spoke. "The night the doctor and Mr. Robinson were killed—we dropped Madeline off at the driveway of her building—right at the entrance," Ernesto said in such a low voice that I had double hearing him. "We saw her go in, the doors are made of glass, you know, so we could see her walk toward the hallway where the elevators are."

"But, you left afterwards, right?" I prompted him. "After you saw her go in?"

They both nodded. Then, it was Stanley's turn to speak.

"Madeline, once we dropped her off at her building, she never comes back out. She likes to go upstairs right away, and watch TV before she goes to bed, Letterman, she loves the Letterman show. Says he comes from Indiana, the Midwest, she likes that."

I thought about what they had said. "Has Madeline ever discussed how she felt about Dr. Steinberg with you?"

"Yeah, she really liked him. She liked him a lot. Said he was a very good doctor, very nice, always made her feel comfortable. All the girls liked him; they all went to him, you know," Ernesto informed me. "Sometimes, he didn't even charge them."

"Yes, I'd heard that," I said, recalling what Suzanne had told me about the good doctor during our lunch at Versailles.

"You know, Madeline would go and have a checkup with him once a week to prove she was a virgin. Her business depended on it. It was part of the deal." Ernesto spoke in a matter-of-fact voice, as if it was perfectly natural for a call girl to have such a checkup. "Once a week, every Thursday morning, eleven o'clock sharp, for over a year. Same appointment. It never changed."

"After each checkup Dr. Steinberg would give Madeline a letter saying she was a virgin," Stanley piped up. "It was always the same letter, always said the same thing: that Dr. Steinberg had examined Madeline, and that she was a virgin. I read it once at the beginning to make sure it said what it had to say, for the business. You know, the clients, they pay a lot of money for Madeline, so it was important to have that proof."

I began to re-examine my initial impression of Stanley as being kind of thick. Behind his thuggish exterior, I suspected there was the soul of a businessman. "What did Madeline do with those letters?" By my calculations, there should be over fifty of them. "Did she ever have to show them to anyone?" The twins looked at me with blank expressions. "I mean, did her clients ever ask to see them?"

The twins continued to look confused. It was clear that although the letters certifying Madeline's virginity were a critical part of their business, they had not devoted much time or energy thinking about what to do with the letters once they had them.

"I think she would put the most recent one in her purse and take it on her dates, but I don't know if she ever had to show it to any of her Johns," Ernesto looked perplexed as he spoke. "But I don't know what she did with the other ones; the letters from the other checkups."

I had asked enough questions about Dr. Steinberg, so I turned to another subject. "OK, let's talk about Woodley Robinson. What can you tell me about him?"

The twins looked at each other. It may have been my imagination, but it seemed that they had both stiffened up just a bit. Why had the subject of Woodley Robinson put them on their guard?

"What do you want to know about Mr. Robinson?" Stanley asked.

"Well, anything you can tell me about him will be helpful," I replied. "Let's start at how he first met Madeline, how long he'd been her client, how often she saw him. Things like that." My interview with the twins had not been exactly clipping along at a fast pace.

"He was a referred from a client of ours from when we

worked at the L'Escort Deluxe Services. Andres said that his friend Woodley had been screwed over by a lot of women, so he wanted one that was young and fresh. And, most important, innocent. A virgin in every sense. Our client had kept in touch with us after we got raided and our boss, Carlos, went to jail, so he knew that we had taken on a new girl, a virgin," Ernesto explained. "Andres, the client, knew all about Madeline, he lives at the Portofino Towers, too, so he'd seen Madeline, and knew what she looked like."

Andres? Portofino Towers? It couldn't be! That would have been too much of a coincidence—and, as we all knew, I did not believe in those. I tried to hide my reaction to what Ernesto had just said, but I felt my heart begin to beat faster. With his drop-dead good looks, infectious charm and enormous bank account, I couldn't imagine that my friend and client, Andres San Pedro, would need the services of an escort company.

I mean, I suspected he was kind of quirky, but to use call girls? That sure didn't fit my impression of him. I had learned early in my career not to be surprised by anything, still . . . Nah, it had to be coincidence. Or, was it? I guessed I really didn't need to know just then. In any case, if it was Andres, I sure didn't want to hear it from the Loredo twins. I would find another way to see if he was the same person. After all, if it was, indeed, Andres San Pedro who had made the contact between Madeline and Woodley Robinson, then he would become part of the investigation.

"OK, so, Mr. Robinson met Madeline, and then started seeing her on a regular basis?" Ernesto and Stanley nodded. "How often did they meet?"

Ernesto thought for a moment; I could almost see the wheels turning in his head as he considered his reply. It was not an attractive image. "He was a regular, about every ten days, maybe twice a month. But, they did meet every month—never skipped a month."

I did the math. "So, Madeline would take in between fifteen and twenty thousand dollars a month just from Mr. Robinson?"

"Not quite. We had to take our cut, of course," Stanley pointed out. "You know, as her managers. We had expenses, costs. All those."

"Yes, of course," I agreed. Madeline was clearly a cash cow for this duo, but as the last thing I wanted to do was alienate the twins just as we were getting along so well, I refrained from making any comment. "And how did Madeline feel about Mr. Robinson? What did they do when they met?"

"Well, we would drive her to his apartment at the Icon." The Icon was a luxury building on South Beach where even the smallest apartment cost more than a million dollars. Mr. Robinson didn't live there; he lived with his wife someplace else. He told Madeline that he had bought the apartment as an investment," Stanley explained. "We would park on Alton Road, by the Burger King, across the street and wait. When she finished, she would text one of us, and we would pick her up and drive her back to the Portofino Towers."

I nodded. "And how long would she typically stay at his apartment?"

Stanley shrugged. "It depended. Each visit was between an hour and two." He looked at his brother as if to consult with him. Ernest shrugged, and held up two fingers. "More like two hours each time. Never longer than that."

"Cash." Ernest suddenly volunteered. "All transactions were in cash. No money trail."

I looked at the twins with newfound admiration as I quickly did the math. God! Four hours a month minimum; five thousand dollars an hour; twenty thousand dollars a month; maybe even more! Even after the twins took out their 'managers' fees', that was still quite a nice chunk of change! Surely, the current Mrs. Robinson, the Venezuelan beauty queen, wasn't aware of that expenditure. A man with assets and income like Woodley Robinson, well, he could pay that out of petty cash.

I wondered how many more men like Woodley Robinson were Madeline's regular clients who could afford to meet her two to three times a month. Suzanne had already given me several names, so I knew Woodley Robinson wasn't the only one shelling out that kind of cash for her charms.

In any case, even if the twins were mercenaries and took out a huge cut of fifty percent or more, whatever was left, Madeline sure wasn't making out badly for someone with an art history degree from Iowa; someone who just a little while ago had been living in a walk-up in Little Havana! No wonder she could afford to live at the Portofino Towers.

In the back of my mind was the nagging, pesky thought of how Madeline dealt with the IRS, but that wasn't my concern. The woman was facing three counts of first degree murder—the IRS was the least of her worries. Well, maybe not—Al Capone came to mind.

I continued the interview. "And did she ever tell you what she did with Mr. Robinson during their dates?"

Both men shook their heads then Ernesto spoke. "She never said, and we never asked. That was their private business, but she didn't have sex with him, that was for sure. No rough stuff, either, with him or with none of the other clients. Remember, every week Dr. Steinberg would write the letter confirming she was a virgin."

"Right. Good point." I smiled. It was clear that the twins figured that for the kind of money her clients paid for the pleasure of Madeline's company, short of taking her virginity, of course, her dates could do whatever they wanted with her. As long as they didn't damage the merchandise, that is, or ruin the profitable scheme they had going. In contrast to the twins alleged lack of curiosity as to what Madeline did with the clients for five thousand dollars an hour, I was dying to know. But, I'd have to wait to learn what it was.

"Can you tell me a bit about how you met Madeline, starting with the gym in Little Havana?" I wanted to confirm what Madeline had told me.

Ernest, the chattier of the two brothers, was the one who told me the story of meeting Madeline, not stopping until she had moved into the Portofino Towers. Except for a couple of discrepancies, mostly to do with the time frame, the story was the same as the one that Madeline had told Tommy and me.

"And, as far as you know, from that day she moved out of the apartment in Little Havana, Madeline hasn't seen Ricardo, the ex-boyfriend, right?" That was critical.

Ernesto and Stanley looked at each other then shook their heads silently. I had the sense they were not telling me everything, but I let it go. I didn't want the meeting to get confrontational.

I looked at my watch and saw that the twins and I had been sitting at the same table at Puerto Sagua for over three hours. I had enough information to work with, so I decided to wrap up the formal aspect of the interview; I could call them later for follow-up.

"One more thing." I smiled sweetly. "I assume you have the keys to Madeline's apartment. Could you take me there so I could have a quick look around?" The twins looked uncertain, so I added, "It's all part of the investigation so I can do my job better. I'm sure Madeline wouldn't mind. When I met with her, she told me to do whatever I had to do to help her," I assured them. "And, I want to look in on Napoleon and Josephine, too. Make sure they're okay."

"Oh, right! The dogs! Napoleon and Josephine" Stanley looked positively stricken at the mention of them.

"We have a set of keys," Ernesto replied. He looked over at Stanley, and then added, "I suppose it'll be OK if we take you there, if it'll help, like you say."

I paid the bill for lunch, neither of the twins made any effort to reach for the check, and we headed toward our respective cars for the short drive to the Portofino Towers. I followed the twins' black Lincoln Navigator to the gatehouse at the bottom of the long, curved driveway that led from the street to the building. At the gatehouse Ernesto, who had been driving, told the security guard there that I was with them. The guard wrote down my license number, then lifted the barrier and let me pass without asking any questions.

Once at the top of the driveway, we pulled in front of the building entrance, and handed our keys to the valet. Inside, we signed the visitors' book, showed our driver's licenses to the front desk concierge and waited while he wrote down our information. I took the opportunity to look around the lobby, and in less than thirty seconds had spotted three security cameras, which meant that there were others in less visible places.

Because of my visits to the Portofino Towers to see my friend and sometimes client, Andres San Pedro, I was somewhat familiar with the security procedures of the building. However, those occasions had mostly been for professional reasons, so I had never paid much attention to them. Obviously, this visit would be different. This time, I was looking to see how easy it would be to enter and exit the building without being observed. From my cursory inspection, it didn't seem simple at all.

The concierge cleared us to proceed, and the twins and I walked toward the bank of elevators that would take us up to Madeline's seventeenth-floor apartment. According to Stanley and Ernest, Madeline had signed a year lease on the place, renewable for another year at the same price.

The twins and I remained silent on the ride up to Madeline's apartment, and did as most people tended to do when riding in an elevator: we stared at the floor. Once on the seventeenth floor, Ernesto walked quickly to Madeline's apartment and inserted the key in the lock. The minute the door opened, he headed for the square box on the right wall, punched in a few numbers from memory, and turned off the alarm.

"Please come in," Ernesto addressed me in a gracious manner, as if he had been inviting me into his own home.

"Thank you." I walked through the small foyer and into the living room. Madeline's apartment was furnished in a simple, utilitarian way, with the kind of furniture one could buy at a Rooms-To-Go. The view, though, more than made up for the decorating shortcomings.

I had thought Tommy's apartment on Brickell Avenue had a magnificent view of Miami, but that had been before I'd stepped into Madeline's. Her unit, although on a lower floor, had a wonderful view of South Beach to the left; to the right was the Atlantic Ocean.

I unlocked the doors to the balcony and stepped outside. It was very windy, so standing outside was a bit uncomfortable, but I didn't mind as the breeze brought up the wonderful smells of the ocean. I counted three enormous cruise ships heading out to sea, as well as several tankers traveling low on the water from the weight of many containers piled high on their decks, steel structures that shimmered in the sunlight. I could see the entire length of the beach, and the people enjoying all kinds of activities: from swimming to running to playing volleyball to surfing to just sunbathing. I would have loved to have been one of them.

"Beautiful view," I commented to Stanley, who had walked up next to me. "I would never get tired of looking out here." I pointed to the sea.

"I know, it's great," Stanley agreed.

Just then, a shout came from inside the apartment Stanley and I looked at each other in alarm and rushed back inside.

"Little fuckers! Fucking mutts!" Ernesto came running into the living room holding his right hand, his face contorted in pain. "Fucking dogs bit me!"

"What happened?" I asked, although it was obvious.

"Fucking dogs were locked in the master bathroom." Ernesto looked at his hand, which was bleeding rather copiously. "I opened the door, and they attacked me! Me! I trained the fucking dogs!"

Stanley and I just stood there watching Ernesto clean off his hand with a pink towel. No sooner had he wiped the blood off than his hand started to bleed again.

"I'm dropping the mutts off at the pound right now—I don't give a fuck how much Madeline loves them. After I tell the people that they're dangerous they'll be put down, killed right away! They'll be dead by this afternoon and it serves them right." Ernesto wrapped the towel around his hand. "Come on, Stanley. Help me get the dogs in their cases. We're taking them right now! They'll be dead in an hour!"

"But, but, Ernesto. We can't do that! They're not our dogs—we trained them to attack. It's not the dogs' fault," Stanley protested. "Madeline loves those dogs!"

"I don't care," Ernesto raged. "You put them in their cases right now or I'm throwing them off the balcony!"

Stanley remained glued to where he was standing, so Ernesto started to walk back toward the bedroom. From the look on his face, I had no doubt he would do exactly as he said. One way or the other, the dogs would die.

I watched the exchange between the twins, and saw the cold-blooded way Ernesto intended to dispose of the dogs, animals he had known and trained. I had no doubt that the older twin was perfectly capable of committing murder. And not just on dogs. The realization chilled me to the bone.

"Wait!" I ran to the bedroom. "I have another idea." Madeline had enough problems without adding two dead Chihuahuas to the list. Needless to say, with Ernesto's mood the way it was, I wasn't able to check out the apartment; I would have to return at a later date. The Chihuahuas would be a good excuse, but just then, my main goal was to get myself and the dogs out of the place alive. Praying they wouldn't bite me too, I threw a big bath towel over the clogs and stuffed them into the Louis Vuitton carrier that was in the kitchen, the same carrier that Madeline had brought them into the office.

That was how I ended up driving back to the office with Satellite Radio blaring oldies, and Napoleon and Josephine sleeping in the case on the backseat. I had just finished going over the seventh scenario in my head as to how I was going to tell Leonardo about our two unexpected guests when my cell phone rang.

"Lupe?" It was Tommy. "Listen, I don't have much time. I just got Madeline bonded out. She's on house arrest, wearing a bracelet, but at least she's out."

"You beat Aurora?" The day was certainly getting brighter. "You got the judge to agree to bail?"

"Yeah, but it wasn't easy. Or cheap. Madeline's lining up the cash now. Listen, I've gotta go." Tommy spoke so quickly, and with the radio still blaring, that I could barely understand him. "I just wanted to tell you that. Call you later."

And, with that, he hung up. Thank God I wasn't going to have to Chihuahua-sit. I turned to Napoleon and Josephine and said, "Well, kids, party time! Your mother's coming home!"

Seventeen

"Oh, Osvaldo, thank you. This looks wonderful, so fresh, and smells even better," Osvaldo had just placed a large dish of the most delicious looking fillet of grouper on top of a mound of yellow rice in front of me. Next to the dinner plate, he proceeded to place a crescent-shaped dish filled with slices of avocado, the only green that I would eat. "Please tell Aida that she's spoiling me."

Osvaldo beamed at the compliments, a broad smile spreading across his wrinkled face. "This fish was caught just this morning. Aida was fortunate to be at Publix just as a shipment was being delivered. This fish was still swimming in the ocean just a few hours ago, Lupita."

The old man busied himself arranging items on the table: the salt and pepper shakers; the dish with three cut-up limes (Cubans smothered their food with lime; no scurvy for us); the water and wine glasses; the cutlery. As he did so, he gave me a comprehensive report as to what each and every member of the family was doing: Fatima and the twins had gone to a movie, Lourdes was at a retreat, and Papi was playing dominos at Tío Henry's house.

Even though Aida had been informed that no one would be

home for dinner, she had still prepared a meal just in case any of our plans changed, something that often happened in the Solano household. That night, I'd been the fortunate recipient of her backup plan.

I knew Osvaldo wouldn't leave until I had tasted the food, so he could report my reaction back to Aida. I was more than happy to oblige, so I filled my fork with a huge mouthful of fish and rice, which I swallowed almost without chewing.

"Oh, this tastes even better than it looks." I winked at Osvaldo. "If that's possible."

The old man swelled with pride. "I will tell Aida." Osvaldo hurried out of the room, leaving me alone for the first time since I'd returned home.

The day had seemed endless. Between dealing with the Loredo twins and the Chihuahuas, I was wiped out. All I really wanted to do was to have a quick dinner, take a bath, then go to bed. I had to be up early the next morning as I had a lot to do. I was so exhausted that instead of drinking the pitcher of mojitos that I had been dreaming about all day, I had chosen to have a single glass of white wine. The last thing I needed was to get sloshed by myself and start the day off tomorrow with a hangover.

I was disappointed to eat alone; even though it had only been three days, an eternity in a Cuban family. I hadn't spent any time with my family since taking on the Meadows case, but the truth was that I was relieved. I could just chill out and not have to be sociable. It had been a long, action-packed day, and I was bone-tired, so perhaps it really was for the best to be on my own.

I would have rather died then and there than admit it, but I still wasn't a hundred percent after having been shot. I tired easily, but then again, that could also be a factor of age. My thirtieth birthday was less than two years away, something I did not particularly want to dwell on. Thinking about my birthday reminded me that my father's was just a couple of days away, and I still had not bought him a present. Tomorrow would be the day, I promised myself.

I was sitting at the card table eating dinner in front of the television while watching the network news, something I hadn't done for a long time. Brian Williams was doing his wrap-up before signing off, but instead of watching him, I was thinking about what had happened that day. Although nothing had gone as planned, the day had turned out pretty well, especially the part where I didn't have to baby-sit the Chihuahuas.

As soon as I had hung up with Tommy, I had made a U-turn on the causeway and had headed back to Portofino Towers to drop off Napoleon and Josephine so they would be there when their mistress came home. The guard at the security gate had been reluctant to let me pass. Madeline hadn't left word to allow me entrance into her apartment, so they really did not have any authorization to let me in. However, after I showed him the dogs, and explained how I just wanted to take them back so they'd be home when Madeline returned, he let me pass on the condition that one of the guards on duty would escort me at all times while I was on the property.

I would have loved to snoop around Madeline's apartment, but I knew that with the security guard watching me like a hawk, that was not going to be possible. Unless I wanted to keep Napoleon and Josephine for the foreseeable future, I was certainly in no position to argue with the conditions of gaining entrance to her apartment. That was the way it had to be.

I had just pressed the up button to summon the elevator when the doors opened, and, much to my surprise, and dread, my old friend and client, Andres San Pedro, stepped out. Of course, I had known he lived in the building, so it shouldn't have been so unexpected that I would bump into him, but still, seeing him like that took me by surprise. I hated being surprised when I was working.

"Lupe!" Andres stepped out of the elevator and greeted me with a kiss on the cheek. "What a pleasant surprise to see you." He took a step back and saw the dog carrier. "What brings you to the Portofino Towers? Are you coming to surprise me?" He asked, with a twinkle in his eye.

I considered how best to answer. The twins had said that not only had Andres been a client of theirs at the escort service, but that he also knew Madeline. Andres may have been an old friend and client of mine as well, but I did not like coincidences, so I decided the best course of action was to be as discrete as possible, without being rude, of course.

"Oh, I've been taking care of a friend's dogs while she was away, but now that she's coming back, I'm returning them," I replied, rather vaguely.

I didn't know exactly how close Andres was to Madeline, or if he had met Napoleon and Josephine before, so I tried to block the carrying cases from his line of vision so he wouldn't be able to see them and identify them. The Chihuahuas were pretty distinctive; even if he'd seen them only once, chances were that he would recognize them; then he'd know that Madeline was my client, something that had to be avoided if at all possible. "I'm so sorry, but I'm running late! I'll call you later, OK?"

I didn't give him a chance to respond, and, instead, blew him a kiss and waved goodbye. The big, burly security guard quickly stepped into the elevator behind me. I didn't want Andres to see where I was going, so I waited for the doors to begin closing before pressing the button for Madeline's floor. The guard took a couple of steps and positioned himself two inches away from me. Either the man had no sense of personal space, or he thought I was going to steal the elevator. Whatever the reason, he was standing so close to me that we were almost touching.

I had seen the frown come over Andres' handsome features as he had taken in the scene: me, the dogs, the security guard, and suspected he hadn't really bought my explanation for being at the Portofino Towers, but there really wasn't much I could do at that point. I would need to do serious damage control later.

The guard and I rode up in silence. After what seemed like an eternity, the elevator stopped and the doors opened. The guard selected a key from an impressive ring dangling from his waist and opened Madeline's door. I obeyed his instructions and waited outside the apartment door until he'd punched in the security code for the alarm and motioned for me to enter.

Of course, I would have loved to have been able to check out the contents of Madeline's apartment more thoroughly, but the guard was sticking to me like glue, so unless I wanted to arouse his suspicions, I had to restrain myself from doing so. By then, I'd been to Madeline's apartment twice that day, earlier with the twins, and now with the guard, but in neither case had I been able to look around.

Since I didn't know how long it would take before Madeline came home, being processed out of the Dade County Jail was never quick, I'd taken Napoleon and Josephine for a little walk before entering the building so they'd have an opportunity to do their business.

Hopefully, that would help them hold out for a few hours longer. I checked their food and water, laid out a couple of sheets of newspaper on the floor in case of a bathroom emergency, and then followed the guard out of the apartment.

Once outside, I thanked the security guard for his services, and before driving away, I slipped him a fifty just in case I needed his help again, a tip he happily accepted. When I'd looked at the clock on the dashboard of the Mercedes, I was shocked to see that it wasn't even four o'clock. I was quite tired, but it was too early to call it a day, and too late to begin a new aspect of the investigation so I decided to go to the office for a few hours and prepare for the next day. I had plenty to do still.

The drive back to the office had been mercifully quiet without Napoleon and Josephine barking their heads off in the back seat. My thoughts turned to Andres. It bothered me that an attractive, wealthy, educated man like Andres would need the services of call girls. According to the twins, he had been a client at L'Escort Deluxe Services, which may have had a grand name, but from what I'd been able to piece together, was anything but.

Before the twins had talked to me about Andres, I would have sworn I'd known quite a bit about him. After all, he'd been my client first, then my friend, and, as such, I'd had an opportunity to learn much about his life, both personal and professional. Andres had always seemed to be a bit crazy—most men who married five times were not exactly conventional—but, still, the fact that he patronized an escort service had come as a shock. Could the reason be that he needed more excitement in his life? Or, was there a deeper problem: a secret life he led that had caused him to be serially married?

I always suspected that he liked to live dangerously, but even so, patronizing call girls seemed out of character for him. Although I was certainly in no position to judge anyone, but I knew that from then on, I would look at Andres in a different manner.

The drive back from South Beach to the office had taken half an hour, allowing me time to think about what I planned to do next. What I really wanted to do was sit Madeline down for a lengthy heart-to-heart, but obviously that would have to wait until she was out of jail. I had a million questions, which would help to steer me in the right direction, if she answered them truthfully. A big 'if' given her track record. I needed to make it perfectly clear that by lying, or failing to disclose certain facts, the two being pretty much the same thing, she was only hurting herself.

While it was important to interview Madeline, there was still plenty for me to do. I hadn't even begun to really check out the victims. Other than having Madeline in common, and being shot with the same weapon, I would need to see what was going on in their lives that may have caused them to be killed.

I had barely scratched the surface on their backgrounds, the reports that Leo pulled from the searches were only a jumping-off point, but I could already tell that all three men seemed to have led complicated lives: Dr. Steinberg, the saintly doctor who treated women who'd been discarded by society, also owned pricey real estate; Woodley Robinson had shady business dealings, expensive ex-wives and fucked-up children; and, last but not least but the closest to her, Ricardo Melendez, the former boyfriend, a practicing Catholic who didn't have sex with Madeline, but carried a gun and beat her up.

And then, of course, there was the matter of the twins. I would have bet my retainer that I would soon uncover other possible suspects. At that point, not even Napoleon and Josephine had been cleared. As far as I was concerned, the case had more suspicious characters than could be found in the waiting room of any of Miami's Department of Motor Vehicles!

On the plus side, Madeline would be wearing a monitoring bracelet, and be confined to her home at the Portofino Towers most of the time. Thankfully, Nestor would not have to conduct twenty-four hour surveillance on her, which would free him up to help me with other aspects of the case.

Tommy hadn't told me the terms and conditions of our

client's release, but I thought it safe to assume that Madeline's activities would be very limited and specific: her lawyer's office, her doctor's office, etc. Most individuals were also allowed to travel to and from their places of employment, but somehow, I did not think that would apply to Madeline. I couldn't exactly see Aurora Santangelo letting her go on dates.

I had just pulled into the driveway of the office building when my cell phone rang. It was Tommy. "Hi, are you still at the courthouse?"

"I'm walking out," Tommy replied. "Heading back to the office to prepare for the trial tomorrow."

Court must have been tough; I could hear the exhaustion in Tommy's voice. "How's it going?'

"God, Lupe! I should have listened to my mother and become a doctor." Tommy laughed.

"That bad, huh?" I teased.

"Worse. I'm lucky if my guy only gets three life sentences instead of the needle—bad luck for him that Florida is a death penalty state," Tommy said. "Listen, on the Meadows case. Before leaving, I called over to the jail and checked in on her. She's almost out. There's some kind of a fuck-up with the bracelet, and she can't get it for a couple of days, so the way it stands, she'll be confined to her apartment. If there's an emergency, she can leave, but basically, only if it's life or death. I gave my word that she would not go anywhere without notifying the court before-hand." I could hear Tommy's breathing quicken as he walked.

"The cops are taking her home, so she'd better stay there, and not fuck around, because if she does, it's back to jail she goes, and next time, I won't be able to get her bonded out." Tommy's voice grew louder. "My ass is on the line along with hers. It was a real fight to get the judge to go along with this; good thing I'm owed some favors."

I thought about what Tommy had said. So much for Madeline not needing twenty-four hour surveillance. Nestor would have to begin right away. "I'll put Nestor on her, just in case she gets cabin fever and decides to go out."

"Good plan," Tommy agreed. It was clear neither of us trusted our client. "Listen, Lupe, I'd suggest dinner, but I have a shit load of preparing to do for tomorrow and I'll probably just eat something at my desk."

"No problem, I have a lot to do myself," I replied. I wasn't too upset that Tommy couldn't have dinner; I had been feeling tired and looking forward to going home and decompressing. "Listen, I just got to my office. I'll call you later to see how you're doing, and, if you have time, I'll give you a report on the case so far."

"Good. Catch you later," Tommy said, and hung up.

It was late in the afternoon, but still hot as hell outside. I sprinted into the building. Leo kept the temperature in our office a bone-chilling 65 degrees year round. Our electric bills were so astronomically high that sometimes it seemed as if I only worked to pay the Florida Power and Light bill.

"Hola, Leo," I called out to my cousin as I entered the reception area. "I'm back!"

Leo came out of the kitchen, stood in the doorway, and looked around the room with apprehension. He was dressed like a normal person, wearing an open-neck man's cotton shirt and blue jeans. It had been a while since I'd seen him dressed in regular clothes, so I was almost as taken aback as he was. "Where are they?"

"Who?" Was Leo frightened of the twins?

"You know who I mean, Lupe." Leo took a few more steps. "The man-eaters!"

"Oh, God!" A light turned on in my head. "You mean

Napoleon and Josephine?" I put my purse down on his desk. "They're back at the Portofino Towers, in Madeline's apartment."

"Thank God!" Leo almost collapsed from relief. "When I heard the client had been arrested, the first thing that came to my mind were those shitty little dogs that wanted to slice off my family jewels and who was going to take care of them while she was gone." Leo sat at his desk and looked at me. "Knowing what a pushover you are, Lupe, I figured you'd get into your martyr role and take them in."

"Well, don't worry. Tommy got Madeline bonded out, so she's going to be home soon," I informed him. There was no way I was going to volunteer to Leo that his worst fears about the dogs had almost come true.

The relief in Leo's face was palpable. "Good." Then, less than a second later, he added, "Tommy got her bonded out? With three first degree murder charges against her? God, he's good, Lupe!"

"Yeah, he's good," I agreed. "She'll have to wear a bracelet, but there's some kind of screw-up at the jail, so it'll be a few days before she's hooked up. She's been court-ordered not to step outside her apartment. As of right now, she's under house arrest. Tommy vouched for her."

Leo didn't skip a beat. "OK, so you want me to call Nestor to make sure she doesn't go anywhere? Or, if she does go some-where, to see where?" Leo, also, did not trust our client. It was interesting that the three of us here assumed that Madeline would disobey the judge's orders.

"Yes, please call him. I'll talk to him now and give him the details." I picked up my purse and headed for my office. Before opening the door, I turned to Leo and asked, "Any calls while I was gone?"

Leo looked down at the pad on his desk. "Yeah, you had a lot of calls: two from Detective Anderson; one from Andres San Pedro; each of the twins called; both of your sisters called to remind you it's Papi's birthday on Friday; and Aida to see if you're having dinner at home. That's it, I think." Leo looked the list over one last time. "*Sí*, that's it." Then, just as I was about to go into my office, he called out, "Hey, Lupe, all of these people tried calling you on your Blackberry first, but the calls had gone straight to voicemail. A couple told me they texted you, too. I really wish you would answer your phone or your texts."

"Oops, sorry," I apologized, closing the door behind me.

The fact that I did not like to answer my cell phone, or, reply to texts, was a running source of friction between Leo and me. I truly disliked cell phones and Blackberries, and although I recognized their importance, I found them to be very intrusive. I would take calls from a select number of individuals: usually from my family (I had listened to the voice mails from my sisters, so I knew what their calls were about); from Leo; from Tommy; from Suzanne; from Nestor and the other contractors who worked for me; any man whom I was involved with at the moment and, in certain cases, from clients. I would eventually return voicemails and text messages, but at a time when it was convenient, and I could concentrate on whatever it was they were calling about. If it was an emergency, I figured that whoever needed to reach me would call the office, and Leo would get in touch with me.

Too tired to even glance out at the parrots in the trees, I headed for my desk. As I sat down, I could feel the exhaustion flow over me. I closed my eyes and hoped the feeling would pass, but, the truth was, all I wanted to do was sleep. There was no way I could be productive in this state of mind, so I gave in to the exhaustion, and lay down on the sofa in the office to take a fifteen-minute nap.

I had just woken up when the phone rang. "Hey, Lupe, I have Nestor on line one," Leo announced. "I clued him in a bit as to what you need him for."

I sat back down in my chair. "Nestor! Hola, you still available to work the Meadows case for me?"

"Sure, I knew you'd call, just like you said you would," Nestor answered. "I came by this morning. Leo said you were in a meeting."

God! Was that really only that morning? I felt my face redden as my mind flashed back to the image of Detective Anderson and I having sex on the couch. "Sorry I missed you," I replied, then went on to explain what I needed him for. Nestor was such a pro he really didn't need much guidance; he knew what needed to be done.

"OK. I'm leaving now," Nestor informed me. "Since the client is still being processed out, it'll be a while before she gets back home, which gives me plenty of time to check out the layout around the building while it's still daylight, and to pick the best place for me to station myself."

"Thanks. Keep me posted." I hung up. With Nestor on the job, there was no way Madeline was going to stray without his being on her tail.

Nestor did not come cheap, but he was the best in the business, and worth every dollar. It might have seemed strange that Madeline was footing the bill for Nestor to keep tabs on her, but I knew from past experience that taking such a step prevented some clients from making huge mistakes. Several of the job requirements for Nestor were that he be part investigator, part babysitter, but, as long as he got paid, he didn't particularly care what he had to do.

After hanging up with Nestor, I decided to ask Leo to make me a cup of his industrial-strength Cuban coffee to wake me up. Once the caffeine kicked in, I planned to write up reports of what I had done that day then work on a plan for the next day. Then, if I wasn't too tired, I would return phone calls. No one had said that their call had been an emergency, so I figured whatever it was could wait until morning. I would head home when I reached the point that I was no longer working effectively.

Despite the coffee, it was only just after six when I had gotten in the car and headed home to Aida and her fresh fish.

Eighteen

That night, I slept a full twelve hours—from nine o'clock at night until nine in the morning. I woke up energized and ready to tackle the day. I bounced out of bed, showered and dressed in my usual uniform of blue jeans and a T-shirt, consumed an enormous breakfast, then got into my car and headed for the office. Before I left, though, yet again Aida and Osvaldo reminded me of Papi's birthday. My window for buying him a present was quickly narrowing.

I turned into the driveway in front of the office building and was pleased to see Leo's black Jeep parked in its usual spot. Although Leo was normally quite responsible about being punctual for work, every so often, whenever there was a full moon, for instance, he would take a bit of latitude and show up on Cuban time. When this happened, he would be anywhere from one to five hours late, depending on his mood. Mindful of Osvaldo's frequent complaints about the sap of the frangipani tree damaging the paint job on the Mercedes, I parked as far away from the tree as possible.

"Leo, *buenos días!*" I called out, opening the outer door to the building.

"Hi, Lupe." Leo greeted me in the disconnected tone of voice he used when he was engrossed in something. Thank

God he was dressed in 'normal' clothes, well, normal for Leo, anyway: bike shorts, white wife-beater tank, a black bandanna tied around his neck, a cowboy hat, diamond cross and red Converse high-top sneakers. Sort of like a redneck, hip-hop Lance Armstrong. "*Buenos días* to you, too."

Leo was sitting at his desk in the reception area, with *El Nuevo Herald* opened in front of him. Lately, Leo had been trying to connect with his 'Cuban roots' and, to him, the first step, apart from eating as much Cuban food as he could stomach, was to improve his Spanish. *El Nuevo Herald* was the Miami Herald's Spanish language paper, and, in some readers' opinions, better than the English edition. In any case, it was a good place for Leo to brush up on his Spanish.

I knew it would be futile to try to hold any kind of meaningful conversation with Leo while he was in the grip of reading 'El Nuevo,' as the paper was known. I'd been very supportive of Leo's efforts to connect with his 'Cubaninity'. I mean, I didn't object to the office radio station being tuned to Cuban stations all day long, nor did I say anything about the television being permanently set to Mega TV. I also didn't make comments about the ever-present smell of pungent Cuban food that emanated from the kitchen all day, but still, the bills had to be paid. I quickly brought Leo back to life in the USA.

"Any calls?" I asked as I walked past him.

With obvious difficulty, Leo tore his eyes away from reading his horoscope; my cousin's day totally depended on what Walter Mercado, the psychic, predicted for him. He looked up at me with a quizzical expression. "Lupe, you seem different," he commented, checking me out. "Have you done anything to yourself?"

"No." I laughed. "I just slept twelve hours last night. Makes a difference. Sleeping."

"Sleeping." Leo kept looking at me skeptically. "Well, you

should do that more often. You look great. About your calls, yes, you've had several from the usual cast of characters: Detective Anderson, Tommy, and one of the twins." Leo read from the pad on his desk. "Ernesto."

"Thanks. I'll call them back now," I said, heading for my office.

Before approaching my desk, I walked to the window and noticed that the parrots were busy building yet another structure. As it was in the beginning stages, I couldn't tell exactly what it was going to be; but at the fast and furious pace they were going, it was obvious it wouldn't be much longer before I could identify it. Maybe they, too, had slept twelve hours.

Even though he would probably be in court, I decided to call Tommy first; I could just leave him a voice mail. I reached for the phone and punched in the first number on the speed dial, his private office number, one that only a very select group of people was privileged to have. Tommy answered on the first ring.

"Hey, Lupe, what's going on? I tried to reach you yesterday afternoon, but you didn't call me back." Tommy sounded annoyed.

"Why aren't you in court?" I countered. I was in a good mood and didn't want to spoil it.

"The judge was sick, some kind of twenty-four hour virus. His secretary called early this morning to let me know. Sad to hear, the judge is a nice guy. But at the same time I'm thankful; I'm getting creamed in there. I need some time to rethink my strategy," Tommy replied. "Anyway, let's get back to why you didn't call me back."

"I'm sorry, Tommy, I really am." I tried to sound as contrite as possible. I hated when Tommy was in a bad mood. "I was really tired last night. I meant to call you, but I fell asleep right after dinner. I slept twelve hours straight; that's how beat I was."

"Twelve hours," Tommy repeated, his voice laced with concern. "Lupe, are you sure you're up to working full-time again? You know, it hasn't been that long since you were shot. Are you sure you're up to carrying a full load?"

"I'm fine now after a full night's sleep. I feel great," I hurried to reassure him. The last thing I wanted was for Tommy to think I couldn't give the Meadows case my full attention as he would pull me off the case in a heartbeat if he thought I was doing his client a disservice. I may have been a first-rate investigator but there were others in Miami who could do a thorough job as well.

"Well, you let me know if you're not up to the job," Tommy ordered.

"I promise," I replied, then quickly changed the subject. "So, what did you want to speak to me about?"

"I wanted to discuss the Meadows case with you, get a status report, talk strategy about what we should do next," Tommy explained.

"I also want to tell you about the bond hearing, but you first. What have you found out?"

I told Tommy about my meeting with the Loredo twins, my two visits to Madeline's apartment, and the strange situation with Andres San Pedro. I explained what I had learned about the three victims so far, telling him that I only had a superficial knowledge about their lives and backgrounds, but I planned to do more in-depth investigations on them next. I relayed that Nestor was at his post, on surveillance.

I emphasized how badly I needed to meet with Madeline to get some answers to some very pointed questions. Why were her prints in the system? She hadn't mentioned having any priors to either of us, so why would Detective Anderson imply that her prints were on file. I also planned to request copies of Madeline's 'A' form, her arrest record. Leo was already searching for any incident reports in which the Miami police had to be called to the scene of any place where Madeline had lived.

Tommy listened without interruption, then said, "You've done a lot in a short period of time, it's all good work, but you still have a shit load to do."

"I know," I agreed. "So, tell me about the bail hearing."

"As you know, the right to bail is granted in pretty much all cases, unless the defendant is a danger to society or a flight risk, none of which apply to Madeline. But she is charged with a capital or life felony. In spite of that, the defendant can still request a bail hearing, an Arthur hearing, which is what I did. If you recall, during these hearings the burden falls on the prosecution, your good friend, Aurora Santangelo, to prove that Madeline was the shooter. Well, the nice judge agreed with my argument that Madeline's fingerprints on the gun was not enough proof that she killed all three victims, so he granted her bail," Tommy explained. "He set it high, though, very high: three million. One million for each victim."

"And, she could pay it?" I tried to keep the disbelief out of my voice. Normally, defendants were required to put up ten percent of the bond, in this case, $300,000. Not exactly chump change. But then, making the kind of money she did on her 'dates', I guessed Madeline had that amount put away somewhere. After all, at her rates, that only represented sixty hours work, probably tax free. Not a bad gig, right?

"Apparently so," Tommy replied. "She asked me to contact a bail bondsman for her. I called Buster, and next thing I knew, she was all set. How she paid him is none of my business. I never get involved in how the clients pay Buster, you know that, Lupe.

The less I know about my clients' financial matters, the better. She made bail, and that's all I know."

In spite of the high bond, and other conditions of her release, it seemed unreal that Tommy had managed to get Madeline bail with three charges of first-degree murder hanging over her; the fact that he had been able do so only served to remind me, yet again, to never underestimate Tommy's legal skills. And, doing all this while he was in the middle of trial. I would have given anything to have been sitting in the courtroom watching Tommy's arguments, and listening to Aurora state her case. Tommy could out lawyer Aurora with his eyes closed, his arms tied behind his back, all the while listening to his iPod.

"Aurora must have been furious that you were able to get Madeline bonded out," I guessed.

"She was not happy, that's for sure." Tommy chuckled. "If looks could kill, I'd be six feet under by now." Then, he turned serious. "She's gunning for you, Lupe, that was obvious, so watch your back. Aurora may be incompetent, but she has a lot of power—those are the most dangerous kind of people. By the way, your Detective Anderson was in the courtroom."

Tommy dropped that last bit of information in a matter-of-fact way, so I let the part about Detective Anderson slide. Instead, I said, "Thanks for the warning about Aurora. Her hate for me is like fine wine; it intensifies with age. So, what are the conditions of Madeline's bail? No, let me guess: *mucho dinero*, an ankle bracelet, curfew, house arrest, all that good stuff?"

"Right," Tommy said. "Pretty much all of the above. She can be on the property of her condo, but she can't venture outside its perimeter. Other than that, she's confined to her apartment unless she has special permission to go to somewhere, my office, doctor's visits, you know the drill, Lupe."

"Well, Nestor's watching to make sure she complies with the terms and conditions of her bail," I reported. "So far, she's been a good girl. Nestor sent me a text last night saying she'd arrived at the Portofino Towers at midnight, and had not ventured outside since."

"Good. I hope she continues doing that. She must be exhausted—she's been through a lot," Tommy said.

"I was planning on calling her at around noon, to ask if I could come over. Of course, I'm dying to speak with her, but for right now, I think it's best if she rests for a little bit," I told him. "Besides, that'll give me a few hours to follow up on some leads."

"That sounds like a plan. Now, listen, I'll check in on you after you've had a chance to meet with Ms. Meadows. I'm going to be in the office pretty much all day. I have to figure out what to do on the case I'm in trial on." Tommy was about to hang up when he suddenly asked, "Do you want to have dinner tonight? If you're not too tired, that is."

"I'd love to," I answered quickly. Dinner with Tommy was always late, so if I was tired, I could always take a quick nap before meeting him. "I'll speak with you later. Bye."

I hung up the phone, and then called Nestor. "Hi, morning. I got your text from last night. Anything going on?"

"Hi, Lupe. No, the client hasn't come outside. I'm in a pretty good spot here. There's a construction site diagonal to the entrance of the building, so I can park where the constructions workers do and no one will notice me." Nestor chuckled. "It's not usually this easy to find a good place, you know, Lupe. I got lucky that it's in the shade!"

"I'm happy for you, Nestor, that's great. Please keep me posted on any developments," I said. "Listen, I'm going to be there around noon to interview her, so you can take a couple of hours off."

"OK, thanks," Nestor replied. "When I see you arrive, I'll go home, take a shower and pack my meals for the next couple of days."

"I'll call when I'm a few minutes away," I told him before hanging up.

Next, I dialed Detective Anderson's cell phone. "Hi, Maxwell, Lupe here. How are you?"

"Ah, Lupe, good to hear your voice. How are you feeling?" I could hear the concern in his voice. We may work on opposite sides of a case, but that didn't prevent us from caring about each other.

"I'm fine, thank you." I supposed I should have been flattered to have two men so worried about my well-being, but truthfully I was still kind of in a fragile state, emotionally and physically, and I didn't want their concern to stem from the fact that I wasn't up to the job on the investigation. Or could it have been that I seemed tired after having sex with the both of them? I shook my head to get rid of that god-awful thought. "So, what's up?"

"On the Meadows case. Your lawyer, Tommy MacDonald, ran circles around Aurora yesterday at the Arthur hearing. If it wasn't for the fact that she's guilty as sin and should be locked up, I probably would have enjoyed it more," Detective Anderson commented. "But, that's not what I called you about." He paused.

"Your client, and I'm speaking to you now as a friend, I hope you respect that I'm going out on a limb by calling you, but you and I, Lupe, we go way back, we have a history. I'm not telling you how to do your job, but Tommy MacDonald stated in court yesterday that his client had a clean record. Now, I don't think he'd deceive the court on purpose, it would not be worth it for just one client, especially on something that's easy for us to verify, so my advice to you is to dig deep, real deep, into your client's background."

I thought about what Detective Anderson said. I knew it had taken a lot for him to call and tell me that, so obviously whatever was in Madeline's past must have been very serious. "Thank you, Maxwell, I will. As a matter of fact, that's what I was going to do in the next couple of days," I said. "I really appreciate the heads-up. I'll certainly look into it. I know it wasn't easy for you to do."

"No problem," Detective Anderson said. "So, maybe I'll see you around?"

"Sure, I'd like that." And, the truth was, I would. "Maybe later on in the week, I'm kind of jammed up right now, or next week for sure."

"Next week, then," Detective Anderson repeated.

Detective Anderson had just confirmed my suspicions about Madeline. Obviously, she hadn't been completely honest with either Tommy or me, and, although it wasn't exactly unexpected, it was annoying as hell. I hoped I would be able to clear up whatever it was she was keeping from us when I met with her in a few hours. The one advantage to having clients under house arrest is that they were always home.

I planned to call Ernesto next, but before doing that, I walked out to the reception area to speak with Leo and give him some assignments. He had finished reading 'El Nuevo,' and had begun flipping through *Vanidades*, one of several Spanish-language magazines on his desk.

"Hey, Leo, could I interrupt you for a minute?" I asked.

Leo looked up from the magazine. "Sure, Lupe." He pointed to the stack of magazines and waved goodbye to them. "I was kind of getting Spanished out anyway. What do you need?"

"Remember that weird feeling I told you I had about Ms. Meadows?" Leo nodded. "I need you to try some more databases, widen the net, see what else you can find out about her,"

I told him. "Also, what else can you find out about the victims? I know you conducted some backgrounds, but I want you to go deeper: check out family members, professional associations, nationwide real estate records, driver's license records, anything you can come up with. I'm especially interested in Ricardo Melendez, the boyfriend."

"Sure," Leo replied. "Should have something back for you by this afternoon." He turned to his computer. "Remember how I asked you if I could sign up for those additional phone, asset and business databases so I could access them directly, without having to go through that company we used? I explained how they would give me quicker access to way more information; that it would save us time and money in the long run."

"I think so." I vaguely remembered Leo asking me that, but I nodded, nevertheless.

"Remember how you told me they would be too expensive, which I knew, but I also knew that they would more than pay for themselves; that it would be a good investment. Well, you weren't feeling well, so I decided not to bother you with such details, and I signed up for them anyway," Leo confessed. "That's why I can have all the information you need in just a few hours, instead of days." Leo beamed with pride.

"Good job, Leo." I congratulated my cousin. Leo may have been a world-class flake in many respects, but he took his job very seriously. I especially had great respect for his abilities in front of a computer. "It's good you didn't pay attention to me. You know much more about that kind of stuff than I do." I began walking back to my office. "Oh, I almost forgot. Can you pull the "A" form for me? It should be ready by now. I want to read about Madeline's arrest."

Leo had already begun to type madly on the computer

keyboard, but stopped long enough to wave to me, his usual indication that he had heard me. The staccato sound his fingers made when they hit the keyboard drove me nuts, so I closed the door to my office after going back inside.

I stopped in front of the window for a few minutes to check out the parrots, but try as I might, I still couldn't make out the structure that they were building. I had hardly sat down at my desk when the telephone rang. "Our client, Ms. Meadows, on line one for you Lupe," Leo announced.

"Madeline! How are you doing?" I greeted her.

"Much better now that I'm back home, thank you, Lupe. Mr. MacDonald was wonderful in court. You should have seen him. I couldn't believe the judge granted me bail." Madeline was speaking so fast that I had a bit of trouble understanding her.

"Yes, he's a great lawyer," I agreed. "I'd like to come and see you; it's important we talk. Would it be convenient if I came by in a little while around noon?" I didn't want to give her a chance to blow me off.

"This morning?" Madeline asked. "I'm quite tired."

"It's important. I have some things I'd like you clear up for me. It'll help the case." I wasn't about to let her off the hook. "It shouldn't take too long, then you can rest."

"Well, OK then," she reluctantly agreed. "See you at noon."

Why would Madeline Meadows not want to see me? If I'd been charged with three murders, forced to shell out three hundred thousand dollars in bail money, and on house arrest about to be fitted with an ankle monitor, I'd be desperate to get out of my situation as soon as possible. Yup, Ms. Meadows puzzled me.

It was almost eleven o'clock. I'd spent most of the morning on the phone, but I had accomplished much. It would take almost thirty minutes to get to the Portofino Towers, so I decided to start getting ready. I didn't want to cut it too close, especially as Madeline seemed none too eager to meet with me. Ernesto's callback would have to wait until I returned from South Beach. However, before leaving, there was one last thing I wanted to do.

I picked up the phone once more and punched in Sweet Suzanne's number. "Suzanne? Hi, it's Lupe. Listen, I need a favor. A big one."

"Sure, honey, what is it?" Suzanne didn't hesitate.

"I need information on Madeline Meadows, anything you can give me. Anything at all, no matter how small, how insignificant you think it might be," I replied.

"Sure, no problem," Suzanne answered. "But, that'll cost you another lunch at Versailles."

"Sure." Oh, God! My hips! My ass! I could feel them spreading as I hung up the phone. A few more lunches with Suzanne there and I was going to have to stop asking her for information. If payment was always going to be a meal at Versailles, people would start knowing what nationality I was from looking at my ass.

Nineteen

"Hey, Nestor, I'm on Washington and Fifth Street." As agreed, I called Nestor to give him a heads up on my arrival. "I should be at the Portofino Towers in about five minutes."

"Thanks, Lupe," Nestor replied, laughing. "I could use a shower right about now; it's hot as hell and I think I'm a bit ripe. So, you still think I have about two hours until I have to be back on post?"

"That's about right," I said. "I'll text you as soon as I leave there to let you know if anything changes. If I'm done with the interview before that, don't worry, I'll find a place to station myself and conduct the surveillance until you return."

"I'll try to make my pit stop at home as quick as possible, Lupe," Nestor assured me. "Oh, I see you now, you're just passing me."

As I drove past, I looked around to see if I could spot Nestor's silver Toyota. Nestor was a master at surveillances, so it was not surprising that he had been so well hidden that not even I, who was on the lookout for his car, could find it. "Hey, Nestor, you're right, you found yourself a great spot; can't see you anywhere," I said admiringly.

"That's why you pay me the big bucks, Lupe, that's exactly why." Nestor chuckled. "Listen, I'm leaving now, keep me posted. Good luck with the interview."

I drove up to the security gate of the Portofino Towers saw that the same guard who had escorted me up to Madeline's apartment yesterday was on duty. I smiled at him. "Hi, nice to see you again."

"Nice to see you too, Ms. Solano." He touched his cap in greeting and lifted the barrier so I could pass. "Ms. Meadows is expecting you—she phoned a few minutes ago."

As I drove up the driveway toward the entrance, it occurred to me that this was the third time in the past twenty-four hours that I had been at the Portofino Towers. I parked the car, gave my keys to the valet and entered the lobby. I headed toward the front desk to sign in and recalled that I still hadn't returned Andres San Pedro's call from yesterday afternoon. I prayed that I wouldn't bump into during my visit.

My sense of déjà vu was becoming stronger by the minute as I also recognized the security guard in the reception area. Just like his colleague at the front gate, he smiled and greeted me in a friendly way. After hurriedly signing the visitors' book, I sprinted toward the bank of elevators around the corner.

Thank God, I made it up to Madeline's floor without incident. One of the guards must have called ahead and announced that I had arrived, because Madeline was waiting for me in the hallway, in front of her open apartment door. For the visit, Madeline was wearing pink cotton pajamas, a worn bathrobe, and bedroom slippers. Her long blond hair was pulled back in a dirty looking ponytail, and there were dark circles under her eyes. One look at her tired, disheveled appearance, and I knew she'd had a rough time of it in jail.

Even though she looked very tired, her exhaustion couldn't completely account for the fact that she seemed quite different, less feminine—a bit tougher. I tried to hide my shock at her appearance, but it wasn't easy. It was difficult to believe this was the same gorgeous woman who had been in my office two days before.

"Hi, Madeline, thank you for seeing me on such short notice," I greeted her and gave her a brief hug. "I'll try not to stay too long so you can rest."

"It's OK, Lupe." Madeline smiled wanly. "I know you need to speak with me." She stood aside so I could enter the apartment.

I took a few steps inside and looked around a bit tentatively. "Where are Napoleon and Josephine?"

"I locked them inside my bedroom so they wouldn't disturb us." Madeline, who had been walking a few steps behind me, suddenly stopped in her tracks. She put her hand up to her mouth and said, "Oh, Lupe, I'm sorry, I should have started off by thanking you for taking care of them while I was away. The twins told me all you'd done for them, how you made a special trip to pick them up, and how you returned them so they'd be here when I came back. That was really, really, thoughtful of you."

"That's all right. I felt bad for them, being here alone and all," I replied. "I'm happy it wasn't necessary for them to be separated from you for a long period of time."

"Yes, that's for sure, thanks to Mr. MacDonald. If it had been up to the prosecutor, I would have been in jail for years." Madeline shuddered, her whole body shaking at that thought. She composed herself, then turned to me, waved her hand around the room, and asked, "Where would you like to sit?"

"The sofa here is fine, thank you," I took a seat on the far left cushion, near a side table.

"Before we start, would you like anything to drink? Coffee? Water? Soda?" Madeline asked. Despite the shit loads of trouble she was in, my hostess had clearly not forgotten her manners.

"No, thank you. I'm fine." I shook my head.

"Well, let me know if you change your mind." Madeline sat in a straight-back chair next to the sofa. After making herself comfortable, she turned to face me. "Now, Lupe, what can I help you with? You said you had some questions."

I took out a notebook from my purse, flipped it open, and looked over the questions I had prepared. Although I'd known beforehand what to ask Madeline, I was aware that that it was very easy to get sidetracked, especially when the interview went off into different areas that were not specific to what I wanted to know.

"Let's start off with your background." I perused my notes. "I see you're the youngest of five children." Even though the background report had stated that there were six children.

"That's right." Madeline nodded. I noticed she did not correct me. Interesting. "I have three older sisters and a brother."

"And, you have an uncle who is a priest and an aunt who is a nun," I continued reading from my notes.

"Yes." Madeline nodded again. "But, why is that important?"

"Oh, I'm sorry, Madeline, I should have explained that it's standard procedure to look into a client's background in a case such as yours." I looked up at her. "I can assure you that the prosecution is doing the same thing, checking out your past for any possible reason why you might be in the situation that you're in right now."

Madeline looked a bit alarmed, but she only shrugged her shoulders. "If you say so."

Sitting near Madeline, I could really see how wan, listless and tired she appeared. Her skin, which had looked so luminescent and smooth yesterday, seemed slightly rough with a bit of gray pallor. The dark shadows being cast on her face made her look unhealthy, as if she'd been underground for a period of time.

Maybe I'd been wrong when I thought she hadn't had any makeup on in my office, that she'd been a natural beauty. Still, spending time incarcerated was no picnic for anyone, especially under the miserable, overcrowded conditions of the Miami-Dade County jail where she had been held, so that could account for the drastic change in her appearance. Those, and the shock of her early morning arrest could account for it. I doubted she would last the two hours that I had informed Nestor that I would be with her.

"Given how Catholic your family was, your upbringing must have been very strict, is that correct?" I ventured.

"Yes, it was." Madeline replied then hurried to add, "I mean, we weren't abused or anything like that, please don't think that, but, yes, we were brought up to be devout Catholics, to obey the laws of the Church."

"And that's why you never had sex, right? With Ricardo, or anyone else?" I was treading on delicate ground, so I had to be careful. "Because the teachings of the Church forbid having sexual relations outside marriage?"

"Yes, that's right." For the first time since we'd begun the interview, Madeline looked away from me. Had I hit a nerve? "It's because of the Church."

Given Madeline's fragile state, I decided against pursuing that line of questioning any further, but told myself that it was definitely something to keep in mind. Madeline may have come from Dubuque, Iowa, but still, Catholic kids there couldn't have been that different from Catholic ones in Miami. Although I hadn't exactly taken a poll, I could safely bet there weren't too many twenty-two-year old virgins here and saving themselves for marriage. At least none that looked like Madeline Meadows.

And, as far as Ricardo Melendez, Madeline's former boyfriend was concerned, there was no way any red-blooded Cuban guy would ever admit to being a virgin—at least, not if he didn't want his heterosexuality to be called into question.

At that point I was under severe time restraints; Madeline could terminate the interview at anytime, so I decided to change course. "Madeline, I know that you said you've never been in any trouble with the law, before this, but are you sure that nothing would show up if the police were to do a background check?" I thought back to what Detective Anderson had said; that I should 'dig deep, really deep' into Madeline's background. "You're completely clean? Even when you were a juvenile?"

"Of course I'm clean!" Madeline stood up, indignant, and began to pace back and forth. Her voice dropped a few decibels as she asked angrily, "You think I wouldn't know if I'd been in trouble before? I told you and Mr. MacDonald I'd never been arrested. That's the truth! You think I'd lie?"

"No, no, of course not," I hurried to reassure her. Her over-the-top reaction immediately let me know I'd been on the right track. She had been arrested, and had a record, somewhere. My bullshit antenna was over the stratosphere: first, she was defensive over her virginity, and now, questions about her background. What the fuck was going on? "I just had to ask. The police are very thorough, you know. I just want to make sure there aren't any surprises."

"Well, there won't be," Madeline fumed. "They won't find anything on Madeline Marie Meadows!" She paced around a bit more then abruptly sat. "So, what else did you want to ask me?" The polite hostess of a few minutes before was gone, and in its place was a wary, distrustful woman.

Madeline's sudden, loud outburst must have agitated Napoleon and Josephine. They began scratching at the bedroom door. Madeline looked over at where the noise was coming from, but, thankfully, made no move to let the dogs out. At that point, I was definitely on borrowed time, so I decided to ask the questions that I really needed answered.

"Your relationship with the doctor and Mr. Robinson. Could we speak a bit about that?" I spoke in my most solicitous tone of voice.

"What do you want to know?" Madeline almost spat out the question at me. Then, without waiting for my answer, she replied, "Dr. Steinberg was the nicest, sweetest man in the world, warm and funny. It couldn't have been easy for him to be so nice. I mean, in his practice, he saw all kinds of terrible things: women who've been beaten; drug addicts; hookers. Really, really bad things had been done to his patients. But he was still so optimistic and sweet" Madeline got a faraway look in her eyes as she spoke. Clearly, Dr. Steinberg was a special person to her. "You know, he had two offices, the one in Coral Gables, on Ponce de Leon Avenue, for his private patients, where I used to go, and one in downtown Miami where he ran a free clinic for women who couldn't afford a regular doctor, or pay for their prescriptions."

"Yes, I've heard he was a very good man," I agreed. "How often did you see him?"

"Once a week: every Thursday at eleven o'clock. He would give me a checkup so he could verify that I was a virgin." Madeline actually blushed. "You know, Lupe, at first it wasn't easy, climbing up on the table and spreading my legs on those stirrups. But, Dr. Steinberg, he made me feel so comfortable that I honestly didn't mind; I even looked forward to going to him. He was so nice that after a while he became more like a friend."

"Did he ever mention that anything was troubling him? Did he have any problems that you knew about?" I wondered.

Madeline shook her head slowly. "No, he was always the same: nice and friendly. After my exam, he would give me a letter for the twins, a letter that would verify that I was a virgin. It was the same routine every time. He would check me out, then he would give me the letter." Madeline's eyes began to water. "I don't know who would hurt Dr. Steinberg. He was such a good man!"

As I listened to Madeline speak about Dr. Steinberg, I wondered how much the good doctor charged the twins for the exam and the letter. Madeline had gone for weekly checkups— four times a month—so the doctor made a tidy sum off of her. Needless to say, those visits were not covered by insurance, so he wouldn't have had to fill out any paperwork for them. Madeline must have been a cash cow for the doctor, too. I wondered how much of his house in North Carolina had been paid for by her weekly visits. And, of course, then there was the matter of his children's tuition.

"Yes, it's very sad. He will be missed a great deal." I waited a moment before continuing the interview. "Now, let's turn to Mr. Robinson. What can you tell me about him?"

"Oh, you mean Woodley?" Madeline asked. I nodded. "He's a sweetheart, such a nice man. So sad that he was killed."

"How often did you see him?"

Madeline took a minute to answer. "It depended: sometimes once a month, sometimes twice. Every so often, it would be three times, but that only happened a few times. He was a very busy man, so he would only ask to see me when he had free time."

Not just free time, I thought, also when he had five thousand dollars an hour to spend. "And what would you do when you met?"

"We would drink some wine, and talk—fool around a little. I have to be honest with you, Lupe. I did take off my clothes in front of him. He loved to look at my body—said I was so pale, that he'd never soon anyone that pale. And, a natural blond, too!" Madeline blushed a deep red. "He was very persistent; he wanted to be the first man to make love to me. All the time we were together, he would try to talk me into it and say he would be gentle with me, that he loved me, that he would never hurt me. Things like that."

"Did you ever consider it? Think about having sex with him?" I asked. "I mean, you did say you liked him. I realize that if you did have sex with him, well, with any man, really, then you wouldn't be able to get such a high price for your services. After all, your virginity was the reason why you were getting five thousand dollars an hour."

I spoke bluntly, she was, after all, the client, but truthfully, time was running out, and so was my patience for niceties. I didn't like being lied to, something that every bone in my body told me that Madeline was doing. I didn't like being taken for a fool, either. I was going to get to the bottom of what was going on with my client, one way or another.

"No, not really. I never thought about having sex with anyone. I still believe in waiting to have sex until I am married; that's what my faith tells me to do, and regardless of how I earned my living now, that's what I plan to do," Madeline stated with conviction. "Woodley kept telling me how he would pay a great deal of money to be my first." She smiled shyly. "He said that he was in love with me. But I'm not sure that was true, that he only said that to get me to agree to have sex. But, he did say that several times—the part about being in love with me."

Shocker! Men lying to get their way—especially as it related to sex! "He said that he would be willing to pay to be your first?" Madeline nodded. I wondered how much Woodley Robinson had been willing to pay to relieve Madeline of her virginity. "Did the twins know about Mr. Robinson's offer?"

"I didn't tell them then about his being in love with me, but, yes, I told them about the money," Madeline answered. "They asked me how much Woodley said he would pay, but I told them we hadn't discussed money. I mean, I turned him down, so there really was no point in continuing the conversation, was there? If I'd kept discussing it with him, then he'd know I was thinking about doing it." Madeline looked down.

"That makes sense," I agreed. I changed the subject. "Did Woodley mention that anything was worrying him? Did he seem preoccupied the past few times you met with him?'

Madeline shook her head. "Well, he was always worried about his business. He always said that real estate in Miami was a crapshoot. You could make piles of money one day, and lose it all the next. You had to have a strong stomach to be in the real-estate business here, especially commercial real estate, like he was. The market has dropped so much in the past year, you know. Everyone has lost money, lots of money. Yes, he was worried about that, of course he was, he explained that the bulk of his money was tied up in real estate. He had a lot of expenses, he said, too, business and family, especially his children."

"But, he could still afford to pay you, so money couldn't have been that tight, right?" I pointed out.

Madeline did not answer. She slumped down in her chair and looked as if she'd been physically beaten. I had a few minutes at most before having to stop the interview.

Among the many other questions I wanted to ask Madeline, I would have liked to delve deeper into what, exactly, had been bothering Woodley Robinson, but I suspected it would be best to move on. I could always come back to discussing him at a later date. After all, as Madeline was on house arrest, she wouldn't be going anywhere. For now, I had to be satisfied with getting my most pressing questions answered; the rest would have to wait.

"Can we talk a little about Ricardo?" I asked as gently as I could.

Madeline's eyes filled with tears at the mention of Ricardo's name. Her reaction to him reminded me that for all their problems, at one point, he had been her boyfriend, and the reason she had moved to Miami. "What do you want to know?"

I knew I had to tread softly. "Tell me about him. What was he like when you met in Iowa, and what made him change once he got to Miami?"

"In Iowa, he was the nicest, most gentle man, a total gentleman," Madeline recalled. "We would talk for hours, go on long walks, go to Mass together on Sundays; his faith was as strong as mine. He believed, as I did, in waiting until marriage to have sex."

"What changed?" I wanted to know.

Madeline took a deep breath, and looked out the window at the ocean. "When we first came to Miami, I swear, the minute he stepped foot in the Miami airport, he changed completely. He became all macho, he was bossy and jealous. He accused me of being unfaithful to him," Madeline started to blink back the tears that were forming in her eyes. "I swear, Lupe, I never looked at another man! I would have never done that! I was in love with him! We were going to get married!"

"It must have been rough. You were here all alone, your family hadn't wanted you to come here with him, and now, Ricardo, the man you thought you knew, had changed, turned into this terrible person," I commiserated with her.

"Yes, it was very difficult." Madeline continued crying, her body shaking quietly. "Lupe, I'm sorry, but I don't feel well." She looked at me with sad, puppy-dog eyes. "Could we continue this conversation later?"

"I'm sorry, I don't want to tire you out." I began to gather my things. However, before standing up, I turned to her and asked, "The gun, Ricardo's gun, the .357 Magnum. It had your prints on it. Can you tell me a bit about the gun?"

"Yes, I know about the gun, I've held the gun a few times. Ricardo told me there was a lot of crime in Miami, and that I should learn how to defend myself." Madeline spoke as she walked towards the door, so I couldn't see her eyes when she answered, but my antenna was going crazy. "But, I haven't seen or touched the gun since I moved out."

"Try to get some rest," I advised her. "I'll be calling you tomorrow, if that's OK with you."

Madeline was so eager to see me go that she almost shut the door on my face, which didn't exactly give me a warm and fuzzy feeling. As I pressed the elevator button, I wondered why Madeline hadn't been more helpful. I understood that she'd just been through a terrible ordeal, being in the Dade County Jail for even a few hours surely was terrifying, but one would think she'd welcome my help. After all, not only was she paying me an obscene amount of money to help clear her name, but also I could possibly help make her nightmare go away. Her attitude clearly perplexed me.

Back in the lobby, I signed out in the visitors' book, and thanked the security guard for his help. After that, I walked outside and waited for the valet to bring my car around. I drove out onto Washington Avenue and circled the block a couple of times searching for the best vantage point to conduct my surveillance.

I decided to park in one of the empty spots across from the building where I could see the entrance, but could not be seen. The interview with Madeline had taken less than an hour, so I still had a while before Nestor was due back at his post. I could always text him, asking him to cut his break short, but that didn't seem right, so I just settled down to wait.

I had just taken a swig from the water bottle in my purse when a familiar car, a black Porsche, raced past me: Andres San Pedro! I thought I could make out that there was someone in the passenger seat next to him, but, with the tinted windows, and from the angle where I was parked, it wasn't possible to see if that was true or who it was. As it had been less than ten minutes since I'd left Portofino Towers, it was lucky I hadn't bumped into him while entering or exiting the building. I don't know what explanation I would have come up with for my presence in the building that time.

It had been a while since I'd been on surveillance, so I had to dig back in my memory to remember how to conduct one correctly. Most people have a preconceived idea that surveillance means just sitting in a parked car: that an investigator can read, listen to an iPod, talk on the phone, etc., but nothing could be farther from the truth. An investigator has to anticipate whatever would and could happen and be ready for it.

One could begin surveillance in a parked car, but end up walking if the mark traveled on foot rather than drove to his or her destination. Or, one could end up at a bar, or a restaurant, or the movies. It was close to impossible to anticipate what could happen, but one had to be prepared for anything.

For me, the most difficult part of being on surveillance was the challenges presented in going to the bathroom. For male investigators, that wasn't so difficult as they kept a bottle nearby where they could pee. For women, that was obviously not an option. Female investigators were known to go for hours without drinking anything so they wouldn't have to pee. Some wore Depends. As I said, it wasn't easy.

In addition, not only can an investigator on surveillance not move their eyes away from the person or the place being watched, but also he or she has to have a camera or video recorder ready at all times to take pictures or video of the mark. All this, plus take notes on any and all activities that take place during the time on duty.

All it took was for the investigator to look away for a second, and the surveillance could turn into a disaster. Many things could still go wrong: the mark could get into his or her car and drive away in a split second to God knows where; or, he or she could meet someone, and the investigator would lose him or her in the time it took to get the camera ready to snap pictures; or, worst of all, every investigator's nightmare: one look away, one lapse in concentration, and one could lose the mark altogether.

Of course, sometimes there were circumstances beyond his or her control that make the investigator lose the mark, but that shouldn't happen to a seasoned pro. Trust me, it was tough explaining to a client who had already spent thousands of dollars in investigator's fees that one lost the mark, resulting in a botched surveillance.

I sat in my parked car for a couple of minutes, watching the entrance to the Portofino Towers when I realized that I needn't have worried about having lost my skills: conducting surveillance was like riding a bike. Although I was a bit rusty, I'd never really forgotten how to do it.

I had just begun to get comfortable watching the Portofino Towers when I received a text from Nestor, telling me he was ten minutes away. I texted him back, telling him where I was parked. I waited until he told me he was back in his spot at the construction site before driving back to the office.

Twenty

I had sent Leo off to get copies of the 'A' form, the formal document in which details of Madeline's arrest are written, so he would not be at the office when I returned. Keeping that in mind, I stopped at his desk to retrieve any messages I might have received while I'd been gone. The first one was from Ernesto Loredo, and the other was from Andres San Pedro—the second time that both had phoned. I needed to return their calls, but, before doing that, I wanted to figure out exactly where I was in the investigation. The last two were from my sisters, reminding me yet again about Papi's birthday.

Andres had called at 1:45 p.m., just when I'd been on surveillance near Madeline's building. And, as he had left his cell phone number, and not his home one, I had to assume he'd called from the street, while speeding past me in his Porsche.

I'd always taken pride in my investigative abilities, especially in seeing through a fog of deceptions, so the fact that Madeline Meadows (street name: Mary) was being less than candid with me drove me crazy. I was used to having clients lie to me but none that had three counts of first-degree murder against them. A worse blow to my professional pride, perhaps, was that even Detective Anderson had put me on notice that

Madeline was hiding something, telling me to 'dig deeper'. At that point in the investigation, I felt I could have dug a hole straight to China, and it still wouldn't have gotten me anywhere.

I had my three best operatives on her trail: Sweet Suzanne was working the street; Nestor was monitoring her moves; and Leo was doing the computer stuff, but still, nothing. Even Tommy had reservations about her, but then again that wasn't unusual. He had doubts about most of his clients, so he was leaving it up to me, his crack investigator, to uncover something. Despite my best efforts, I'd come up dry.

Interviewing Madeline had been like trying to break into Fort Knox with a screwdriver. Even though I was desperate, I wasn't about to try to hit Detective Anderson up for more clues about what exactly it was that I was 'digging' for. I had a reputation to maintain. I didn't want there to be any hint that I may have lost any of my skills as a result of getting shot. To the world, I had to be as sharp, or sharper, than before I was shot. In this business, reputation was everything.

As far as the Meadows case was concerned, deep down I was confident that eventually I would get a break and find out what Madeline was hiding. My instincts told me that some of the answers were right in front of my face, and that all I had to do was to look over the information that I'd already gathered to see it but I had to do so with fresh eyes.

I went back to the very beginning of the investigation, specifically the file on Madeline that Leonardo had compiled. I read the notes on the front page, hoping that by now, I would be able to answer some of the questions that I had raised red flags earlier: Madeline's mysterious background; skeletons in the closets of Dr. Steinberg and Woodley Robinson; Andres' connections to call girls, for starters. Then, of course, there was the matter of the gun, the .357 Magnum. Unfortunately, I couldn't cross any of them off the list, as sadly, if anything, the list of unanswered questions had grown.

The fact that Madeline's fingerprints were on file with the police continued to be a red flag, one that waved and flapped loudly. I just couldn't get past that. Madeline had vehemently denied ever having been in double, either as a juvenile or as an adult. If I were to take her statements at face value, a criminal record would not be the reason for her prints being in the system.

Leo had used the social security number that Madeline provided to conduct background checks, both civil and criminal, in several nationwide databases, but even though he had done so several times to make sure he had not missed anything, there was no record in any of them for Madeline Marie Meadows. According to the public record searches, 'Mary' was as pure as her street name.

Tommy had said that he had specifically asked Madeline why her prints had shown up as a match to those lifted off of Ricardo's gun, but she had just shrugged and said that yes, she had touched the gun a few times during the time she'd lived with Ricardo. The next time I met with Madeline, I would begin the interview by grilling her about the gun: the last time she had touched it, seen it, etc. I had to establish a timeline for the gun.

For now, though, I had enough work to keep me busy for the rest of the afternoon, at least, until I left for my dinner with Tommy. Meals with Tommy were always succulent affairs, and my mouth began to water at the thought. I hadn't had time for lunch, and as 'food-in-mouth-time' was still hours away, I reluctantly pushed the mental and vivid image of a steaming-hot plateful of food away.

I reached for the phone and dialed Andres' number.

"Lupe! Hola! How are you?" Andres greeted me with the kind of joy and enthusiasm that brought to mind the television commercials where individuals (usually dressed in their rattiest clothing) react to being told they've won the lottery.

"I'm fine, thank you, Andres," I replied sweetly. "And, you?"

It was strange to think that if not for the Meadows case, I would never have known that Andres used the services of call girls. I had resolved not to let that fact change my opinion of him, but I knew that it would. I mean, the man had been married five times, obvious proof that he could attract women, so why would he need to use a call girl service to satisfy his urges? Was it because such an exchange was strictly a business proposition, cash traded for services, and he would not get emotionally attached? I supposed that was for his shrink to figure out; all I could do was thank God I'd never had sex with him. I'd come close, true, but something, maybe my strong survival instincts, had prevented me from doing so.

"I'm fine, also, thank you," Andres said. "Listen, it was great bumping into you yesterday on South Beach, but it reminded me how much I've missed you. It's been way too long since we saw each other." I heard Andres take a breath. "Do you want to get together soon?"

"Sure, I'd love to," I replied casually.

"Well, I know this is short notice, but what about tonight?" Andres asked. "We could go to dinner; wherever you'd like."

I thought about the dinner plans I'd already made with Tommy, and was about to refuse his invitation, but then reconsidered. According to the twins, Andres was the reason why Madeline had moved into the Portofino Towers, so I could use a nice, relaxed, casual dinner to delve into what he knew about her. I didn't want to stand Tommy up, through. "Oh, I'd like that, but I sort of have tentative plans. Would it be a problem if I checked with my friend to see if she still wants to meet, or if I could reschedule our dinner?" I purposely used the female pronoun when referring to my 'friend'. I didn't want Andres to think I had a date. "We kind of left it open."

"Sure, go ahead and ask her," Andres agreed. "Just call me back when you know."

We said our goodbyes and hung up. I wasted no time calling Tommy at his office. "Hi, Tommy. Listen, I know we agreed to have dinner tonight, but something has come up." I told him about the situation with Andres, and how I hoped to turn the dinner from a social event into a fishing expedition for information about Madeline.

"Listen, Lupe, you go ahead and have dinner with your Mr. San Pedro and wring as much information from him as you can. It sounds like a good opportunity to try to get a bead on what's going on with our client." Tommy sounded distracted, which meant that he was probably looking at his computer screen as we spoke. "Listen, don't feel too bad about blowing me off. I may have had to do the same thing to you. Just before you called, I had another call, one from the judge's secretary to tell me that the judge was feeling much better, and trial would resume tomorrow morning as scheduled, which means I'd better stay here and prepare."

I was relieved that Tommy had let me off the hook. I hated to change plans with anyone, much less Tommy, at the last minute. Still, I did want to see him, so I countered, "Well, can we have dinner tomorrow night instead?"

"Yes, sure," Tommy agreed. "Now, Lupe, do your thing and squeeze all kinds of information from Mr. San Pedro. You're good at getting men to talk. Ply him with wine and food, and flirt a lot, the way you do so well; then ask him what you want to know. He won't be able to resist you!" Tommy laughed. "Call me later, if you want. I'll be here pretty much all night."

"Well, good luck with your preparation," I replied. "I'll call you on the drive home after dinner. It probably won't be too late."

I didn't volunteer that it wouldn't be a late night because I was tired and wanted to go to bed. The beneficial effects of my twelve-hour-long snooze fest from the night before had begun to wear off. Also, I wasn't that excited about spending time with Andres, now that I knew he went with call girls. I was seriously trying not to be judgmental, but I was finding that harder than I expected.

I hung up with Tommy, called Andres back, and told him I would be able to have dinner, but asked if it could be on the early side, as the next day would be a busy one, and I still had work to do. Andres volunteered to pick me up whenever and wherever I wanted. I didn't want him coming to either the office or the house, so I told him that I would meet him at whatever restaurant he chose.

I was informally dressed—I still had on the same blue jeans and T-shirt that I'd put on that morning—but luckily I kept several changes of clothing in my office closet, so I could spruce myself up and go to dinner looking somewhat respectable.

"How about we go old style and have dinner at Christy's?" Andres suggested. Christy's was a steak house in Coral Gables that had been around for decades. It was very traditional, serving dishes not often found on menus, such as Baked Alaska. It also happened to be one of Tommy's favorite restaurants, but I did not let that stop me from accepting Andres' suggestion.

"Perfect. I'll meet you there at seven, or is that too early for you?" I suggested.

"No, that's fine." Andres chuckled. "I'm getting hungry just thinking about one of those big, juicy steaks."

"I'll call and make a reservation," I said before hanging up.

So as not to forget, I quickly placed the call to Christy's. I had been about to call Ernesto back when I heard a commotion coming from the reception area.

"Leo," I called out. "Are you back?"

No one answered, so I called out again, "Leo?" Still nothing. As far as I knew we weren't expecting any visitors. Our clients never dropped in on us, nor did we have any 'walk-in' business. I knew there was someone out there, though, and it wasn't one of our regular visitors: FedEx, UPS or the water company delivery man to replace the empty bottles as they would have answered back. My heart began to beat faster. Slowly, I reached for my purse on the floor next to my chair, and avoiding looking at the bullet hole on the side, took out the Beretta. As quietly as possible, I took off the safety, got up, and, gun in hand, tiptoed toward my office door.

My heart was racing so fast that I was having trouble controlling my breathing. In that agitated state, if I were going to have to shoot someone, I would certainly miss, so I desperately tried to compose myself. With the vision of being shot again creeping into my mind's eye, I knew I was on the verge of having a flashback to that horrible day. I slowly counted to ten as I tried to regulate my breathing. I extended my right arm, my normal shooting stance, and gun pointed, stepped into the doorway.

"Who's there? I swear I'll shoot if you don't answer me!" I shouted. I hoped whoever it was didn't notice my hand was shaking.

"Wait! Wait! Don't shoot!" A man's panicked voice came from the far corner of the room, by Leo's office. "It's us, Ernesto and Stanley!"

A wave of relief flooded over me. I didn't know whether to shoot them or kiss them. I did neither, and instead, screamed at them. "What the fuck do you think you're doing? Don't you ever creep around my office that way again. Do you realize I almost shot you?"

Ernesto and Stanley may have been big, tall, brutes, but the sight of me, all of five feet tall, and one hundred pounds, had reduced them to a shivering mass of jelly. It must have been the business like way that I was holding the Beretta that made them come close to peeing in their pants.

The twins were dressed in black from head to toe: black pants, black T-shirts, black belts, black patent leather boots, clothes that made them look like extras in a bad mob movie. Tony Soprano would have been embarrassed. The twins sure as hell were not disciples of John Gotti, the 'Dapper Don.'

"We're sorry to come here this way, but you didn't answer our calls, so we thought we would come by and see you," Ernesto explained. "We're sorry we frightened you."

Slowly, I lowered my arm, but kept my finger on the trigger. I still had not put the safety back on. "So, what was it that was so urgent you speak to me about?" I could have been a bit friendlier, but I was in no mood. They had almost scared me to death, and I was not in a forgiving mood. But they were right, I hadn't returned their call. Still, that wasn't a valid excuse for scaring the shit out of me.

"It's that man we told you about. Andres San Pedro," Stanley spoke for the first time.

"What about him?" The twins coming to speak with me about Andres San Pedro was the last thing I expected.

"He's been bothering Madeline," Ernesto reported.

"Bothering her?" I repeated. "What do you mean?"

"Ever since she got out of jail, he's been coming to the apartment. He lives in the building, so he can go anywhere he wants. He's come by three times already; he says he wants to help her, but she doesn't want him around," Ernesto explained. "She can't call the police, or tell anyone, you know, with her problems, that she didn't know what to do, so she called us."

I thought about what the twins had just told me. "So, she asked you to tell me about this?" It seemed strange that Madeline wouldn't call me herself. After all, I'd been there just a few hours earlier.

"No! No!" Ernesto and Stanley shouted at the same time. "She doesn't know we're here."

"We asked her if we should tell you, and ask for help, but she made us promise not to tell you. She made us promise," Ernesto said again, almost beside himself with worry about what they had done.

"So, what are you supposed to do then, with this information?" I figured I would think about why Madeline did not want me to know about Andres until later. Right now, I had to deal with the twins and see what I could do to solve the immediate problem.

"Well, she wants us to move in with her, to protect her. She's scared of him, but, Lupe, I'm not sure if that's a good idea," Stanley said. "We're not exactly upstanding citizens, you know. Me and Ernesto, we have records, and if there's any trouble, well, you know, it's not good for us to get involved."

Clearly, I had not known Andres as well as I had thought. I had never considered him to be violent, just as having terrible judgment. "Does Madeline feel threatened in any way? Does she think he's going to hurt her?"

Both men shrugged their shoulders and looked at their feet. "It's like he's stalking her. He keeps bothering her, calling, showing up," Ernesto answered.

It was difficult for me to visualize Andres acting that way, but I had no choice but to believe the twins. "Seeing as how I'm not supposed to know about this situation, I'm not sure what I can do to help. I have to give it some thought." I couldn't exactly tell them I was going to dinner with Andres San Pedro in a couple of hours.

"Please help Madeline," Ernesto pleaded. "She's in enough trouble already and she's scared of him."

"Look, her apartment has an alarm, right?" I had seen it, so I knew there was one. "Tell her to set the alarm, and to call the security guards downstairs and tell them that she's been hearing weird noises out in the hallway; have them think maybe it's rats. They'll look at the security cameras on her floor, and they'll also send someone to check up on her periodically. Then, Madeline should make one call to Mr. San Pedro and tell him she's alerted the security guards that someone's been stalking her, threatening her and that they'll be roaming around on her floor constantly, and checking up on her. She's not to answer the door, or her phone, either. That should discourage any more visits from Mr. San Pedro, at least, for now, until we can come up with a more permanent solution."

The twins listened solemnly, as if I'd been the Oracle at Delphi. I, of course, knew that Andres San Pedro would not be bothering her for the next few hours because he would be with me, so I wasn't overly concerned about anything happening to her that night.

"Thanks, we'll do that," Stanley said.

There really wasn't much more to say after that. I mean, it wasn't as if we were going to exchange recipes or shopping tips, so after expressing their concerns once again, the twins left. I was still very shaken and wanted to forget the unpleasant episode as quickly as possible. After locking the front door, the first thing I did was to walk back to my office, and return the Beretta to my purse.

I had intended to continue reading the files that Leo had compiled, but instead, I walked into the kitchen, opened the door of the refrigerator, and chose a bottle of white wine from the dozen or so that Leo always kept on hand. I needed some sustenance, and figured that a glass or two, for that matter, of Morgan, a Chardonnay from California that I'd recently discovered, and which had quickly became a favorite, wouldn't hurt. I poured myself a glass, and still standing in the kitchen, drank it. I refilled it and returned the opened bottle to the refrigerator.

I walked back to my office, deep in thought as to why Madeline didn't want me to know about Andres San Pedro. So much bothered me about her, and the questions kept piling up, but unfortunately, I couldn't for the life of me come up with any answers. How the hell could someone from Dubuque be so complicated? I would have thought that all that farmland and fresh air would have produced a much simpler person.

Back at my desk, I tried to work on the files, but without much success. Despite the two glasses of wine I'd drunk, I was still quite shaken by my unexpected visitors. There was only one hour remaining before I had to leave to meet Andres at Christy's, so I decided that rather than sitting at my desk and pretending to work, I would, instead, lie on the sofa and observe the parrots. Unlike me, at least they were doing something constructive.

Twenty-One

Andres San Pedro may have been a stalker and a patron of call girls, but he sure as hell wasn't a picky eater. I'd forgotten what an enormous appetite the man had. Christy's was known for its delicious food and huge portions, and, at dinner, Andres certainly did them proud. Throughout its long history, no one ever got up from the table hungry and that night was no different.

Andres had begun the meal by demolishing the breadbasket and almost licking the plate clean of the complimentary Cesar salad. After that, he inhaled an appetizer of six jumbo shrimp, polished off one of the biggest sirloin steaks on the menu, and an entire baked potato, accompanied by side dishes of mushrooms and creamed spinach. But he hadn't stopped there; he had eaten most of the Baked Alaska we had 'shared' for dessert. As I watched him consume a meal that would have satisfied two, possibly three individuals, I couldn't help but think how unfair it was that he could eat such prodigious quantities of food and still keep his figure.

Most of the conversation during dinner had been about everyday, mundane matters: hurricanes, Miami politics, real estate, nothing particularly memorable. Andres owned a very successful business, one that supplied parts to airlines and, naturally enough, was quite knowledgeable about the airline business, so I kept him talking about that, asking him lots of questions.

He had started his company on a shoestring budget twenty years before and had built it up into a hugely successful enterprise, an accomplishment he was justifiably proud of. Apparently, he had recently gotten into the security business, and was starting a company that manufactured and sold alarms for homes and businesses. Whatever Andres' failings may have been as a human being, he had the Midas touch as far as business was concerned. Andres loved talking, and the conversation, helped along by two bottles of Cabernet Sauvignon, flowed easily. As we sat across from each other, taking our time over dinner, it was almost like old times.

Andres became especially animated and lively when discussing his work, which made him seem quite attractive; not that he needed anything else for that to happen. His looks alone would have been enough. For dinner, he had dressed casually in a light blue cotton button-down shirt, no tie, navy blazer, khaki trousers and loafers, no socks. Had I not known about his visits to call girls, I might have been tempted to take our relationship to a different level, but that knowledge was a real passion killer.

I had decided to follow Tommy's advice and wait until Andres was relaxed, full of food and even better wine, before bringing up the topic of conversation that I was most interested in: Madeline, and his relationship with her. Even though Andres had consumed most of the wine himself, I knew that his mind was as sharp as if he'd been drinking water. I had to question him in a way that wouldn't tip him off that I was focusing on her. We had finished dinner and were enjoying our espressos, when I decided that it was now or never.

"So, you still enjoy living at the Portofino Towers?" I prodded him. "It's such a great building."

"Oh, yes, it's great," Andres answered. "I love it."

"You've been living there for what?" I paused. "Five years?" I asked, even though I knew the answer.

"Just over; closer to six, actually," Andres gently corrected me.

"Do you know many of the other residents of the building?" I asked, speaking as innocently as possible. "Seeing as how you've been there so long, I mean."

Andres shook his head slowly. "No, actually, I don't know anyone there. I'm so busy, you know, with work and travel. I barely have time to enjoy the amenities: the gym, pool, all that."

"Oh, that's too bad; it would be nice to have friends in the building, people to do things with," I commented, a bit vaguely. I would have definitely liked to pursue that line of questioning a bit further but was apprehensive about arousing his suspicions, so I held back.

A couple of seconds later, though, I reconsidered that decision; another opportunity might not present itself, and I needed some answers. Figuring the risk was worth the reward, I was about to open my mouth to ask Andres another question when I saw that he was about to speak.

Without warning, Andres' warm and friendly attitude changed, and he began to stare at me intently. "When I bumped into you, yesterday afternoon, you said you were taking care of some dogs for a friend, someone who lives in the building and you were returning them." I nodded. I knew what was coming, but it was like riding in a runaway car, I was powerless to stop it. "Maybe I know your friend?"

It was clear by the way he said it that Andres was hoping I would tell him the name of whoever it was that I had been visiting. I took my time before answering, to get a sense of what he wanted from me. Was he trying to see if I would say Madeline's name? Or, did he really not know that I'd been carrying Madeline's dogs, and was simply making conversation? I felt as if I was walking into a trap and had to tread very lightly.

"Probably not. I really don't think so." I shook my head and took a sip of my espresso.

Normally, I didn't drink coffee at night. Contrary to popular belief that we Cubans are able to consume vats of the stuff at any hour without it affecting us, whenever I drank coffee after noon, I would pay the price with an extreme case of insomnia. However, I still hadn't gotten any information about Madeline from Andres, so I'd had no choice but to prolong the dinner, and, if that meant drinking a double shot of espresso, then so be it. Every sip I took meant one additional hour for me to fall asleep, but, nevertheless, in the spirit of giving my clients my all, I continued to sip.

Andres didn't say anything; he just continued to stare at me in a disconcerting manner, making me feel as if I had to offer an additional explanation. "I really doubt you would know my friend. She lives out of the country and only uses her apartment a couple of times a year," I replied. "Besides, you just said you didn't know any of the residents of the building." I hoped I wasn't too forceful in my answer.

As before, Andres didn't say anything, he just continued looking at me. Then, he shrugged his shoulders, as if to let it pass. His body language made it clear that he hadn't believed me, but had decided not to pursue it further.

"Would you like anything else, Lupe?" Andres asked, his manner changing back to the soft tone of voice he had been using.

I was so relieved he had dropped the subject that I blurted out. "Oh, Andres, I'm so full! It was all so delicious. I don't think

I'll be able to eat anything for days! Great idea you had to come here."

"Yes, that was delicious, wasn't it?" Andres reached across the table and took my right hand in his left. "I've missed you Lupe, I really have," he declared, looking into my eyes.

His abrupt change of attitude took me by surprise, and I hadn't been prepared for it. Once again, I was amazed how quickly my opinion of Andres had changed once I'd learned about his forays into the world of call girls, and now his stalking of Madeline. Just a few days ago, I would have considered him a close friend, and now I could barely hold his hand without wanting to pull it back. I may have been a seasoned private investigator who wasn't easily shocked, but still, learning that unsavory detail about him had been a surprise.

"I've missed you, too," I replied. I pretended to yawn. "I'm so full that I think I'm about to fall asleep." I smiled. "Food coma, you know."

"I'll get the check, then." Andres signaled for the waiter, then after catching his eye, pretended to write in the air with his right hand—the universal sign for requesting a bill.

The waiter brought the check right away. Without looking at the check, Andres slipped his black American Express card into the leather folder, and handed it back to him. Less than a minute later, the waiter reappeared with the folder. Andres quickly calculated the tip, the dinner was expensive, I saw him add fifty dollars to the total, and snapped the folder closed.

"Ready?" Andres smiled at me.

"Thank you so much again, Andres," I replied. "Dinner was wonderful."

We walked out of the restaurant, and because we had parked next to each other on Ponce De Leon Boulevard, continued together until we reached our cars. I, of course, was still desperate to extract information from Andres, but I didn't know how to do it without arousing his suspicions. The sad truth was that I had learned next to nothing during the dinner, so I kept thinking of how to salvage the time we'd spent together.

We reached my car first. It was now or never, so I took the plunge. "Andres, the night passed so quickly. We really haven't had much chance to discuss our personal lives. I meant to ask you earlier, but we got to talking about so many other things." I tried to look as innocent as possible. "Are you seeing anyone?"

"Actually, yes." Andres nodded. "For a few months, I've been seeing an American girl; she's very nice, but, sadly, I think it's ending."

"Oh, I'm so sorry," I commiserated. "What happened?"

Andres looked down at the sidewalk. "I'm not really sure. I think part of the problem was that she was very young, in her early twenties. She's twenty-two; even for me, that's a big age difference."

"Twenty-two?" It had to be Madeline! My heart skipped a beat. "Yes, that is young," I agreed. "You said she was American," I repeated. "She wasn't from Miami, then?" There were almost no Americans (non-Hispanic whites, as they were referred to in the demographic studies) in Miami.

Andres shook his head. "No, she was from the Midwest—a total change for me, from the women I normally am involved with."

Madeline was twenty-two, from Iowa, and a call girl; Andres was forty, Argentinean businessman, who'd been married and divorced five times. No wonder it hadn't worked out.

For a minute, I feared I would pass out from excitement from what I had just learned and it took all my self-control to continue speaking casually, as if nothing Andres had said had surprised me. "Ah, the Midwest, she's very young and from the Midwest."

I repeated, as if that explained everything. "Well, maybe it's not really over," I added, making sure to insert a hefty dash of hope into my voice so that Andres would think I was encouraging him. "Maybe it's just a brief breakup, she'll reconsider, and you'll get back together."

"I don't think so," Andres said, his voice cracking. "She made it quite clear that she doesn't want to see me anymore. She doesn't want to ever have anything to do with me again." Andres was visibly upset. "I'm in love with her, Lupe, but she isn't interested in me anymore."

"Oh, I'm so sorry." I repeated as I put my hand on his arm, and patted it to comfort him. So, maybe Andres wasn't a stalker, maybe he had been Madeline's actual boyfriend, they'd broken up, and he was upset about it. Maybe that's why he'd shown up at her apartment so many times. However, the twins knew him back when he'd been a client at L'Escort Deluxe Services. So, what was it? Was Andres the brokenhearted former boyfriend as he claimed to be, or was he a client-turned-stalker as the twins said? Or, was he both? I'd have to find out.

"Thanks, Lupe." Andres looked at me. "I appreciate your sympathy. And, your encouragement, too, that it might be a temporary break up."

"Well, it's getting late, I'd better get going." I stood on my tiptoes, and kissed him on the cheek. "Thanks again."

Andres, ever the gentleman, reached down, and opened the driver's side door of the Mercedes. "My pleasure, Lupe." He waited for me to slide into the seat before shutting it. "Good night. Drive safely."

I waved, and after making sure the road was clear, pulled out of the parking space. It was still early, just before nine o'clock. I waited until Andres could no longer see me before reaching for my phone, and punching in Tommy's office number.

"So, Lupe," Tommy answered on the first ring. "How did it go with your Mr. San Pedro?"

"It went OK, I guess. I just left Christy's and I'm on my way home," I replied then, without meaning to do so, blurted out, "Oh, Tommy! I'm more confused than ever."

"Confused? No, I don't believe it!" Tommy laughed. "You, Lupe Solano, crack detective, confused?"

"Don't make fun of me, Tommy, please don't," I pleaded. "I'm not in the mood."

"Well, are you in the mood for something else, then?" Tommy spoke in a playful tone. "When you called, I was about to leave the office and go home. I've done all I was going to do tonight," he explained. "You feel like meeting me at my apartment in about fifteen minutes?"

It took less than five seconds to answer. After all, the espresso I drank after dinner, it would be hours before I would be able to get to sleep, so I figured I might as well do something fun and enjoyable to pass the time—and burn the calories off, of course. "I'm making a U-turn now."

"Good. I'll have a glass of champagne ready for you when you get there," Tommy said before hanging up. "You'll feel better and see everything clearer then."

I was already doing that.

Twenty-Two

Needless to say, when I'd accepted Tommy's invitation to meet at his apartment, I knew that that meant we would end up in bed, or, rather, as had been the case, start off there. It was very late; light was beginning to streak ever so lightly across the sky. Tommy, who wanted to get an early start to the day, had set the alarm for six, less than thirty minutes from now. I planned to get up when he did, but instead of going to work, go home.

At that early hour it would be highly unlikely that anyone would be up yet, so no one would notice that I'd spent the night out. I may have been a twenty-eight year old woman who carried a gun, but I still had to respect my family and honor their traditions. The double espresso I had at dinner with Andres earlier that night still coursed through my veins, and I hadn't been able to get any sleep.

My brain was on overdrive; I couldn't stop thinking about the Meadows situation. I'd worked some complicated cases but none that I'd devoted so much time and effort to, and none with such paltry results. Every twist and turn, instead of leading me to answers and clarity, just led to more twists and turns. Was that just the nature of the case, or was it because of my shortcomings as an investigator? Had getting shot caused me to lose my investigative abilities, and not be able to do my job properly?

I knew Tommy had a formidable adversary in Aurora Santangelo, and not because of her legal abilities. Tommy was an outstanding criminal defense attorney; I had complete confidence in his abilities, but Aurora played dirty, and she was willing to use every one of her the dirty tricks against him. Besides, Aurora had the weight of the State Attorneys' Office behind her, lawyers who, although they might have despised her and would have loved to see her fall flat on her face, wished to bring Tommy down even more. His impressive win/loss record had been achieved at their expense, and everyone in the law enforcement community knew it.

Both Tommy and Detective Anderson had made it very clear that Aurora was out to get me, something that I never doubted for a minute. Tommy relied on my investigations to build the defense for his cases, and it would be disastrous if I were to give him wrong or incomplete information. As a result, not only was I feeling pressure about not screwing up because of my injuries, I was worried that I might fuck up the investigation because it was so complicated and complex! Ay! Given all that, it wasn't just the coffee keeping me awake.

For the past hour I had lain awake on my side of the bed, my eyes wide open, staring blankly at the ceiling, as if the answers to my questions would miraculously appeal. Even though I had a very busy day ahead of me, by then I'd given up hope of sleeping. I kept trying to sort out all of the aspects of the Meadows case with such fervor that I was surprised Tommy hadn't been able to hear the wheels of my brain turning. It was difficult to believe that only a few days had passed since that Saturday afternoon, when he had first mentioned Madeline Meadows to me. I felt Tommy move next to me.

"Hey, Lupe," Tommy whispered. "Have you slept at all?"

"No." I moved several inches closer to him, and put my head on his chest. "The Meadows case; it's driving me crazy."

"I can tell." Tommy kissed the top of my head. "Look, you want to discuss it some now? I know we just have a few minutes before the alarm goes off, but we can start, if you'd like." His hand began stroking me, tracing the scars the bullets had left. The first time I'd gone to bed with Tommy after getting shot, I'd been embarrassed about my body and had insisted the lights be turned off, but he had made me feel so comfortable that my shyness had worn off. Surprisingly, I didn't mind his touching me there.

I sat up. There was no way I could have a serious conversation with Tommy while he was playing with me that way. "Well, to begin, I think she's lying through her teeth."

Tommy shrugged his shoulders. "God, Lupe, she's not the first client you've had who's lied to you," Tommy said in a dismissive tone. "What else?"

"I know, I know. That's not what's really bothering me. What's killing me is that I can't find out what she's lying about," I replied.

I briefly considered telling him about what Detective Anderson had said about 'digging deep' into Madeline's background, but decided against it. Lying there, in bed, naked, was not the best time to bring up Detective Anderson's name to Tommy. Although he would never admit it, I knew that the subject of the detective's relationship with me was a bit sensitive.

"You'll find out, you always do, Lupe," Tommy reassured me. "It's just a matter of time."

"Thanks for the vote of confidence." I smiled as I reached over and kissed him hard on the mouth. "I also want to know about Madeline's relationship with Andres San Pedro. What, exactly, is their relationship? Boyfriend? Client? Stalker?"

"From what you've told me, he might be all three," Tommy commented. "He could have started out being her client, then became her boyfriend, and, when she broke up with him, became her stalker."

"Could be." I nodded slowly. "Also, I know what she does professionally, of course, but, is that really and truly where all her money—and, there's a lot of it—comes from? And, of course, where does it go? I realize that at $5,000 per hour she was making bank, but that's a hell of a lot of clients to sustain her lifestyle. Remember, she lives in the Portofino Towers, she pays the twins, and she still has enough money, hundreds of thousands of dollars, left over to post bail? Tommy, there's not enough hours in the day—or, enough clients—to earn the kind of money to afford all that."

"Once you look at her financials, you'll figure that out," Tommy said. It was reassuring to know he had such confidence in my abilities; I only hoped it wasn't misplaced. "What else?"

"The big question: If she didn't kill Dr. Steinberg, Woodley Robinson and Ricardo Melendez, then, who did?" I asked, not expecting an answer. "These were not random killings—why is it that she had a close relationship with all three? Why were all three men shot with the same gun? And why were Madeline's prints the only ones on the weapon? I mean, it was Ricardo's gun, after all, and she said she hadn't seen it after she moved out."

Tommy smiled as he looked at me. "Lupe, by the way you ask that, I have a sneaky suspicion you don't believe our client is innocent."

Now it was my turn to smile. In all the years I'd worked as Tommy's private eye, he'd never once asked if I thought a client was innocent or guilty. He would make comments like, "Lupe, is there anything I should know about the client before I go to trial?" Or, "Am I going to get blindsided by the prosecution?"

Or, my all-time favorite, "Is there anything about our client that's going to come back and bite me in the ass?'

"I'm not saying that, Tommy," I answered quickly. "It's just that I don't like coincidences, and I especially don't like being lied to."

"That last thing, the lying, I fully understand," Tommy agreed. Just then, the alarm rang, and Tommy reached over and turned it off. "So, what are you going to do now?"

I took a deep breath; this was going to take a while. "I'll start by telling you the easy, least labor-intensive information: I have Nestor on surveillance, and he's reporting that Madeline is staying put, that's a good thing, but I'll check in on him anyway. I'm waiting for Suzanne to get back to me with what the word on the street is on Madeline. As you know, there are very few secrets in that business, so I should hear back soon; I'm going to look into Madeline's financials to see what's going on with the money; Leo should have the 'A' form back this morning; I'll call our favorite bail bondsman, Buster, at his office, and ask how, exactly, Madeline paid the $300,000 bond; I'm going to try to interview relatives of the victims, although I'm not sure they'll speak with me, seeing as I'm working for the defense; I'm going to try to speak with several of Madeline's clients that Suzanne told me about; I'm also going to contact Madeline's family in Dubuque, to get some background information on her. Hopefully, they'll want to help." I took another breath. "Then I'll really get working on the case."

Tommy swung his long legs over the side of the bed. "Well, that should keep you busy for an hour or so," he joked. "Let me know how you make out with all those."

"I'd like to be able to take my time, but I know Detective Anderson is working 24/7 on this case. Aurora is on his ass about it, so I don't have the luxury—every minute counts." I told him.

"Listen, Lupe, I'd love to be able to stay with you longer to discuss the case, but I have to be in court in less than three hours, and I still have some preparation left to do." Tommy bent down and kissed me before heading off to the bathroom to take a shower.

I yawned, and then stretched my entire body, a move that turned out to be a major mistake as it made me realize that I was getting sleepy. My eyes were closing at a fast rate—I could be sound asleep in less than a minute. Shit! Why couldn't that have happened hours before, when I could have used it?

I gathered my clothes from the places I'd flung them the night before in the throes of passion. Tommy took very long, very hot showers, so rather than waiting for him to finish, I headed to the guest bathroom to shower and get dressed. It was getting late, and my window for arriving home before anyone woke up and spotted me was narrowing. I had to hurry unless I wanted to do the 'walk of shame' into the house.

I quickly showered, put on my clothes, and fixed myself up to look as presentable as possible, which wasn't easy considering I'd had no sleep, was slightly hung over and was wearing the same wrinkled clothes from the night before. Before leaving, I stopped by Tommy's bathroom and called out to him that I was going.

"Good luck in court today," I shouted into the steam-filled bathroom.

"Thanks," Tommy answered. "I'll call you later to see how your day went."

I blew him a kiss, picked up my purse and headed towards the front door. I quietly let myself out into the hallway, and while I waited for the elevator, took out my BlackBerry and checked my messages.

The first missed call had been from Nestor. I saw that when he hadn't been able to speak with me, he had sent me an e-mail.

"Subject left building at 1:00 A.M., took dogs out to building dog park, couldn't see much because park is out of line of sight. Didn't want to risk being burned. Subject spent one and one half hours in park. Mutts must have diarrhea."

I smiled as I read that last sentence; it was so like Nestor. As I'd taken Napoleon and Josephine myself to the building's dog park, I could easily picture what Nestor meant when he had said he couldn't keep Madeline in his sight the entire time. It was true, the building did block part of the dog park from the street. Next, Andres had called to tell me what a lovely time he'd had. The last call was from Suzanne, informing me that she had found out some interesting information about Madeline. It was about time something like that happened!

Once downstairs, I headed to the entrance of the building and gave the parking ticket to the valet. By then, it was almost seven o'clock, and the day was starting. The shower I had taken in Tommy's guest bathroom had woken me up, so I figured I might as well get to the office early, and, if I got tired, I would just go home. On a practical level, I could take another shower in my office bathroom, and as I kept several changes of clothing in my closet, no one would ever be the wiser. I planned to call Aida later and tell her I'd worked through the night, that way she wouldn't worry.

And so, when the valet brought up the Mercedes, instead of going home to Coral Gables, I headed to Coconut Grove. At that hour of morning, there was little traffic on the road, and I made the trip in less than ten minutes. I figured I would have around two hours there to myself, as Leo never arrived at the office before nine o'clock and that was only if the stars were aligned correctly.

Careful not to park under the frangipani tree, once in the driveway of the office building, I reached into my purse for the keys to the front door before turning off the motor. As had become my habit, I looked around to make sure no one was around before exiting the car. Keys in hand, I walked up the driveway to the front entrance.

I was about to insert the key in the lock when I sensed that something seemed wrong. My heart began pounding as I slowly put my hand inside my purse, and took out the Beretta. I debated dialing 911 and waiting for the police to arrive before going inside, but dismissed the thought. After all, everything looked perfectly normal, and, really, it was only a sense that something was amiss. I would feel pretty stupid if I had called the police, and everything was fine. Besides, what kind of a private eye wouldn't go into her own office just because she had a 'feeling?' The old Lupe would not have even hesitated.

I crossed myself, said a brief prayer to Mami in heaven to protect me, then, holding the Beretta in front of me, inserted the key in the lock, and turned it. I took a deep breath and pushed open the door. The first thing I noticed was that the alarm had not gone off. A very bad sign. I took another breath, and slowly, with my right arm holding the gun still extended, entered.

One look at the reception area told me that my worst fears had been confirmed; the entire place had been ransacked. Papers were strewn everywhere, file cabinets were opened, and the contents spread all over the floor.

My first instinct was to rush in and see what had been stolen, but mindful of what had happened to me before, I decided to play it sale. Instead, I went outside and called the police. Although it was probably unlikely whoever broke in could still be inside. Less than a minute later, I heard the sirens of police cars, first faintly, then increasingly louder. Two cars with two officers inside each pulled up simultaneously.

"Were you the one who called it in?" The lead officer addressed me. He took one look at me standing there, the Beretta in hand, and without waiting for me to reply, spoke again, in a very unfriendly tone of voice. "Put the gun down slowly, and let me see some identification, please."

Oh, God! It just hit me! Did the cops think I was the perp? Was I the one who was going to be arrested?

"It's OK, officer. I know her. She has a license to carry." I heard a familiar voice say behind me. Detective Anderson!

"Detective Anderson, what are you doing here?" I was never so happy to see anyone in my life.

"I heard the call on my police scanner and recognized the address. I was on my way to work just a couple of blocks away, so I thought I would swing by and see if you needed help," Detective Anderson replied. "So, what's wrong? Why did you call us?"

We were still standing in the driveway, with the five men— four police officers and Detective Anderson forming a protective circle around me. "When I opened the door to the building, the alarm was turned off—I immediately saw that the place had been broken into and ransacked. I wanted to go in and see what else had happened, but I thought I should call the police, and wait for backup."

"Good—you did the right thing." Detective Anderson knew I had acted that way because I'd been reminded of the time I'd been shot. "Let's go in." He reached for his holster and took out his Sig Sauer.

I waited outside, standing in the driveway, while the officers went inside to investigate. If the reception area looked like that, I hated to think of what the rest of the rooms looked like.

Solano Investigations had operated out of that building for eight years without any problems. I knew there'd been a few cases of breaking and entering in the neighborhood, but those were minor; mostly kids looking for a quick hit, nothing as destructive as what I had seen in the reception area.

From the way things had been tossed around, whoever had done this knew what they were looking for, but I'd been in and out of the reception area so fast I hadn't really had the time to see what was missing. Apart from the plasma television in the gym, the only real items of value we had were the office equipment: computers, printers, fax machines, etc I couldn't imagine that kids would be interested in those. Leo would have a fit when he saw the damage to our office.

Five long minutes passed before Detective Anderson re-emerged in the doorway, still holding his gun. "Hey, Lupe, can you come in here, please?"

"Is everything OK?" I dreaded what I would find inside.

"Just come here now, OK?" Detective Anderson repeated in a louder, sharper, no-nonsense voice.

Detective Anderson had never raised his voice to me—he was the most calm and collected person I knew. It frightened me to hear him speak that way. "OK, I'm coming," I said, hurrying.

When I stepped inside the building, Detective Anderson took my elbow and gently led me through the reception area to my office. Then, standing in the doorway, he took a step back so I could pass by him. Once I was inside the room, he pointed to the couch and asked, "Know him?"

Andres San Pedro was sitting up very straight in the middle cushion of the couch. His head was tilted back, and his mouth was open, seemingly taking a nap. It was surreal seeing him there, sitting like that, on my couch; I had trouble believing it was he. I approached him, wanting to get closer to make sure my brain had correctly registered what my eyes were seeing.

The first thing I noticed was that he was wearing the same clothes he'd worn for dinner at Christy's last night: light blue cotton button down shirt, no tie, navy blue blazer, khaki trousers and loafers, no socks. The main difference in his appearance, though, was that last night there hadn't been a red, angry-looking welt around his neck.

"Yes, I know him."

Twenty-Three

It was after one o'clock when the last of the crime-scene techs left, and the police allowed us back into the building. The coroner, thank God, had removed Andres' body after a couple of hours. It was close to unbearable having him there, sitting upright on my sofa, as if waiting for me to join him. I'd seen a number of corpses, but the fact that I'd had dinner with this particular one just a few hours before really affected me. I could not get over the fact that he was still wearing the same clothes I had last seen him in.

Although it looked as if Andres had been strangled, the medical examiner would conduct an autopsy as the law required of any unexpected death like his. I had met Dr. Peony Liu, the Miami-Dade County chief medical examiner, on several occasions, and knew her to be very thorough and extremely competent. I felt confident that whatever her findings would be for the cause of death, it would be correct.

More importantly, she'd be able to establish time of death, and whether Andres had been killed in my office or someplace else. Dr. Liu would conduct tests to determine if he had been drugged, and, if so, what drugs were in his system at time of death. As part of her investigation, she would scrape under his fingernails to see if she could recover DNA from his assailant and search the government databases for a match.

Dr. Liu may have been a tiny woman, she made me look like I could play for the WNBA, but she had enormous stature in her field. Students came from all corners of the earth to watch her conduct autopsies, and interpret her findings. Miami, being the violent, crime-ridden place that it was, had a seemingly endless supply of victims—all ages, genders, and races—for Dr, Liu to work on, so the individuals who came here to watch her work were privileged to get an all-around education.

Detective Anderson had told me that microscopic yellow fibers had been found around Andres' neck, so he may have been strangled with some kind of cord. He said they had searched the office, but had not found any item that could have been the murder weapon. Dr. Liu's findings would determine how Andres had been killed. We would just have to wait for her report.

I had telephoned Leo immediately after Andres' body had been discovered to let him know what was going on. Leo, after the initial shock had worn off, had immediately volunteered to rush over to be with me, an offer I had accepted without any hesitation.

My next call had been to Tommy who, naturally enough, had been shocked. He'd been on his way to his office, and, after making sure I was fine, tried to persuade me to go home. I refused, so he had made me promise to check in regularly. Last, I called the house, to let Aida know that I was OK, and that I would be home later. By the time I'd finished making my calls, the place was swarming with all kinds of people: at least a dozen police officers; several crime-scene investigators; a couple of photographers; homicide detectives; individuals from the media, who had heard the news on their radio scanners, and so forth. Detective Anderson was still around.

Leo lived close by the office, in a carriage house in Coconut Grove, so I knew it wouldn't take him long to arrive. I was aware of how sensitive he was, and how he would be affected by the sight of Andres' body, so I waited for him in the street to prepare him for what he would find inside the building.

After the discovery of Andres' body, one of the first things the police had done was to cordon off the driveway that led from the street to the building with yellow crime-scene tape. Any vehicles coming to Solano Investigations had to park on the street. At that point, there were so many vehicles that late arrivals to the scene had been forced to park two blocks away. Television trucks were blocking the street, so access to and from the scene was difficult.

I was familiar with the route that Leo normally took from his house to work, so I wasn't worried about missing him. The moment his car appeared, I waved him down and pointed toward an empty spot on the street that I'd been saving for him. As soon as he finished parking, I got into the passenger seat and explained the situation, this time slower and in more detail than during the earlier phone call.

"But, Lupe, I don't understand." Leo had heard me out without saying anything. "How did whoever did this get into the building?" He wondered, thoroughly bewildered. "We always set the alarm at night as we lock up. I know I did it last night before I left."

"I have no idea, Leo." I shook my head. "I know you always set the alarm; you never, ever forget." I hurried to reassure him that I never, for a moment, thought it might have been his fault. Suddenly, I had a thought. "You know, Leo, during dinner, Andres told me he was starting a new business—a security business—one that supplied alarm systems to commercial and private properties. Maybe he turned off the alarm himself.

Knowing how thorough and hands-on Andres was in his businesses, he might have learned how alarms function, and exactly how to shut one off."

Leo didn't make any comment about what I'd just said. He was following his own train of thought. "I came back from pulling those reports for you. I put them on my desk so you would have them first thing in the morning." Leo was painstakingly trying to reconstruct his movements from the day before. "You had already left for your dinner with Andres."

"Well, the door was closed, but unlocked when I came in this morning," I told him. "Whoever broke in obviously knew how to disconnect the alarm." I had not given up on my theory that it had been Andres who had been responsible for the alarms being turned off.

"Do you think it was a pro?" Leo wondered. "Those guys know how to disconnect alarms. Ours is a good one—serves our purpose—but if a professional wants to get in, alarms won't stop him."

"We really don't have much of value for the junkies to pawn—I mean, they don't normally take computers and printers and fax machines," I pointed out. There was no point in speculating as to who had turned off the alarm. I thought it had been Andres, and Leo thought it had been some pros. At that point, we were both guessing. Still, why would Andres have turned off the alarm so he could get into the office, and then be killed there? Clearly, then, he hadn't been alone. Or had he broken in by himself, and someone followed him into the office and surprised him?

"Oh, God! Lupe!" Leo turned to me with a stricken look. "The fact that Andres was killed—does that mean we're in danger?"

The thought had occurred to me but I had not wanted to bring it up—at least not until I'd had time to give it more thought. "I hope not." I reached over and patted Leo's arm. "Come on, we'd better go inside." I looked at him. "You sure you're OK? The place is a mess, I'm warning you. There's a hell of a lot to clean up."

"Wait, Lupe—one more question." Leo took a deep breath. "Did whoever broke in take anything?"

"I couldn't tell, I really didn't have time to look around, but from what I could see, all the equipment was still there. But they did a job on our files—papers everywhere, drawers opened, really chaotic," I answered candidly. I wanted to give Leo as realistic a picture of what to expect, but didn't want to scare him so much that he would drive off. I was walking a fine line with Leo, and we both knew it.

"OK, well, let's go." Leo opened the door, and stepped out of the car. We walked the two blocks to the driveway in silence.

In spite of preparing Leo, I must not have done a good job because I thought he was going to pass out when he saw the mess in the reception area—the only room he'd entered, and then, only a foot or so inside the room. Because Andres' body was still in my office, and the crime-scene techs were not yet finished processing the room, no one was permitted further. In fact, after I'd identified Andres' body, the police had not allowed me back in, either.

It may have seemed silly to do so with Andres San Pedro's body still on my sofa, but I worried about the parrots in the avocado tree and the effect that the ruckus going on inside the room was having on them. They could see into my office just as easily as I could look out the large bay window and observe them.

Apart from the bad weather that accompanied the occasional hurricane, the parrots were not used to commotion. They were largely undisturbed as they went about their business, so I hoped that all the excitement in my office would not adversely affect them. Of course, it did occur to me that my lovely, feathered friends had witnessed what had happened in my office, but they could not talk, so obviously, I could not interview them.

Detective Anderson had been standing in the entrance to the building when I'd entered with Leo, and, although he had not said a word, I sensed that he wanted to speak with me. However, instead of stopping Leo and me from going inside to look over the reception area, he had let us take our time to inspect the premises, that was, what we could see from the doorway.

The scene inside the building was an even worse disaster than I remembered. The crime-scene techs were only doing their job, but still, they had trashed the place. Cleaning up was going to be a bitch. At that point, I hadn't even begun to consider what had been taken. I couldn't stop thinking about poor Andres and speculate as to who had done this horrible thing to him.

Leo was so shaken by what he had seen inside that Detective Anderson led him outside, to sit in one of the two chairs there. After making sure he was OK, the detective had handed him a bottle of water, and waited until he'd drunk some before moving away. Leo gulped from the bottle as if he had been stranded in the desert—thankfully he soon began to look a bit better.

Detective Anderson waited until Leo had calmed down before taking my arm gently and leading me outside, away from the building. I would have rather stayed with Leo, as he really did not look very well, but there was not much more that we could do for him at that point. Leo had always been fond of Andres, so I knew his death had been quite a blow, and not just because his body had been found in my office. I knew how Leo's mind worked: at the back of it was the fact that with Andres' death, we had also lost a good, regular, cash-paying client.

Arm in arm, Detective Anderson and I walked until we

reached the frangipani tree, under which his car was parked. Remembering what Osvaldo said about the sap, I briefly debated advising him to move his car, but decided against it: the man clearly had more important things on his mind than a few stains on the paint—like the dead body inside, for starters.

We reached Detective Anderson's dark blue, government-issue, four-door sedan, and both of us instinctively leaned up against it. Anyone observing us might have gotten the impression that we would fall down if it hadn't been there. By then, it was close to ten o'clock, and the oppressive heat was almost intolerable. However, neither of us made a move to change our location and get out of the heat; doing so would have simply required too much effort.

"Lupe, look, I know you're upset, but can we discuss what's happened for a few minutes?" Detective Anderson was speaking in a low tone of voice. I nodded. He took a deep breath. "I'll make this as quick as I can, but I have to get a statement from you."

"It's OK. I figured you would have to." I smiled. Then, without warning, a wave of exhaustion came over me, and I shuddered. The sleepless night, the stress of that morning, and the fact that I had not yet eaten had caught up with me. Right then, all I wanted to do was to go home, get into bed, pull the covers over my head and sleep for the next twenty-four hours.

"Good, I'll try to be as quick as possible," Detective Anderson said. He flipped his notebook open. "Now, let's start at the beginning." I nodded again. I had already told him that I had no idea why Andres was in my office, how he'd gotten there, or who had killed him, so at least we didn't have to go through that again. "Back there, you identified the victim as Andres San Pedro. How you know him?"

"Andres was a client of mine. I've known him for years. I met him when I worked the first of his divorces," I replied.

"The first of his divorces?" Detective Anderson asked.

"Yes," I answered. "There were five in all."

Detective Anderson scribbled on his pad. "You have the names of his ex-wives, right?" I nodded. "Were the divorces friendly? I mean, as friendly as divorces can be?"

"Yes. Andres was a gentleman. They were all treated very well by him; he was a very generous man." There was no point in trying to hide anything from Detective Anderson—all divorces in Florida were a matter of public record. "If you're going to ask me next if I think any of his ex-wives were responsible for killing him, in my opinion, no, they aren't." Even though few women would have had the strength to strangle a man, especially one as big and heavy as Andres, I had known where Detective Anderson had been going with his line of questioning. Exactly where I would have if I were working the case.

Detective Anderson just smiled. "And were you working for him now?"

"No, his last divorce was two years ago, and he hasn't remarried. We've stayed friendly. As I told you earlier, I had dinner with him tonight, last night, actually," I corrected myself. "We had dinner at Christy's. We met there and we each drove our own cars," I said, then added, "Everything was normal; he didn't seem upset or worried. Mainly, we just caught up on what was happening in each others' lives. It was an early night."

I was anticipating Detective Anderson's questions, even answering them before he'd had a chance to ask them, but I couldn't help myself. I was very familiar with investigative techniques, so it seemed natural to do so. So far, Detective Anderson did not seem to mind, besides, it was my way of controlling the interview, steering it as much as I could in the direction I wanted it to go. Or not go.

The reality was that, as a private eye who was working on behalf of an attorney, all of my work on the Meadows case was confidential, considered attorney/client privilege, so legally I didn't have to divulge any aspect of the case to Detective Anderson. Still, I felt that I had a moral responsibility to help him find out who killed Andres, so I was willing to answer his questions, as long as I didn't reveal confidential information about Madeline's case in the process.

Even so, I really didn't feel the need to volunteer to Detective Anderson that Andres had been somehow involved with Madeline. I wasn't technically withholding information because I did not know for sure that Andres and Madeline were boyfriend and girlfriend, or client and call girl, or anything at all. Honestly, I didn't have any hard proof that they even knew each other. My information had come from the twins, and only the twins, and we all knew what fine, upstanding citizens they were!

Besides, Madeline was in enough trouble as it was. If Detective Anderson found out that she knew Andres—the fourth murder victim who could be linked to her—well, she'd be back in jail, and then there would be nothing that either Tommy or Buster, the bail bondsman, could do for her. I resisted the urge to ask Detective Anderson what he meant about 'digging' into Madeline's past just then; keeping Madeline's name as far away from Andres' murder was my main goal.

"OK." Detective Anderson was busy writing in his notebook. "Where did you go after you left Mr. San Pedro?"

I waited for a moment before answering. Detective Anderson and I were no longer involved, but that didn't mean it wouldn't hurt him to learn that I'd spent the night at Tommy's, especially in view of the fact that we'd had wild and crazy sex in my office just a couple of days ago. This was a murder investigation, and a man I knew had appeared dead in my office, so I wasn't about to lie about my whereabouts to spare Detective Anderson's feelings. As it was, the victim had been found sitting on the very same sofa that we'd had sex on just a few days before, a detail that I was sure had not escaped him. It certainly had not been lost on me, either.

I took a deep breath and began to speak. "I went directly to Tommy MacDonald's apartment and I stayed there all night I came to the office this morning, at 7:30, which was when I discovered the break-in and Andres San Pedro's body." I felt like a cheap whore.

Detective Anderson just kept writing. "And you have no idea why the victim was in your office, how he got there, who could have done this to him, or why?" He looked at me intently, as if he was daring me to tell him a lie. "Have you been working on a case that might be connected in some way to Mr. San Pedro's murder?"

"No, none that I can think of." I shook my head, and prayed he would not bring up Madeline's name. If he did, I wouldn't be able to lie to him. That would be obstruction of justice, a very serious crime. "I wish I did have some answers, but, honestly, Maxwell, I don't know why, or how, Andres ended up dead on my sofa." My voice had started to crack.

"I guess for right now, we're going to have to wait until Dr. Liu finishes with the body, then, hopefully, we'll get some answers. I have to tell you, I'm especially interested in those yellow fibers around his neck. I've already called Dr. Liu and told her to put a rush on the autopsy, that time is critical. Andres San Pedro is a priority." Detective Anderson closed his notebook and placed it back in his pocket. "Lupe, I don't want to frighten you, but you may be in danger. I'm sure that's occurred to you, so I'm not telling you something you haven't already thought of."

"I know," I replied. "But I don't know from whom."

"Well, the minute the scene is released, I want you look over everything and tell me if anything's missing and what you think whoever did this was looking for." Detective Anderson smiled and patted my shoulder. "You know the drill. Sorry if I'm repeating it to you but I have to. It's procedure."

"I promise I'll call you with any information." I began walking up the driveway toward the office. "I'd better go see how Leo is doing."

"He was pretty shook up," Detective Anderson agreed. "Look, I know you're not going to like this, but I'm going to post an officer outside your building for your safety. Just in case."

"Really, Maxwell, I appreciate it, but that's not necessary," I protested. The last thing I needed was to have a police officer monitoring my comings and goings. "Leo and I will be fine, really, we will."

"I'm sure, but better safe than sorry," Detective Anderson insisted. He looked around and saw that most of the people who had been swarming the property had either left, or were in the process of leaving. "In a few more minutes, everyone will be gone, and you can start cleaning up."

"We have a hell of a job ahead of us." The first thing I planned to do, after checking on my beloved parrots, was to get rid of the sofa in my office. There was no way I could keep it knowing that Andres had been on it for hours, and had possibly been killed there.

I walked to where Leo was still sitting and plopped myself down in the chair next to his. We stayed there for half an hour, not speaking, just watching the officers collect their gear and pack up. After the last person had left, I turned to Leo. "Detective Anderson feels better if there's a police officer watching the place for a few days."

"That's probably a good idea," Leo answered, looking relieved. "Let's go inside and check the place out."

I had just stood up to go inside when my phone rang. I didn't want to speak to anyone just then. I had let the other calls go to voicemail, but, this time, it was Sweet Suzanne, so I answered.

"Hi, Suzanne, what's up?" I asked.

"Remember how you asked me to dig a little deeper into Ms. Meadows? Well, I did." Suzanne sounded like the cat that had swallowed the canary.

I began to feel excited. "And, so, what did you find out?"

"At Versailles, when we had lunch, you told me that Dr. Steinberg had been shot, that Ms. Meadows was a patient of his, and I had told you my girls went there. Remember?" Suzanne was beside herself with excitement.

"I remember," I answered. "Suzanne, you're killing me. Please, just tell me what you found out."

"I know it's not really ethical, but his receptionist, Magda, has been on my payroll for years, so I asked her about Madeline Meadows. As a personal favor," Suzanne explained. "It's not that I don't trust my girls, but I want an official report as to their checkups. In my business, I need to know what's going on. I can't have one of my girls giving a client crabs or an STD or God forbid, getting pregnant. It's bad for business, bad for my reputation."

I should have guessed that Suzanne would check up on her girls. A madam did not stay at the top of her profession as long as Suzanne had done by taking other people's word for what was going on. "'Trust but verify,' as President Reagan said about the Soviets and their nuclear weapons," I commented. "So, what did you find out? What did Magda tell you?"

"Oh, Lupe, she told me a lot. And, you're going to love this!" Suzanne exclaimed.

And I did. I certainly did.

<h1 style="text-align:center">*Twenty-Four*</h1>

I watched Leo as he went inside the building to assess the damage. There was a lot of cleaning up to do, but I wanted to stay outside a bit longer and think about what Suzanne had just told me. I was very fortunate to have a wonderful, loyal friend like her who had great contacts; on some occasions, even better than mine.

Suzanne hadn't been lying when she'd said that she'd learned a lot about what went on in Dr. Steinberg's office from Magda. But the more interesting information had been what the receptionist had not told her.

Magda had revealed to Suzanne that, from what she knew, Dr. Steinberg did not keep a file on Madeline—at least, if he did, it was not kept in the drawers along with those of his other patients. Apparently, when Madeline came in for her checkups, he didn't order the same kind of tests as he would for his other patients. Perhaps, most telling, though, was that when Dr. Steinberg examined Madeline, he wouldn't insist that there be a nurse present, as was office policy. According to Magda, Dr. Steinberg definitely treated Madeline differently than his other patients.

Magda was not able to give Suzanne much more information about Dr. Steinberg's relationship with Madeline because he would not let any of the nurses, clerks, secretaries or other staff members interact with her when she came in for her checkups, every Thursday at eleven o'clock. She always arrived punctually at the Coral Gables office, and, once there, she would be immediately ushered to one of the examining rooms. Dr. Steinberg's other patients were always directed to the bathroom first, where they would give a urine sample, something that, as far as Magda could tell, Madeline had never done. Magda reported that Madeline's special treatment was quite strange, but it had been going on for so long that everyone who worked in Dr. Steinberg's office was used to it and accepted it.

As I listened to Suzanne, I recalled my interview with Madeline at her apartment after she'd been released from jail. I remembered she had said how Dr. Steinberg would examine her, checking her out while on the table, her legs up in stirrups. If Dr. Steinberg conducted an examination that way, wouldn't he want a nurse in the room to protect himself from accusations of sexual misconduct? What Magda said, and what Madeline had told me, were at odds with each other. Who was lying, and why?

An idea as to what had been going on with Dr. Steinberg and Madeline began to formulate in my mind, but, at that point, all I had was a suspicion, and nothing else. I would have to wait until I had more definitive information to act on it. Besides, my idea was so improbable that I sure as hell wasn't going to go out on a limb unless I had proof to back up my suspicions.

I was standing close enough to the building to hear Leo banging around inside as he went about straightening up the place. Leo's flurry of activity made me feel guilty that I wasn't helping him, so I went back inside.

"So, Leo, anything missing?" I saw my cousin kneeling on the floor, holding a pile of papers in his right hand.

"It's weird, Lupe, but, no, not that I can tell." Leo stood and pointed out the different items in the reception area. "The computers are still here, the printers, the fax machine. I just finished checking out the gym, and everything is still there, too: the plasma television, the equipment, the heavy bag and weights, all there. From what I can tell, they're all there. Nothing is missing in the kitchen, either: the bottles of wine and champagne, the chocolates. Everything's accounted for."

Leo looked at me with a puzzled expression. "What kind of break-in was this, Lupe? They didn't take anything, but they left us a mess and a dead body. What the fuck?" He shook his head at the wonder of it all. "I swear, only in Miami, only in Miami, does this kind of burglary happen! No wonder we have the kind of reputation we do—the nutcase capital of the world!"

I left Leo muttering to himself as he went back to cleaning and I headed to my office. Leo was correct: what kind of crazy break-in was this? Usually, when people broke into and entered a property, they were interested in taking stuff out, not leaving stuff behind. Like, in this case, Andres' body.

My office was such a mess that it took me the better part of an hour just to clear a path from the door to my desk. I tried to concentrate on what I was doing, but my eyes kept straying back to the sofa where Andres' body had been found. Although I'd seen him with my own eyes, I still could not believe that just a few hours ago, he'd been sitting there, as he had on so many other occasions. Only, this last time, he'd been dead.

I knew I was being ridiculous, but the truth was that I felt responsible for what had happened to Andres. After all, he'd been my friend and client; I'd had dinner with him a few hours before; and he'd been found dead in my office.

Every few minutes I would take a break from picking up the papers and other items scattered on the floor, and would walk over to the bay window to check on the parrots. From what I could tell, they were none the worse for having witnessed what had happened in the office. It would have been terrible if they had been traumatized by what they had seen take place before their beady little eyes. I was pleased to see that they were busy building yet another structure. I couldn't quite identify what it was going to be, but from the foundations they were laying, I could tell that it would be quite impressive.

I went about restoring order to my office, checking around to see what might be missing, but, thankfully, as far as I could tell, nothing had been taken. All of my office equipment—the computer, printer and fax machine—were still there, just as they had been in the reception area. I had never kept anything of value in the office so, really, there wasn't much to take. There was one place I hadn't checked yet, but, as I really didn't want to know whether or not the murderer had taken anything from there, I had left that for last.

Working diligently, I had made a significant dent in picking up the mess, but I still had a long way to go. I couldn't put off doing what I should have done first, so I walked over to the sofa and pushed it against the wall, across from the bay window. I held my breath, and stepped on it, standing as far away as possible from where Andres had been found. I balanced myself as carefully as I could, took down the painting of the Cuban landscape that hung on the wall, and placed it on the floor, against the sofa. To my relief, I saw that the wall safe appeared undisturbed.

I twirled the knob in the center of the safe this way and that, whispering the combination until I heard the familiar click that preceded the opening of the lock. Still holding my breath, I reached inside the small area with my right hand, dreading what I would find, or, not find. I could have wept with relief when my hand touched the barrel of the Beretta I kept in the office, safely nestled inside the black Kate Spade bag.

Before removing the gun, I steadied myself on the sofa; the last thing I needed was for the Beretta to discharge while I was standing on the same cushion where Andres had been found. The safety was on, so it was unlikely I could have shot myself. Still, given my history, I couldn't be too careful.

I slowly and carefully brought the Beretta up to my nose to smell it to see if it had been fired recently. From my preliminary examination of it, it didn't seem as if whoever had broken into the office had touched the gun, but I still needed to convince myself of that. I inhaled deeply, but thankfully, I could not smell any cordite. The Beretta was in exactly the same condition that it had been in the last time I had taken it to the range, the Sunday before I'd begun working the Meadows case.

I gave the gun one more once-over before returning it to the safe where it would remain, hopefully untouched by hands other than mine. Then, I locked the safe and re-hung the painting over the opening. After doing that, I pulled the sofa away from the wall, and pushed it back to where it had been, making a mental note to call someone from St. Anthony De Padua to come and get it. I'd be sorry to see it go. It was a good sofa, a designer piece that I'd bought it years ago at a floor sample sale from one of the stores in the Design District, but I just couldn't keep it. I would always picture Andres sitting on it. I was sure that the good folks at St. Anthony would put it to good use.

I sat down at my desk, picked up the phone, and pressed the first number on my speed dial. "Tommy?"

"Hi, Lupe," Tommy answered on the first ring, as if he'd been expecting my call. "How're you holding up?"

"I'm OK, I guess," I replied. "Everyone just left. Leo and I are picking up the mess."

"Do you want me to come over? The trial just broke for lunch. I can call the judge's office and tell his secretary that I had an emergency, maybe even try to get the trial continued until tomorrow morning. It's not a big deal, really. I'm sure the other side wouldn't be upset. We're not on a full schedule, and the judge is starting his calendar after lunch by hearing motions for other cases, so, at most, we'd be there for a couple of hours," Tommy said. "Really, Lupe, it's not a problem, just let me know, but I'd have to call the judge now so the jurors can be dismissed. It wouldn't be fair to keep them hanging around if trial's not going to continue."

I considered Tommy's offer, but tempting as it was to ask him to come over, I couldn't accept it; it wouldn't be right to interrupt his trial just because I was spooked. I was a seasoned private investigator after all, so finding a body shouldn't have been enough to send me running for Tommy's protection.

"Tommy, thank you very much, but I think I'm OK, just shaken up, that's all," I replied. "But could we meet later on, maybe? I'd like to discuss the case with you."

"Of course," Tommy quickly assured me. "Let me know when and where, and I'll be there. But before I hang up, promise me that you'll call if you change your mind and want me to meet you earlier."

"I promise," I answered. "And, again, thank you for the offer. Good luck with the trial, and I'll see you tonight."

I wanted to look over the Meadows file again, so I reached down for the desk drawer where I kept the folders of active cases. I opened the drawer and was shocked to find it was empty. The Meadows file was missing! Thinking that maybe I'd misplaced it in one of the other drawers, I searched the other five, but the file was definitely gone.

"Leo!" I called out. "Leo, come here, please."

It took Leo less than five seconds to arrive. "Lupe! Lupe, are you OK?" He asked breathlessly, looking around the room. "What's wrong? Are you all right?"

"The file! My personal copy of the Meadows file! You know, the one with my notes and observations. Did you take it?" I asked him.

Leo shook his head. "No, I didn't take it. I just have the office file. Isn't it in the drawer where you always keep the files of cases you're working on?"

"Look." I showed him the empty drawer. "It's gone."

Leo and I looked at each other in alarm as the significance of the missing file hit us at the same moment.

"It's no wonder that whoever broke in didn't take any of the equipment," I pointed out. "They were after the Meadows file. That's what they wanted."

"I think you're right, Lupe, that's the only thing it could be." Leo nodded. "What was in the file? All your notes, right?"

I tried to reconstruct the contents of the file in my mind. "Yes, that's right. I mean, some of the information on the case is still on file on my computer, but you know my system, Leo. Ever since my computer crashed two years ago and I lost most of the information I had stored there, I print out all my reports and notes; that way, I'll always have a hard copy. Just in case."

"So, once they read what's in the file, whoever has it will know the work you've done on the case," Leo mused.

"Yes," I answered miserably. "Everything. I'd just updated all the information yesterday, before leaving to meet Andres for dinner." I began to cry.

All of a sudden, it seemed as if the world was collapsing around me. Had I come back to work too soon? Had I lost my edge as a private eye? The last time I could recall breaking down like this had been when my mother had died. This, of course, was nowhere near as serious, but, for some reason, I felt as if I was on the verge of a breakdown. Oh God! Was I in such a fragile state that a missing file could cause me to collapse like that? Were my days as a private eye coming to an end? How the fuck was I going to be able to stand up to that bitch Aurora Santangelo if I began acting like a girl? Maybe getting shot had affected me more than I had previously thought. It hadn't been all physical, that was for sure.

I sat at my desk and sobbed until I had nothing left in me. Then, just as suddenly as they had started, the waterworks stopped. I wiped the last of my tears with a bunch of Kleenex, blew my nose, and with that, the breakdown was officially over. I was ready to get back to work.

Leo, who had never before seen me cry like that at the office, hurried over to where I was sitting to console me, but, as the floor of the office was still a mess, it took him a while to get to me. "Lupe, it's not your fault that the file is gone. We've never had a break-in before; we have a good alarm system, we lock up, we're careful, we do everything right." He was so shaken by seeing me break down that he was stammering and stuttering. Poor Leo. For his sake, and mine, of course, I had to get a grip on myself.

"I know, but, still, Leo, I fucked up." I confessed. "I know that I have most of the information that was in the file saved on Microsoft Word, but some of the other things, like the notes and observations I jotted down on the margins of the reports, stuff like that, those I can't reconstruct," I told him in a matter-of-fact tone. "And those are some of the most important parts of any file; the notes I write to myself." I blew my nose for the last time. "You know, those notes and observations are what I follow during the course of an investigation. They tell me where I've been on the case, what I think, and, of course, where I want to go." Now, I was all business.

Leo looked thoughtful. "Lupe, one thing. If whoever broke in was looking for your personal copy of the Meadows file and found it in the desk drawer, why trash the place? After all, it took a while to make this mess, and every minute they spent here was risky." Leo gestured to the stuff that littered the floor of my office.

"I don't know; maybe they were looking for something other than the file, and, remember, we still don't know why Andres was killed, and why his body was here," I reminded Leo. "At least now we have proof that they're connected: Andres' death and the Meadows case." I pointed out.

"Well, I'd better get back to cleaning up. There's a shit load of crap out there still for me to pick up." Leo started to walk out of my office, but, before leaving, he turned to me. "Well, this might not be the right thing to say right now, but I was overdue in cleaning out some of the stuff we had piled up. I'm just sorry that it came at the price of Andres San Pedro's life."

"You're right, Leo, it's not right thinking like that, but I know what you mean about having to clear out the place." I looked around my office floor that was covered wall to wall with sheets of paper. "I should have deep-sixed a lot of this stuff years ago."

Less than a minute later, Leo poked his head into my office. "Hey, Lupe, are you going to tell Detective Anderson about the file? After all, something was stolen from here, even if it didn't have any monetary value."

"It's funny you should ask, Leo. I was just wondering about that," I answered. "Don't know yet. I have to think about it."

"Please let me know what you decide, so I'll be on the same page in case I'm asked any questions about that," Leo said. "Oh, Lupe, by the way, I've already started downloading the information from my computer about the Meadows case. I'll bring the papers in as soon as I'm done."

"Thanks, cousin, you're the bomb," I called out to him.

I turned my attention back to my computer and started printing out information so I could start my own new Meadows file. Less than an hour later, I'd downloaded everything and was ready to incorporate it with the pages that Leo had brought in a few minutes before.

Although the file that Leo had reconstructed wasn't as complete as I would have hoped, it was missing my all-important handwritten notes and observations, it was still quite thick. Thankfully, I hadn't yet found out what Suzanne had told me about Magda—otherwise that juicy bit of information would have been in the file as well. If it were to get around that Dr. Steinberg's receptionist had been reporting on his patients, who knows what the repercussions might be.

A few hours later, after I'd done as much administrative work as I was going to do for the day, I turned my attention to my investigative duties. I picked up the telephone and called Nestor.

"Hey, Lupe." Nestor sounded sleepy, no surprise there, the poor man had been on surveillance for God knows how many hours. "What's up?"

"Shit, Nestor, lots going on here, none good," I replied then proceeded to tell him the horrible fate that had befallen Andres San Pedro. I also told him about the missing file.

Nestor digested my information. "Look Lupe, apart from that hour and thirty minutes last night from one o'clock to two-thirty that your client was at the dog run with her mutts, she hasn't left the building. I can vouch for that as I haven't left my post."

"Well, if you can assure me of that, then I know that's the case." I told Nestor. "One thing that I'm wondering, though, is there any way that she could sneak out of the dog park without your seeing her? Any blind spots at all in the dog park setup?"

"Give me a second, Lupe," Nestor said. I could almost see him picking up the binoculars he kept on the seat next to him, and looking across the street at the dog park. "Well, I can see pretty much the entire park—except for a couple of dark areas—but at night the place is quite lit up."

A feeling of dread came over me. "Nestor, is there any way, any way at all, that the client could have snuck out during the ninety minutes she was in the dog park, without you spotting her?"

Nestor was quiet for a moment. "Let me think back, Lupe. Look, I can swear the dogs were there the whole time; they're off leash while they're in the park. It's an enclosed area, so they can't wander off. I remember looking at them, thinking what a pair of shitty little dogs they were. They were yapping so loud that I could hear them across the street" Nestor snorted. "If they'd been quiet, I sure as hell would have noticed, so, yes, Lupe, the dogs were there the whole time."

"Nestor, think back, it's important. Could you see the client the whole time? Is it possible that she left the dogs there and snuck out of the dog park unnoticed?" I remembered the twins had said that Madeline was scared of crime on South Beach, so she was reluctant to go out at night alone. Did being at the dog park qualify as being outside, at night, alone?

"Well, now that you ask, Lupe, I suppose that was possible," Nestor conceded reluctantly. "But not probable. If she did leave, then she left the mutts in the dog park alone and she didn't drive out that I know. I checked out every car that came in and out of the building."

"Nestor, look, I'm not pointing any fingers. I'm just asking questions, trying to solve this." I could tell that Nestor was getting increasingly testy, not that I could blame him. He was exhausted, which made it difficult to maintain a thick skin. On

top of that, I was seemingly questioning his professional abilities, something that I had never had done before.

"I know that Lupe. I know it's not personal," Nestor answered
in an unconvincing tone. "You're just doing your job."

"I was thinking, do you want to get someone to replace you
for a few hours?" I was worried about my investigator. I knew
I was treading on thin ice, but, still, I had to ask. "Please don't
take this the wrong way, but you sound exhausted."

"Listen, Lupe, I don't need anyone to replace me." Nestor
sounded indignant. "I know how to do my job. If you want,
you can fire me, that's your right, but don't tell me I need to
sleep."

I should have known that Nestor would instantly take offense
at my suggestion. One of his favorite claims to fame was how,
years before, while working a criminal case, he'd been able to
conduct surveillance for five days without falling asleep. "Nestor,
no, of course I wasn't implying that you weren't doing your job.
You're the best there is. I'm sorry if I gave you that idea, I would
never think that. I'm just worried about you, that's all," I said,
backpedaling as fast as I could. "I'm so sorry," I repeated.

"It's OK, Lupe, no offense taken." Nestor backed off. "I'll call
in if there's anything to report."

"Thanks again, Nestor," I was relieved.

Thank God I'd managed to mollify Nestor; I couldn't afford
to alienate him. Still, I was worried about Madeline having been
out of his line of vision for some of the ninety minutes that
Napoleon and Josephine had been in the dog park. It was something that I would have to keep in mind.

I looked at the clock. It was just after three in the afternoon.
I was exhausted. I only hoped I didn't look as bad as Nestor
sounded tired. I was completely sleep deprived"not only had
I not slept properly at Tommy's the night before, but all the

activity of the day had drained me of energy. I would have given anything to get in my car and drive home, but I quickly dismissed that thought. Going home was still hours away.

I placed my right hand on the telephone, and slowly raised the receiver to my ear. I punched in a number.

"Madeline? Hi, it's Lupe." I spoke as soon as Madeline picked up the phone. "I was wondering if it was convenient for me to come by to see you this afternoon. Say, in about an hour?" I didn't want to give Madeline time to think. "Good. I'll see you in a bit."

I walked over to the bay window to check out the parrots. They were busy putting finishing touches on their structure. As I watched them, it seemed as if every bird participated in the process and had a specific task. Each one knew exactly what he or she was doing. As I picked up my purse to go and see Madeline, it occurred to me that for that one moment, I envied them.

Twenty-Five

"Hey, Leo, can you come in here a second, please?" I called my cousin on the intercom.

Leo appeared in the doorway of my office less than a minute later, and without saying a word, headed straight for one of the client chairs. No sooner had he sat down, that he let out a huge sigh. "Christ, Lupe! What a mess! I've been straightening stuff out non-stop, but I'm still far from finished. And I'm not leaving tonight until it's all done." Leo sighed again. "I just can't face that in the morning. I just can't." He looked at me. "So, what's up? You wanted to see me?"

"Leo, when does the city pick up the recycling?" I asked.

Leo looked at me as if I'd gone crazy, and, maybe I had, but I needed to follow up on a hunch that I couldn't shake. Madeline Meadows was lying to me, and after much thought, I had come up with a way to verify her story.

"Recycling?" Leo repeated. I nodded. "First thing Monday morning; the city picks up at dawn. Do you mind if I ask why you're asking about recycling, Lupe? Is Solano Investigations going green?"

I ignored Leo's question. "Monday morning. Good. Today is Thursday, so that means the bottles that we've used all week are still here, in the recycling bin?" Without waiting to hear Leo's answer, I got up from my chair and sprinted toward the kitchen, where the green plastic bin was kept.

"Lupe, are you OK?" Leo got up from his chair and started after me. "Why don't you go home and rest? It's been a difficult day for you. You need rest."

At that point, I was so busy pulling out the bin from the closet in the kitchen that I barely heard what he was saying. Madeline was lying to me, and I was going to get to the bottom of it; if that meant starting at the very beginning, well, then, so be it. After all, it was her money that I was spending, so it served her right.

"Leo, when Madeline was here on Monday morning, you offered her some water. I remember you gave her a bottle of Perrier from the refrigerator. That bottle should still be here, right?" I knelt down and carefully began to sift through the two dozen or so bottles in the bin. I thanked God that neither Leo nor I drank many bottled drinks during the day. We were strictly Cuban coffee and wine types.

"Yes, it should be." Leo knelt down on the floor next to me and watched as I slowly pulled out the lone bottle of Perrier from the bottom of the bin.

"Aha! Here it is!" I announced triumphantly, holding up the bottle between my thumb and forefinger.

"Lupe, really, are you OK?" Leo looked at me with concern. "I honestly think you should go home."

I knew I looked like a nutcase, sitting on the kitchen floor, holding on to a Perrier bottle with my thumb and forefinger, but I didn't care. "Leo, please call Hernan and ask him to come here ASAP, tell him to bring his kit."

Hernan Martinez was a former FBI fingerprint agent who, after retiring from the bureau, began freelancing as an expert. I had used him on previous occasions, and had always found him to be the consummate professional: serious, dedicated, accurate. Best of all, he was quick. He would come to the office with his fingerprint kit and raise prints from just about any surface, even partial, smudged ones. It was amazing, but in this day of computers and high-tech equipment, Hernan was still able to compare fingerprints by just using a magnifying glass. As a matter of fact, he once told me that was his favorite method of working. The man was truly gifted.

Not only was Hernan a fingerprint expert par excellence, but he also had outstanding connections, and, if necessary, would call on his former colleagues for assistance in running prints through the system. Nestor had originally introduced me to Hernan, something for which I would be eternally grateful. He had proved to be an invaluable resource.

"OK." Leo seemed relieved that I had given him something concrete to do. "I'll call him right away."

"Leo, look, I'm not crazy." I needed to give my cousin some kind of explanation as to what I was doing, and why. "I want Hernan to run Madeline's prints. I don't think our client has been completely honest with us."

Leo looked at me with a thoughtful expression. "So, Lupe, by having Hernan run her prints, I gather that you don't think Madeline Marie Meadows is really Madeline Marie Meadows."

I shrugged. "Well, she wouldn't be the first client to lie to us, would she?" I smiled. "It wouldn't hurt to check out her story; there's just something about her that rings false."

"Yeah, checking her out would be a good idea." Before walking out of the kitchen, Leo stopped and turned to me. "Hey, Lupe, I just remembered, I poured some water into a bowl for the mutts. I think she touched that, too. I think it's still on the floor of the kitchen."

"Excellent. The more samples of her prints Hernan has to lift, the better." I got up from the floor and returned the recycling bin to its proper place. "Remember, Leo, Aurora Santangelo is the prosecutor on the case, so I can't afford to let anything bite me on the ass," I pointed out. I was tempted to tell Leo that Detective Anderson had advised me to look into Madeline's background, and even though I was sure my cousin wouldn't say anything, still, I couldn't betray such a confidence. I also needed him to continue to believe in my abilities.

Soon, I could hear Leo calling Hernan on the phone. I had just sat down at my desk when Leo buzzed me on the intercom. "I just got off the phone with Hernan. He said our timing was perfect. He just finished a huge case, and had just e-mailed the final report to his client. He's on his way and should be here within the hour."

"Thanks Leo." I debated what to do. I had told Madeline I would be at her apartment in an hour. As it was, I was already running late. However, I was very interested in hearing Hernan's report about Madeline's prints, so I decided it would be best to wait and see Madeline once I had it. In my business, along with timing, information is everything.

I dialed Madeline's home number. "Hi, Lupe, what's up?" She asked in a guarded voice.

"Listen, I'm really sorry, but I won't be able to see you this afternoon. Something has come up, an emergency. I apologize for the short notice. I'd like to reschedule for tomorrow morning, say, around eleven o'clock?" I figured that by then Hernan should have had plenty of time to run the prints and give me the results.

"Tomorrow morning? Eleven o'clock?" Madeline repeated. I had a strong sense that she was relieved our meeting had been postponed. "That's OK." Madeline took a breath. "Your emergency—does it have anything to do with my case?"

"No, it's something else. Don't worry," I hurried to reassure her. "So, I'll see you tomorrow morning," I said, hanging up. I purposefully did not mention Andres to her. I didn't want Madeline to know that I was aware of the fact that they knew each other.

I looked around the office and considered how best to spend the next hour while waiting for Hernan to arrive. There were still papers and files strewn around that needed to be picked up, but I decided that wasn't of utmost importance. The Meadows file was more pressing, especially now that Hernan would be on the job. I wanted to be ready for his report.

I picked up the phone again and dialed Nestor. "Nestor, how're you doing?"

"Oh, hi, Lupe," Nestor greeted me. "I'm fine, thanks. Hanging in here."

I was pleased to hear Nestor sounded like his old self. The truth was, he was a pro, and he wouldn't let a little misunderstanding affect his work. Still, I would have liked if he'd been able to confirm that Madeline had not left the dog park the night Andres had been killed.

"Good," I replied. "Anything going on?"

"Nope. The client has not left the building, not even to take the mutts to the dog park," Nestor reported. "I haven't moved from here," he hurried to assure me. "I haven't taken my eyes off the building."

"I'm sure you haven't." I also felt the need to offer my assurances.

"Lupe, you know I'll call and let you know if there's any activity going on," Nestor said.

I wanted Nestor to know what was going on, so I changed the subject. "Listen, Nestor, I think there's something funny going on with the client. Hernan is coming over to lift her prints and run them."

"You're running your own client's prints?" Nestor asked. "Even for you, Lupe, with your weird clients, that's a big step."

"It's the only way I'll find out who she really is. I don't buy her story, Nestor, I just don't. Prints don't lie; I'll get to the bottom of this."

"I'm sure you know best," Nestor said. "Just keep me posted, OK?"

"Sure will," I replied. "I'll call as soon as I know anything."

I was just about to make another call when I heard the front door to the office open, followed by Hernan's voice calling out. "Hey, Leo, how're you doing?"

Although Leo and Hernan weren't exactly friends, they were friendly enough with each other, so I figured they would spend some time catching up before getting down to business. I put those five minutes to good use and called Suzanne.

"Hey, Suzanne, it's me. I need another favor. A big one." I knew Suzanne well enough that I could skip the pleasantries. I didn't feel the least bit rude, she would do the same with me whenever she needed something important.

"Sure, Lupe," Suzanne replied. "What is it?"

"Listen, Magda, the receptionist at Dr. Steinberg's office?" I asked. "Is your relationship with her tight enough that you can ask her to copy part of a patient's file and fax a couple of pages to you?"

Suzanne didn't answer for a while. "I've never asked her to do anything like that. The way it works is that she gives me a verbal report. She answers my questions about a girl, tells me pretty much everything I want to know, but as far as my getting any kind of paperwork from her, no, I've never asked for that." Suzanne took a deep breath. "Her information has always been reliable, so I've never asked her to back it up with any kind of paperwork. I mean, Lupe, if she were to copy a patient's file and send it to me. That would be a serious breach of confidence. She could get fired or worse for doing that."

"OK, I understand." I thought about what Suzanne had just told me. "I won't ask for any copies of records then, but do you think she would answer a couple of questions for me about Madeline Meadows?"

"I really don't know," Suzanne replied. "I guess it would depend on the questions, and, of course, I would have to vouch for you. It would be tricky."

"I'd pay her, of course," I hurried to assure Suzanne that I didn't expect Magda to give out such sensitive information for free. "I'd pay her well." Then, a moment later, I added. "Maybe you could point out the fact that Dr. Steinberg is dead; that might affect the issue of patient confidentiality." I ventured.

Madeline had given Tommy a big retainer, so I wasn't particularly worried about where the money would come from. Besides, she was lying to us, so I felt justified in spending her cash to get to the truth. We were still working on her defense, and, after all, these were the costs associated with doing exactly that. It wasn't my fault she wasn't being truthful.

"I'll call Magda right now and ask her," Suzanne said. "I'll get back to you right after I've spoken with her, OK? I'll play the patient confidentiality card only if I need to. Don't want to mix up too many issues—that might scare her off. Dr. Steinberg had two other partners in his practice—she would probably worry about them, too. It's not that simple, Lupe, to get confidential medical information."

"Thank you, Suzanne—I know you're doing me a huge favor—and that Magda is going out on a limb with tins—but, she wants to find out who Dr. Steinberg's killer is, doesn't she?" I pointed out. "Hint to her that it would really help if she were to agree to do this. Thank you again for doing this. I'm asking a lot, but I wouldn't ask you if I didn't feel it was totally necessary, I promise you."

"I'll get back to you, Lupe, but remember, I'm not promising anything." Suzanne said before hanging up.

It was a long shot that Magda would help me, but it was worth a try. However, I couldn't only count on her for answers. I had to pursue other avenues, as well, to get to the truth. Hernan was waiting for me, so I got up and went out to the reception area.

"Hola, Hernan," I greeted the fingerprint expert. "You're looking well." As I kissed him, I was relieved to see a large black leather case by his feet. Hernan had come prepared.

"You too, Lupe." Hernan smiled at me. Hernan had twice sent me flowers while I'd been at home recuperating after being shot.

Hernan was a gentleman from the old school. Even in the hottest, most miserable days of summer, he was impeccably dressed in a suit and tie. Hernan's classic looks made it impossible to guess his age, but I imagined him to be in his late sixties. He had retired a few years earlier after a long and distinguished career in the FBI, but less than six months later, he had started his own company. He claimed he had gone back to work because Clara, his wife of forty years, had made him, but no one believed him. According to Hernan, Clara said he was driving her crazy puttering around the house, but the truth was that catching bad guys was in his blood.

"Thank you for coming on such short notice, Hernan. I really need your help on a case I'm working." I took him by the arm and led him into the kitchen. I pointed to the green Perrier bottle and the glass bowl that Leo had placed on the kitchen counter earlier, and asked, "Can you lift prints off of those? And, if yes, can you run them for me? I don't know if the individual whose prints I'm interested in are in the system—I'm trying to verify the identity of a client."

Hernan looked at me with an amused expression. "You're trying to see if your client is who he or she says they are?" he chuckled. "You've always had interesting clients, Lupe."

"Too interesting, sometimes," I agreed. "So, can you lift prints from these?" Again, I indicated the items on the counter.

Hernan turned his attention to the Perrier bottle and the bowl. "They're both glass, a good surface for prints." He leaned down and, without touching the items, carefully inspected them. "I see several prints here—I imagine some of them are yours and Leo's, so I'd have to print you both to eliminate those, and then I can concentrate on the others. We can begin by doing that."

"Great," I said, relieved. "Just tell us what to do."

"Let me get my case and I'll begin." Hernan straightened up. "I assume you want me to run the prints for you right away, Lupe?" Hernan smiled in that knowing way of his. "Everything with you is always at top speed. But, I have to say, you pay for that requirement without any complaints."

"Of course, that's the least I can do." I laughed. "You know me too well."

"Well, let's get started, then." Hernan was all business. "He looked over the bottle and the glass bowl. "I think I can lift some good ones off these—hope those aren't yours, that they belong to the client—and some partials, but I'm not promising anything." He looked up at me as if to make sure he was clear in what he was telling me.

"I understand, Hernan. Just do the best you can." I assured him. "We'll just hope for the best."

While we'd been talking, Leo had brought the fingerprint case to the kitchen, so Hernan wasted no time in spreading the items he needed for his work on the table. I was amazed at how much he could fit into that one large briefcase.

"OK, Lupe, you first, then Leo." Hernan took my right hand and quickly and methodically began applying the black ink on the bottoms of my fingers. After doing that, he rolled my fingers one by one on a sheet of white paper. I was amazed at how clear my prints came out. The whole process took less than a minute. He did the same with Leo.

"OK." Hernan looked up at me. "Now I'm ready to get to work. I'll start with the bottle."

Leo and I watched as Hernan placed a box filled with small, square, thin plastic sheets on the middle of the counter. He opened it and took a single sheet out from the top. After carefully inspecting the bottle, he placed the sheet over the glass and then lightly rubbed the plastic square until he had made a clear imprint of a fingerprint. After that, he carefully put the sheet into a paper envelope, labeled it and returned it to the box. He repeated this process perhaps a dozen or so times. After finishing with the bottle, Hernan began working on the glass bowl that Leo had reported that Napoleon and Josephine had drunk from. Those, unfortunately, had not come out that clearly.

"I'm going to run these right away; I'll start with them as soon as I get to the lab," Hernan announced as he packed his case. "If all goes according to plan, I should have something for you in a couple of hours. I'm very aware that this is a rush job."

"Thank you so much, Hernan. You're the best," I said as I walked him through the reception area. "I'll be here, waiting for the results."

I had just closed the outer door to the office when the phone began to ring. Leo picked it up.

"Hey, Suzanne, how's it going? When are you coming by the office to visit?" Leo loved Suzanne.

"Leo, I'll take it in the office," I called out as I hurried by his desk.

"Hi, Suzanne," I greeted my friend. "I hope you have good new for me."

"Good and bad," Suzanne replied. "The good is that Magda will answer some of your questions; the bad is that she won't speak with you directly. She'll only do it through me." Then, she added, "And, I have to warn you, getting that information is going to cost you plenty of bucks; doing something like this is outside my normal arrangement with her."

I thought about what Suzanne had just said. The expense, that I was expecting—getting sensitive information was never cheap. But how it would work? Using Suzanne as an intermediary, that aspect of the transaction I hadn't. "Through you?" I repeated. "So, I tell you the questions, you tell them to her, she answers them, and you report what she said back to me?"

"That's right," Suzanne chuckled. "Not exactly the most efficient method, but those are Magda's rules, and, right now, she's setting the rules. I tried to convince her to speak directly with you, but it was a 'no go.' She feels as if she's not breaking such a trust by going through me. She figures she already has a relationship with me, so it's just kind of the same thing. She's not into breaking new ground."

I had to admit, I could follow Magda's logic. "Is that OK with you? I mean, I don't want to put you in a tricky position."

"Fuck, Lupe!" Suzanne answered. "How long have we known each other? Tricky situation! You should hear yourself! You sound like a total nerd."

"Sorry. For a moment, I forgot who I was speaking with." I burst out laughing. "So, you have a paper and pencil handy to write these questions? I only really have a couple, but, I have to warn you, they're doozies."

"I'm ready," Suzanne announced. "Shoot!"

I took a deep breath. "OK. Here goes." I began speaking slowly, to make sure there were no misunderstandings.

If Suzanne was surprised at what I wanted to know, she didn't let on. She just wrote down what I said. "I'll call you back as soon as I have the information."

"Thank you so much. I owe you big time for this," I said. "I'll be here at the office."

Now, it was simply a matter of waiting for the reports from Hernan and Suzanne. I'd never had much patience, so that wouldn't be easy. I looked out the window and saw that the parrots were busy with their construction. I continued straightening out the office, and, as I worked, I was comforted by the fact that at least I would be in good company while I waited for answers.

Twenty-Six

"Hey, Lupe, I'm going home now. I'm so tired I don't even know my own name." Leo stuck his head in the doorway to my office. "How much longer are you going to stay here? It's late; almost seven o'clock." He yawned as if to make his point.

"I'm not sure, hopefully not much longer. I'm tired too, and I still have to get Papi a birthday present for tomorrow before I can go home and relax," I answered. "Don't worry about me, Leo. Remember, Detective Anderson still has one of his officers stationed outside. He'll be there until we lock up for the night."

"I know, he's a nice guy. I went out to speak with him an hour ago; he's young, just graduated from the police academy," Leo chuckled. "I think this is his first assignment."

"I hope he doesn't have to shoot anyone! It would be a bad start to his career," I commented.

"God, Lupe! Don't talk that way—it's not funny, especially after what happened here today." Leo clutched his heart in mock alarm. "So, what are you going to buy Papi for his birthday?"

"I don't know yet, I feel terrible, I haven't seen anyone in my family for a week. For some reason, every single person seems to be so very busy, especially me, since the Meadows case began.

I miss getting together with everyone, so tomorrow will be nice. I'm looking forward to it." I stood up and stretched. I'd been sitting for so long that my entire body was stiff. "I'm exhausted, Leo. If I don't hear back from Hernan and Suzanne by eight o'clock, I'm going home."

"They can call you on your cell, you know, Lupe. Text you, too. It's not as if calling the office is the only way they can reach you," Leo pointed out quite logically. Clearly, my cell phone use, or, rather, lack of it, was still a sore point. "Why don't we leave together in a few minutes? I'll wait for you." Leo volunteered.

Leo was right. Both Suzanne and Hernan had my cell phone number, so if they couldn't reach me at the office, they would try me there. Still, I had told them I would be here, and as much as I was tempted to leave with Leo, I felt obliged to be here; at least until eight o'clock.

I had just finished telling Leo that I would be staying a bit longer when the phone rang. I looked at the called ID and saw that it was Suzanne, so I quickly picked up the receiver.

"Hey, Lupe, I have a report from Magda. Your hunch was correct. Ms. Madeline Meadows isn't who she says she is. Well, at least not physically, that is," Suzanne laughed. "I knew there was something weird about that woman, and it wasn't just the virginity crap. I never bought that story. It's good to know I haven't lost my bullshit meter."

"So, talk to me. Don't keep me in suspense, Suzanne, come on," I begged. "Tell me everything that Magda reported, and, please, don't leave anything out. I want to savor the moment."

Suzanne confirmed what I'd suspected about Ms. Meadows. I was quite gratified to learn that my instincts were as sharp as ever; being shot may have affected me physically, but, thank God, it had not affected my investigative skills. I waited until Suzanne had finished her story before asking, "Did Magda suspect anything was wrong? I mean, did she have any inkling as to the real reason for all the secrecy?"

"Well, Magda did tell me she thought there was something puzzling in the special treatment that Ms. Meadows received, but she said that she and the others who worked in the office figured that it was because she wasn't the normal kind of patient—call girls who came in with STD's, or for pregnancy tests and conditions like that. According to Magda, they all knew about the arrangement that Dr. Steinberg had with Ms. Meadows about verifying her virginity situation," Suzanne reported.

"But, because she'd never read the file, until now, of course, she didn't know the real reason Dr. Steinberg treated her the way he did."

"Well, now that Magda has read the Meadows file, we can see why the doctor insisted on all the secrecy, can't we?" I asked. "It's clear that there was a lot riding on the contents of it staying secret and it wasn't just about the money. Reputations are at stake, too; important people's reputations and careers," I pointed out. "Thank you so much, Suzanne. You've helped me a great deal."

"Anytime, Lupe, anytime. You know I'm always happy to be of help to you. But this time, the results of doing so have been especially sweet and satisfying," Suzanne declared. "Please keep me posted on any developments in the case. As you can imagine, I'm very interested. I'm happy to see the bitch exposed. As for me right now, I'm going to open a bottle of Dom Perignon and pour myself a glass or two. You may think it's shallow of me to do this, but I'm off to celebrate Ms. Meadows' downfall."

"No, Suzanne, I don't think it's at all shallow of you at all. You don't have a single shallow bone in your body. It's natural that you would want to celebrate the exposing of someone who has been living a lie and profiting handsomely by the deception," I hurried to assure her. "Again, thank you so much for your help. You've been invaluable."

"Oh, Lupe, before we hang up, don't forget, you have to give me some cash to pay Magda for the information. She's a single mom with two kids in college—the boy is at the University of Florida, and the girl is at Florida State. The money will go towards the kids' tuition," Suzanne reminded me. "I'm going to be seeing her tomorrow so, if you want, I can front her the three thousand she wanted. You can pay me back when you see me."

"That would be great. Thanks again, Suzanne." I knew that Suzanne kept a safe with a significant amount of cash in her closet, so it wasn't as if she was going to have to hit ATMs all over Miami to pay Magda. Still, she had done me a huge favor, so it wasn't right to keep her waiting to be reimbursed. "I'll call you as soon as there are developments on the case, I promise. I'll pay you within a day or two at most, as soon as I get the money from Tommy."

I was quite aware that I was going through the retainer that Madeline had given Tommy at warp speed, but that couldn't be helped.

These expenses were necessary—Magda, Nestor, Hernan, etc.—but at the rate I was spending money, we would soon have to hit her up for another chunk. Besides, I told myself again, a significant amount of the money I was shelling out was as a direct result of her deception, so really, she couldn't complain about the costs.

After hanging up with Suzanne, I reached for the Meadows file that Leo had made to replace the one that had been stolen. I was pleased to see that he'd been able to reconstruct just about all the papers and documents that had been in the original. My notes, of course, were missing, but in light of what I'd just found out from Suzanne, that wasn't really all that terrible. I kept a lot of information in my head, anyway, so I was able to remember quite a bit without needing all the notes.

I opened the file to the section that contained the notes and comments from Tommy's initial interview with Madeline and didn't stop reading until I came to the section that contained the background information. Before he agreed to represent someone, Tommy's normal operating procedure was to know as much as possible about them, so he made his potential clients fill out an extensive questionnaire that asked for all kinds of information both personal and professional.

The form was quite thorough, beginning with background information from the client's childhood to the present. Just then, I was interested in the list of family contacts—names, addresses and telephone numbers—that Madeline had supplied. I looked at the clock. It was seven-thirty in Miami, which meant that it was six-thirty in Dubuque. Hopefully, there would be someone there at the Meadows home.

I decided that I might as well call the parents first. I took a deep breath and dialed their home number. The phone rang a few times before an older man answered.

"Hello. Good evening. Is this the Meadows home?" I spoke in my sweetest voice.

"Yes. Who's this?" The man spoke in a guarded tone.

"I'm trying to reach a Miss Madeline Meadows," I said. "Could I speak with her, please?"

"There's no Madeline Meadows here," the man shouted. "And don't you ever call back!" The man slammed the phone down so hard that my ears began ringing.

It was clear that Madeline had not left her family on good terms. I picked up the phone again, and dialed the next number on the list: Madeline's sister, Rose, the married social worker with no children.

"Hello, good evening," I greeted the woman who answered the telephone. "I am trying to reach a Miss Madeline Meadows. Is Miss Meadows available, please?"

"Why are you calling here?" The woman, who I assumed was Rose, instantly turned suspicious.

"Miss Madeline Meadows wrote this telephone number down as her contact information," I replied. "Does Miss Meadows live there? I was told she lives there. I need to speak with her, please. It's important."

"Your information isn't correct. It's totally wrong. There isn't anyone called Madeline Meadows living here now, and never has," the woman hung up.

Yet again, Madeline had alienated a family member to the point that her own sister denied her existence. Given the negative reaction from her father and sister, I figured that the other members of her family—her two sisters and a brother—would have the same, so, really, there was no point in continuing to go down the list.

When I'd first come up with a working theory as to who had killed the four individuals, Dr. Steinberg, Woodley Robinson, Ricardo Melendez, Andres San Pedro, I had thought that I was crazy. But now that I was actively pursuing that angle and the facts kept backing it up, I wasn't so sure. I was still waiting on Hernan's fingerprint report, but I had a feeling that his findings would corroborate my theory.

I wanted to call Tommy and tell him my suspicions, but I held back. Tommy, as much as he trusted my instincts, would want hard evidence to back up my theory. And frankly, given how out there it was, I didn't blame him. Right now, all I had was a report, and, a secondhand one at that, of confidential information contained in a file that had been read by an assistant in Dr. Steinberg's office and two telephone calls to Madeline's family in Dubuque. And, of course, Detective Anderson's confidential recommendation that I delve deeper, way deeper, into Madeline's background, something that Tommy knew nothing about. Those, plus, lots of guesswork on my part.

But the more I thought about it, the more confidence I had my theory. Really, it was the only one that worked. However, all of that didn't exactly add up to compelling evidence. Hernan's report would be the one thing that would back up my theory. Hernan had told me he would call when he had something to report, but I was so eager to learn what he'd found out that I called him.

"Hernan, hi, it's Lupe," I began. "I hate to bug you but my curiosity is killing me. I know you said you'd call when you had something to report, but waiting is so hard!" I threw myself at his mercy. "Could I have an interim report, please?"

"Ay, Lupe! You need to have patience. I told you I'd call you when my report was ready," Hernan chided me, making it clear he was annoyed at the interruption. "It's not ready, but I can tell you this: I was able to lift some partial prints off the glass bowl, the one Leo gave water to the dogs in that she touched. I was also able to get some clearer partials off the Perrier bottle, but as of right now, the glass bowl offers the best opportunity for good, reliable prints. But, neither are perfect." Hernan warned me.

"I hope some of those belong to the client's." I commented.

"Remember, I still have to separate the prints from Leo's and yours. It's slow, painstaking work," Hernan reminded me. "That'll take a while longer. Then I have to run them. All that takes time, Lupe. I'm going as quickly as I can, but I can't rush it, you know that. I'm sorry."

"I understand, Hernan. I'm sorry I bothered you," I apologized. "I'll just have to wait. Thank you for your help."

"I promise I'll call you as soon as I have something; should be a couple of hours longer. Now I'd better get back to work or it will be even longer before you get your results." He reminded me.

"Thank you, Hernan," I said again, before hanging up.

I looked at the clock on the far wall. Eight o'clock. The time that I had told Leo I would be going home. By all rights, I should have been exhausted, instead, I found myself wide awake, and deciding what to do next. Hernan had warned that it would be at least a couple more hours before he would have anything to report, so there was really no point in staying at the office.

I sat at my desk and looked out the window to see what the parrots were up to, but they were sleeping. I considered my options: I could shop for a birthday present for Papi's party tomorrow night; I could go home, have dinner and get to bed early; or, I could follow up on another hunch and do a bit of investigative work.

Not surprisingly, considering the mood I was in, I was on the hunt, the investigative work won out. I gathered my purse, made sure the office was tightly secured for the night and made my final preparations to leave. There really wasn't much left to do; Leo had taken care of the locking up before he left, but still, it didn't hurt to double check.

I waved to the young officer stationed in the driveway, then walked over. "I'm leaving for the night, officer. Thank you so much for taking care of us. I felt much safer knowing you were out here."

Even though it was dark outside, I could see the young officer blush. He was so young that I didn't even think he shaved. "Thank you ma'am. It was my pleasure." He actually tipped his cap to me. "Good night. Would you like for me to follow you home?"

"No, thank you, officer." I tried to keep a straight face. It was quite touching, really, that the officer felt he had to protect me. Actually, I should not have been surprised; there had been a body found in my office that morning. "I don't live very far from here."

I got in the Mercedes, started the motor, and slowly drove out the driveway toward the street. However, instead of turning left, south, to go home to Cocoplum, I turned right, north, towards South Beach where I had some unfinished business.

One way or another, I was going to find out the truth about Madeline Marie Meadows. And, given how crazy my theory was, the more proof I had about that, the better. Madeline was going to regret having lied to Tommy and me.

Twenty-Seven

I had just passed Star Island on the MacArthur Causeway when I punched Nestor's number into my cell phone. "Hey, just to give you a heads-up, I'm headed your way," I warned him.

"You're coming to see the client now?" Nestor sounded puzzled. "Does that mean that you got Hernan's results? You found out who Ms. Meadows really is?"

"No, unfortunately, I don't have the results yet, but will soon, I hope. I called Hernan a little while ago and he said it would be still be a couple more hours before he'd have anything for me. I didn't want to wait that long."

Nestor's silence spoke volumes. I knew him so well that I swore I could see the wheels turning in his brain as he decided how to respond. Nestor was a very cautious man. He liked to wait before all the facts were in before doing anything. However, given what had happened earlier that day, when he hadn't been able to eyeball Madeline for the few hours Napoleon and Josephine had been at the dog park, he knew he had to tread lightly—almost as if he was on probation.

"Well, if you think that's best, Lupe," he finally said. "I'll be here in case you need anything."

"Thanks, Nestor, I appreciate that," I said. "I shouldn't be too long. I'll stop by and see you on my way out."

Nestor didn't know it, but I wasn't going to see Madeline; I was going to poke around Andres San Pedro's apartment. I knew that Nestor would have insisted on accompanying me if I'd told him my true intentions, but, after much thought, I decided it would best if I was alone while I looked through his place. Even though I had a set of keys, I did not have authorization to be in Andres' home. In any case, if there was any trouble, I didn't want Nestor to be involved.

Years ago, when I'd worked Andres' first divorce, he had given me a set of keys to his apartment, and, truthfully, I'd forgotten to return them to him. He hadn't asked for them back, either, so I didn't feel too bad about keeping them. Andres had thought that his first wife was going to try to clean him out of a valuable art collection, paintings worth a considerable amount of money, and he needed to get them far away from her grasp. Right after filing for divorce, Andres had been called away on an emergency trip to Buenos Aires, and he needed someone he trusted to supervise the fine-arts packers as they prepared his paintings for shipping, so he'd given me the keys to his apartment. I'd spent all day there, not doing much, just cataloging the dozen or so paintings and watching the packers wrap them up and place them into crates so the movers could transport them to storage, safely away from the soon-to-be former Mrs. San Pedro.

As the packers went about their business, I really didn't have much to do, so I had plenty of time to check out Andres' apartment. Everything had seemed normal, except for a locked door in the hallway between the master bedroom and the bathroom that appeared to lead to a closet. The door had two Medeco locks protecting it, the expensive kind that can't be copied. Medeco locks were usually used to protect outside doors and entrances, not inside residences, so whatever was inside the closet must have been quite valuable to merit that kind of security. Andres had not removed the two Medeco keys from the key ring he had given me. I'm not sure if it had been an oversight, or if he hadn't had the time to take them off, or if he trusted me not to look inside the closet. Whatever the case, the keys were still on the ring.

It was that particular door that I intended to open that night. True, I hadn't been in Andres' apartment for a few months, but on my last visit I could recall that the door to the closet looked just as it had years before, well, at least the Medeco locks had still been on it. I felt safe to assume that he had not changed the locks.

Before leaving the office, I'd taken five crisp hundred dollar bills from the emergency stash of a thousand that I kept next to the Beretta in the wall safe. It wasn't much money but it would be enough for my purposes that night.

When I'd gone to supervise the packing of the artwork at his apartment, Andres had placed me on the list of visitors who were approved to go into his apartment anytime; he had even named me as an emergency contact, but so much time had passed that I wasn't sure if my name was still on the list. As I made my preparations to go there that night, I figured an offering of several hundred dollars could be quite persuasive.

I hoped my friend, the security guard that had escorted me to Madeline's apartment the day before when I'd returned the Chihuahuas, was on duty. I'd already given him a fifty, so I knew that he was receptive to receiving cash gifts. However, if he wasn't there, it wouldn't be the end of the world, as I was confident I could come up with a plausible story about why I needed to get into Andres' apartment.

As I drove up the driveway to the Portofino Towers, I was pleased to see that my friend, the security guard, was on duty.

"Hi, how are you?" I greeted him warmly. "So nice to see you again."

"Yes, ma'am." He tipped his cap at me. "You're going to Ms. Meadows' apartment?" He began to reach for the phone to call up to Madeline to announce that I had arrived.

I took a deep breath before answering his question. "Actually, I'm not here to visit Ms. Meadows." I gave him a sad smile. "I'm here to go up to Mr. San Pedro's apartment."

Suddenly, the guard was all business. "I'm sorry, but I'm afraid I cannot allow you to go up there." He stepped outside the guard-house, and approached my car. "You know about Mr. San Pedro?"

I shook my head slowly and blinked. "Yes, I know. It's so very sad." For a minute, I debated telling him that Andres' body had been found in my office, but I decided against volunteering that particular nugget of information—there was no sense in complicating matters.

"The police have been here, looking through his apartment. The last of them left less than an hour ago," the guard informed me. "They searched the whole place."

Thank God, I'd missed them! "That's proper procedure. Even though he wasn't killed here, they were looking for clues as to why he was killed, and who might have been responsible for his death." I reached into my purse and brought out the key ring that Andres had given me. "Mr. San Pedro and I were friends, you know." I held out the key ring, and said, "We were such good friends that he gave me a set of keys to his apartment. I'm on his list of approved visitors." This was the point where I would find out how persuasive my charms, and the amount of tip I'd given him on my previous visit, would turn out to be.

It may have been my imagination, but I could have sworn the guard was blinking back tears. "Mr. San Pedro was a fine gentleman. We will miss him, that's for sure."

I took a deep breath. "I need to ask you for a big favor." I looked into the guard's eyes. "It's a very delicate matter." I had the guard's complete attention.

"Of course," he said.

"Mr. San Pedro's mother and sister are flying up from Buenos Aires tonight. They will be arriving in Miami in a few hours and will be coming to Mr. San Pedro's apartment." The guard didn't say anything; he just listened with a curious expression on his face. "You are probably aware of some of Mr. San Pedro's interests in his private life. I mean, there aren't many secrets here. Mr. San Pedro lived here for a long time, and you told me earlier you've worked here for almost all that time as well, I'm sure you know what I'm talking about."

A troubled look came over the guard's face. Although I was pretty confident of what I was hinting at, still, I wasn't one hundred percent certain. I had to tread lightly. The last thing I wanted to do was to besmirch Andres' reputation and alienate the guard.

"Mr. San Pedro was a nice man, he treated everyone with respect. He was very nice to everyone, he was one of our favorite residents," the guard stated.

"I know that, he was my friend, too, but we need to get back to why I'm here." I looked the guard straight in the eyes. "I would not want Mr. San Pedro's mother and sister to find out about his 'private' interests. Being such respectable, conservative ladies, they probably would not understand his lifestyle. They might be shocked, and they certainly don't need any more shocks right now, in their moment of grief, don't you agree?" Desperately adlibbing—I was counting on there not being any secrets in the building, I kept making my case, so as to not give the guard time to respond. "I'm here as a friend of Mr. San Pedro, out of respect for him and for the family, to clear out anything in

Mr. San Pedro's apartment that might upset or offend them. I need your help in letting me do that. Not just for Mr. San Pedro's memory, but for the sake of his family."

The guard just looked at me, but I could tell his mind was racing a million miles an hour. I had said my piece, now it was up to him to give me permission to enter Andres' apartment. The guard seemed to be a decent man, so I hoped he would buy my admittedly flimsy argument.

Finally, after what seemed like an eternity, the guard spoke. "Mr. San Pedro was a good man. Whatever he did in his private life is not my business, but I know he deserves to have respect. I'll allow you to go up to his apartment. I know you said you're on the list of approved visitors and you do have a set of keys, but I can get into trouble for letting you go up now. Miguel, the guard at the reception desk, he wasn't so fond of Mr. San Pedro, so I can't tell him what you're going to the apartment for. I'm going to have to distract him, so you can walk past the desk without him seeing you. Don't sign in. Just wait until you see him get up from the desk, then go to the elevators and up to Mr. San Pedro's floor."

"Thank you so very much. You've done a good deed here." I hated to have put the guard in such a difficult situation, but it was the only way I could think of to get inside Andres' apartment. I reached into my purse, and took out the white envelope with the five hundred dollar bills. "Here, for your trouble. Mr. San Pedro would have wanted you to have it for helping him," I said as I handed it to him.

In spite of the cash I had just given him, it was obvious that the guard was not comfortable in doing what he was about to do, but, thankfully, his sense of decency had won. "But, please, don't stay very long; no more than thirty minutes, at most. Please."

"Thank you again. You're a good man for helping Mr. San

Pedro and his family at a difficult time like this." I smiled at the guard, and then drove up the driveway toward the guest parking spaces at the side of the building.

I parked the car and walked up the driveway until I was close enough to the building that I could look into the reception area without being seen. Sure enough, less than a minute later, the guard behind the reception desk got up and walked toward the back room. I quickly opened the front door of the building and raced across the lobby toward the bank of elevators at the end. As I pushed the button for the doors to open, I suddenly had a nightmarish vision of Madeline emerging from the elevator with Napoleon and Josephine, going to take them for a nighttime romp in the dog park.

Thankfully, that never came to pass, as I didn't encounter a single person on my way up to Andres' apartment. Andres lived on the penthouse floor, and although the elevator ride probably took no more than thirty seconds, it had seemed endless. Once on the top floor, I raced down the hall to his apartment, and let myself into the place as quickly as possible.

I was most grateful that the police had not wrapped crime scene tape around the door and sealed the apartment. It was one thing for me to let myself into Andres' apartment without having properly signed in downstairs, though, in my defense, I did have a set of keys. But it was another thing for me to have broken into an apartment that had been sealed by the cops. I may have been dedicated to my job, but I was not stupid, especially when I knew that Aurora Santangelo was gunning for me. She would have been celebrating for the next decade, or, at least until Fidel Castro died, if she had been able to prosecute me for breaking and entering.

I closed the apartment door behind me, and felt along the wall of the foyer until I located the switch for the lights, and flipped them on. It was eerie standing in Andres' brightly lit living room, knowing what had happened to him but, as it wouldn't be very productive to get creeped out by that fact, I shook off the thought as best I could.

I walked into the middle of the living room. The apartment seemed to be reasonably neat, but it was obvious that some kind of search had taken place. Andres had been meticulously tidy, making sure that every object had a proper place. It was easy to see that certain things had been disturbed: the mail on the dining room table was scattered around, as if someone had been sifting through it; the cushions on the sofa were not exactly in the right place; the pictures and paintings on the walls were hung just a bit crooked, etc. Nothing major, more like a song was being played just off-key, but just enough to know that Andres had not been around to straighten up.

I would have liked to explore at my leisure, but I had given the guard my word that I would only be in the apartment for thirty minutes. I had a specific agenda, so I headed for the hall closet and quickly inserted the keys into the Medeco locks.

Although it gave me no pleasure to have been proven right, the enormous walk-in closet contained exactly what I thought it might: it was stacked floor-to-ceiling with all kinds of women's clothing. What I didn't expect to find was the section on the right side of the closet that was taken up by the items that Andres used for sex play. From what I could see, in addition to being a cross dresser, Andres had also been into some serious bondage. Even though the proof was right in front of my eyes, I could hardly believe what I was seeing: a cross-dressing domi-natrix? Was that even possible?

Andres San Pedro clearly led a complicated life: by day he was a heterosexual businessman, and by night, he was a cross dresser who was into bondage. Or, did he alternate his preferences? One night, Andres was a cross dresser, and the next, a dominatrix? No wonder he had been married five times. I felt really stupid, for as well as I thought I had known Andres, I had not suspected any of this was going on in his life.

I was mesmerized. Standing there, in the middle of the walk-in closet, gawking at my friend's secret life served no other purpose than to make me feel like a voyeur. It was time to go. What I had seen in the closet had been the final proof of what I had been searching for. It was too bad that my memories of Andres would be influenced by knowledge about his secret life, but that couldn't be helped.

I had just turned to walk out of the closet when I heard a noise behind me. I froze in my tracks, my heart pounding in my chest. I held my breath and prayed that it had been my imagination, or that it had been the guard from downstairs who had come up to check on me. No such luck. I looked over my shoulder and saw Madeline Meadows standing a scant five feet away from me.

"So, Lupe, smart girl detective that you are—you think you're the only one with keys to Andres' apartment?" Madeline snickered.

"Oh, hi, Madeline." I slowly turned around, and greeted my client in as calm and composed tone of voice as I could muster. Madeline was not alone; she was carrying Napoleon and Josephine under each arm. More ominously, there was a yellow nylon rope hanging loosely around her neck.

The individual standing in front of me was Madeline Meadows, but, then again, it wasn't. I was so fascinated by her physical appearance that, in spite of the fright she had given me by showing up that way in the closet without warning, I took the time to look her over. True, she still had the long, silvery blond hair I had so admired the first time I had met her in my office, as well as the crystal clear blue eyes, but the rest of her was slightly off. Her skin wasn't as translucent as I recalled, nor as smooth looking. Madeline definitely looked bigger, bulkier, stronger—and the grey pallor on her face way more pronounced than the last time I had seen her back in her apartment a couple of days before. The more I looked at her, the more convinced I became of my theory.

Madeline was wearing a navy velour tracksuit and sneakers, an outfit that did nothing for her femininity. She didn't have any jewelry on—no earrings, no watch, no necklace—nothing. Madeline's hair was tied back in a no-nonsense ponytail, a style that made her look quite severe. The yellow nylon rope that hung loose around her neck conjured an unwelcome reminder of Andres San Pedro sitting upright on my office couch.

Napoleon and Josephine were sleeping soundly under each of her arms. I had to admit they looked angelic, but I didn't trust them to stay that way. I had witnessed firsthand how vicious they could be. I recalled how quickly they had gone from attacking Leo in the office, to going back to sleep, and hoped the situation would not repeat itself: that they would go from being sound asleep to attacking me.

"How're you doing?" Although my heart was thumping a mile a minute, I greeted her as if bumping into her in Andres' closet, a room filled with women's clothes, bondage equipment and rubber sex items, was the most normal thing in the world. Madeline was blocking the doorway of the closet so, unless I was able to somehow force her to move aside, something she did not seem to be in a hurry to do. I was trapped with no way out.

"Oh, fine, thanks, and you?" Madeline replied.

"Fine as well." I began to feel increasingly uncomfortable standing in the closet. Still, I didn't want to aggravate the situation, so I remained as calm as I could. "Do you mind telling me how you knew I was here?"

"I guess there's no harm in telling you. Magda, from Dr. Steinberg's office, called to tell me that you'd been asking about me. FYI, your friend, Suzanne's payroll is not the only one she's on. She told me the questions you wanted answers for, so I knew where you were going from that. I'm kind of a detective myself, sort of like Nancy Drew. Or, maybe more like Sherlock Holmes, but then, you knew that already, didn't you?" Madeline smiled. She was clearly enjoying herself, while I was becoming more fearful by the minute. "I have to stay on top of things, you know. I'm in a very competitive line of work."

"Ah, Magda," I repeated, rather stupidly. I should have known. I thought it best to keep Madeline talking, at least until I figured out a way of getting out of the closet. I had a lot of questions for her, and she seemed to be in a chatty mood so I decided to take advantage of that. "But, I'm not sure I make the connection of how the information you got from Magda led you to the fact that I would be here."

"You know, Lupe, if you keep asking questions like that, my opinion of your skills as a private eye is going to deteriorate at a very rapid rate." Madeline shook her head at my naïveté. "The guard downstairs, Miguel! He saw you bolting across the lobby floor without signing in. He assumed you were going up to my apartment, so he called to let me know. When you didn't show up, I figured you had taken a little detour instead and come here."

"So, you knew I was friends with Andres?" I was curious.

"Sure. From the beginning, he'd talked about you, how you had helped him during his divorces. He told me all about you; what a great private eye you were. That was one of the reasons I retained Tommy MacDonald to represent me. Besides his being the best criminal defense attorney in Miami, I knew he'd hire you to work as his investigator." Madeline snorted, a very unattractive sound. "I knew you had dinner together last night, the night he died." Napoleon and Josephine had woken up and started to fidget so much that it became difficult for Madeline to control them. "Unfortunately, Lupe, you were too good of an investigator for your own good. You found out my little secret, and I can't have that, can I?"

To my amazement and total disbelief, Madeline Meadows began a complete metamorphosis before my very eyes Now completely gone was the pale, perfectly natural, delicate beauty that had appeared in my office four days before seeking my help. That person had been replaced by a wiry, muscle-y, tough-looking blond one, who looked perfectly capable of inflicting serious bodily harm. Although Madeline was still struggling to keep the dogs under control, she had now assumed a most aggressive stance: legs wide apart, head forward, muscles of her upper arms rippling. She oozed bad news.

There was no point in beating around the bush, so I asked, "You mean the fact that you're a man and not a woman? That little secret? The fact that four men had to the so you could keep it a secret and continue to make shit loads of money from it?"

"Yes, that little secret," Madeline agreed. She took what I had just accused her of in such a matter-of-fact way that I knew I was in serious trouble. "And, it's going to stay a secret, 'cause you, Lupe, are not going to have the opportunity to tell anyone about it." Madeline looked at me menacingly.

"Hey, Madeline, it's OK. I won't tell anyone, I promise. Just let me go. It'll be our secret, I swear." I knew it was useless to plead for mercy, but I had to try. Four men were dead; why would the killing stop now? There was too much at stake for Madeline; she wouldn't just let me go, and we both knew it.

"Hey, Lupe, time for a reality check. I bet no one knows you're here. You're a lone wolf, like me. This closet is locked with special Medeco keys; there are no other copies. Andres informed me of that when I would come up here for our sessions of fun and games." Madeline began playing with the nylon rope. "You could be here for a quite a while before the smell started, gives me time to come up with a way of getting rid of your body. I figure if the air conditioning were turned up really cold, well, that would help with the smell, wouldn't it? Even in the heat of a Miami summer. The cops have already been here so it's unlikely they'll return."

Madeline was obviously enjoying herself. I had a million questions that needed answers, but I had to figure out a way to get out of this mess. After getting shot by Carlos Suarez, I figured I'd already had my share of near-death experiences, and I certainly didn't intend to go through another.

However, just then, I had no idea how to get out of my predicament, so to buy time, and, of course, to get some answers, the best strategy was to keep Madeline busy talking. "Look, Madeline, you definitely have the upper hand here, but before you do whatever it is that you're planning to do to me, could you please answer some of my questions? At least then, I'll know if I was on the right track." I smiled in as an encouraging manner as I could muster. "It would mean a lot to me."

Madeline looked at me as she played with the rope. "I guess there's no harm, Lupe. After all, you sure worked hard on my case. And Andres was correct. You're good, you're really, really good." She smiled in a really scary way; it wasn't much of a smile, more like she bared her teeth at me and showed her gums. "Too bad I won't be able to recommend you to anyone. You won't be taking on any more clients."

"Who are you, really? I mean, I know you weren't born a biological woman. That much I'm sure of. I know that Dr. Steinberg was giving you hormone shots to bring out your feminine side, that's why you went to him, and why he treated you differently. And last, but not least, why you paid him so much money: to keep your secret." At that point, I didn't have much to lose by disclosing information. I had to keep talking until I could come up with some kind of a plan.

"That's right, Lupe," Madeline agreed. "I wasn't born Madeline. I was born Matthew Mark Meadows, Madeline's twin. And, you're right about Dr. Steinberg and the hormone shots. I was getting ready for my sex-change operation; that's why I needed to get so much money, why I agreed to the scheme that Ernesto and Stanley had proposed: to become a call girl. It was perfect, really—I would make lots of money fast without anyone finding out I was not a biological female. It was positively a genius solution to my predicament. I couldn't believe how well it all worked out. During the first six months, I'd made enough quickly to have my penis removed. Dr. Steinberg recommended the surgeon—it was all very quiet and efficiently done; next was the reconstruction part. That was way more difficult and expensive, the process by which I would become a woman. And now with all these problems, all this legal stuff hanging over me, well, that might not happen right away."

Madeline looked at me with an expression of such sadness that I found myself feeling sorry for her. One look at the yellow nylon rope, though, and I instantly came back to reality.

"I was born into the wrong body. I should have been a girl like my twin sister Madeline, but the doctors explained that something went wrong in our mother's womb, and I came out a boy." Madeline was pleading with me to understand the circumstances. "Somehow, I had to fix it, to become what I was supposed to be, a real woman. I was positive that I would only be happy when that happened. And then, everything changed when Madeline was killed in that car accident junior year in college—it was a stupid accident, should have never happened, I was driving—it was so easy to just become her. I just took over her identity—she wouldn't have minded, I'm sure of that. Maddy loved me and she supported me all the way." Madeline sighed. "Now, I'd like to ask you a few questions of my own."

"Sure." I nodded. I'd think about what Madeline was telling me later, if there was a later, that was. At that point, I would have agreed to pretty much anything to gain time. "I'll answer the best I can."

Madeline took a few steps closer to me. "When did you begin to suspect that I wasn't who I said I was?"

"It wasn't just one thing, lots of little things didn't add up. To begin with, I never believed your story from the first I heard of it. Men may be stupid, but they're not that dumb. No man will pay that kind of money just for the pleasure of your company, even such a gorgeous woman as you. I knew there was more there, to the story, than what you were telling us." I decided that definitely, my best shot at getting out alive out of that closet was to keep Madeline talking.

"You never believed me? Not from the beginning?" Madeline was curious.

I shook my head. "To begin with, I had a problem with your street name: Mary. No one as Catholic as you claimed to be would choose that as a street name; you were in the system, that's how the cops ran your prints, but didn't give an explanation for that; I called your family—your relatives hung up on me—they didn't want to talk about you; when I saw your apartment after you'd been released from jail, you looked very different, almost masculine. The change in your appearance was startling, very revealing. Then, there was the secretive way Dr. Steinberg treated you. When I checked his financials, and discovered that large sums of money was being wire-transferred

to him, I began to suspect there was more to it than just verifying you were a virgin."

"OK. When you take all those things together, I can see
why you were skeptical," Madeline acknowledged. She began
stroking the dogs that had thankfully quieted down again. "You
have my interest. What else?"

Even though I kept talking, I kept looking around to see how
I was going to get out of that closet alive. I had no doubt that
Madeline was perfectly capable of killing me. Her secret was
that important to her; she had proved it already. "Oh, there
were lots of other clues; your relationship with Ricardo never
made sense to me; you had access to the gun; your relationship
with Andres. Like I said, there were lots of other clues that told
me that you weren't who you claimed to be, and that you were
responsible for the murders. But, I have to tell you, it was the
information that Magda gave me that told me I was on the right
track."

"Well, Lupe, it's been nice chatting with you. I'm sure you
have other questions you want to ask me, but, unfortunately,
all good things must come to an end." Madeline looked at me
with a cold, hard stare. "I'm afraid it's time to get down to
business."

Madeline bent her right arm, moved Napoleon from under
that arm, and placed him under her left, where he nestled
next to Josephine. Her right arm now free, she reached for the
rope around her neck, and began to walk toward me. I took
a couple of steps backward, until I was pressed back into the
rack of dresses in the closet. I couldn't believe what was about
to happen. Even though my body was paralyzed with fear, my
brain worked furiously as I tried to figure out how to get out of
my predicament.

I knew that unless I did something to defend myself, I was

going to die. Madeline may have been about my size, but she was stronger and definitely fitter. And she was holding a rope that she fully intended to strangle me with. Madeline carefully placed the Chihuahuas on the floor, petting them as she did so, making it clear that she was enjoying this to such a degree that she was going to take her time in killing me.

I looked around the closet for a weapon, but couldn't see anything that I could use to overpower her. Stupidly, I'd left my purse with the Beretta in it back in the living room, so that was no help. No, I would have to find a weapon in the closet.

Suddenly, a vision of the dogs attacking Leo back in the office appeared in my mind, and that gave me an idea. A crazy one to be sure, but I didn't have any other option. I counted to three then darted to the side of the closet where the bondage equipment was displayed, and grabbed all the black latex unitards hanging at the end of the row. With all of my strength, the adrenaline kicked in just at the right time, I rushed Madeline, pushing her down to the floor, and in one move flung the unitards on her. Napoleon and Josephine's killer instincts took over, and just as they had been trained by the twins to do, immediately turned on her, and attacked.

I knew Madeline would probably be able to bring her dogs under control quickly, but that I would have just enough time to run to the living room and get the Beretta out of my purse before that happened. I figured right. I dialed 911, gun in hand, and reported my emergency.

I had just enough time to make the call before Madeline appeared in the living room, followed by Napoleon and Josephine. The dogs, thank God, were quiet because, if they hadn't been, I surely would have shot them. Madeline took one look at me, in my shooting stance, and she knew I meant business, just as she, herself, had meant it just a few seconds earlier.

I was pleased to see she was bleeding slightly on her face and arms from several scratches the Chihuahuas had made during their attack.

"That's brilliant; using the latex! I always knew you were smart." Madeline was laughing, not exactly the kind of reaction I would have expected. "Come on Lupe, you know I wouldn't have hurt you!" Now no longer laughing, Madeline took a few steps towards me. "I promise I wouldn't have done anything to you. I just wanted to scare you into telling me what you knew, that's all."

"Don't come any closer. I swear I'll shoot you." I pointed the gun straight at her. "You're full of shit, Madeline. After all, you broke into my office and stole my file on the case—you and Andres. You broke in to see what I knew, so don't come to me with that story."

"Okay, okay, you got me there, Lupe." Madeline smiled sheepishly. "I do have your file. I had to stay ahead of you so that I knew what information you'd uncovered about me, then I could figure out what to do and how to act."

I shook my head slowly. "Madeline, if you'd been honest with Tommy and me from the beginning, you wouldn't be in the mess you're in. Ricardo would be alive, as well as Andres. Tommy could have probably gotten you a good deal, but, you'd be a lot better off than how you are right now: facing four counts of murder."

The sirens in the distance were coming closer. All I had to do was to hold Madeline off for a couple more minutes and I would be safe. The dogs had hopped onto one of the sofas, and were now softly snoring, looking positively angelic. If it hadn't been for the fact that I was holding a gun aimed at Madeline's chest, an observer would assume we were having a quiet evening at home.

"Yeah, well, Lupe." Madeline scowled at me. "We can't have everything, now, can we?" She grinned. "So, do you think they're going to send me to the men's jail, or the women's? Last time I was in the women's." The sirens had stopped by now. The police had arrived at the building. Madeline shrugged. Then, suddenly she asked. "I gave Mr. MacDonald a very large retainer. I'm sure he hasn't burned through it all yet. So you think he'll continue to represent me?"

The police began knocking at the door, so I was spared from having to answer. If I had, I would have told her that I couldn't see Tommy representing her when she'd tried to strangle his private eye. At that point, I was just glad it was over.

I had just finished giving a brief statement to the police about what had happened when my cell phone rang. I looked at the caller ID. It was Hernan.

"Hey, Lupe, I have some information for you. I was able to identify a set of prints from the partials I lifted from the glass bowl. But I thought you had said your client was a woman." Hernan sounded curious. "The prints belong to a man—a Matthew Mark Meadows."

"I know, it's all been quite confusing for me too—that was part of the problem." I was exhausted. All I wanted to do was to go home and go to bed. "Listen, Hernan, I hate to do this to you after all your hard work, but I'm in the middle of something here. Can you e-mail me your findings? And your bill, too? I'm so grateful for your work, but I'm really in a bind here."

"Sure, Lupe, no problem. I'll e-mail them to you right away," Hernan, ever the gentleman, agreed. "Take care of yourself, would you, please do that? I know it's not my business, but you really do sound exhausted. remember, you're not 100 percent yet."

Was I ever going to be? I picked up my purse to leave Andres' apartment. Well, I may not have been 100 percent yet, but the fact that I had not either died or had to shoot anyone that night, just then, at whatever percentage I was, seemed a pretty good number to me.

Twenty-Eight

I had intended to go home after leaving the Portofino Towers, but, instead, I ended up pulling into the driveway of Tommy's building on Brickell Avenue, probably more fitting, considering that Tommy's apartment was where I'd first heard of Madeline Meadows.

After giving my statement to the police, I had called Tommy and told him what happened. He immediately volunteered to go to Portofino Towers, but I turned him down. I'd been surrounded by police at the time of my call to him, so I hadn't been able to give him too many details. At that point, all Tommy knew was that Madeline Meadows had attacked me and that she had been arrested—again—as a result.

Before leaving Andres' apartment, I had called Ernesto and Stanley and told them about Madeline. I didn't give them too many details and asked them to take care of the Chihuahuas, something that they agreed to do. Although I still found the twins quite creepy, I was starting to become fond of them, in a weird kind of way.

Tommy was standing at the entrance to his apartment, waiting for me as I came out of the elevator. "Lupe! Are you all right?" He raced toward me and hugged me tightly. "Let me look at you. Are you sure you're OK?"

"I think so." I managed to mumble. "Just exhausted."

"Come inside and rest." He closed the apartment door behind us, then took me by the hand and led me into the bedroom. Once there, he gently helped me onto the bed. "Can I get you anything? Water? Champagne?"

"Just water, thank you." I lay back on the bed and closed my eyes. It couldn't have taken Tommy more than a couple of minutes to get a glass of water, but I had been so exhausted that by the time he returned, I had almost fallen asleep.

Tommy watched as I drank the entire glass without stopping. "Would you like another?" He asked, concern in his voice.

I shook my head. "No, thank you. That was perfect." I closed my eyes again. Suddenly, I had a flashback to Madeline approaching me with the yellow nylon rope in her outstretched arms, and my entire body began to shiver uncontrollably. Tommy looked at me with alarm, and immediately ran to the closet where he got a thick comforter.

"It's OK, Lupe, you're safe now." Tommy adjusted the comforter so that it covered me completely, then leaned down and kissed me softly on the forehead. "I'm so sorry, Lupe, I really am. If I hadn't been consumed with that trial, I would have been paying more attention to the Meadows case, and this could have been prevented." Tommy sat on the edge of the bed and began stroking my hair with a gentleness I hadn't thought possible.

"It's OK, Tommy. Don't beat yourself up over this. There probably wasn't much you could have done anyway." I reassured him. "I shouldn't have put myself in a position where my personal safety could have been in danger, especially after what happened with Carlos Suarez." I closed my eyes. "I honestly thought it was safe, that I could go into Andres' apartment, check out my suspicions, and get out. Who would have guessed?" My words trailed off.

"Look, Lupe, there's no point in second guessing what each of us could have done. It's over, you're safe now." Tommy continued stroking my hair. He spoke again a moment later. "I don't want to rush you, but whenever you feel up to it, I'd love to know what happened tonight."

I would have given anything just to burrow down deeper under the comforter and sleep for the next twenty-four hours, but that would not have been fair to Tommy. He deserved to hear what had happened-and the sooner the better, so he could figure out what to do next.

Madeline Meadows, after all, was still his client. That was, until he decided otherwise, something I suspected he might do.

In any case, I would eventually have to tell him what had happened, so I might as well get it over with. Discussing the events of the night, and what led up to them, would give clarity to the situation and help me come to terms with them, something I desperately needed, especially to process the conversation I'd had with Madeline at Andres' apartment. It had all happened so fast that it was still a blur.

"You know, Tommy, I never made a secret of the fact that I never really believed Madeline's story. I mean, she might have had that fresh-faced, virginal, Iowa farm girl look about her, but my bullshit antenna went crazy every time I saw her," I began. "There was just something about her that seemed off; nothing I could put my finger on, just something."

Tommy smiled. "Well, Lupe, your instincts have always been sound. I've learned to trust them, and to let you run with them. That's one of the reasons I pay you your exorbitant lees. For that bullshit antenna of yours."

"Thanks." I smiled back. "Anyway, I continued working the case as if I believed her, but, at the same time, I was on a parallel course, checking out her story." Even though we were exchanging confidences, I wasn't about to reveal to Tommy that Detective Anderson had advised me to look deeper into Madeline's background. Honestly, there was no percentage volunteering to anyone that a homicide detective was telling me how to run my case especially as I was going to do that anyway.

"Not exactly the first time you've had to do that, right?" Tommy pointed out.

"No, not the first time," I agreed. "But I think the reason I pursued it so aggressively was that Madeline's attitude bothered me. She set off vibes as if she could fool all of the people all of the time.

"You really don't like that attitude, Lupe, that one of your clients thought she could fool you," Tommy teased me. "That's what got to you."

Tommy knew me too well. I continued. "Anyway, I found myself working just as hard on proving Madeline's innocence in the three murders as I was in digging into her background."

"So, what was the first clue you had that Madeline Meadows wasn't who she said she was?" Tommy asked, just as Madeline had done a few hours earlier. This time, I gave a more in-depth explanation. Tommy didn't have a yellow nylon rope hanging around his neck, telling me he was going to kill me, so I wasn't under any pressure to hurry.

"Well, in the beginning, it wasn't anything really concrete; it was just common sense. I just didn't buy that virginal Catholic girl stuff. A girl that looks like that doesn't stay a virgin for long, especially one with a serious Cuban boyfriend. Now, I'm Cuban, and no Cuban guy I know would put up with that 'waiting until after we're married to have sex, and then we'll only fuck to have babies' crap. At some point, the guy's going to insist on her putting out. So I figured if she was lying about being a virgin, even though she had a serious, long-term boyfriend in Ricardo, then I was going to assume she was lying about other things. So I began with the assumption that Madeline was hiding something—people don't usually lie unless there's a reason—and, the logical thing she would be hiding was that she wasn't a virgin. If that were to have come out, then her whole shtick would go out the window—along with the thousands of dollars she was making, of course."

I'd been talking so much, I wanted to tell Tommy everything and all at once, that I had begun to get a bit breathless. I made myself calm down before continuing. "It was only in the past couple of days that I began to think that Madeline's 'secret' wasn't that she wasn't a virgin, but, that she wasn't Madeline at all. At that point, I didn't know that Madeline was a man. I thought 'our' Madeline had, in effect, 'invented' herself in Miami."

I had already told Tommy that Madeline was a man, so he knew that. What he didn't know was how I had come to that conclusion. Tommy had not exactly been shocked at the revelation: as a top-notch, experienced criminal defense attorney in Miami, there was the fact that few things ever surprised him. He was more interested in hearing the details of my investigation, and how I'd arrived at my conclusions, than in the fact that Madeline had turned out to be a man.

"I didn't know exactly why her prints were in the system— that was how the cops had been able to identify them on the gun that killed Dr. Steinberg and Woodley Robinson. But, nothing, absolutely nothing, showed up in any of the background checks that Leo conducted. And, Tommy, we know how thorough Leo is. If he says there's nothing in the system under Madeline Marie Meadows and the d.o.b. she gave us, I know I can trust his information."

"Yes, Leo is thorough; I'll say that for him." Tommy had defended Leo on drug charges on a couple of occasions, so he knew him in different capacities. "I would have taken his word for that as well."

"So then, my approach to the case became: who is Madeline Meadows and what is she hiding from us? What is the secret that was so big, so enormous that she was keeping the truth from her lawyer and her investigator, even though she was in deep shit and Florida, as we well know, is a death penalty state," I pointed out. "The background hadn't given up anything, so I sat down and thought, 'Who would best know a girl's secrets? The most intimate part of her?' "

"Her ob-gyn," Tommy answered. "Dr. Steinberg."

"Go to the head of the class!" I chuckled. "But, of course, doing that was a bit problematic, as Dr. Steinberg was dead. So I did the next best thing. I went to Sweet Suzanne. If anyone knows everything there is to know about Miami's working girls, it's Suzanne. I'd already run Madeline by her, so she was aware of her existence. It was Suzanne who gave me a bit of background on her. She also told me Madeline's street name was Mary, which could have been a play on her middle name, Marie. But a true practicing Catholic would never mock the Virgin's name that way. At least, no Catholic that I know would ever do that. That was another red flag that she was not telling the truth. At that point I didn't have anything concrete, just circumstantial information, but the deception just kept piling up. Anyway, Suzanne also told me that her girls were patients of Dr. Steinberg's, so she was familiar with him and his operation. Remember, Steinberg was the one who used to verify Madeline's virginity, so he was a key player in this scheme."

"So, what was the story with Steinberg?" Tommy asked. "Besides verifying Madeline's virginity, what was his role in this? At least, I assume he had another role, or he wouldn't have gotten killed."

"I had Leo run Steinberg's financials. You know my motto,

Tommy, 'follow the money', and discovered that, in addition to the cash that he received from the twins for checking Madeline out the first of every month, he received a wire transfer into his account for ten thousand dollars from a bank in Miami; the sender was an MMM Corporation," I explained. "Dr. Steinberg was doing more than checking out Madeline's private parts. And, while I was trapped in the closet, Madeline confirmed that Dr. Steinberg's role was much bigger than I had suspected. He had been instrumental in preparing her for sex reassignment surgery: gave her hormone shots; introduced her to the surgeon that performed the operation; facilitated all the procedures for her to move the process along."

"So, now you were zeroing in on what it was that was worth the ten 'G's a month to the good doctor," Tommy said.

"You got it. It was time to seriously follow the money, right? That point was when Madga, the receptionist at his office and Suzanne's longtime spy, who, by the way, was double dipping information, became invaluable." I told myself to slow down or I was never going to finish my explanation. This was the second time that night that I'd been describing some of the details of my investigation. All that talking and thinking was taking a toll.

Tommy got up and, without asking if I wanted anything, went into the kitchen and returned with another glass of water. "Take your time, Lupe, really, there's no rush."

"Thank you." I took several sips of the water, and placed the glass on the bedside table. "So, I asked myself: what could Dr. Steinberg be doing for Madeline that was worth that much money and was it the same thing that got him killed? It had to be. Magda had told Suzanne that Madeline was treated differently from Dr. Steinberg's other patients: she wasn't given the same tests, her file was kept in a different place; it was all quite puzzling. I mean, Dr. Steinberg treated plenty of other hookers, so there had to be a specific reason why she was treated differently, and I didn't think it was about her virginity. That wouldn't have been enough of a reason to shell out all that money or to get Steinberg killed.

"I recalled Madeline's appearance that first time I went to visit her at her apartment just after she'd been released from jail, and how shitty she had looked. That, in itself, was not surprising. No one looks as if he or she is ready for a glamour shot after being released from the Dade County Jail. What made me suspicious was that Madeline seemed different; her appearance had changed, and it wasn't just from stress and exhaustion. Those would have been expected. She wasn't the dainty woman I had seen in the office before. Back home in her apartment, she hadn't seemed so feminine; she looked kind of rough, not quite right. Remember, she hadn't been able to go to see Steinberg for her shots in a while, so her masculine side was kicking in."

Tommy looked at me with admiration. "Lupe, you don't miss a trick, do you? You don't take anything for granted, not even a person's gender." He chuckled.

"Hey, don't knock it, that's what makes me a good investigator." I smiled back. "But I needed to confirm my hunch, so I gave Suzanne a list of questions to ask Magda, and requested that she look in Madeline's files and see what, exactly, Steinberg was doing to her in private. Sure enough, Steinberg was giving Madeline massive amounts of hormone shots, injections that could only be suppressing her masculinity, and making her more feminine. The plan had been brilliant, really. Madeline would go once a week to Steinberg's office, but not for the reason everyone thought. Thanks to Steinberg, Madeline was able to continue fooling everyone, and making plenty of money while doing so."

"So, then what?" Tommy asked. "Where did you go from there?"

"Well, I still didn't know who Madeline really was, that's why I pulled in Hernan to lift the prints. I remembered that Madeline had to be in the system; the cops had found her that way so I knew that if Hernan could lift those prints, we would know who she was, and go on from there."

"God! Lupe, why didn't you ever tell me any of this?" Tommy asked, sounding annoyed.

"I wanted to be sure. I mean, you have to admit, it was kind of a crazy theory, right?" I pointed out. "Would you have believed me if I'd told you that Madeline Meadows was a man? If I recall, you were quite taken by her." I didn't want to point out that he'd been busy with the trial so he had pretty much told me I was on my own.

Tommy scowled at me. "Keep going, I'm fascinated, this is like the plot to a novel."

"Once I'd figured out what Madeline's secret was, well, then, everything fell into place." I had to admit, I was rather proud of myself for having discovered that. "Madeline killed all four men because of her secret. Some of this Madeline confirmed while we were in Andres' apartment, but a lot of this is just plain guesswork. There's still more digging to do. But as best as I can figure it went this way: Woodley Robinson got killed because he grew tired of playing games with Madeline; he wanted to get down and do the nasty with her. He even proposed marriage. Madeline couldn't hold out much longer, so, unless she was going to confess, or put out, he would have to go.

"I'm not sure what, exactly, happened with Steinberg, but from what Leo found in his financials, he was in way over his head: lots of expensive real estate, four kids to put through college, for starters. He was probably trying to extort more money from her, after she'd had the first surgery. Madeline figured she could find another ob-gyn, so off he went." Talking while lying down was becoming difficult, so I sat up. I was beginning to get my second wind. Telling Tommy about the case had been easier than I'd thought.

"Ricardo. Now, that was interesting. Remember the huge fight that he and Madeline had the night she moved out? Where he beat her up within an inch of her life? I figured he got tired of her 'good Catholic girl' story, and that it was time to get laid. Maybe he tried to rape her and that's when he found out she was a guy—remember, she hadn't had any surgery yet—she probably got hormones from some pharmacy that sold them illegally, or off the internet. None of that is easy to do. She knew what finding out that the woman you loved and were going to marry was really a man could do to a man's ego. Especially one who'd been claiming she was such a devout Catholic girl. Ricardo wasn't any kind of a saint, but that was just too much. Madeline knew what awaited her, so she got the hell out, and went to the twins."

Tommy thought about what I had just said. "So, if she got out, why'd she have to kill him? Especially two years after the fact. Doesn't make sense."

"The twins told me they'd bumped into Ricardo on South Beach several times in the past few months. Madeline had told the twins that Ricardo hated South Beach and would never go there. The fact that he had been there could have been an indication that he was looking for her. Maybe she figured it was just a matter of time before he would find her and expose her. Ricardo was too much of a loose cannon to leave running around. After all, she'd already killed two men who would be able to expose her, so a third wouldn't be too much of a problem.

Madeline hated Ricardo for the way he'd treated her, so maybe she felt that he deserved it."

Tommy nodded. "When you explain it that way, it makes sense." He looked at me. "And the gun?"

"Ricardo's gun, the .357 Magnum?" I asked. "I'm assuming she took it with her when she left the apartment in Little Havana. She admitted that he had given it to her to use for protection when she first moved in."

"And, your friend, Andres San Pedro?" Tommy asked. "Why did she get rid of him?"

"Ah, Andres! Poor, romantic, Andres!" I sighed. "His mistake was that he knew too many of her secrets. He had fallen in love with Madeline, and had fallen hard. He knew what she really was, and you know what? He accepted her and loved her anyway—given his tastes, he might have loved her because of who she really was." I looked at Tommy. "After all, he had plenty of secrets of his own. So who was he to judge others?"

Tommy thought about what I had said. "I'm not sure I understand what you're saying. If Andres loved her and understood her, then why'd she kill him?"

I shook my head at the irony of it all. "Because he loved her too much; he wanted to take her away from the life she was leading and keep her only for himself."

"But, why kill him in your office? Why not someplace else, someplace not so risky?" Tommy asked.

"Madeline knew I was putting together a file on her. She told Andres that I was coming close to knowing everything about her. If she could read the file I'd been putting together about her, personally, then she would know what I knew about her. Remember, Madeline was a total control freak. She needed to control the investigation, and reading the file would allow her to stay one step ahead of me. Madeline correctly assumed that I would find out who she really was, but I was moving too fast. From the very beginning, she sensed I didn't trust her.

My attitude toward her during the interview at her apartment confirmed it, Plus, I imagine she spotted Nestor on surveillance. She knew I was on to something, and reading the file I was putting together on her gave her power. With Madeline, it was all about control: control of Ricardo, control of Dr. Steinberg, Woodley Robinson, the twins. Yes, Tommy, even you and me."

"I'm not sure I understand. We were trying to help her; she was in deep shit, and we were only trying to help her," Tommy wondered. "Why sabotage our efforts? She was only harming herself."

"People like Madeline have to control every aspect of their lives, and what happens around them, even if it ultimately ends up hurting them, as it usually does. They're narcissistic. They're convinced that the world revolves around them, and they only feel happy when they control people and events. Madeline knew you'd get her off—you were the best criminal defense attorney in Miami—she'd researched you and me, too, by the way. She knew hers was the kind of case you'd love to work on. She was pretty savvy. She knew men well, that was for sure. She went to you and worked you over with her innocent farm girl bit and charmed the hell out of you, doing it so successfully that she was confident she could control you. Me? I wasn't so easy."

"I suppose you're right." Tommy smiled a bit sheepishly, as though his admission was not easy to admit. "So, what about Andres?"

"He was so in love with her that he would do whatever she asked him to do," I replied. "If she wanted to read the file, and the only way she could do it was by breaking into my office, then he would help her do it. He was a security expert, too, so he knew how to break in without getting caught."

"But why kill him?" Tommy wondered.

"Probably because he had become a nuisance. He wouldn't

leave her alone. He was in love with her and, of course, he knew her secret. What if he were to talk? Suppose he tried to black-mail her? The twins had said that he was close to stalking her, he was so obsessed," I explained. "I'm not sure if she planned to kill Andres in my office ahead of time, but remember, she still didn't have the ankle bracelet. She had been put on notice that that would happen the next day, so her window for getting rid of him was closing quickly. Not just that, but she had a perfect alibi; Nestor was watching her while she was in the dog park. It was the perfect opportunity to get rid of Andres."

Tommy nodded. "That does make sense. She certainly had all three components necessary to commit murder: means, motive and opportunity."

"In all four cases," I agreed. "Our Ms. Meadows was quite a girl. Or guy, for that matter," I corrected myself.

"So, where do the twins come in?" Tommy wanted to know.

I laughed. "Amazingly enough, the twins were the only inno-cent ones in this whole deal. For all their sleaziness and petty criminal lives, they really believed in Madeline. Hard to believe that, given their backgrounds, right?"

"Hey, don't judge a book by its cover and all that, eh, Lupe?" Tommy asked. "Listen, you've been talking long enough, it's time you got some rest." He kissed me again. "But, before I let you do that, I have one question: who the hell is Madeline Marie Meadows?"

"Madeline Marie Meadows was actually Matthew MARK Meadows. Madeline, when you interviewed her, said that she was the youngest of five. When I had Leo run a background check on her, he found out that actually there were six siblings—a set of twins—a boy and a girl: one called Madeline and the other called Matthew. When she had talked about her family, first with you, then with me, Madeline had not said she was one of a set of twins. I thought that was quite unusual, seeing as how one of the first things twins do, is to mention that they are twins. Why had she neglected to tell us that?

"Also, when I called the members of the Meadows family in Dubuque to discuss Madeline, none of them would even mention her name. They knew I was really asking for Matthew. I checked with the high school, St. Mary of the Hills, and found out that, indeed, there had been a set of twins in the graduating class of 2003, and that one had gone on to study at Iowa State. I also went online and looked up the class yearbook from St Mary of the Hills, and checked out the photos of the Meadows twins." I made myself more comfortable in the bed.

"Tommy, the twins' resemblance was uncanny—they were fraternal twins, but they could have passed for identical. The other, the boy, Matthew, was a total fuck up—strung out on drugs and alcohol, so he had never gone on to college after graduation. He just drifted. No one in the family had anything to do with him except for the 'real' Madeline while she was alive. She loved him, and understood him. Well, it was this love that got her killed—he was never charged with her death— it was ruled an 'accident'. While on the drive here, I had Leo research the death certificate record, to confirm the official cause of death, and he just texted me the information. What Madeline told me in the closet was true—for once, she didn't lie." I shook my head sadly. "Matthew took the identity of his twin sister, Madeline. He always felt he had been robbed of his correct gender, and when the opportunity presented itself, I assume he did just that. He sure looked like her, so that would not be a problem."

Tommy thought about what I had just said. "It all seems so weird, I mean, to take his dead twin sister's identity. Why not just invent one of his own?"

"I think it was because the beloved twin sister was dead, and she wasn't ever coming back." I replied. "The 'real' Madeline Marie Meadows died during junior year at college, drunk driver killed her, missed a curve and smashed into a tree. The accident report Leo pulled confirmed that, gave details. While we were in the closet, Madeline admitted that he had been driving, that he was the one who killed his sister. Being twins and looking almost identical, he just assumed his sister's identity. Obviously, Madeline already existed, so it was easier to take on his sister's identity than to invent one of his own, especially as he was planning on living as a woman. Remember, Madeline was clever, very clever; criminals on that level usually are, so she was able to carry out the deception."

"And the prints? Did you find out why they were in the system?" Tommy asked.

I was quite tired, and all I wanted to do was go to sleep, but I owed it to Tommy to answer his questions, so I was determined to soldier gamely on. It was a relief to finally get all the information I had been hoarding off my chest. Besides, we were almost done, and I would be able to rest soon. I had told him most of the important details of the case, the rest I could fill in later.

"You're going to love this: Matthew Meadows, the total fuck up, if you can believe it, before he became Madeline, had been interested in becoming a police officer and had submitted his application. Part of the requirements had been that a background check be conducted on him. Maybe he wanted to straighten his life out, who knows?"

"How ironic!" Tommy cried out. "Had Madeline/Matthew not wanted to become a police officer, the police here in Miami would have never connected him/her to the murders."

"That's right—the final joke was on Matthew/Madeline," I agreed. In spite of my best intentions, I couldn't go on any more. "Tommy, I'm really tired. I'm falling asleep."

"Sorry, Lupe—go to sleep—you've certainly earned your rest." Tommy kissed me gently on the forehead. The exhaustion that I had managed to hold off finally took over, and I never even heard him walk out of the bedroom. The last thing that came to my mind as I drifted off to sleep was that I was actually quite pleased that I was finished with the Madeline Meadows case. Apart from this being one of the weirdest cases I had ever worked, I had never really liked her much; nor her dogs, either, though they had saved my life.

Twenty-Nine

We had just finished singing a spectacularly off-key version of 'Happy Birthday' to Papi, but he looked so pleased that he probably didn't even notice. As I looked around the dinner table at my family: Papi, at the head; then Lourdes, Fatima and her twins, I realized for the millionth time that God had certainly given us many blessings, but the ability to carry a tune had not been one of them. Not even Osvaldo and Aida had been spared from being tone deaf.

I had been so consumed by the Meadows case that a full week had passed since I'd seen my family. That may not have seemed long by today's standards, but if one is Cuban, it is considered to be justifiable cause to file a missing person's report after a family member doesn't check in every couple of hours. I had greatly missed being with my family, so it was wonderful to get together with them again, especially for such a happy occasion: Papi's birthday party.

As I watched Aida cut the birthday cake, my mind wandered back to the scene that had taken place a few hours earlier in Tommy's apartment, when I had given him the details of the Meadows case. Earlier that day, Tommy had explained to me that he felt obligated to continue representing Matthew/

Madeline, especially now that it was very obvious that she had serious mental problems. His focus now, though, instead of trying to get her off completely, would be to try to get her help, something she desperately needed. He really had no choice but to change his strategy, as the evidence against Madeline was overwhelming: four murders and an attempted murder (me). Tommy was a great lawyer, but no one could get her off on all of those charges. Besides, as she was so mentally ill, and it would not be in her best interests—nor for society at large—to have her walking around a free woman.

As per her request, Leo had given Tommy a rough estimate of how much the investigation had cost to date. Even taking into account all of my costs and expenses, there were still enough funds left in Madeline's retainer for Tommy to continue working on her behalf, at least a while longer. Madeline had tried to kill me, true, but I knew she desperately needed help, so I wasn't going to begrudge Tommy for continuing to represent her. However, I made it crystal clear that there was no way I was going to keep being involved with the case. I was a firm believer in the Constitution, especially where the part where it states that everyone charged with a crime is entitled to a defense, but I drew the line at Madeline Meadows. The scene in Andres' closet, especially the yellow nylon rope, was still very vivid in my mind, and would be for a while longer.

Detective Anderson, of course, had been immediately notified as to what had happened at Andres' apartment, and had contacted me several times to discuss the Meadows case. I had not obliged him, citing confidentiality issues. Even though it had been Maxwell who had urged me to delve deeper into Madeline's background and I was indebted to him for that, I really didn't want to reveal the details of the case.

It was still an ongoing investigation, so the information I

had uncovered was privileged. And I certainly did not want to discuss the scene in the closet. Besides, Detective Anderson would have been rightly furious with me for having put myself in a potentially dangerous situation, knowing what I did about Madeline, and how she'd already killed four people. I still had feelings for him and definitely wanted to see him, just under different circumstances.

As I looked around the table at my family, it was difficult to believe that twenty-four hours before I had been in very real danger of being killed, strangled in a closet by a cross-dressing dominatrix who was undergoing sex reassignment surgery, and had only been saved by two Chihuahuas who hated latex. There was no way anyone in my family would have ever believed it, but it was a moot point as they would never even hear about it. There was no way I would ever discuss any part of the Madeline Meadows case with them. I had always made a point to keep my personal life as separate from my professional life as possible. Only Leo knew how drastic the differences between the two were.

"*Gracias*, Aida." I smiled at Aida as she handed me a plate with an enormous slice of chocolate cake. Aida had no concept of portion control. As far as she was concerned, we were all just hours away from starvation. Aida had made her very special cake for Papi's birthday: a triple chocolate layer cake with an extra layer of chocolate chunk frosting. There was no question in my mind that if Dr. Mendoza, Papi's cardiologist had been there, watching him happily inhale the cake—and have seconds—we would have had to call paramedics to revive him.

And it wouldn't have just been the chocolate cake that would have put Dr. Mendoza into cardiac arrest. He would have passed out if he had witnessed Papi lighting up one of the Montecristo Numero Uno cigars from the box that I had given him as a birthday present. It was illegal to buy Cuban cigars, but Tommy had them smuggled into the States by one of his less reputable clients, and, knowing what a dream it was for Papi to smoke one of his favorite cigars, I'd debated asking Tommy for a box to give my father as a birthday present.

All week I'd meant to take time off to buy Papi a special present for his birthday, but I had been working the Meadows case pretty much non-stop, so I hadn't had time to go shopping. I'd told Tommy that, and, without my asking, insisted on giving me a box of his Montecristos to wrap up for Papi. I'd had a bit of a moral dilemma in doing so; the Castro government had confiscated the cigar company from its rightful owners without giving them any kind of compensation. But in the end, I gave in and accepted the gift, telling myself that, after all, I hadn't spent any money for it. Tommy's client had given it to him, so he hadn't paid the Castro brothers, either. Watching Papi's face light up with pleasure as he enjoyed that first puff made up for my accepting the gift from Tommy. I could worry later about my lack of moral compass.

It was difficult for me to believe that the Meadows case had only lasted six days, from the Saturday afternoon that Tommy had first told me about it, to early this morning, when I'd finished debriefing him on the details. It had felt like a lifetime. After dinner, I planned on going upstairs and sleeping until Monday morning.

Just then, Aida was walking around the table, offering seconds on cake. Even though I knew I couldn't afford the calories, I happily accepted her offer. As I took a big bite of the huge slice she had cut for me, I figured it was better to be fat and alive in Coral Gables than thin and dead in a closet on South Beach.

Acknowledgments

First and foremost, I would like to thank my faithful readers, the ones who contacted me and encouraged me to write another mystery featuring Lupe Solano. It is because of you that I brought her back, and I'm so grateful that I did, for being with her again brought me many hours of pleasure. I had not realized how much I had missed her (had it really been nine years since the last Lupe book was published?) until I sat down to write *Bloody Twist*.

Next, I must thank my family (my daughters: Sarah, Antonia and Gabby, of course; my sister, Sara; my brother, Carlos; my mother, Lourdes; my nephew, Richard) for their unwavering support for my endeavors. There are certain individuals who I must thank: Andrew Delaplaine and Brian Antoni from South Beach; Dr. Scott Hall from Key West; Ruth Latterner; etc.)—for their friendship. If I ever get into trouble, I would not hesitate to call Peter Raben, Miami criminal defense attorney extraordinaire (I've programmed his number on several telephones). Peter was very helpful in guiding me through the various legal procedures described in the book, and I'm most grateful for his assistance.

Finally, special thanks goes to my literary agent, Gregory Aunapu, for his support and friendship, but mostly for his faith in me.

About the Author

Carolina Garcia-Aguilera is a Cuban-born American writer. Her books have been translated into twelve languages, and her seventh novel, *One Hot Summer*, was made into a film for Lifetime Television. Born in Havana, she came to the United States when she was ten years old, eventually graduating from Rollins College in Winter Park, Florida, with a B.A. in history and political science. Going on to become a private investigator, Garcia-Aguilera is now the author of ten books, including seven in the Lupe Solano Mysteries series. She lives in Miami Beach with her three daughters.

Find a full list of our authors and
titles at www.openroadmedia.com

FOLLOW US
@OpenRoadMedia